Beyond Our

Mothers'

Footsteps

by
Breggie James

Library of Congress Catalog Number: 98-093797

ISBN: 0-9659042-1-0

BeeJay Publishing
P.O. Box 1373
Alpharetta, GA 30009

Acknowledgements

A very special *thank you* to the best parents in the world, Frank and Fannie James.

Much love to Diana and Malinda, two very special jewels.

Many thanks to Nicola Bridgeforth, Darrell Bohannon and Merian Randall for offering their support and talent.

A very big *thank you* to Cheryl Black for commiting 100% to the project.

To the little one who never had
a chance, you will always be a
part of me.

Breggie

Chapter One

Barbara heard Catherine and Debra talking again, but this time she listened. Both of their daughters were in trouble and they needed a favor, one more time. She could see them as if they were in college again. It was when they were in the prime of their friendship. Each taking a vow of loyalty to one another and later deciding to join a sorority to maintain the bond.

Barbara met Catherine on the first day of school. They were roommates. Barbara was impressed with Catherine at the initial meeting. She was glamorous and sophisticated, being one of the few whose education was paid for. Her fair complexion with red undertones did not make her beautiful. Nor was it the twenty-two inch waistline she so proudly displayed. She was able to walk into a room with confidence and catch eyes from both men and women. Barbara could sense Catherine was vain and spoiled. It didn't bother Barbara because she was the oldest of seven and only had the luxury of attention one time. That one time proved to be detrimental.

Barbara first caught whim of the calculating Catherine when she was introduced to the president of Phi Kappa Psi sorority. Catherine charmingly asked a Kappa to introduce her to the chapter president. Catherine was honored when she received news that her request would be granted. On the day of introduction, a happy Catherine waited patiently for the well manicured young woman to acknowledge her by name. It didn't happen. The Kappa's president did not acknowledge Catherine and offended her by refusing to return her smile. The president looked at her sorority sisters and asked the whereabouts of her boyfriend. Barbara's five-feet-nine inch, lanky frame stood back as the five-feet-three, gentle but explosive Catherine used her soft voice to tell the sorority's president that she could give her the name of a good beautician.

The young woman was insulted by Catherine's suggestion, but Barbara was fascinated. Catherine gave a big smile and told the president that they would talk soon. The incident stayed with Barbara for a few days until she gathered the courage to ask Catherine, "Why?"

"The quickest way to get noticed is through controversy. I only have four years to get what I want and that's not a very long time," Catherine responded.

"But why the president of Phi Kappa Psi?" Barbara asked.

"Because I met her first," Catherine answered with a wicked grin.

News about Catherine and the Kappa's president spread quickly around campus. Catherine received stares and greetings from fraternity men. Interestingly enough, the Kappas spoke to Catherine, with the exception of three, all high ranking sorority officers. Everyone ignored her sidekick, Barbara.

A month later, Barbara and Catherine were on their way to dinner in the cafeteria when a short, light brown girl passed them. Her tight beige skirt, showing off shapely legs, made them take notice. Her shoulder length hair was pulled back into a neat ponytail. Her close fitting cotton blouse gave emphasis to a bustline that most girls her size didn't have. Catherine noticed her first. The girl carried the same air as herself, but not with glamour. They were both on a mission. The girl walked swiftly. She did not have time to waste.

Catherine turned to Barbara and asked, "Who is she?"

Barbara shrugged her shoulders.

"Barbara Ann, please don't hunch your shoulders. My mother says a lady should never hunch her shoulders," Catherine chastised.

Barbara grinned. Catherine's mother was just like the fashion magazines and books that she read. It was always good hearing wisdom from Catherine's infamous mother, even if she only existed in the etiquette books and magazines in their dorm room.

Catherine walked to the table first. The girl did not look up. Catherine cleared her throat softly but the girl continued with her dinner. "May we join you?" Catherine politely asked.

Finally the girl looked up and said in a southern accent,"Of course, Catherine."

Catherine was surprised. She smiled at what would soon be her competition, which she already knew. Their eyes met and squared off while Catherine took her time sitting. Crossing her legs at the ankles. She continued to take mental inventory of the girl. The girl's face was young but her eyes seemed older. Her complexion with its red undertones, reminded one of cinnamon.

Catherine took a closer look at her real competition. The girl's beauty mark over the top lip was much more noticeable than Catherine's beauty mark which was on her left cheek. The girl's clothes, which were obviously second-hand were clean and neat. Her shoes were worn. Outside the rummaged clothing, Catherine sensed the girl's spirit had character.

"Why don't you have a seat, Barbara?" the girl said.

Barbara looked at Catherine first and then sat.

"Since you know who we are, who are you?" Catherine asked in a delicate tone.

"Deborah. . .Deborah Orville," she said with a deep southern accent.

"Is it Debra Arville or Arvell?" Catherine asked.

The girl's smile stretched wide across full lips. The beauty mark seemed to grow as the lips spread wider. She liked the name Debra Arvell. The way Catherine pronounced it, it sounded important. "It's Debra Arvell."

Catherine liked the name Arvell. It sounded European. She also liked the girl, including the rough edges. It added difficulty in seeing how well they connected. It was Debra who spoke next. "So tell me, what does the popular Catherine Peterson want from me?"

Catherine was flattered. "So you've heard of me?"

"It's more like hearing about you. I see the Alpha's president didn't get a chance to meet you first," Debra said.

Hearing Debra make that comment excited Catherine. They were connected! "Good or bad?" Catherine asked, wanting to pick the girl's brain.

"If you wanted to get noticed. . .well, you have, but it won't last long, especially if you have nothing to back it up," Debra said and chuckled. The laughter grew husky like an older woman. Catherine looked at her for an answer. It appeared to take forever.

"If you are going to sell wolf tickets, then make sure there's a wolf show," Debra said and turned her eyes to Barbara. "Where you from?" she asked, taking on authority. The room seemed to be hers now.

Barbara looked curiously at Debra before speaking. "Alabama. Why?"

"Let that be your secret. Other words, don't tell another soul."

"Where you from?" Barbara asked with a gentle southern accent.

Debra looked around the cafeteria. "Nowhere. We both need to lose our twang before people find out about us," Debra said in complete control.

Barbara looked with suspicion and interest at the stranger.

Barbara's own interest was growing and Catherine knew it and became jealous.

"Barbara and I are going to pledge Kappa. What about you?" Catherine asked, looking Debra squarely in the eyes. For Debra to stay a contender, she had to agree to pledge Phi Kappa Psi, a sorority mainly for girls who took etiquette as a career.

Debra saw the challenge and wanted to take it. Joining a group whose focus was on the polished woman was not her interest. Her interest was more in line of another group.

"Hangin' round a group of uppity women ain't never been my thang. Why Kappa?" she asked.

"Why not? It's about time the sorority embarked upon a different breed of women. One who is elegant, yet strong. One who is glamorous but yet smart. Women like us," Catherine said with a smile. Something in her smile told Debra there was more to Catherine's plan than breaking the class barrier.

"Ha! How we gonna git the Kappas to vote us into their sorority? You already done tore your drawls with them," Debra said, becoming more common.

Catherine was gaining strength from the girl's ignorance and vernacular. She decided to use her weapons as needed.

"You're right. It's time to lose that southern twang," Catherine said. Debra looked slightly embarrassed but agreeable. "What do you want most?" Catherine asked Debra.

Debra wanted to answer truthfully, but didn't trust the two people who had invited themselves into her life. She said matter-of-factly, "A husband. Why does a girl go to college?" Debra burst into laughter as she read Catherine's hand.

"Good. We should all make good sorority sisters. We want the same thing."

The group met Susan and JoAnn a month later. They were roommates. The two were fairly attractive girls with cunning minds. Both were from poor backgrounds and both drawn to Catherine's magnetism. All five girls kept low profiles as they ended their first semester.

It was Debra and Barbara who worked in the homes of wealthy white families to earn money for school. Neither had families to go home to during holiday breaks. Barbara went home with Catherine for Thanksgiving. Debra stayed in Jefferson City to work.

After the group came back from the holiday break, Debra presented them with clothes. She lied, saying that her employer gave them to her. The group was apprehensive, questioning Debra's integrity. "If we want to become Kappas, we must look the part. These dresses and skirts are expensive. What do you care where they came from?"

Barbara found out that Debra helped herself to the white women's property. They didn't seem to miss them because Debra took those clothes that were hardly worn or shoved into the corner of closets. She had stolen the clothes over a period of time. Sometimes she received clothing as gifts but nothing like what she took. Debra shared everything with the group. They became comfortable with Debra's stealing because they could wear new clothes. They all became her accomplices in removing items from the homes.

Barbara had a job cooking and cleaning for a Jewish family on the weekends. One evening, Debra came by the house while everyone was away. Reluctant to let Debra inside the house, Barbara continued with her duties. She stopped when she saw Debra pick up a small statue.

When Debra saw the concerned look on Barbara's face, she eased the statue down. She continued to survey the house but then stopped. "I wouldn't do nothing to hurt nobody unless they hurt me first," Debra said. Barbara remained quiet and continued to polish the furniture.

"One day, I'm gonna have a nice big house like this and a husband and a little girl. I'm gonna make sure my daughter won't have to worry 'bout a thang. I won't give her away to some white folks like my momma did us. She won't have to fight off dirty old men either," Debra said and walked beside Barbara.

"So ya don't have a momma?" Barbara asked out of curiosity.

Debra gave a light chuckle. "Oh, I have a momma. I just have to find her," Debra said.

"You said she gave y'all away and that white folks raised ya. You got other family?" Barbara asked.

Debra became quiet for a couple of seconds. "They didn't raise us. We raised ourselves. We were their live-in-maids, pretty colored girls without a home. I don't mind taking from white folks. They ain't been nothin' but trouble to me. Don't you have a story?" Debra asked.

"Everybody's got a story. These folks ain't white. They're Jews. I have to finish my chores. I don't want to lose this job," Barbara said.

"Now I can show you how to make money without a rag," Debra said.

"What kind of job are ya talking about?" Barbara asked, not being interested.

"Are you good with a knife?" Debra asked and laughed.

It was a month before the Lambda's Cotillion. The sororities began the week of Informal Rush. The group, with the exception of Catherine, attended the Alpha's rush. The women seemed nice but at arm's length. Susan and JoAnn felt comfortable with the women. Barbara missed Catherine's presence and Debra was lost. She recognized a classmate talking to some Alphas after Rush. The young woman was Debra's rival, they both were straight "A" students.

Debra was about to leave when two Alphas approached her. They talked to Debra as if they knew her. Debra was slightly uncomfortable but answered their questions. They knew her as the first person to make an 'A in Mr. Hawkins' science class. They were impressed.

Before Debra left, she bumped into a girl who sat alone most of the time in the cafeteria. She was mocha brown with short hair. She always wore dark and extremely conservative clothes. Debra had heard Catherine tease the girl behind her back, calling her a preacher's daughter. One thing Debra liked about the girl was that she minded her own business.

"Excuse me," the girl said shyly. Her smile was pleasant.

Debra returned the smile. "I should apologize. I almost knocked you over. You're interested in pledging Alpha?" Debra asked.

"They seem much more pleasant than the Kappas," she said.

"They are. Why don't you go to the Kappas' Rush before making a decision?" Debra said but the girl frowned. "You can go with me and my girl friends. At least you won't be alone," Debra said. It was something about the elusiveness behind the girl's eyes Debra liked. The girl seemed timid but strong.

Finally she nodded. "Okay. My name is Marilyn. What's yours?"

"Debra. . .Debra Arvell."

The group, along with Marilyn, walked back to the dorm. They had to cross an area what the students called "The Yard." The Greeks socialized and performed their step-shows there. All, but Debra, were slightly nervous as they walked by the area. A young man called out, "Hey legs! Wait up baby. I got something for you."

Everyone turned to look at Debra. She was the one noted for her shapely legs. She turned around to see a bright smile from the president of Gamma Zeta Tau fraternity. She smiled with an enormous amount of confidence and crossed her arms. She stepped her foot out and pointed her toes the way Catherine taught her.

"Ya talkin' bout me?" she asked teasingly with a slight southern accent. Catherine had rehearsed Debra and Barbara on their diction so that the plan could go as smoothly as possible. The young man looked at the sexy beauty mark on Debra's lip and began to drool. He ignored the rest of the group. He handed Debra an envelope. She stared at it curiously, waiting to get to her room before opening it.

"Who else am I talking to? Are you busy Friday night? We're

stepping on The Yard," he said with a demanding grin.

"Let me check my calendar. By the way, Benny, what did you get from Mr. Hawkins?"

"Uh 'C, thanks to you. I'll see you Friday night," he said and walked off to join his fraternity brothers.

The girls continued their walk until someone called out, "Hey gorgeous. You look nice tonight."

Debra saw the boy that she held a secret crush on. He was tall with a baby face. He had a beautiful copper brown complexion. He was standing with his dark curly hair friend whom every girl, including seniors, were going crazy over. The boy smiled too much for Debra. She could never trust anyone who always showed their teeth.

"Hey Bill! How ya doin'? Ya hangin' round the big boys now?" Debra teased.

Bill just smiled at the girl of his dreams. He had seen how the president of the Gammas smoothly asked her out. He didn't have the courage to do the same. Too many boys liked her. Although many girls made an eye at him, he still did not think they were interested. He felt that they liked his friend better. Bill believed that one day, he would have any girl he wanted.

"What do you mean I'm hangin' round the big boys? Don't you think I'm a big boy too?" he asked teasingly, slightly bashful.

Debra twisted as she grinned at him. He was so handsome. She didn't understand why he was so shy. He looked better than all the fraternities presidents, but he wasn't as confident as them.

"Hello ladies. Hi Debra," the friend said.

Everyone spoke to the curly hair friend with the exception of Debra. She just waved and took off walking. The group decided to follow. They continued their journey to the dormitory. Marilyn went to her room while the rest of the group rushed upstairs to Barbara's room to talk to Catherine. She was up waiting to hear the details.

Everyone talked at once. Debra opened the envelope that Benny had given her. She gasped out loud. Everyone jumped and turned around.

"What's the matter, sweetie?" Catherine asked gently with her hands on her chest. Not only did her mother use the word "sweetie" a lot, but Catherine had heard wealthy white women acknowledge each other with the word, therefore, it was a good name to call someone.

Debra could not speak. She handed Catherine the envelope. She took it and her mouth dropped open. Something nagged her. Jealousy. How dare they do that to her? She fought for control. She had to maintain respect among the group. Finally she smiled. "Congratulations, honey! You are in the big times now!" Catherine said, trying to sound excited. Everyone looked puzzled. Catherine had to explain. "Debra has received an invitation to be on the Gammas' court."

Everyone congratulated Debra, but she wasn't happy. She couldn't smile. She was afraid. She could not find any honor in being a fraternity queen. She turned her head away from the group. Catherine was curious. She didn't understand.

"What's the matter? Don't you want to be a queen?" Catherine asked softly.

Debra could not respond. Her almond-shaped, hazel eyes were filled with tears. She turned her back quickly. Catherine stepped in front of her. For the first time, she saw fear in Debra's eyes.

"Honey, this is a once in a life time affair. You are an unknown freshman who has been noticed. You didn't have to ruffle anyone's dandruff. Don't worry, I'll help you. You are going to be beautiful," Catherine said, giving a sincere smile and embrace.

Barbara walked over to Debra and placed her arms around Debra's shoulders. "We are going to be at the Ball with you. I'll make your dress. . ." Barbara said but was interrupted by Catherine. "It's a gown Barbara Ann."

Barbara nodded. Her diction was getting better and so was her appearance. She took Debra's advice and helped herself to the clothes she believed Mrs. Bernstein didn't want anymore. Unlike Debra, Barbara's employer liked her and gave her things freely, including perfume. When Mrs. Bernstein realized that Barbara cooked well and had an eye for presentation, she immediately changed her attitude toward the sweet colored girl by being human.

"Remember ladies, it's all for one and one for all. If Debra is invited as a contestant on the Gammas' court, we are all contestants. We will all wear gowns," Catherine declared. She pranced around the room like a ballerina. All eyes were on her then she spoke. "Let nothing come between us. Not even a man."

Debra paused a little before speaking. Catherine had a crush on Benny Hayes. Everyone in the group knew Catherine liked Benny. Since Catherine had made her statement, Debra decided to tell. "Benny Hayes invited me to the Gammas' step-show on The Yard, but I'm not going."

Catherine stopped prancing and stared at Debra. Everyone in the room became still. Catherine had the toughest time maintaining her composure but she did. "What did you do, sleep with him?" Catherine asked jokingly.

Debra was insulted. Although Benny was handsome, Debra thought he was the dumbest person she knew. Even Catherine said that Benny was stupid. "I didn't have to," Debra said defensively.

Catherine knew she had to keep control of her emotions. She had started off wrong in her first year at Lincoln. She could see that men liked the innocent type, girls who did not exude self-confidence. She still believed men liked mystery. It was time to shift gears and change her approach. It was going to take time to master it but she was a quick learner. She had lost valuable time.

"Of course you didn't sleep with anyone. Have fun with Benny. You know he's not too smart, but he does give nice gifts," Catherine said and began coordinating everyone's wardrobe for the Kappa's Informal Rush.

They walked quietly back to the dorm after the Kappas' Rush. They were well dressed in wool or tweed jackets and skirts with silk or crepe de chine blouses. Some of the Kappas were happy to see Catherine. Two talked to Debra, the vice president and the chaplain. Catherine could not rest knowing the vice president had an interest in Debra. It wasn't until the young woman approached her that she knew she did not want to be around the vice president. She was medium height and pretty with a coffee and creme complexion. She had slightly wide hips. She stared at Catherine the way men did at Lincoln.

Barbara broke the silence and revealed that one Kappa told her that her eyebrows were not even. Susan apologized for causing the damage and complained about one staring at her shoes. JoAnn said one told her that she was a little heavy.

"Can you believe one told me that I was too dark to wear red?" a fragile voice said.

Everyone turned to see the person who invited themselves into their conversation.

Catherine gently brushed her long black wavy hair from her face. "Honey, you're not too dark for red. It's your makeup. It's missing. Barbara Ann, your eyebrows look like parenthesis. You should have polished your shoes Susan. And JoAnn, what have I told you about eating ice cream all of the time?" Catherine said, eliminating Debra from the discussion. She didn't want to insult her because she was the one who got them the new clothes. But Catherine's personality would not allow something to go unnoticed.

"Debra, you must stop slouching," Catherine said and paused. "By the way, who are you?" Catherine asked the new member. Catherine already knew the young woman, the preacher's daughter.

"My name is Marilyn. Did you know Bernadette and Harold are not together anymore?" Marilyn added for flavored. The group gasped.

"How did you know?" Catherine probed. How did any unknown person know the Kappas' president and her boyfriend, the president of Lambda Phi Chi, were not together anymore.

"I'm helping Harold with an English paper. He told me that

they broke up two weeks ago. She's been begging him to escort her to the Lambdas' Cotillion," Marilyn said.

The group got their first earful of good campus gossip. Because they kept to themselves, they hardly knew the latest on campus. Hearing the news made Catherine's heart leap with joy. Knowing the Kappas' president was begging her ex-boyfriend to take her to the Cotillion was good news. She thought about how good it would feel to even the score.

Catherine wondered about Marilyn, a very plain looking person who was able to get a top dog in the Greek world to share the information. What would make the president of Lambda Phi Chi tell her those things? Catherine couldn't understand why Bernadette dated Harold. It had to be for his money. He came from money. He was not a good looking man.

As they continued to walk, a group of freshmen boys passed them and whistled. One shouted out, "Hello legs!" Debra turned and gave an innocent wave. Catherine was convinced that Debra was the one.

"We are all going to the Lambdas' Cotillion. We are going to look fabulous," Catherine said.

"I hear the Lambdas' Cotillion is very fancy," Barbara said shyly.

"It is! I saw pictures of last year's Cotillion," Susan said breathlessly.

"We are going in nice cocktail dresses. Every head will turn to see us walk into the room with dates," Catherine said joyfully.

Debra smiled at Catherine's excitement. "Where are we going to get dresses? And who are going to be dates to six unknown freshman?" Debra inquired.

"You mean four unknown freshmen. Barbara will make our dresses, something original. We have to get fabric so that she can start on them immediately. We want to be sophisticated ladies from well-to-do homes. Before I go on, Marilyn, we don't take quickly to strangers. It's all for one and one for all. There is something about you that make men spill their guts. Have you noticed?" Catherine asked Marilyn. She shook her head.

"It's called a therapeutic personality. We could use one in the group. What we say and what we do is our secret. You understand?" Catherine asked softly. Marilyn nodded. Catherine turned to Debra. "Why don't you use your charming personality and get us dates for the Cotillion."

Debra was ready to faint but smiled. She liked the challenge. "Who should I get?"

Just then, two boys walked by smiling. They spoke to every girl by name, except Catherine. The tallest one was too shy to look at Catherine. He held his head down a little and grinned.

"What's the matter? Cat got your tongue?" Catherine asked of him playfully. He gave a bashful grin, not looking at the person whom he regarded as the most beautiful woman on earth.

"Sorry ma'am. Hello," he said with a southern accent.

"I've got a name. It's Catherine. You've got a name?" Catherine asked, looking intensely at the very shy person. She defeated him with her glare and she knew it.

"Bill. . .Bill Smith," he stuttered. His friend gleamed at the sight of Catherine. He too was fairly shy about speaking.

Catherine turned her attention to the friend. "My name is Catherine. What's yours?" she asked of the dark curly hair boy. She already knew.

"Charlie Johnson," he answered with a giant smile and little confidence.

Catherine slowly brushed her hair from her face. She smiled shyly, not wanting to be too forward. "Nice to meet you Charlie. I hope you two speak the next time you see me," she said in a voice that could charm bees. The two agreed quickly and said something to Debra before being excused by Catherine, who followed by her entourage, simply walked away.

"You can start with those two first and make sure you get the Kappas' ex-boyfriend. I know Marilyn can help you with him," Catherine said, looking directly into Marilyn's eyes with a very pleasant smile.

When Barbara woke up, she could weakly see Linda and her husband Edward. Linda looked worried and Edward looked sad. Barbara was so weak that she could not speak. She decided to go back to sleep. She wanted to remember. She wanted to continue to listen.

Chapter Two

Barbara's chest did not feel tight anymore. She felt better than the day she collapsed. She refused to open her eyes for fear of seeing visitors. At one time, she enjoyed company, but now she was regressing, going back to the days in Titusville.

Because she was tall as a child, she was considered an anomaly, except by her uncle. He knew she was a shy teenager. Even her own mother didn't notice her nor did she listen to anything she had to say. The one time she wanted her mother to listen, she was slapped across the face and was accused of lying on her uncle.

She could still smell the whiskey on her uncle's breath as she washed herself off. She felt ashamed. As she bled, she cried internally, wondering if she were going to die. She was only thirteen the first time it happened and fifteen when it stopped. Like before, she bled again, but this time it was a miscarriage. Thank God for people like Miss Askews. She was the one who helped her get away. It wasn't good for her to stay at home Miss Askews told her. She was the one who confirmed that her uncle had committed a crime. He murdered Barbara's innocence.

Barbara stayed with Miss Askews two weeks after the miscarriage. Miss Askews marched to the shotgun house that housed the Wright family. She didn't get a chance to come to the door because Barbara's mother, Effie Wright met her at the road.

"Your daughter is smart. She can be a teacher one day," Miss Askews said.

"Can she stay with you?" Effie asked, not responding to the

teacher's compliment.

"You have other girls, don't you?"

Effie looked away. Her very frail daughter Birdie had told her what her husband's brother Jay had done to her too. The only thing Effie could do was to make sure that Birdie was always in her sight. Effie said nothing to Jay.

"Miss Askews, do what you can to help my girl. I don't want her coming back here." Effie walked away before Miss Askews had time to respond.

Barbara felt a warm hand on top of hers so she decided to take a peek to see the owner of the hand. She decided to close her eyes again, to remember the good times.

It started the night of the Gammas' Ball. Debra was on court. She did not place, but it was a big boost for the group. Something dreadful happened that evening which brought three members of the group closer together. They had a common enemy, Benny Hayes. He was Debra's escort. He didn't take her back to the dorm. Instead, he drove her to a deserted part of town. Debra wasn't afraid because Catherine told her that Benny was soft and dumb.

Debra and Benny were in the backseat of his car kissing. Benny began caressing Debra's breast. She shifted away and straightened the old second hand gown she had stolen from her employer.

"What's the matter?" Benny asked.

"I want to go back to the dorm," Debra answered. The mere touch of Benny made her want to puke.

"Don't you like me?" he asked.

"I do, but I don't want to do nothing."

"All we're doing is a little kissin'. You are a great kisser. Did I ever tell you that?"

"I just kissed you for the first time tonight."

"Your kiss ain't like some little girl. It's like a woman." Benny leaned toward Debra to kiss her again. She kissed him back. She could feel his hand travel up her dress. When she tried shifting, he scooted her to him.

First Debra tried being sassy, telling Benny to take her home but it didn't work. He continued to roam his hands under her dress. She became angry and slapped him. He was stunned and became angry. He slapped her back. Many girls liked him and she was playing hard to get.

He handled her roughly, pinning her arms down. Debra kicked him but it was useless. She was defenseless because she had left her best friend at home, her knife. Benny had her where he wanted. He held both of her hands down with one of his and the other went into his pants. He made two quick stabs inside of her, causing her to scream.

She muscled enough strength to push him away when he tried inserting his penis again. Strangely enough, he stopped. He looked embarrassed. He thought she would enjoy it. He could tell she wasn't a virgin. He got in the front seat and drove back to the dorms. Debra was quiet and very still. She didn't know how to protect herself. When he came to a stop sign, she jumped out and ran as fast as her legs could take her. She was near The Yard. She heard someone call her name but she didn't stop.

Footsteps were behind her. They were getting closer. She was out of breath and her legs were giving way. The footsteps kept the same pace as her. Finally, his finger tapped her shoulder. He grabbed her arm and she screamed. He looked innocently at her, not knowing what had happened. She didn't cry. She just panted. He looked childlike, wanting to help. "What happened?" he asked.

She finally caught her breath. "Benny. . .he," she stopped. She couldn't tell him. It was difficult. He would know she wasn't a good girl. He had always been polite and helpful. "I cain't tell you Bill. I just cain't," she said, letting her southern past slip.

"It's going to be alright. I'll take you to the dorm."

"What are you doing out so late?"

"I just got off work."

Debra went to Catherine's room because she had no place to go. She knocked on the door softly. Not wanting to wake them. Barbara opened the door and immediately knew something was wrong. Debra walked in slowly and stood in the center of the room. "Are y'all sleepin'?" she asked in her southern voice. She sounded very young.

Catherine turned onto her side and looked at Debra. Catherine could feel something bad had happened. "What happened Debra?" she asked, but Debra was incoherent for a couple of seconds.

"What did Benny do?" Catherine insisted.

Debra still didn't answer. She sucked in her jaws. Catherine got out of bed. She walked to Debra and escorted her to the bed, trying to make her sit but she wouldn't. Debra buried her face in her hands as she breathed hard.

"He took me Catherine. I didn't want to. He took me," Debra whined.

Catherine's face flushed with anger. It was her idea that Debra ride around with Benny after the Ball. Catherine wanted Debra to be seen with the Gammas' president. Catherine thought since Benny never made a move toward her, Debra would be safe. She made a terrible mistake. Her friend suffered the consequences.

"What are we going to do?" Barbara asked.

Catherine didn't know. When Debra shivered, so did she. "Can you keep a secret Barbara Ann?" Catherine demanded. Barbara nodded quickly. "What happened to tonight is a secret, our secret. No one is to know, especially Marilyn. She talks too much," Catherine said. She walked to Debra. "Benny is going to pay for this," Catherine said. Debra nodded, knowing Catherine was a woman of her word.

Catherine paced the floor. She had to do something before word got out that Debra had sex with Benny. No one could know that any of them were spoiled. It would ruin their chances of pledging Kappa. Benny would be graduating in a matter of months. Catherine had to think quickly.

No one knew how, but Benny's senior paper was missing. He swore up and down he turned it in. The teacher remembered seeing it, but Benny had to redo the paper in four days. Benny wanted a quick fix. He called on reliable Debra who was ready. She had been coached well by Catherine. She typed his paper and turned it in for him. Benny was happy. But his senior professor denied him permission to graduate because the paper had too many grammatical errors and typing mistakes. As a result, Benny had to go to summer school. The incident bonded three of the six women. It was their secret.

The night of the Lambda's Cotillion brought all six closer. After four Lambdas escorted four freshmen to the school's most exquisite gala, they became famous overnight, something they had never imagined. They were all grateful to Catherine or was it Debra?

The Kappas' internal conflict caused a delay in the pledge class that year. Several seniors did not want the group of six. The newly elected president, Carol Bradley made a motion to postpone the pledge class until the Fall of the new school year. It gave the members time to reevaluate their standards. Several seniors feared the new president's motives, calling it destructive. It didn't bother Carol, she was intrigued by the six. She had heard from a reliable source about Benny and Debra and what happened to Benny's senior project. Carol was elated. She hated Benny because he received so much recognition even being the dunce that he was. Carol wanted to see how smart the group of six really was.

The pledge class of Fall, 1953, was ten cherubs. Catherine had the most elegant pledge mother. Barbara had the meanest. Susan's and JoAnn's pledge mothers were fairly nice. Debra had the president of the sorority and Marilyn's pledge mother changed daily. Each time Marilyn arrived for her hourly visits, she was instructed to go to another Kappa. It was rumored that she was unwelcomed.

The group worked hard to earn their eleven diamonds,

especially Barbara. Her pledge mother was not gentle in reminding her on etiquette like Catherine's pledge mother. The young woman was often cruel to Barbara to the point of humiliating her. Although Barbara didn't cry like Marilyn did, she was deeply hurt and hid her feelings very well. Debra accompanied Barbara many times to visit her pledge mother but was told to leave each time.

Debra also accompanied Marilyn on her visits to her ever changing pledge mothers. Debra did that to keep up Marilyn's spirit. Debra knew that Marilyn regretted not pledging Alpha.

It wasn't until the election, that Spring, when their friendship was challenged. Catherine was voted second Vice President and Debra was first Vice President for the next year. The bomb was lowered when Carol explained the leadership process. Only the pledge daughter to the president was allowed to be president. She must receive two-thirds majority vote. It wasn't a written rule, just an oath some Kappas took several years ago. Somehow it wasn't fair, especially to Catherine. The rest of the group felt the same, even Debra, at least for a little while. It didn't matter how anyone felt. They all took a vow to the sisterhood. They had given their word. Nothing could change the process.

Catherine seethed over the sorority's leadership process, saying it was undemocratic. There was nothing in the sorority's by-laws and constitution stating such a ruling. She brought it up in the sorority's last meeting of the year. Some Kappas became a little agitated over Catherine's persistence so she stopped complaining and started planning.

The following year, Catherine spent less time with the group of six and more with other members and girls who were interested in pledging. She was selected to be on the Lambdas' court and won queen. As Catherine silently went about her scheme to become president of the sorority, she got the lift she had been waiting on. It came from a broken hearted Marilyn. She came to confide in Catherine about a secret rendezvous between Paul and Debra the previous Spring. Debra was promised to Bill, whom she dated in their sophomore year. Bill became angry finding out about his brother and Debra, so he pledged Beta to spite him.

Marilyn continued with more gossip about how Bill lost his virginity the night of the Lambdas' Cotillion last year, thanks to Debra. Because Bill was so trusting, he told his brother Paul that he was in love with Debra. Paul was known as a Casanova. He actively and persistently pursued Debra. She turned him down several times but gave in when she needed some money. It only happened once but Bill found out and was hurt by it. He decided to call it quits with Debra.

Marilyn continued to talk and Catherine listened. For some strange reason, men liked talking to Marilyn, trusting her with information. As Marilyn continued, Catherine soon came to realize that Marilyn had a relationship with either Paul or Bill.

"It seems like Paul likes you. He probably wants you as a girlfriend," Catherine guessed, wondering what else she could find out. Marilyn blushed.

"I really like you, Marilyn. You have a great love for the sorority. If I became president, I would want someone like you as vice president," Catherine lied.

Marilyn was from Springfield, Missouri and was extremely naive. She was the daughter of a Pentecostal minister. He was a very strict and abusive man. Marilyn received beatings from him if she stepped out of line. She was not allowed to date or keep company with anyone. No one visited her on school breaks nor did she visit anyone. When her father saw her in makeup the first time, he drug her to the bathroom and washed it off, calling her a Jezebel. She hardly had any friends. The group was not only her friends, but she also viewed them as family too.

"Don't you think it's ridiculous that only the pledge daughter of the president has the right to become president?" Catherine asked. Marilyn nodded. "Oh well. What's done is done. How about visiting me during the summer. We will have so much fun. I bet my brother Carleton will go crazy over you," Catherine said.

Marilyn's heart pounded. She had heard of the handsome Carleton Peterson. She smiled at Catherine.

During the girls' junior year, tension mounted. Everyone found out the first suspicious thing about Debra. She was only nineteen ready to turn twenty. Everyone else was twenty one. They were a little suspicious of her because she lied on the school application but it wasn't bad. It only proved she was smart. It wasn't until another comment made about Debra that raised the group's eyebrows.

Several Kappas were in Catherine's room talking. First the conversation was on men. Then it went to last year's president Carol Bradley. Comments about her sexuality surfaced. She was pretty but yet masculine. Then Marilyn said it, "I saw Debra and Carol hugging."

The group was stunned and looked at Marilyn. They could not believe it. Even Marilyn felt bad blowing the close embrace out of proportion. She had walked in on the two when one Kappa told Marilyn that Carol was her pledge mother that day. Marilyn knocked on the door. She thought she heard Carol say "come in." When she walked in, the two were embracing. Marilyn rushed out.

Debra saw her later that week and asked why did she leave so quickly. Debra went on to tell Marilyn that she had asked Carol to be her pledge mother too. Carol decided not to be Marilyn's pledge mother but help Marilyn through the process. Carol made sure

that Marilyn was treated fairly. Marilyn said nothing about her
relationship with Carol, an independent thinker. Some of Carol's
wisdom help shaped Marilyn later on.

"We can't have another bulldagger in the sorority. We are
getting a lot of recognition from fraternities. What are we going to
do Catherine?" one Kappa asked in a high pitched voice.

"What can we do? We took a vow to uphold the rules that
govern the sisterhood. It was only a little exchange between one of
our own. It's not like Debra is a whore," Catherine said cunningly.

"She has been known to fool around with a few men around
campus too," Marilyn added.

The other Kappas were almost breathless. They knew Debra
had a playful spirit. She was the only Kappa to be asked on two
fraternities court. She had won the title of Miss Beta Gamma
Delta. It was the first time in five years that a Kappa won over an
Alpha.

Barbara watched quietly as Debra's reputation was tarnished
by people whom she trusted. It wasn't the same anymore. One of
them had broken the rule and it wasn't the outsider, Marilyn.

From the sounds of the conversation in the room, Catherine
was winning the presidency. But what Catherine didn't know was
Debra wasn't interested. She knew Catherine was. Debra thought
about resigning after receiving the office so that Catherine could
automatically take over. Only Barbara knew Debra's plan.

Catherine caught a glimpse of Barbara out of the corner of her
eye. Barbara looked deceived. Catherine came to the quick
realization that being president of the sorority wasn't worth
tarnishing her word, "all for one and one for all." The slogan
became the sorority's motto. Catherine really liked Debra. The
quest for the presidency wasn't worth losing friendships over.
Catherine also wanted a fair clean fight.

"Let's stop this foolish talk. We must go with the process our
sisters before us started. We can work with Debra," Catherine
said but it was too late. She already had an audience.

"No Catherine! Like you said, we can't be afraid to stand on
principle. It is a stupid rule. Debra cannot be president of the
sorority. We need someone like you," one said. Another agreed
and then another. The rest of the room agreed, except Barbara.
She continued to watch.

Catherine's attention went to Barbara. Catherine felt she had
lost credibility with Barbara. It was at that point Catherine
realized how much she respected Barbara. She was loyal to the
end.

It was a month before the election when Debra received word
about the mutiny. She was flabbergasted. She and several
Kappas were scheduled to visit the campus at Missouri State
University to start a chapter of Phi Kappa Psi. Although starting

the chapter was Debra's idea, something she and her new friend Ruby Lane discussed often, Debra could not imagine traveling with a group of girls who were once her friends and her sisters as well. Carol talked her into going anyway.

The group took the Greyhound bus to Harrisburg. The air was tense. Hardly anyone talked. Debra looked out of the window the entire trip. When they arrived on campus, they walked around slowly, looking strangely at the predominantly white student body. Lincoln University was the college in Missouri most blacks attended.

The Kappas met with the Dean of Women. It was a good meeting. They decided to walk around campus to meet potential members. They walked through the school's Student Union. It was newer, much nicer than Lincoln's Student Union. The group walked to the back of the building near some steps. It was there Debra lost control. She turned to Catherine and snapped. "How dare you ruin my name to become president!" Debra said and gave Catherine a hard shove.

Catherine had to regroup. She had made it known that she had no interest in being president. After the discussion in the room that day, she and Barbara talked about their loyalty to Debra at great length. Everyone in the room that day promised not to tell Debra.

The scene was odd to everyone. Debra never had a harsh word to say to Catherine, not to think to fight her. Debra began accusing Catherine of the plot against her. Catherine tried hopelessly to defend herself verbally. She told Debra the truth about wanting to be president, but deciding it wasn't worth risking their friendship. Catherine went on to say that Debra was smarter than her. Debra brought out other devious acts Catherine orchestrated. At the time of plotting, no one saw the acts as devious. Debra went on to tell Catherine that she was jealous that Charlie Johnson had shown an interest in her.

Catherine called Debra a liar and told her that Charlie had been seeing her since the start of winter. Debra became furious and slapped Catherine across the face. Catherine turned red, not knowing how to fight with her fists and not wanting to. Barbara stepped in between the two. Catherine walked away in tears. The friendship was never the same and neither was the sorority.

Debra did not show up for the election but Carol Bradley and some others who graduated did. They thought Debra would come to the sorority meeting but she didn't. The older members chewed out the younger ones badly. It was Carol who spoke the most. She called them out by name starting with Catherine.

The internal conflict escalated to the point that other Greeks found out. Instead of everyone becoming angry at Catherine for starting the confusion, the new members bonded closer with

Catherine and became angry at the older members for
embarrassing the sorority. The new members created a process
that selectively chose the people they wanted. One invitation per
member. Catherine became president and Debra strengthened
her friendship with someone that was her equal, Ruby Lane,
another straight 'A student. The two spent an enormous amount
of time together.

Many Kappas accused Debra of sharing the secret of Missouri
State to Ruby, but the secret was shared at the time Debra
brought it up at a sorority meeting. It was both Ruby's and
Debra's idea. They talked about starting chapters at other
schools. Catherine just added the finishing touches. Then the
Alphas enacted the pledge mother/daughter process. The group
grew further apart from Debra.

It was never the same. Even when they all went their separate
ways, it was different. Marilyn married the first man that asked.
She was desperate to leave home. Susan married an engineer who
was fifteen years her senior. JoAnn married an insurance agent
but was divorced ten years later. Barbara married a doctor like
she said she would. Catherine married Bill and Debra was left out
again.

Debra found out later it was Marilyn who ruined her
reputation. Debra used Catherine's own motto against her and
everyone else in the group.

Barbara, Marilyn, Susan and JoAnn continued with the
sorority after college. All the ones living, lead separate lives apart
from each other. They have grandchildren now and new friends.

Barbara moved her head from side to side. The memories were
not good anymore. Too much had happened without an apology
or the truth. She opened her eyes when she no longer felt the
hand. She looked up to see Paul standing by the bed. She dosed
off again.

Paul was the oldest of four. Bill was next, two years younger.
Then came a sister and last another brother. Paul was very
popular with the girls at Lincoln. He was handsome with mature
broad features. His beard was always trimmed. He was tall like
most Lambdas at the time. He was a starter on the basketball
team.

Paul had to leave school two months before he graduated
because their mother took off walking one day and did not return
until a neighbor found her wondering. It was Alzheimer's. At that
time, neighbors declared her crazy. Naturally, his sister should
have been the one to take care of everything, but she suffered
from muscular dystrophy. Folks in the neighborhood said it was a
curse.

"I'm leaving today. Are you going?" Paul asked Bill.

"Why are you leaving? You only have two months to go. I'm finishing school. I took care of Mildred. I'm not taking care of momma," Bill said. Every time he thought about his sister, he became ill. The first time he changed her make-shift diaper, not only was he embarrassed, he was disgusted. He took care of her until he left for college.

Paul took one last look at his selfish brother and headed for the bus station. He couldn't understand his brother. He thought Bill would pledge Lambda, but he chose Beta. His brother was still angry over the one night stand with Debra. Paul couldn't understand.

Maybe it would have been different if their father was still alive. An accident on the job took his life before Paul graduated from high school. The only thing the family received from the foundry was a month's wages. Paul had to work to help the family.

Their mother insisted one summer that Paul go away to college to make something of his life. Paul decided to leave Tennessee. He went to Missouri on the advice of a family friend who had relatives living there.

Paul was good with his hands. It was something his father taught him. He could lay carpet and do plumbing before he turned fifteen. His father taught him how to weld and do electrical work too. Paul worked in St. Louis for a year before going away to college.

He was able to get help from a church while away from home. The pastor admired his determination and asked the congregation to help Paul get through Lincoln University. It was the college in Missouri that most black students attended. As soon as the other boys found out he could play basketball very well, he became the team, averaging thirty-eight points a game. His free throw was at eighty percent. Then he became popular, which made him handsome. Everyone saw him as a ladies man because he was gentle. His attitude changed. It wasn't appropriate to date girls he liked. They were too plain.

Paul never forgave Bill for abandoning the family. Paul was relieved of his obligations when their sister died two years after he quit school and their mother passed away less than a year later. By then, the youngest brother was ready for college. He decided on Tennessee State. Paul gave the young man two hundred dollars and a good luck wish. He was to make it on his own.

Paul decided to leave the memories of his failed dreams to go back to the place that gave him his start, St. Louis. He went back to the same church to do maintenance work. The congregation was glad to see him despite his inability to finish school. They were proud to hear the story of him caring for a dying mother and sister. They promised Paul that the Lord would take care of him and bless him abundantly. They gave Paul hope when there was none.

He became better with his hands. He went to night school to become a certified electrician. He worked with construction crews, mainly white ones, to perfect his trade. He was cheated many times by white contractors. To earn extra money, he built caskets for funeral homes.

Finally, Paul got his break. He was given a contract issued by the St. Louis Housing Authority, to maintain one of the fairly new housing projects. He ran across Debra again. She was different, not as innocent or caring.

He was happy with his job because he got a chance to see Debra often. The more he visited her, the more he wanted to make her happy. He worked harder, still providing the church with maintenance, and building caskets for funeral homes on the side. He saved his money and shared some with Debra. He was convinced that Debra would become his wife.

One day, he went to the jeweler to buy a ring. He planned to propose to her on her birthday. He talked to the pastor of his church about his soon-to-be-bride. The older man was not too set on the idea. He had not seen Debra at church. He felt there were many good Christian women that were better choices.

On Debra's birthday, a Thursday night, Paul decided to surprise her. He was well dressed, and the ring box was lodged in the inside pocket of his suit jacket. He was nervous. He had rehearsed his speech over and over; "Debra, you are a very beautiful woman. I can't remember the last time I've been so happy. I want to make you happy. Will you marry me?"

He took the stairs to the fifth floor. He took deep breaths as he climbed the stairs. Apartment 501 stared him in the face. He took another deep breath and lifted his fist to knock. Before he got a chance, his brother walked out of the apartment. It was the first time in six years he had seen him. They were face to face, neither being able to speak.

It was Debra who broke the ice. She came to the door wearing a robe. First she saw the look of disappointment on Paul's face. Next came the anger.

"What is he doing here?" Paul asked angrily.

"Selling insurance. He was leaving," Debra said.

"Hello, Paul," Bill said.

Paul straightened his suit jacket. In comparison to his younger brother, it was cheap. He turned sharply and took off down the stairs not wanting to take another look at the past.

"Paul, where are you going? I need to talk to you!" Debra shouted.

Paul heard Debra call to him in a distance, but he was able to shut her out when he reached the bottom floor.

Paul's anger turned into isolation. He could not do maintenance in Debra's building anymore. He asked to be reassigned but was denied. The projects were becoming dangerous, so he quit. He wanted more than just to be a maintenance man. He remembered Debra making him scrub down hard before coming to bed. He tried convincing her that he was clean but she wanted to know for sure. She probably chose his brother because she didn't respect a maintenance man. But his brother was married. There was no reason for him being at Debra's apartment.

Paul was excellent in construction, but there was not enough steady work for him to earn a decent living. The white contractors could not believe he did not have an engineering degree, so Paul lied and said he did. He worked with the white contractors again still getting paid less than his white counter parts.

One day, a church member called about lighting problems in his home. Paul was reluctant to go but he did. He fixed the problem quickly. The church member and a visitor were pleased with his performance.

The visitor, a Jewish gentleman by the name of Mr. Klein, asked Paul a series of questions about buildings and foundation problems. Paul's answers impressed him. He asked Paul to come to Kansas City to take a look at a building of his. Paul was reluctant, but decided to go. Meanwhile, Debra called and told him that she was pregnant. What she said made sense. She was far enough along for the child to be his, but he ignored her.

Paul went to Kansas City to survey Mr. Klein's building. He came to the conclusion that the building was built on ground that had not hardened before pouring the concrete. The building was sinking. The man had a case against the construction company, but no one with strong credentials wanted to take it because of his remaining finances. Everything was sunk into the project.

Mr. Klein asked Paul to be an expert witness, but he couldn't. He didn't have the credentials behind hm to make a good case. He gave Mr. Klein valuable information on material composite and how everything had to work in order to make a foundation stable. Mr. Klein went up against the company alone. It was a long and trying fight, but he prevailed.

Mr. Klein paid Paul for his consultation. Paul accepted it without questioning the amount. Mr. Klein told Paul something that changed his life. "If you don't think you're worth more than what I'm offering you, then you are nothing."

"That company tried to cheat you. I'm only trying to help," Paul said.

"Everything comes with a price. I got more money than the building's worth. You were the one who won it for me. Son, you

can't be too soft in this kind of business," Mr. Klein said and
wrote Paul another check. "If ever you are in Kansas City, look me
up. There are more people like me who could use your talents."

When Paul returned to St. Louis, he found himself the father
of a six pound baby girl, according to Debra. He couldn't believe
her and refused to see the child. He gave Debra most of the
money that he received from Mr. Klein and then disappeared. He
took Mr. Klein's advise and went back to Kansas City.

Paul did well as a subcontractor. He wasn't frivolous,
therefore, he saved a great deal of money. He lived in Kansas City
four years without anyone knowing. On a sunny Mother's Day, he
felt his mother smiling on him. He found a church near his
apartment and attended.

He stood when visitors were asked to stand. He received warm
inviting glares from women in the congregation. Their looks made
him shift, so he decided not to go back for awhile. He dated off
and on, but he wasn't ready to trust again. He did what many
construction workers did, went to the bars. He ran across
fraternity brothers from Lincoln. He was introduced to girlfriends
of wives. It was obvious that they were out to catch.

Five years went by. Paul's appearance changed. He grew a big
Afro, and once again, became handsome. He bought a small
house in a not so quiet neighborhood. It was a brick home with a
good foundation. He put up with the noise on the block in order
to have a sturdy house.

It was Mother's Day that year. His mother was smiling once
more. He decided to go back to the church that was near his old
apartment. When he walked through the doors, a familiar face
was in the congregation. She had to be special because there were
so many faces in the room. He didn't want to be noticed, so he
kept his focus at the pulpit. After service was over, he decided to
wait until everyone exited before leaving.

He walked out of the door smiling at women, as they asked
him to come back. He saw the back of a woman as she yanked a
pre-teenaged girl who was frowning. He thought back to his own
mother. She always had a strap in her purse in case if any of his
siblings stepped out of line. His attention could not leave the
openly rebellious little girl and the mother whose patience had
worn thin.

When the woman looked up, Paul recognized her. It was the
familiar face in the congregation. He was her first time. She cried
hard afterwards. He tried convincing her that he loved her, but
she didn't believe him. She had a right to. Had he known she was
a virgin, he would have left her alone, but he was drawn to her.

She was fairly plain at that time. She was beautiful when she
wore makeup. He liked her physique. She wasn't thin like many

girls at that time. She had hips and legs. That was in college. Now, she was trim and attractive without makeup. She wore an Afro, large earrings and had an attitude.

Paul wanted to leave before she said something, but it was too late. They had made eye contact. Her eyes were not the same as in college. She looked at him as if he were intruding.

"Hello Paul," she said.

"Hello Marilyn. How are you?"

"Fine. Are you living in Kansas City now?"

Paul nodded. He looked at the little girl who dared him to finish the conversation. The oldest boy wasn't welcoming either. The attitudes on the children's faces made him laugh. They looked cute to him.

"Don't tell me you're giving your mother a hard time on Mother's Day," Paul said to the girl. She crossed her arms and poked out her lips.

"I ain't giv'n her a hard time," she said with sass.

Marilyn pursed her lips. "Gina, I don't want you to use the word *ain't* again. Unfold your arms and tuck in that lip before I spank you."

The little girl unfolded her arms and sucked in her bottom lip. Marilyn introduced her three children to Paul before leaving. He looked around for the father, but Marilyn piled the children into the car and drove away.

Paul wanted to see Marilyn and the children. He had to go back to the church again. Some Sundays he was disappointed because she was not there. The Sundays she was there, everything seemed bright. He soon asked about her husband. He was absent and Paul was happy. The man could stay gone as far as he was concerned. Paul had taken a liking to the man's children the first time he saw them. He had a much stronger liking for the man's wife since she had shown no interest.

It wasn't easy for Marilyn to date again. The courtship was rocky. The children were rebellious and Marilyn was constantly on duty at the hospital. She was the head nurse at a hospital in a very rough part of Kansas City. Paul found out immediately that Marilyn was not submissive. She was not the same fretful young woman she had been at Lincoln.

They dated two years. It was time to have a family and a loving wife whom he could trust. He had always trusted Marilyn in school. His mind went back to the little girl in St. Louis. He had never seen her and wondered if she was really his, but he had to let that part of his life go and move on.

Once again, he talked to his pastor. This time, the pastor was pleased because Marilyn was a nice Christian woman who needed a father for her children. The pastor wasn't pleased with Marilyn's Afro. But all in all, he gave his blessing. Paul took the ring, that was meant for Debra, to be cleaned and polished. It had been too big for Debra. It was as if the ring was meant for Marilyn. This time he made a date with Marilyn. He didn't want to take any chances. He rehearsed his lines again: "Marilyn, I love you. I love your children too. I want us to be a family. Will you marry me?"

Marilyn said, "Yes."

Barbara opened her eyes a little. No one was there but Debra and Catherine. They looked as if they were friends again like in college, in their twenties. They asked Barbara if she would help their daughters. She didn't know. They asked her if she would join them. She told them not right now.

Chapter Three

Barbara heard talking. Her eyes slowly focused to a man and woman in white lab coats, both with stethoscopes around their necks. Before Barbara went back to sleep, she caught glimpse of her daughter aging before her eyes. Linda had been by her side since the day she collapsed. It bothered Barbara that her daughter was weak. Linda never had to struggle. Catherine's daughter was strong. Melanie got through the tough times of being unemployed with a hearing impaired child. Even Debra's daughter proved she was a fighter and survivor. Barbara knew between the three of her friends, she was the strongest, but her daughter was the weakest.

Surprise leaped into Barbara's soul when she saw Bill. He gave her a kiss on the cheek. She blushed internally. He gently rubbed her forehead whispering something to her. She couldn't understand what he was saying because Catherine and Debra were talking to her. Barbara tried hard to make out Bill's message. The dead had her attention, therefore, she couldn't say anything. She saw Bill walk over to Linda and hold her in his arms. He kissed her on the forehead. Linda shook her head and wiped her eyes.

Barbara felt happy seeing Bill again. He now goes by William and lives in Colorado as a big shot at Allstar Breweries. He decided to stay single. Good choice, Barbara thought. Bill meant well in everything he did but ruined a few lives in the process. All he wanted was to be noticed, to be somebody. He thought Catherine could do it, but he came to the realization that he had to do it himself.

Bill tried playing basketball in college, but he didn't have it. He tried out for football and got hurt. He made the baseball team but didn't get a chance to play. He was excellent in track, but girls only liked basketball and football players.

Bill was a very shy person with a baby face. He was a kid inside an adult body. He never did much as a teenager, therefore he knew very little when he left home. His mother and sick sister were his world growing up. He took good care of his sister, but when he went off to college, he never saw them again because he never went back home. He was the first to see their mother decline. One day she was cooking. She stopped suddenly and went to her bedroom to get her purse. Bill asked where was she going. She told him to church. She did other strange things before the convicting episode. But that particular incident was the strangest because he could not convince her it wasn't Sunday.

Bill thought his mother was going crazy. How could he tell anyone? He didn't know what to do. Everyone in school didn't think much of him because he was only smart. He didn't play sports. He didn't go to parties. He didn't tell jokes. No one really recognized him. He probably would have been good at sports if he had gotten the chance to practice after school. He had to go home everyday to help his mother with his sister. All the other kids were having a good time in school, except Bill. Nobody liked him because nobody knew him.

Bill followed his brother to Lincoln University. He didn't know where else to go. His brother was popular in school, which made Bill proud. All the girls were wild about Paul, the star basketball player.

The most unusual thing that happened to Bill in his freshmen year is when the prettiest girl he had ever seen befriended him. She was playful with a southern accent. The boys on campus said she was Creole and to beware. She knew Voodoo. Bill couldn't imagine such a pretty tiny creature with gorgeous legs being so dangerous.

Bill was awkward around her at first. She was the first person to make him feel important. She said it was because he was smart. She liked smart men. He found himself falling in love with her silently. She couldn't possibly want him. So many other boys, who looked better than him liked her.

The night he saw her running for her life made him want to run off and marry her. She would never be afraid if they were married. She turned him down, but they became closer as he shared his feelings and his secrets. To her, what he said were not secrets and she told him so. He was embarrassed so she kissed him. He blushed while looking up at the sky. He always loved the stars. She kissed him again. She was the second girl he had kissed and the first to kiss him. She taught him how to gently place his tongue inside her mouth and move it around. He did. He was more in love.

It was the first Saturday in March of 1953. She became his on the night of the Lambdas' Cotillion. He was her escort. She made the first move by telling him to watch the stars with her. He was excited. He talked about the Big Dipper and the Milky Way. Although they couldn't see either one, he imagined them in the sky. She giggled as he talked. She stretched out on the grass. He saw her as she rubbed her stomach. He turned his head quickly because he felt a rush of excitement. The embarrassment was growing.

"What's the matter?" she asked sweetly.

He shook his head with a smile, not really looking at her. She took his hand to explore her body. For the first time, he felt a woman's breast. It was covered with clothing, but he felt the sensation the other boys talked about. She told him to do what he wanted. He waited a few seconds before leaning over to touch the beautiful dark wavy hair. It was silkier than he imagined. He gently rubbed her face with his hand and then he touched the beauty mark on her lip.

She smiled at him. He stopped. He did what he wanted to do. He stretched out beside her smiling with hands covering his groin. She grinned a little and then took the initiative. When it was over, he was convinced she belonged to him. She made him feel safe and secure. But, girls with her experience were considered taboo.

Bill couldn't wait to tell his brother about his adventure. To Bill, it was the moment of his life. He was in love. To Paul, it was another notch in the belt. Paul didn't possibly think his brother was serious about a girl who wasn't a virgin.

Debra and Bill dated until he pledged Beta Gamma Delta the Spring of their Sophomore year. The relationship between them fell apart after Paul pursued Debra relentlessly until she gave in. She was not as sensitive with Paul as she was with Bill. She treated him as a business transaction, but Paul didn't know. He had to pay for what he wanted. Paul had to buy a book for one of Debra's class.

Bill found out about his sweetheart and his brother. He was deeply hurt. He couldn't speak to Paul or Debra for a long time. Debra couldn't lie to him, but she could not convince him that it was nothing. She couldn't understand that to share herself with another man was not acceptable whether it meant anything or not.

When Bill's mother became ill that year, Paul could not convince him to come home and help the family. Bill had pulled away from everything he trusted.

In his junior year, Catherine came into the picture. She saw something in Bill that he did not see. He was a tall attractive man, something other girls commented on, but passed by. Her long time interest Charlie Johnson, Bill's best friend, was becoming more popular. The dark, curly hair, young man was receiving an enormous amount of attention. He was voted the president of Lambda Phi Chi fraternity. He was on the basketball team. He was president of the Negro junior class. His popularity made him untamable.

Catherine convinced Bill to join the debate team. He was an excellent speaker. His voice quality was strong with a steady tone. Catherine taught him how to smile and give small talk. She wanted to groom him to be a lawyer or the president of the United States. She believed Negroes were moving in that direction. Her time was running out. She only had one more year in college before she had to find a husband.

Bill ran track in the Spring. He ran hurdles. He had the best time in the state at his first meet. He broke his own record by the fifth meet. The coach looked for Bill to be a gold medal contender in the next Olympics. Surprisingly, girls came to the track meet with the help of Catherine. She saw it as a way to neutralize Charlie's popularity.

Tragedy struck when Bill was practicing for the final meet of the year. He went out for a practice run. He wanted to beat the last record he had set. He took off fast, coming up on hurdles at record speed. He felt energy from another source. It was the same feeling he felt when his mother would tell him to ignore the cruel children. For some strange reason, he lost his focus and crashed into a hurdle. He hit the ground knees first. He stopped running.

Bill was voted president of Beta Gamma Delta that year, but he lost Catherine. Charlie became interested in her again. Catherine smoothly transferred her time from Bill to Charlie. According to Catherine, she and Bill never really dated. They were just seen together. It wasn't much of a surprise to Bill. He was curious as to why Catherine had shown an interest in him in the first place.

The Thursday before the Lambdas' Cotillion that year, Bill saw Debra in the library alone. She looked sad. He had cut ties with her after hearing about her and his brother, but his heart went out to her. He never hated her. He was just angry at her.

He was doing last minutes research on a term paper. He decided not to go to the Cotillion. He couldn't stand to see Catherine and Charlie enjoying themselves as a couple. Bill took the initiative and decided to speak to Debra.

"Hello legs."

Debra slowly looked up and said a low "hi." She quickly went back to her reading.

Bill checked out his book and came back to the lonely table. He sat across from her. "Are you going to the Cotillion?" he asked. Debra shook her head.

Bill wondered if Debra was still angry with him for treating her badly when she tried explaining what happened between her and Paul. Bill believed it was probably his brother's fault. Paul probably pushed himself on her.

"What's the matter Debra?"

"I can type your paper if you want me to."

"I'm almost finished with it. What's the matter?"

Debra broke down and told him how her friends, her sisters, turned against her. She blamed Catherine for everything. As she told the story, she cried. Bill thought about how Catherine used him too. Although she didn't give him any promises or commitments, she still took advantage of him.

"Let's go to the Cotillion," Bill said. He wanted to show both Catherine and Charlie that he was still a contender. Debra shook her head.

"How about if we go and look at the stars, the Big Dipper and the Milky Way like we did in our freshmen year," Debra counter-offered. Bill smiled. He hoped the magic would come again.

Everyone made plans for life after college. It would have turned out fine for everyone if things went well between Catherine and Charlie. A few months after graduation, he told her that he could not marry her. He fathered a child out of wedlock and felt a responsibility to the girl. Catherine was devastated. She had started wedding plans. She tried pleading with Charlie, but he wanted to do the right thing. It hurt him more than Catherine to call off the wedding. He believed that Catherine was the perfect woman. She was smart. She could read his thoughts. He grudgingly took off to Tennessee to be with his soon-to-be-bride.

Bill lived in St. Louis and worked as an insurance agent. He ran across Catherine in a department store. He was always awkward around her. Even during the times when they were seen together. He was so bashful that he tried leaving, but she saw him. She approached him with a glamorous smile. He blushed upon her arrival. She complimented him on his looks and achievements. Then she threw out the bait. She invited him over to dinner. He couldn't turn her down. He had never said "no" to Catherine. He decided to break a date with Debra in order to go.

Dinner went well and so did other dinners. Catherine cooked fairly well. She looked pretty in her apron, as she moved around the kitchen. Not once did Bill see her out of character as a well presented housewife. She was sophisticated and classy. At the last dinner, she brought up the idea of marriage. Bill was shocked. He never imagined Catherine ever wanting him. It was an honor. Now the problem was calling it off with Debra. He figured instead of telling her, he would simply ignore her, hoping she would go away.

Bill talked to Charlie about the confusion. He sided with Catherine. He felt he owed her something. He disliked Debra ever since the time she wrote a plagiarized term paper.

A month later, Bill proposed to Catherine. Debra was informed upon a receipt of a wedding invitation. She was crushed. Once again, Catherine humiliated her, but Bill was the real animal. How dare he misuse her? Debra knew Catherine was being nice by sending the invitation. Catherine did not expect her to attend, but she decided to make a surprise visit.

It was uncomfortable for everyone, including the maid-of-honor, Barbara. Her wedding was the following month. Debra waited until the reception before approaching Bill. She stood in front of him saying nothing. He was speechless. It wasn't until Catherine came over smiling that someone spoke. Debra turned a deaf ear.

"Bill, sweetie, we must take pictures now," Catherine said.

Bill lowered his head and nodded. He continued to stand still.

"Are you coming?" Catherine asked.

"Yes," Bill answered.

Before Catherine left, she turned to Debra and said, "I'm glad that you could make it. I didn't get an RSVP."

Debra walked away.

Bill found out early in the marriage that he had made a mistake. He couldn't talk to his wife nor did she look the same as when they were dating. She was still pretty, but it wasn't the same as in the courtship. She didn't wear an apron when she cooked or while doing housework.

Bill was happy when Catherine announced she was pregnant. Although he wanted a boy, he was just as happy with his daughter Melanie. He couldn't take his eyes off of her in the hospital. He constantly stared at her when they took her home. He hoped she would turn out perfect, no defects or abnormalities like his mother and sister.

Reality set in again. Catherine spent most of her time with the growing baby, ignoring Bill. He complained, but Catherine was able to make him see how foolish his behavior was by being jealous of a baby. Bill spent most of his time working. He had to earn more commission to take care of his family. His long hours didn't seem to bother Catherine.

One day, while going door to door selling life insurance in one of the buildings in a housing projects, he came across his first love again. She said nothing and just stared at him. He didn't know what to say. He was ready to leave. She broke into a high pitch laugh and invited him in. He walked in obediently and sat down. He still could not talk.

Bill looked around the scantly furnished apartment. They said nothing for a few minutes. She did not have the same smile or innocence as in college. She was a smoker now. She blew rings of smoke into the air. She had a piercing look. She looked at him in full control. "What brings you to these parts of town?" she asked. The southern accent was gone.

"I'm working," Bill mumbled.

She finished her cigarette and smashed the butt in the ashtray. She walked to the door and opened it wide.

"Come back when you have something to say," she said. Bill got up and left.

Bill couldn't get her out of his mind. He felt guilt, love and lust when he thought of Debra. After thinking about his marriage, he had plenty to talk about so he came back several times. She sat and listened as he talked about the mistake. He apologized for his behavior toward her. She just listened. He said Catherine was trying to become more interested in the marriage, but he didn't want her. He continued to complain. Then it happened. She made the first move again. She sat on his lap and kissed him. He kissed her back.

One night, he stayed at her apartment late. He was too ashamed and afraid to go home. Catherine didn't ask of his whereabouts because she was already in bed. He went back to Debra's again, each time it became easier. He told her that he was leaving Catherine soon. Debra became happy again. He saw the glow she once had in college.

His visits were getting sporadic. He couldn't stay late anymore. Debra pressed him about marriage continuously. She wanted to know when was he leaving Catherine. He gave a different story each time.

One day, he decided to tell Debra the truth. He couldn't leave Catherine because he didn't know if he really wanted to leave. Debra released a long sigh and told him to leave and to never come back. When he walked out the door, he came face to face with his brother Paul. Bill wondered what was he doing there and Paul wondered the same. Debra came to the door and saw Paul. She told him to come in, but he rushed down the stairs. She called for him, asking and pleading for him to come back.

Bill walked away casually. He had another appointment. He didn't bother to apologize for getting her hopes up again. She saw that he had no feelings of commitment to her nor his wife. He was searching for something else. She felt the coldness of his spirit that she never felt before. It was only until she had absolutely nothing that she saw Bill for what he really was, selfish.

One night, Catherine waited for him. He came home late as

usual. For the first time, she wanted to know where he had been. He actually worked late this time, but she didn't believe him. Her eyes x-rayed his thoughts. He became uncomfortable. She told him about Debra's visit. She came to see the baby. Catherine told Bill what Debra told her. He had spent many late nights at her apartment. She thought that he was divorced until she talked to Barbara and found out that he was still married, Debra lied. She called Barbara asking questions to set up the scene well.

Catherine had a small pink sweater in her hand. She extended it to Bill. "Debra described your daughter's birthday gift," Catherine said low. She asked about other things.

Bill could not deny anything because it was all true. He waited for Catherine to ask about the affair. But she didn't. Everything she said was in the form of hints and innuendoes. Then she told him that Debra was pregnant. She was due in five months. Bill was surprised. Debra said nothing about being pregnant.

Catherine got Bill's attention when she slapped him hard across the face. Then she began throwing things. He tried explaining, but it came out wrong. He blamed her for the failed marriage. Catherine was furious. She stopped throwing things. She told him that he would pay for all of the pain he caused her and their daughter.

Bill did everything he could to make up for the disappointment he caused his wife. He stopped working late. He spent time with his daughter. He noticed how smart she was. She looked just like Catherine. He loved Melanie more than Catherine.

In the mean time, Charlie Johnson came to St. Louis several times. He was an engineer with an appliance manufacturer and was doing well. He tried convincing Bill to come to Tennessee but there were too many bad memories for Bill.

Seven months later, Catherine announced that she was pregnant. Bill became excited and Catherine became silent. The whole pregnancy was in silence. At one moment, she thought the child was dead because it did not move for days. A smile came across her face. She was ready to go to the hospital, hoping it was a still born, but immediately, she felt a gentle kick. It made her sad, realizing the baby was alive.

Two months before the due date, Catherine felt severe pains in her back and pelvis. Her brother took her to the hospital. She made him promise not to tell Bill, who was in Tennessee looking for a job.

It wasn't a difficult delivery. The baby was not expected to live longer than two days. Catherine became happy, believing the baby would not survive, but *she* became ill too.

Catherine's mother was on her way to the hospital when the telephone rang. It was Bill. He had been calling Catherine for two days and received no answer. Miss Mattie told him that the child and mother were in the hospital fighting for their lives. Bill rushed home.

Bill wanted desperately to see the strong little girl who fought the odds. He heard about the child's questionable development skills and became angry. At first sight of the infant, he choked. He knew she wasn't his. Her color was too dark for him or Catherine. He could only think of one person, his best friend. Catherine had always loved him, they were supposed to get married.

Catherine tried explaining as Bill packed. Hearing about Debra had driven her into the arms of Charlie. It wasn't serious. Little Melanie watched as her father threw clothes into a suitcase. Bill left Catherine, their daughter and the illegitimate child. He didn't leave any money nor did he send any. What surfaced was "It was only good for the gander." Catherine vowed that he was going to pay.

A couple of years later, Catherine died in a car accident. She and Bill were still married. Bill took the insurance money and half of Catherine, their daughter Melanie. He loved his daughter more than anything. He did his best to care for her. Although he spoiled Melanie, she was his pride and joy.

Bill married Dora, his second wife, four years later. He took his family to Kansas City to get away from the strange mother-in-law who talked to spirits. His little angel, Melanie, was never to go near anyone who could hinder her development.

It was a few years later before Bill met up with his brother, Paul, and some old friends from Lincoln University. With the help of his brother and a few contacts, Bill landed a job at World Airlines in the Community Affairs division. He made sure Dora understood the requirements to be the wife of a successful businessman. She agreed, but it didn't help. No matter what she did, it wasn't enough. It was the constant comparison to wives of white counterparts that got Dora's attention.

Dora tried hard but the marriage failed. Although she and the bratty teenage daughter didn't get along, Dora tried hard to be the missing link for the girl. It wasn't until Barbara stepped in that added balance to the stepmother-daughter relationship. Barbara also helped Dora to slightly understand Bill's humble beginnings. It was useless. Again, Bill blamed Dora for the problems. All of his attempts at success had failed. Dora wanted him to come to terms with his shameful past. It never happened.

Years later, Bill married a white woman, Jean. She had been married to an executive at the telephone company in Dallas. Bill did things for Jean that he had never done for anyone else. She was constantly showered with gifts and compliments. Bill was even willing to adopt her children, but her ex-husband was not willing. His money and power gave him custody of the little boy and girl. When the children visited, Bill did something he never did before. He spent an enormous amount of time with the children.

The marriage went well until Bill was a contender for a big promotion. He wasn't selected. He knew he had to leave the company. Jean became another problem to him. Her constant inquiries and suggestions about his future at International Foods made him uneasy. Failure began to surface. Bill ignored Jean until she went away, taking a large portion of his assets. He didn't care because out of the two he had married, he respected her the most.

Barbara couldn't hear the dead anymore. Instead, she heard the familiar rhymes of Green Eggs and Ham. She opened her eyes to her grandson reading his favorite book. He read and spoke very well to be such a young age. She smiled as he put expression to the "would nots and could nots" of Dr. Seus' famous story. Barbara muscled enough strength to clap. Her grandson jumped with excitement.

"Look mommie! Grandmother eyes are opened," he said.

Linda spun around almost dropping her three-year-old daughter Indie. Linda and Barbara made eye contact for the first time in three days. Barbara saw the worry leave Linda's face instantly. Before Barbara said anything, she saw a beam of light around Indie. Barbara saw her first granddaughter Camille when she looked at Indie. The little girl had come back to her. Barbara was ready to say something, but Camille went away. Barbara closed her eyes.

"Don't tell me you are about to go to sleep again," Linda complained.

"Bring her to me," Barbara mumbled.

Linda walked to the bed with Indie. The little girl looked at Barbara as if she were a stranger. She hardly ever went to Barbara. It was understood. Barbara made it her business not to bond with the little girl for fear of another loss.

Linda leaned Indie to Barbara. She touched the child and felt electricity surge through her body. She became warm. Instantly, she could feel strength. Barbara knew Indie was not an ordinary child.

"Thank you sweetie," Barbara said dryly. Indie smiled.

Barbara's visitors, Marilyn, Paul, Bill and Edward came back into the room. Her husband, Edward, approached her bed solemnly. He took her very thin hand and stroked it. He couldn't look at her, but he had to tell the truth.

"Barbara, they must operate in order to prolong your life. One valve is not functioning properly and the walls are getting thinner. You must reconsider," Edward said.

They knew the diabetes would not allow Barbara to heal quickly if she had the surgery. They knew that Barbara was not one for surgery of any kind. Barbara smiled her usual big grin. She had strength from another place.

"Edward, I don't want to discuss surgery. My baby sister is turning fifty in two months. I want Malinda to meet her. We'll take the baby. It's going to be a girls only trip," Barbara said slowly.

Linda looked around the room suspiciously. Indie looked at Barbara questionably. She beckoned for Indie. Linda carefully sat Indie on Barbara's bed. Indie looked around the room. She looked up at Linda and then at Barbara.

Barbara saw Jennifer's face come into focus then it left. Melissa's face appeared as Indie continued to look at Barbara. She realized that she had made contact with the dead. The conversations with Catherine and Debra were not a dream. Barbara decided to do her friends a favor, but she wondered if they would like it? She knew she had to help her daughter first. Linda had to become strong to handle what might soon happen.

"How is my precious grandbaby," Barbara cooed. She gently rubbed Indie's cheeks.

Indie giggled and then spit out, "Hi Barba."

Barbara gasped at the little girl and then looked at Linda for an explanation.

"Well, you said you hated the name Big Momma," Linda said.

Chapter Four

Linda was in the kitchen cooking breakfast at Barbara's house. Barbara sat still at the dinette listening to her grandson read. After reading each page, he turned the book around for Barbara to see the pictures. She smiled at him. He smiled back. Barbara was very close to little Edward. She was at his birth. At the time of his birth, his father, Keith was delivering a baby at another hospital for one of his patients. Linda was at Barbara's house when she went into labor. It happened so fast that Linda did not need an epidural. Edward Steven Reed came into the world giving his mother little problems.

Indie Melissa Reed was a different story. Linda's pregnancy was difficult. She was sick for five of the nine months. When the little girl's head appeared at the opening, Linda pushed hard to relieve herself of the tiny giant. Indie's lungs proved well developed when she belted out a scream upon her entrance. Linda immediately had her tubes tied.

Linda finished dressing a plate of brown rice, cottage cheese, two slices of tomatoes and four slices of fresh peaches. She garnished it with a strawberry and parsley and placed it in front of Barbara. She looked at it and lost her appetite. The meal wasn't anything unusual for her to eat, but she craved for a southern meal. The hospital food was bad enough, but what she saw on the table looked worse.

Barbara commended Linda on the presentation of the tasteless meal, but it wasn't mouth watering. She wanted a more filling meal. "Malinda, dear, I must have turkey sausage and toast too," Barbara complained.

"The doctor said. . ." Linda started.

Barbara waved her hand. "I know what the doctor said, but I must enjoy my meal on the first day home," Barbara insisted.

"Grandmother, you have to eat what mommie cooked. We don't want you to die," little Edward said.

"Don't worry, honey. Your grandmother is too mean to die," Linda said without looking at Barbara. Little Edward looked bewildered. He gave Barbara a confusing stare. She smiled at him.

"There's turkey sausage in the refrigerator," Barbara said. Linda hesitated and began cooking the sausage. She filled the toaster with wheat bread.

"Where is Indie?" Barbara asked.

"Sleep," Edward answered.

"Honey, it's asleep," Barbara corrected.

"Asleep," Edward replied.

Barbara had to be careful with her next question. She didn't want to upset her daughter, but it had to be asked. "Have you talked to Lauren? Her birthday will be here soon."

The toast popped up. Linda removed them from the toaster. She placed a slice on Barbara's plate along with the turkey sausage. Then she began preparing eggs for herself and Edward.

"I haven't talked to her recently and her birthday is not until September. I think she's spending the summer with Lionel," Linda said with her back turned. She poured two glasses of orange juice and put plates on the tables.

Barbara decided to drop the subject. She took a fork full of brown rice and savored the flavor. She had to admit it wasn't what she expected. Linda experimented with spices often. The rice dish had a sweet flavor. Barbara couldn't determine the spice. She enjoyed her meal in silence.

Linda began clearing the table. Edward blurted out, "Grandmother, mommie's running for office."

Barbara was surprised. She looked at Linda for a response. When the younger women of the Kansas City Alumnae chapter of Phi Kappa Psi sorority broke away four years ago, Linda worked hard to position herself in the new chapter. She created a program in conjunction with a government program that helped immunize hundreds of children in the city. She became active in several health fairs to the economically disadvantaged. She pulled the likes of her husband, father and family friends, who were physicians or nurses. Linda insisted on free screening tests for blood pressure, diabetes, hearing and sight checks. She added a flair to new directions in medicine by including a physical therapist, massage therapist, iridologist and herbalist. They too offered free services.

With all the hard work Linda performed within two years, she did not receive recognition from the sorority. Many pictures were taken and featured in the sorority's quarterly journal, but Linda's name was not mentioned, only Lori Collins, the chapter's president. Linda was overlooked at election time. She did not receive one nomination, not even from the person she regarded as her best friend who was elected First Vice President. The two had discussed Linda's desires to become an officer. The whole thing had left a bad taste in Linda's mouth.

Linda removed herself from the sorority physically. Her mother encouraged her to go back. She decided to attend meetings at the old chapter where cultural programs and fund raising were most important.

Barbara only made appearances at those functions ranking high in program status, funding or where her close friends were chairpersons. She occasionally saw Linda working with the fussy older women. Her daughter did her best to accommodate the women, but it was almost a lost cause. She hardly ever got her message across. Experience ruled over the thirty-something doctor's wife and mother of small children. Linda got frustrated and vowed to never work with the old outdated women again, but it was back to the meetings next month because one of the old women would call to check on her. They knew she was a hard worker and good listener. They enjoyed her conversations. The older women seemed to like her.

Barbara took a deep breath. "What office are you running for?" she asked. She was concerned. She knew Linda did not stand a chance at winning anything but secretary in the chapter that had an active membership of three hundred and fifty. The members were older and had reputations exceeding anything Linda had ever hoped to accomplished. Barbara felt Linda was better off trying to make a try in the new chapter with a membership of little over one hundred.

Linda was slightly offended at how her mother asked the question. It made her a little nervous. She knew Barbara disapproved already. She never encouraged her daughter to do much of anything in the sorority. When Barbara saw her at the functions, she treated the older women much better than Linda. Barbara was even happy to hear that Melanie was voted First Vice President.

"What do you care? You were happy to hear about Angel being voted Vice President and you knew I worked harder," Linda said, quickly putting up the defense to keep her feelings from becoming further damaged.

"If I didn't care I would not have asked," Barbara said sluggishly. She felt tired for some reason. Something was pulling on her strength, but she managed to hold on. "Yes you worked harder than Melanie, but she is better at being recognized for doing little. There is a difference in working hard and working smart. If you are going to run for an office, you must learn the difference between the two."

Barbara decided to let the issue rest. She did not want to fight with Linda. They had begun to get along much better since Edward's birth. Something was driving a stake between the two.

Barbara stood to leave. Linda didn't want to offend her mother. She did not look at her when she said, "I'm running for Regional Director."

Barbara almost had heart failure again. Her daughter was virtually unknown in the chapter not to say within the region. Linda was sure to be embarrassed at the conference, not to mention that Barbara would be too.

"What! Regional Director?" Barbara said in a pant.

Linda smiled a little. "Mrs. Massey says I have a good chance at winning," Linda said proudly.

Barbara was confused. She had been out of the local level loop for a little while, but she did have contacts. Someone would have told her about Linda's quest for regional director, especially Floristine Massey. They were friends. Barbara was the one who nominated Floristine as chapter president. She was good at politics. She had strong contacts throughout the region.

"Floristine told you that?" Barbara asked, almost calling Linda a liar.

The game was getting good to Linda. She had her mother where she wanted. "Yes ma'am. Mrs. Bircher is supporting me too. By the way, she wants you to give her a call when you get on your feet," Linda said happily. She shook the suds off of her hands and rinsed the plate. She handed it to Edward who was drying.

Barbara had no choice but to remain silent for a little while. Gloria Bircher was not only another past chapter president, but a past regional director and past first national vice president. She and Barbara were good friends in and outside the sorority. Gloria was one of Barbara's best customers at the old shop.

Barbara stared at Linda's back. She had grown up without her noticing. Barbara was proud of her.

Linda could feel the intense stare. She got enough courage to turn around. Her focus went past her mother to the little giant that was approaching the kitchen. "I took a lot of nonsense off of those old broads. They are willing to support me for Regional Director. *I* will be representing the chapter. I don't know if that is working hard or smart."

Barbara grinned. "I must say it's both."

She reflected to a statement made by Gloria last year. She called Linda a young Barbara Stevens with a heart. Sounds of little feet caught Barbara's attention.

"Hi Barba," Indie said.

Barbara gave Indie a chastising look, but it didn't move the child. She kept walking toward Linda as she rubbed the sleep from her eyes.

"Eat, mommie, eat," Indie demanded.

Linda sat her in a chair. Barbara sat down at the table beside Indie and brushed her arm. She felt electricity again.

"Sweetie, I'm your grandmother. You must call me grandmother, not Barba. You understand?" Barbara asked gently.

Indie couldn't comprehend everything the woman was telling her, but she gave her usual response. "Kay," Indie said innocently.

Barbara leaned forward and placed a kiss on Indie's forehead. It made Indie shut her eyes. Barbara got up and walked toward the kitchen opening. Without turning around she said, "Tell Gloria I'll give her a call in a couple of days. We need to talk."

Linda had just gotten off the telephone with one of the fussy older women. The news the woman shared was not good. Linda was going to have tough competition in the election. The older Kansas City Alumnae chapter usually sent the candidate to represent Kansas City in the regional election. Now there would be two candidates. Lori Bass-Collins was running too. Kansas City produced several past regional directors. Linda knew the election would be tough having Lori in the picture.

Lori was the catalyst that created the new chapter in Kansas City. Upon its inception, she was voted president and served two terms. It was obvious that she was moving toward bigger things. She had received an enormous amount of exposure over the past two years in the sorority's national quarterly journal from Linda's health fairs. Lori had several pictures taken of her talking to participants. There were none of Linda, the person who had coordinated the programs.

Linda tried to forget about the telephone call, but it was difficult. She wanted to call her mother, but she did not want to hear a lecture. Linda still believed Barbara was not convinced she could pull it off. Linda was accustomed to following plans and schemes of others and not setting a plan for herself. She thought the move to go back to the old chapter was a shrewd one. There was hardly anyone under the age of forty active. She thought if she worked hard and proved that she was a good worker, she could become an officer. The idea alone seemed unrealistic. The thirty-something doctor's wife had nothing in comparison to the accomplishments of the old fuss-boxes. Some had received city and state recognition for their careers and for volunteer work.

Linda thought about working on her Master's degree. It was

only a thought. The more she was around the nagging old women, the more their Ph.D.s encouraged her to do something more. Despite the old women's personalities, they seemed to like her, except for a few. They still had a bone to pick with her mother.

To Linda, the ones who nagged and fussed the most were just lonesome women with children who did not care enough to spend time with them. Occasionally, Linda called them or dropped by with Indie for a visit. When Linda visited, they hardly ever wanted her to leave.

Linda continued to pack for the trip the next day. Barbara barely received a release to travel. The doctor was dead set against it. Barbara told him that she was going regardless. He placed strict orders for her not to do a lot of walking and to watch her diet. Before Barbara left his office, she used the receptionist's telephone to make reservations.

Linda heard Keith enter the house. She could hear little Edward running to his father. It was the usual scene. Keith would pick Edward up and toss him in the air several times. The boy squealed with joy as his father spent no more than thirty minutes with him before retiring to bed. Indie was usually in bed. She only saw her father in the mornings. Tonight she was still up, preoccupied in Linda's bathroom. Suddenly, there was a loud crash in the bathroom. Indie came running out.

"Bro' mommie bro'," the child panted and pointed back to the bathroom.

Linda rushed into the bathroom to see the bottle of her favorite fragrance splattered on the floor. Normally it was on the bedroom dresser, but she took it in the bathroom and forgot to bring it out.

Linda wanted to kill Indie. The odor from the perfume was getting stronger. Indie knelt to the floor and patted her hands in the liquid. She rubbed it on her arms. Linda had to take a deep breath. "No honey. You are going to cut yourself. Don't!"

Linda took Indie to the hall bathroom to bathe her. Keith looked up the stairs and blew a kiss. Linda closed her eyes and turned her head.

"What's the matter?" Keith asked with a crease in his eyebrows.

"Your curious daughter just broke my bottle of Boucheron," Linda said disgusted.

She went into Indie's room and got a gown and bath toys. She rushed back into the bathroom before Indie got into something else, but it was too late. Indie was in the bath tub with her clothes on. She had turned on the faucets to start the bath water, but the shower nozzle was on instead. Water was splashing on the floor.

Linda smacked Indie's hand. "I said, *no*. Do you understand?"

Indie let out a scream. Linda roughly removed the little girl's clothes. Linda was down to the training pants. They felt damp.

"Did you wet your pants again?" Linda snapped. Indie looked fearful.

"I'll pick you up another bottle of Boucheron tomorrow," Keith said.

"We're going out of town with mother tomorrow for two weeks. Remember? Never mind. I don't want it," Linda said, avoiding eye contact. Indie looked pitiful at the only person who could save her.

"You seem edgy lately. Is something wrong?" Keith asked. He was exhausted but always made time for his family. It was the first time in a long time he saw his daughter in the evening.

Linda ignored him and continued to bathe Indie. Keith decided to leave Linda alone. He waited until she was finished tucking Indie in bed before he snuck in and gave his daughter a kiss on the forehead. She opened her eyes and then closed them again. He walked back to the room and undressed. Linda walked sluggishly around the bed. She was not in the mood for sex. It had been almost a month since the last time. Either she was exhausted or Keith came home too late from delivering a baby. Sometimes, one of the children would join them in bed.

Linda turned off the lights and slipped into her side of the bed without facing Keith. He decided to mop up the mess in the bathroom. It surprised him that Linda left it in the middle of the floor. He came back into the room and turned on the lights.

"Maybe you need to consider going back to work or open that catering business you've been talking about. Why not go back to school?" he said for small talk. Linda adjusted the covers.

"Tell me what's going on," Keith said. He walked over to her side of the bed and sat down. He looked at the stressed expression on her face. He bent forward and placed a soft kiss on her neck.

"Not tonight Keith," she said. It seemed to be her favorite line lately.

"Okay," he responded without hesitating. "Your mother is going to be fine. She's a fighter, just like you. She has beat death twice," Keith said.

Linda shook her head. Her mother was not going to be fine and her mother was the fighter, not her. Barbara Stevens never considered giving up. Her mother was testing fate by going to see her baby sister. Linda knew she would never entertain the thought if her health was on the line. Only Barbara Stevens could be so brave.

"Mother is not going to be fine, Keith. She hasn't been to this Titusville place since I was a baby. No one wants to see her. She hasn't kept in touch with those people in years. They all probably hate her. She is going to be hurt when they don't welcome her into their homes. They say old people go home before they die," Linda preached before breaking into tears.

"Your mother is going to be fine. She's a strong woman like you," Keith said as he stroked Linda's hair.

"You're always saying that! I'm not strong! I'm not running for Regional Director!"

"Why not?"

"Lori is running. She's had way more exposure than me. There is no way I can beat her."

"You're talking like this because you're exhausted. When you get back, we need to discuss putting Indie in daycare. You've taken her along on enough visits. She needs to behave like a little girl."

Keith stopped stroking Linda's hair. "Lauren called me at the office today. She asked if she could spend a night to see Edward and Indie."

"I don't care."

"I want you to care. She's our goddaughter and a good one too. We haven't seen her in months. I don't want this conflict between you and Melanie to cloud our responsibilities to Lauren."

Keith turned out the lights. He walked over to his side of the bed and slipped under the covers. He scooted to Linda. "Since it will be two weeks before I get a chance to see you, I want to hold you in my arms tonight," he said. Linda eased back into his arms. He kissed her on the neck.

Barbara and Edward senior stood outside the gate at the airport waiting for Linda and Indie. Barbara saw Keith walk through the doors with Indie in his arms. Little Edward saw his grandfather and broke into a run. Indie bounced in Keith's arms. Barbara smiled at little Edward as he hugged her around the legs. She looked up at Indie and continued to smile.

"Hi Barba," Indie said.

Barbara stopped smiling. At one time the child called her "Mudda" trying to say "mother" like Linda. Barbara complained continuously. Now the child called her "Barba."

"Indie, I want you to say grandmother," Barbara said.

Indie looked around. Then she looked at Linda. "Don't look at me," Linda said.

"Say grandmother, sweetheart," Barbara insisted.

Indie put her fingers in her mouth and looked shyly at Barbara.

"Oh well, forget it," Barbara said. The group took off for the gate. Edward senior asked an airport attendant for a wheelchair. Barbara openly refused. She continued to walk slowly, taking her time.

They stood around the gate talking until it was time to leave. They boarded the plane and bid everyone farewell. The plane was half empty on it's way to St. Louis for an hour layover. Barbara had a seat in first class, leaving Linda and Indie in coach. Linda didn't care. She did not want to debate her mother about going to a place she had only heard horror stories about during the Civil Rights struggle. She had no interest in meeting her mother's people. They probably felt the same.

Once in St. Louis, Linda and Barbara each found a telephone and called friends until the plane was ready to board. They lost more passengers as they started loading. In a little more than an hour, Barbara and Linda would each make sight of the past. Barbara was a little nervous and Linda was uncomfortable. Indie sat in her seat busy with the doll Linda brought along.

Chapter Five

Upon their arrival to Birmingham, Linda found out that no one was greeting them at the airport. She was shocked to learn that no one expected them. Barbara never went anywhere uninvited. It was out of character for the woman who considered herself an expert in etiquette.

Linda asked the attendant at the rental counter about the location of either a Kmart or Wal-Mart. She needed a carseat for Indie. Barbara stood still the entire time. Linda managed to keep her temper under control as she got behind the steering wheel. Barbara remained quiet throughout the ride to Wal-Mart.

Linda made the necessary turns and parked the car on the lot. Barbara helped Indie out of the car. Indie broke out into a run. Before Barbara could catch her, a car came to a screeching stop. Indie was face to face with the bumper. A white woman with a deep Alabama accent rushed out of the car to see if Indie was hurt. Linda was breathless. She and the woman talked. Everything was fine. When the car pulled off, Linda was steaming. She started chastising Indie.

"Yelling at her will not keep her safe," Barbara said.

Linda gasped a little. She could remember many times being yelled at by her mother. Now since Barbara was a grandmother, the old parenting habits were obsolete. Linda ignored Barbara and carried Indie in her arms.

Indie was caramel brown with very thick hair which seemed unmanageable like her personality. She was tall for her age and leggy like her grandmother, Barbara. She had Keith's big clear eyes and long lashes. She had her mother's small plump lips and pug nose. Linda cooked healthy meals, so Indie, just like her brother Edward, was lean.

When they were inside the store, Barbara pulled out a cart.

"I didn't think we were going to shop," Linda said irritated.

"It's for Indie. Unless you want to chase her around the store," Barbara responded.

Linda put the precocious little girl in the basket. Indie looked around gravely until Linda began pushing. She went on her merry way to find a small portable carseat.

Barbara looked in the jewelry cases. She asked the sales associates about the watches and necklaces. She met Linda at the check-out with a bag in her hand.

"Don't tell me you bought jewelry from here," Linda said. Barbara nodded with a smile. "You bought your sister cheap jewelry for her fiftieth birthday?" Linda added with sarcasm.

"The watch may be cheap, but it tells the same time as the two hundred dollar watch on your wrist," Barbara said and walked away.

As long as Linda could remember, her mother never bought cheap jewelry. Every piece of jewelry Barbara had was expensive, even her scarf clips. So many things were not clicking to Linda. She decided to let it pass and complete the trip in peace.

The group got back into the car and headed to Titusville, which was pronounced Tit-tus-ville. It was twenty minutes on the outskirts of the city. As they left the city limits of Birmingham, Linda noticed some small frame houses were in need of repair. She hoped that they would look better but was slightly disappointed. She was use to new things. The houses were not bad but to her, they were old.

As Barbara gave directions onto a main strip outside Titusville. Linda's small excitement about seeing her relatives dwindled. Some houses looked like shacks. She drove the car almost into the yard of an old beige house. It looked a little better than the other houses she had seen along the way.

Linda was disgusted. It was the first trip to the South and it reminded her of pictures she had seen of the rural South after reconstruction. There was no way she was staying in the dainty house that could not have had more than five rooms. She took a deep breath. "I'm not staying here. No one is expecting us, so why are we doing this? Mother this is crazy!"

"Dis is qua-see," Indie said in the back seat with lips poked out.

Barbara gathered her bags and purse. "You don't need an invitation for country people. And why are we doing this? Like I said, it's my baby sister's birthday. Another thing, you don't have to stay here," Barbara answered and got out of the car. She walked up three steps onto a weak porch. It still looked the same, fragile.

Barbara looked at her mother's brass cross on the front door. It was in desperate need of polishing. A great deal of work had been done on the house. The screen door had been replaced but the new one was rickety. Barbara knocked on the door. She fought for what to say. It had been over thirty years since her last visit and twelve years since she last spoke to anyone. Rose was the baby sister who lived in their parents' house. She was the only one who stayed in Titusville.

A little chubby boy, around four-years-old, opened the door. His undershirt was too small for his belly. He had round cheeks and little marble eyes. He looked strangely at the tall woman. Barbara smiled. "Is Rosie Jones here?" she asked politely.

The little boy nodded and took off running and yelling, "Grandma, somebody's at th' do'." Barbara stood still, daring not to walk inside. She took deep breaths. Linda and Indie were standing behind her.

The little boy appeared again with his grandmother. She was medium height and very brown. She had strong legs and broad shoulders, covered by a cotton shift. Her several strands of gray hair were pinned up. Her expression was blank until Barbara called her by name.

"Hi Rosie. It's me, Bobbie."

Rosie's grin spread wide across her face. She was in shock. Tears filled her eyes. She put her hands to her mouth. "Oh Lord! I can't believe you came home. I always knew you would. C'mon inside."

Barbara walked inside the old and what was once familiar living room. It was wider since the heating stove had been removed. The walls were bright with flowered wallpaper. The furniture was different. The house was different. Barbara began to relax as she looked at Rosie.

"Happy Birthday Rosie. I bought you something," Barbara said pleasantly and gave Rosie three boxes.

Rosie slowly opened them and gasped at the sight of the gifts. Her eyes continued to water. "These are so beautiful. I can't believe you remembered my birthday. Thanks Bobbie." Rosie gave Barbara a big hug. It took awhile before they released the embrace.

"You look wonderful, Rosie. I guess it's been a long time. Over thirty years but you knew how things were."

"You know you're welcome whether it's thirty years or forty. We're family. We all still love you. My God, Bobbie, you look good. You still with that doctor?" Rosie asked earnestly.

"Edward is fine. This is my daughter Malinda and my granddaughter Indie. I have a grandson too. This is your Aunt Rosie," Barbara said to Linda. She tried looking happy, but the house was fairly warm. Linda hated heat.

"Nice meeting you. . .Rosie," Linda said professionally.

Rosie chuckled. "I bet you married a doctor too," she said. Linda gave a half smile. "You look just like your momma. How long y'all staying?" Rosie continued.

"For a week. We're going to get a room at a hotel in Birmingham," Barbara said.

Rosie shook her head. "Y'all staying right here. I got plenty of room. There's another bedroom in the back."

Rosie's grandson asked if Indie could go outside and play. He tried crossing his fat arms over his pot belly.

"Sure. Y'all be careful, you hear?" Rosie said.

The little boy escorted Indie out the back. Linda was jittery. She didn't know how outside looked. Indie had never been outside unchaperoned. She had always been in a controlled environment.

"Maybe Indie should stay inside for awhile," Linda rushed to say.

"She'll be fine. She's safer here than in Kansas City," Rosie said.

They sat on the sofa, catching up on the family. Barbara knew that two of her siblings were dead. Only five of the Wright children were still alive. Barbara had thirty nieces and nephews. Eight died either by murder or at birth. Rosie alone had six.

Barbara got the strength to ask about Uncle Jay. Rosie hesitated. "He's still alive, barely. He ain't got much of a memory left."

As they talked, Linda found out that Rosie had been very active in the Civil Rights struggle in Birmingham. She was a participant in the March on Washington to witness the famous "I Have A Dream" speech. Rosie gave up a college education to partake in the struggle. As Rosie talked, Linda became more fascinated. She forgot about the cubby house.

"Why did you give up college? You could have had so much," Linda said.

Rosie smiled. She had a very pleasant face. She and Barbara had the same eyes, but Rosie's eyes looked inviting. Barbara's eyes questioned people.

"Some of us had to be soldiers and some had to get the education to help with the legal matters. It was hard for me to do both. I liked what I did. I have no regrets. Everything turned out fine," Rosie said.

Indie and her new friend came into the house happy. Indie rushed to Linda holding something in her hands. "Look mommie," Indie said and lifted her hands high in Linda's face.

Linda screamed at the creature. She almost jumped off the sofa. "Indie no! Put that thing outside," she said and pushed Indie's hands away. Rosie and Barbara laughed.

"Chile you are too city-fied for me. Chunky, you and India go outside with that frog," Rosie ordered.

Linda wanted to correct Rosie on Indie's name but decided against it. She began fanning herself with a sheet of paper as they continued talking.

"The more you fan, the hotter it gits. Just relax and enjoy yo' self," Rosie said.

"It's very warm in here. I don't like heat," Linda said but she stopped fanning. She tried relaxing, but it was still difficult. She began to fidget.

"Bobbie, I want you to see the library your sorority donated. It has your name on a plaque in the inside. Everybody in town knows Barbara Wright Stevens is a homegirl," Rosie said loud and proud. Barbara nodded.

Linda questioned Barbara about the library. Rosie told the story. It was ten years ago when Barbara had a good friend from the Birmingham chapter to start a fund raiser to help the community. They decided on a library. It took a few years to purchase and renovate an old building to become not only an educational facility but a place for job training and to socialize. The big problem was funding salaries for the staff. The sorority had done all that they could do. So the good grass root people of the community became involved and got the state to fund the library. That took an additional four years.

When Barbara received the settlement from the sale of her boutique, she made a contribution of a couple of computers and fixtures to the library. She also help extend the holdings and renovated a room for reading.

"So Malinda, what do you do?" Rosie asked in anticipation of knowing the niece to the sister she admired so much was probably socially active too.

Linda became embarrassed immediately. She had done nothing but worked in the sorority since she resigned from World Airlines. The way she had been treated by the sorority, she figured what she had done was nothing. She decided to tell Rosie about the programs she developed with the new chapter.

Linda started with the multi-cultural week at her son's grade school and then elaborated on the health fairs. When the smile came across Rosie's face, Linda relaxed.

"I knew you was as strong as your momma. Dr. King's dream was to see a multi-cultural week. Having a health fair that goes back to the old medicine is a good idea too. You never know what they prescribing these days. It ain't doing nothing but killing people. Bobbie, I know you proud of her."

"Yes I am. Malinda has been a big help to me. She's also running for an office in the sorority. It's on the regional level," Barbara said, not emphasizing or bragging.

Linda wondered what her mother would say if she knew of the change in plans? Linda figured Barbara wasn't too keen on the idea of her running for regional director anyway. Linda concluded Barbara would choose Lori over her any day.

Lori gained Barbara's respect by doing something no one thought she could pull off. She was able to convince fifty members of the old chapter to leave and establish a new one. Melanie convinced sixty more to join within two years. All members were a little over forty years or younger. The chapter received recognition from Nationals within two years after the split.

Rosie walked into the kitchen to prepare dinner. Her husband Calvin was expected home in two hours. Linda reluctantly retrieved the luggage from the trunk of the car and hauled them to the proper bedrooms. Barbara went into the kitchen to help Rosie with dinner. Indie and Chunky were outside playing.

Soon they heard the front door open and footsteps. Calvin was home. He was a tall brown stout man with sleepy eyes and a humble spirit. He had on a sanitation uniform. When Rosie introduced him to Barbara, he just smiled and said, "Nice meeting you ma'am." He began his usual routine by going into the bathroom to clean up for supper.

They sat down to smothered pork chops, fried corn and sweet potatoes. Linda saw cholesterol written all over the entire meal, but she had to try it. Barbara ate the meal without hesitating. Indie ate as if she were starving. Linda took a small bite into the pork chop. The first awareness was, it wasn't salty. The onions, garlic, celery and peppers added zest to the meat. The only time Linda saw fried corn was at Miss Mattie's house, but she didn't try it. She took a small fork full of the corn and slowly wrapped her lips around it. She was hooked. She was determined to make Rosie share the recipe.

After dinner, they went into the living room, which Rosie called the front room. They sat down with full stomachs. Indie and Chunky sat on the wooden floor and played with a puzzle. Rosie brought out the family photo albums. She gave one to Barbara and another to Linda. Rosie sat between the two.

Linda opened the book and saw old photos of people she had never seen before. Rosie gave names to everyone on the page. Some were aunts and uncles. Some were second and third line cousins. Linda turned to a picture of a girl at a carnival. Her head was pressed through a poster board of a mermaid.

Rosie roared with laughter. "That's Bobbie!"

Barbara leaned over to see the old photo. She was fifteen when it was taken. She gave a light chuckle. Linda flipped a few pages and came across the missing link. It was a picture of the grandmother she had never seen or heard of. Linda's eyes asked

Rosie the question.

"That's momma. She was so pretty then," Rosie said.

Linda didn't think the picture was so pretty. The woman's face was too wide for the hairstyle. The eyes looked sad. She had on a cheap fancy dress that emphasized a heavy chest. Linda stared at the picture hard. The woman looked more like Rosie than Barbara.

Linda flipped another page. A fair complexion man with processed straight hair was staring her in the face. He looked like a gangster in the hat. He was posed in a stiff position. He was tall and skinny with slits for eyes.

"That's daddy. He was one fine man," Rosie said.

Linda gawked at the picture. The man looked like a slickster.

"Bobbie, I called Sugah Doo and Babe Bruh. They're coming over tomorrow to see you. We're going to barbecue," Rosie said, hoping Barbara gave her approval.

"It should be a fantastic birthday celebration. I'm going to get some rest. Malinda, I'll get Indie ready for bed. Come sweetie," Barbara said to Indie.

Reluctantly, Indie obeyed Barbara and followed. As Barbara ran the bath water, Indie sat quietly on the floor waiting. Exhaustion was all over the little girl's face.

"Barba, I taka bath?" Indie asked.

Barbara nodded. She felt weak. She looked down at the little girl. Melissa's face appeared. Gradually, it went away.

"Stand up sweetie so that grandmother can undress you."

Indie stood and lifted her arms. Barbara eased Indie's shirt over her head. The electricity began to flow between Indie and Barbara. She became warm. She wanted to call for help.

Indie removed the rest of her clothes and climbed into the tub. She splashed in the water. She tried reciting Green Eggs and Ham like her brother. Barbara sat on the toilet seat and let Indie bathe herself. The trip was taking a bite out of Barbara. It was time to rest.

Rosie and Linda stayed up talking. Linda learned more about her mother's unknown family. Her grandmother, Effie Cole Wright was a blues singer, who became pregnant at the age of sixteen by a man who owned a jook joint across the railroad tracks. The tall, smooth-talking, skinny man they called "Po Boy" was forced to marry her.

Effie sang a few more months at the jook joint after Barbara was born before she started showing with her next child Gertrude, the one they called Birdie. Effie's career ended after the third child was born. Effie continued to give Po Boy more children, seven all together. He even fathered two children by a woman who lived in a shotgun house up the road. They called her Hotsy Roxie. All the men came to her house to buy liquor and to gamble. Po Boy spent most of his time with Hotsy Roxie until he got pneumonia. It was Effie who nursed him until he passed on.

Rosie was five-years-old at the time their father died. His brother Jay moved in to help the family. That's when the trouble began. Rosie paused for a second and changed the topic. She told Linda about the uncles and aunts. Sugah Doo, Nellie Ann, was the middle child. She was what they called a "high stepper", a fast woman. She moved to Birmingham after graduating from high school and lived there ever since. She tried a music career but had no luck. Now, she works at a factory, divorced and has three sons and one daughter. Rosie talked about how tough Sugah Doo was. She stabbed her first husband while he slept, for beating her.

Babe Bruh, Irvin Lee, was the youngest boy. He's a sanitation worker in Birmingham. He followed his favorite sister, Sugah Doo. He was one year older than Rosie. He's married with four children. He, Barbara and Birdie looked like their father.

Birdie was the mystery sister. When she left Titusville, she never came back, not even for their mother's funeral. Linda noticed it didn't bother Rosie that their sister pretty much wrote off the family. Rosie smiled as she talked about Birdie. There was still a sense of respect and honor. Linda soon found out that Birdie married a big time politician in Nashville and has two daughters who were suppose to be pretty. Birdie worked at a law firm as a para legal.

Rosie touched on the two that were dead, A.C. and Odie Lee. Odie was the oldest boy and the third oldest child. He was shot at a craps game. A.C. was two years younger than Sugah Doo. He died at the hands of a white police officer during one of the protests in Birmingham.

Linda asked about Barbara. Rosie smiled and told Linda how Barbara had all kinds of dreams. She worked hard at everything she did. Nothing came easy for her. She left the family after graduating from high school and only came home for their mother's funeral. Barbara was the mother when their mother had to work. Barbara cooked well and sewed even better. She made all of their clothes.

Linda could feel the effect of the plane ride. It was time for bed. "Rosie, I'm going to retire now. Thanks for dinner."

"You don't have to thank me for dinner. You know you're always welcome. Let me get you a blanket. I saved you the back room. You should enjoy the country air," Rosie said. She removed the sleeping Chunky from the floor and put him in bed.

Linda walked by her mother's room. She and Indie were tucked away sleeping. It was an unfamiliar sight to Linda. Her mother only slept with her father. She never allowed Linda or the grandchildren to sit on her bed.

Linda continued to the back room. She hoped that she would sleep comfortably in the strange bed. She only slept in hotel rooms while traveling. She stood in the doorway of the back room. It was the newest room, which wasn't saying much. It was spotless. Linda opened her overnight bag and went into the bathroom. There was no shower curtain. She had to run bath water. She gave a huff and turned on the faucets.

The next evening, Sugah Doo and Babe Bruh came to Rosie's house for the barbecue. Sugah Doo was the darkest of everyone. She had the same face shape as the mother but with bigger eyes. She looked fairly young for her age of fifty six. She smiled a lot and wore very trendy clothes for a woman her age.

When she saw Barbara, all she asked was, "You still with that doctor?" Sugah Doo sat down and lit a cigarette.

Babe Bruh hugged and kissed Barbara. He cried a little, telling Barbara how great she looked. Barbara's eyes began to mist. Babe Bruh was tall and skinny like their father. He was the lightest of everyone. He had a square face with slanted eyes like their father. Babe Bruh was soft spoken with a humble attitude.

The two family members welcomed Barbara home without any explanation. It had been a little over thirty years since they had seen her. Everyone, except Linda, knew why Barbara left. They didn't care that she refused to pick up the telephone to see how they were doing. Rosie was fine with the notion that Barbara had a library donated to their community and not once laid eyes on it. All was well. To Linda, it was strange. Her mother's siblings were the most forgiving folks she had ever met.

They talked about old times and old sweethearts. It became clear that every man Sugah Doo dated was eventually scared of her. She took no mess off of anyone. She was the family fighter. Even Barbara and Birdie, the two oldest, had to give her respect.

They talked about their favorite singers and then began to sing. They started off singing church songs, harmonizing melodiously. They knew their cues without practice. The real talent started when each sang their favorite songs in their own style. Rosie sang gospel with her soprano voice. Sugah Doo did a little jazz in the style of Sarah Vaughn. Babe Bruh sang some Nat King Cole. It was Barbara's turn. They had to prod her into singing her once favorite, the blues.

"Look hussy, g'on and sing," Sugah Doo said.

Barbara smiled a little. Then in a raspy voice, she bellowed a couple of Billy Holiday songs. Linda sat in amazement as her mother stepped out of character and sang of being mistreated. They all clapped when Barbara finished.

Sugah Doo turned to Linda and said, "I know you can sing. Let's hear it."

Linda was a little embarrassed. She enjoyed singing, but only in the shower. She never sang in front of anyone. Even in college, the sorority knew Linda could sing well, but she never would do it.

"Come on chile. Sing one of your favorites," Rosie said.

Linda looked at Barbara. "Why are you looking at me? You know any songs?" Barbara asked sharply. Linda looked at the smiling faces in the room and became more nervous. Even Indie smiled at her.

"Honey, take a deep breath and let it roll from your chest," Sugah Doo said.

Linda looked down. She took a deep breath and lifted her head. She began singing Whitney Houston's, *All The Man I Need*. When she finished singing, everyone clapped including Chunky and Indie.

"Girl, that song is one of my favorites. All the man I need, um, um, um," Sugah said.

The family connected when they entertained Linda by joking and teasing one another. They talked about Birdie, the one that was next to the oldest but behaved as if she were the oldest. They commented on how Barbara invited the family to the wedding of the doctor, but Birdie didn't invite anyone to see the politician. No one had seen the likes of Birdie's husband. But they were proud that their sister married a politician. He was someone they could brag about.

Barbara came up with the idea of calling Birdie. Everyone stopped talking and looked at her nervously. Rosie and Babe Bruh looked jittery at one another. Sugah Doo broke into a loud chuckle. She always enjoyed the rivalry.

"Rosie, do you have Birdie's number?" Barbara asked.

"Let her be, Bobbie. She don't won't to be bothered with nobody. We're having a good time. Let's not spoil it," Rosie said almost stammering.

"I say g'on and call her. Bobbie got herself a doctor. I bet he makes more money than that politician of Birdie's," Sugah Doo said.

"Don't worry Rosie. Birdie and I speak the same language. This will give her an opportunity to wish you happy birthday. Do you have her number?" Barbara asked a little more firmly.

Rosie looked around the room and then disappeared. Sugah Doo lit another cigarette and began singing.

Rosie came back with her phone book. She handed it to Barbara. She took it and then pressed several numbers on the key pad. Rosie looked on curiously. "Why you punching so many numbers?" she asked.

"It's my calling card number. This way, you don't pay for the call," Barbara replied. It was odd that Rosie knew nothing about a calling card.

"Oh hello, may I speak to Gertrude please. . .Birdie, this is Bobbie. How are you?" Barbara said gaily. There was a long pause before Birdie spoke. Barbara's eyebrows raised. After being on the telephone for ten minutes, she walked to a corner to finish talking.

Rosie and Babe Bruh were tense. Something was wrong. Every time the older ones turned their backs meant something was wrong. Sugah Doo blew rings of smoke in the air. She turned to Linda. "So you got yourself a doctor too, huh? You go girl! I wished I could find a doctor to marry me. It makes life a little easier," Sugah Doo said with a smile.

Usually, a comment like that would have offended Linda. But such a comment from Sugah was part of her personality. Linda liked Sugah Doo's mental and physical toughness. The stories Sugah Doo told about defending herself against an abusive husband and having to fight women because they liked her second husband, Linda could tell Sugah Doo was an attractive, fast woman in her day. The old photo showed big legs, big hips and a small waistline. She had been married twice and had nothing to rebound from after each time.

After twenty minutes of talking, Barbara turned around and handed Rosie the telephone. "It's for you," Barbara said.

Rosie hesitated before taking the phone. She slowly brought it to her ear. "What should I say? She don't won't to be bothered with us," Rosie complained.

"Don't talk loud. She will hear you," Barbara shushed.

Rosie struggled to keep the phone to her ear. She took a deep breath and spoke. Her eyes got big and she eyed each of her sibling. Soon a smile broke across her face. Babe Bruh smiled too. Sugah Doo extinguished her cigarette and blew the last smoke.

"Let me talk to that uppity hussy. I ain't talked to her in ten years," Sugah Doo said and took the phone from Rosie who wasn't quite finished. Rosie sat next to Babe Bruh and looked up at Sugah Doo.

Sugah Doo talked loud. "So when we gonna to see that man of yours. . .You don't sound good. What's the matter?" There was a long pause before Sugah turned her back. The two youngest looked fearful again. They knew something was wrong with Birdie. Sugah Doo turned around and spoke low but everyone could still hear her.

"Are you sure you want your family around. . .Oh." Sugah's voice trailed off. She talked to Birdie for several minutes. Babe Bruh got the courage to stand next to Sugah, extending his hand, asking for the phone.

Sugah flashed Babe Bruh a quick look and frown. "Bruh wants to say something...Okay Birdie. See you soon."

Sugah Doo gave the telephone to Babe Bruh and walked over
to Barbara. Babe Bruh grinned as he talked to Birdie. They
waited until Babe Bruh finished his conversation. He was excited
when he hung up. He turned around into three solemn faces. As
always, they had discussed something without him.

"Birdie's got cancer. Same thang momma had," Sugah Doo
said.

Babe Bruh's joy turned sour. He shook his head and looked
sadly at his sisters.

"She's coming to visit us as soon as she's strong," Sugah Doo
added for comfort. Babe Bruh nodded. He took his mother's death
terribly. He cried a long time at the funeral and withdrew for
awhile. All of his sisters were important to him, but Sugah Doo
was his favorite. She was the most patient.

"I want to take you and your families out to dinner. I want to
meet my nieces and nephews," Barbara said to break the
stillness. She watched Babe Bruh's eyes light up with hope.

"You don't want to take all of our chilluns out. Most of them
grown. Hell, they eat like horses, specially Rosie's chilluns. Look
at that fat-tail grandson of hers," Sugah Doo said. Everyone knew
she was talking about Chunky.

"That's enough, Sugah," said the maternal Barbara.

Everyone gathered around to cut the cake. The group sang
more songs. Barbara decided to visit Birdie. There was still more
forgiving to do.

Chapter Six

Linda and Barbara sat in the comfortable home of Barbara's friend from the Kappa's chapter in Birmingham. The woman was a widow. She and Barbara were friends from during the time Barbara traveled as a national official. They small talked about the old days. Barbara pulled Linda into the conversation by commenting on her hard work with the Kansas City Alumnae, the old chapter. The woman asked about Floristine Massey, Gloria Bircher and several others. Linda answered knowingly because she talked to the women at least once a week.

Barbara mentioned Linda's quest for the Central region's director position and how Floristine and Gloria were supporting her. The woman lit up.

"You must be very special if Floristine is supporting you. Sometimes young women are a little too eager to make changes. Everything has it's proper place and time," said the woman.

"You're right Edna. When the young women decided to leave the chapter, we were devastated. We tried talking them into waiting until they were ready. Sometimes, I think their decision was a little hasty. The leadership is lacking a little wisdom," Barbara commented, causing Edna to shake her head.

Linda almost choked on Barbara's spiel. She remembered Barbara and a few others supporting the younger women on their quest. The older women wanted the young ones out of their hair. Barbara made sure that a reception was held when the new chapter started.

"Young people are just too impatient. Malinda, you're doing the right thing by learning from the experiences of mature women like Floristine and Gloria. I have several friends in the Oklahoma City, Denver, Ohio and Indiana Alumnaes. I think I will give them a call. You are such a sweet girl," Edna said to a smiling Linda. She complimented the woman's decor. Edna started on her story about wanting to be an interior designer. Linda commented on the right cues and asked the right questions.

"Malinda, you are such a bright girl. I will call my friends today. I want you to visit them. I can't wait for them to meet you," Edna said as if her friends lived in the neighborhood. Linda nodded. She knew once she had given her word to the old woman, she was expected to act upon it within a couple of weeks. They all expected her to respond immediately.

"Barbara, how is Ed?" Edna asked.

Barbara began talking about Edward. The conversation later went to grandchildren. Barbara pulled out pictures and Edna brought out a photo album. Both had the smartest and cutest grandbabies in the world. Linda politely offered to get them something to drink. Edna smiled the biggest.

"She's such a sweet girl," Edna commented to Barbara who also smiled.

After the women drank a glass of lemonade, they continued looking at pictures. Finally, Barbara made the first move to go. They had to get back to Titusville to pick up Indie. Barbara and Edna hugged each other. Edna gave Linda a tight hug.

"Now don't lose that list of names. I want you to give me a call after you visit them," Edna said.

"Thanks, Mrs. Mosley. I'll be talking to you within two weeks," Linda said.

They were on the plane to Nashville. Barbara rode in coach, a seat in front of Indie and Linda. Indie kept transferring between seats. Finally Barbara made her sit with Linda. That put an end to the little girl's excitement.

When the plane landed, Linda went to pick up a rental car. Indie stayed with Barbara who called Birdie for directions. It was a twenty minute drive from the airport. Linda was impressed as she drove through the beautiful neighborhoods with well kept lawns. She felt at home. According to the directions, they were close to Birdie's house. They arrived at a fairly large size house, located in a private neighborhood. Rose bushes outlined the front of the house.

Linda parked closest to the sidewalk of a three car driveway. Before she got out, she looked at an exhausted Barbara. "Are you okay?" Linda asked. Barbara nodded weakly. She had to get some rest. The trip was taking it's toll. The heavy eating wasn't helping her condition. She decided to watch her diet for the duration of the trip. For what Barbara remembered of Birdie's cooking, it wasn't going to be difficult.

The front door opened without them ringing the doorbell. Barbara was still for awhile and so was Linda. She could have sworn she was seeing her mother's twin. Birdie was a couple of inches shorter than Barbara. Both had the same hairstyle, a salt-n-pepper Toni Braxton look.

Barbara spoke first. "Hello Gertrude."

"Hello Barbara. Come in," Birdie said.

Barbara introduced Linda and Indie to Birdie. Then she and Barbara embraced. Birdie was very thin but her presence was fairly healthy. She took them around the house. Each room had its own personality. The living room and dining room was Victorian. A side room which Birdie called her Tea room had a sunny California look. The library was filled with black art. The sunroom was Oriental and the kitchen was old country. To Linda, the house was interesting.

"How long are you staying?" Birdie asked.

"Until Sunday. We're staying at the Opryland Hotel," Barbara answered.

Birdie's eyebrows raised. "So you know about Nashville?" she asked.

"I've traveled this way several times for the sorority," Barbara said.

"Which sorority?"

"Phi Kappa Psi."

"I'm an Alpha. My two daughters are Kappas," Birdie said dryly and walked into the kitchen. Linda and Barbara raised eyebrows to one another. "You don't have to stay in a hotel. You can stay with me. We have plenty of room," Birdie said.

"Thank you, Birdie. So how are you?"

"Just over five months ago, I was sitting in the doctors office with a small lump in my breast. I didn't think much about it. When they did the biopsy, it came back malignant. At times, I wished I had never gone to the doctor."

Barbara did not want to stare at the obvious. Birdie's top was very large. No one could tell. "Did you have a double mastectomy?" Barbara asked. Birdie nodded. Her attention went to Indie. She sat patiently at the table enjoying the conversation. Birdie thought how well behaved Indie was in comparison to her granddaughter.

"Hello precious. How are you?" Birdie cooed to Indie.

"Fine tank coo," Indie answered. Everyone chuckled.

"My daughter Kelly is coming over for dinner tonight. She's married to an architect and has a two-year-old daughter named Aundrea. My daughter Deidra recently married a dentist. She lives in Philadelphia," Birdie said, slightly bragging.

"So what does Kelly and Deidra do for a living?" Barbara

inquired.

"Kelly teaches and Deidra will probably live off her husband. That child is lazy!"

Linda waited for Barbara to begin bragging about Keith and little Edward. It didn't happen. They sat watching Birdie as she went to the refrigerator. She struggled to remove a tray. Linda rushed to help. She took the platter from Birdie and sat it on the table. It was a fruit tray with a crab salad in the middle bowl. Birdie removed a small covered basket from the oven. It was filled with breads.

Birdie walked over to the cabinets to get the plates but turned to Linda. "Sweetheart, could you take down four salad plates and three tea cups. The baby can drink out of a plastic cup," Birdie said. Linda obediently followed the instructions.

"My husband, Carl and I are giving a dinner party. I want both of you to attend," Birdie said. She took out the serving utensils and placed them on the platter. "There's a nice restaurant downtown. I thought we could go there tomorrow for dinner. Friday night, we can go to a dinner theater. I think you will enjoy it."

Everyone's plate was filled, except Birdie's. She didn't have much of an appetite. Linda bit into the crab salad and knew right away it was store bought. She didn't want the rest. Indie ate heartily. She always had a huge appetite. To Linda, it was a good sign. She didn't want the same thing that happened to Camille to happen to Indie. They said it was SIDS but Linda thought it was from nutrition.

Barbara ate a small portion of the crab salad. She came to the conclusion that the rest of the week would be either restaurants or store prepared foods. Birdie brought out an apple pie from the refrigerator. She was about to heat it when Barbara and Linda immediately declined. Birdie was about to cut a slice for Indie until Linda stopped her. She didn't allow her children to eat sweets.

"So Carl is a politician?" Barbara asked.

"Not now. He works for a law firm and is a law professor at the university. He served a few terms in the House of Representatives. I was glad when he gave it up. It was too much of a compromise and I wanted out of the district we lived in."

Linda excused herself to get the luggage. She walked sluggishly to the car and pulled out the suitcases. They were getting heavier.

"Where Chungy?" Indie asked as she walked beside Linda.

"He's at home with his grandmother. He is going to visit you this summer," Linda said. They walked inside the house. Birdie directed Linda to the guest rooms at the east wing of the house. Linda walked up the stairs and became more impressed with the decor.

All the rooms were freshly painted. Linda selected a room painted soft blue with a dark blue, orange and green starlet print border. There were double beds for her and Indie. Linda put her mother's luggage in the bedroom with miniature figurines on the dresser and a queen size bed. The room had it's own bathroom.

Linda went back to her room and unpacked quickly. Her wardrobe had dwindled after giving Sugah Doo two pairs of shoes and a scarf. Rosie's teenage granddaughter was given a pair of shorts, jeans and shirt. Linda still had enough clothes to last her the duration of the trip.

She decided to take a shower and nap. She assumed Indie was tired too but bored. She continually asked for Chunky whom she called "Chungy." The pair played well together. Indie stayed dirty during their stay in Titusville. She loved the very shallow creek that was behind the house. She enjoyed searching for frogs and insects too.

Birdie's house was familiar to Linda. It was just like home. Although she rested well in the back room with the country air, she felt at home with Birdie. Linda undressed Indie and turned on the shower nozzle. Indie complained, saying she wanted to take a bath. The baths at Rosie proved relaxing, but Linda was used to showers. As Indie sang about taking a bath, Linda blew out air. She ran bath water. She used the bath oil balls she saw on the basin counter. She got undressed and eased herself and Indie into the tub.

Indie splashed around for awhile. Linda saw a mark on the back of Indie's left shoulder. It was in the shape of a small patch. She tried rubbing the mark until Indie complained. It was the first time Linda noticed the little patch. It reminded her of the same birthmark Camille had on her left thigh.

Indie wanted to get out. Linda made her stay a little longer, but Indie had too much energy. She turned faucets on and off. She splashed the water wildly. Linda could not relax. She finally yielded to Indie's demands and got out of the tub. She took a plush towel and patted Indie dry. Linda turned the towel on herself and began drying off until Indie took off running naked down the hallway. It was the usual routine, but Linda was nude too.

Linda caught Indie who was giggling with joy. Linda laughed, too. She gave Indie a big kiss on the cheeks.

"Mommie, Barba," Indie said, pointing down the hall.

"No. Indie must take a nap."

"No!"

Linda put Indie on pajamas and put her in bed. Indie lifted her head in retaliation. Linda put on a gown and laid beside her. As Linda waited for Indie to sleep, the rejuvenation process kicked

in, causing Linda to drift off to sleep. Indie eased off the bed and
went down the six steps to see her grandmother.

Barbara and Birdie looked curiously at Indie who looked
guilty. "Mommie sheep," Indie said and walked into the living
room. She walked around the cocktail table, admiring the shiny
objects that rested there.

"Pwetty," Indie said with a smile. She put her hands behind
her back.

"She's very obedient," Birdie said.

"Malinda is too lazy to put up her nice things so she has
trained both children not to touch," Barbara commented.

"You were telling me that her first baby died?"

"SIDS. She was about three months old."

"She seems to have handled the death fairly well."

"Not really. She hasn't worked in five years. She volunteers at
my grandson's daycare. Most of her time is spent with the
sorority. She's running for regional director for the Central
region."

"Great! It should be a good experience."

"She needs to toughen up a little. She's a little soft. When
things become frustrating, she's more likely to leave it alone. She
only has patience with older people and that's not saying much. If
she wants to become regional director, she must learn how to
negotiate. You know how it is working with egos."

Indie came running out of the kitchen. "Eat!" she shouted.
The two women got up and went into the kitchen.

Linda heard noises downstairs. She slowly turned her head to
the other bed and saw no Indie. Linda looked at the clock on the
dresser. She had been asleep four hours. She quickly got up and
dressed. She walked downstairs and saw more guests in the
house. She assumed the older gentleman was Carl and the
younger one was Kelly's husband, the architect. There was a little
girl standing beside a young woman in her early thirties. It had to
be Kelly and her daughter Aundrea.

The host and the hostess finalized dinner plans. Barbara went
upstairs to freshen up. Linda and Indie rode in the Explorer with
Kelly and her family. Barbara rode in the Mercedes with Birdie
and Carl. On the way to the restaurant, Linda came to the
conclusion that Kelly was accustomed to entertaining. She was
extremely polite, not friendly. Linda thought back to Sugah Doo,
Rosie and Babe Bruh families. Everyone was relaxed and inviting.
Linda should have been comfortable with Kelly. She was what
Linda was accustomed to.

A table was waiting in the back of the restaurant upon their
arrival. The waitress found boosters for the little girls and handed
out menus. Indie looked across the table at her cousin. She

stared back curiously. The adults looked through the menus in silence. Linda decided on oysters and Barbara wanted the cold salmon.

The group talked as needed. Kelly turned to Linda and asked,"What does your husband do?"

Although Kelly was polite, Linda was a little perturbed. She never enjoyed discussing Keith's profession as if he were her trophy. Before she responded, the arrogant look on Kelly's husband's face made Linda speak loudly. "He's an obstetrician gynecologist," she said pleasantly.

"Oh! How's business?" Carl asked jokingly.

"Booming!" Linda said, extending her arms from her stomach. Everyone gave a light chuckle.

"What do you do Malinda?" Kelly's husband asked. His attitude had changed some. He had a genuine smile.

"Right now, I volunteer at my son's daycare. Most of my time is spent with the sorority. This Fall, I'll be working on my Master's."

"I was hoping Malinda would start a catering business. She's excellent," Barbara said.

"Mother, why don't you ask Malinda to cater Saturday night? Her cooking has got to be better than yours," Kelly said, making a joke. Birdie was not at all flattered with her daughter's sarcasm. She gave her an unwelcome look.

The waitress brought out the entrees. Linda took her time, assisting Indie with her meal. Indie used silverware but still had a difficult time coordinating with hand and mouth. She used her hands to help her meal along.

Kelly gave Aundrea a plate to fend for herself. She too had problems with the fork so she ate with her hands also. Kelly began lightly chastising.

"Kelly, I told you she is going to eat with her hands until she's able to handle the silverware," Birdie said calmly.

"I don't want her growing up like a pig," Kelly snapped.

"Then feed her," Birdie said firmly. She did not let her eye contact leave her daughter. Kelly blew steam and assisted Aundrea with her meal.

"Aunt Birdie, I can cater Saturday night if you like?" Linda offered.

"*Aunt Birdie?*" Kelly shrieked.

Birdie was about to lose her patience. "My brothers and sisters called me Birdie growing up," she said.

"I'm sorry Aunt Gertrude," Linda said. Birdie waved her hand as to say "forget it." The group finished their meal in silence, just what Linda was use to.

Linda was in Barbara's room watching her mother prepare for

bed. Linda couldn't tell if Barbara was tired or ill. She moved slowly. Indie jumped on the bed and tried getting under the covers. Linda tried coaxing her into sleeping in her own bed.

"Let her stay. Thank God she isn't like that obnoxious brat of Kelly's," Barbara complained, turning up her nose. Linda laughed. Aundrea did not behave well. She gave everyone a fit except Birdie. She took her to the restroom and Aundrea came back with watered eyes.

"Night mommie," Indie said.

"Good night, baby," Linda responded.

Linda went to her room. She tried getting comfortable in the pretty bed but couldn't. The house was too quiet. Soon it wasn't. Linda heard arguing from down the hall. It wasn't loud, more on the line of a discussion. Linda knew Birdie and Carl were having a fight.

Soon a door slammed. Linda tried closing her eyes to sleep. All she could think about was Birdie without breast and Carl not finding her attractive anymore. Linda wondered how Keith would handle a mastectomy. He would probably be more understanding because he was a doctor. But he was a man first. Linda concentrated hard on going to sleep. It wasn't her business.

Friday morning, Linda took Birdie to the grocery store. They small talked for awhile. "Your mother tells me that you are running for Regional Director," Birdie said. Linda closed her eyes in exasperation then shook her head.

"What's the matter? Don't you want the office?" Birdie asked.

"It's not that. Mother talks too much," Linda said.

Birdie looked at Linda out of the corners of her eyes as they searched the aisles for items. "Politics is a self absorbed business. Politicians liked the idea of people knowing they are running for office. It helps get votes. You can't be afraid to get out there and sell yourself, figuratively speaking," Birdie said. She picked up a can of tomato paste and put it into the cart. Linda took it out.

"I like using fresh tomatoes when I cook. I'm not afraid. I just don't want Mother telling everyone. It's not that important," Linda said, trying to convince an old pro. When Birdie gave her an unbelieving look, Linda turned her head.

"If you were running for chapter secretary than I would say it's not that important. You must want a little spotlight if you are running for Regional Director. So what if everyone finds out? The purpose is to get votes. You can't be afraid of losing," Bird said. She picked up a box of white rice and put it into the cart. Linda took it out.

"I want wild rice with the cornish hens," Linda said and put the rice back on the shelf. "A very popular person in one of Kansas City's chapters is running too. It's unheard of for two candidates to represent the same city. We usually support one candidate metro wide. This person has received recognition in the national journals. I won't stand a chance against her," Linda confessed. She searched the shelves for olive oil.

"Carl ran against an incumbent on his first try. He won. Nobody could have ever imagined it. The game is not for soft skin people. If you don't win the first time out, then try again. When does your sorority journal come out again?"

"In two months."

"Um, June. When is the deadline for submitting an article for publication?"

"The end of next month."

"When is the conference?"

"Near the middle of July."

"The June journal is going to be a very important piece of campaign literature. It will wrap up the entire year, regardless of what has been said prior. Your mayor's wife is a good friend of mine, my soror, of course an Alpha. I will get him to write a letter to the sorority, thanking it for the fantastic job and to mention your name several times. He will thank you for the previous work you've done. I will ask him to take a picture with you, shaking hands under your sorority crest. How does that sound?" Birdie asked and put a box of macaroni and cheese in the cart. Linda leaned forward to take it out. Birdie stopped her. "I like the fake stuff," Birdie said.

"Do you think the mayor will do that for me?" Linda asked shyly.

"I asked how does it sound." Birdie picked up a jar of spaghetti sauce and turned to Linda. "I'm going to eat this when you leave."

"Sounds great. I can't wait to tell the others," Linda said anxiously.

"They will like it. I know Gloria Bircher. We went to Tennessee State together. She was the only Kappa I liked. Kappas were what the kids call wannabees. I'm surprised you pledged," Birdie said arrogantly and walked to the seafood counter.

Linda frowned at the shrimp inside the case. Birdie told her about a market nearby. Linda bought several items from the grocery store and drove back home. Birdie decided to stay home with Barbara. She left Linda and Indie to finish shopping alone.

Birdie and Barbara went to the entertainment room. A large screen television was in the middle of the floor. A bar was in the back. A stereo was in the corner. The room had a nice plush black leather sofa with matching love seat and ottoman. Birdie turned on the stereo and went to the bar and took out a bottle of

Scotch. She offered Barbara a drink. She refused. She made it her business not to be around alcohol. But she was tempted.

Birdie put a compact disc in the stereo. The voice of Ella James rang throughout the room. Barbara always liked Ella James. She sat comfortably on the love seat and hummed. She and Birdie small talked for awhile. They talked a long time about their siblings. Then they talked about their children and few grandchildren.

The more Birdie drank, the more she talked. She was quite relaxed now. Two hours had passed. She began complaining about Kelly. According to Birdie, she was disrespectful because her father had spoiled her. She had not come by to help Birdie through the crisis. She was selfish. Deidra was much more pleasant. She was willing to come home to help her mother but Birdie said, "No."

Another forty minutes passed. Birdie started in on Carl. She suspected him of cheating on her. Since the mastectomy, he had not slept in the same bed with her. Birdie began to cry. "The son-of-a-bitch won't even try to fake it, Bobbie."

Barbara tried consoling her by making excuses for Carl, but it was useless. Birdie was always head strong. She continued to drink while singing along with Sarah Vaughn. Barbara sat quietly. It was time to go home.

Birdie finally said it. "Why did that son-of-a-bitch do it! We were only kids. He stole our childhood. He took our innocence. Momma said nothing, the bitch!"

"Birdie that's enough! Respect the dead."

"Dead my ass! She let that bastard rape us. Isn't that why you left us? He had the audacity to apologize. But he had to stop. Sugah Doo would have cut his throat if he tried it with her."

"What's done is done. There's nothing we can do to change what happened."

"How do you live with it Bobbie?"

"I forgave momma when she came to my wedding. She couldn't relax. She felt out of place, constantly pulling and tugging on her dress. She told me that I had everything she had ever wanted. She warned me not to look back or come home. She was willing to call herself a failure to save me. I had no choice but to forgive her. Momma cooked very well and sang better. Those are the good things I can say about her. She did her best."

"I can't let it go."

"It's not going to help you. You can't kill momma because she's already dead. You keep her alive with your anger and memories of those terrible times. It's time to enjoy your daughters and granddaughters."

Three and a half hours passed. Birdie started complaining about Kelly again. Then she turned her head and sang the song that was playing, *God Bless the Child* by Billie Holiday. Birdie had a voice like Aretha Franklin. Barbara joined in taking the low notes. They sang together for the first time since Barbara left home. Suddenly, something loud came from the kitchen. They sprang from their chairs and rushed into the kitchen.

Linda was looking at Birdie's cookware and a pot dropped. Linda kept her head turned. "It's just a pot," Linda said.

Barbara saw how nervous Linda was. She probably had been home for awhile. Barbara hoped she had not heard them talking. Her past had to be her secret. Even her husband didn't know everything. Barbara continued to watch Linda move around the kitchen without seeing.

"Aunt Birdie, I told Kelly to come by tomorrow to help. You shouldn't be lifting anything," Linda said.

"Thank you, sweetheart, but it will be a cold day in hell if she does."

"I just hope the evil people wear coats tomorrow."

It was a setting for seven, three couples and Barbara. Carl was entertaining the new partner of the firm, a political friend and their spouses. Carl wanted the new partner to meet a few people from Congress. The new partner was a fifty year old black man with a peanut shaped head and a gut. His frumpy wife's gut was equally matching. They were very friendly. The new partner and his wife were lawyers, but the wife stopped practicing after she had the second baby.

Linda started with a shrimp cocktail. It was set up in the entertainment room. Cut flowers laid around the table. The couples enjoyed the appetizer as they sipped drinks. The men talked together and so did the women.

Kelly looked happy as she sliced fruits. She had never prepared a dinner such as the one Linda arranged. Under Linda's instructions, Kelly placed the fruit on a tray and stuck it in the oven for a couple of minutes. When they were done, she placed them in half moons on each plate around a cornish hen stuffed with wild rice, mushrooms and peppers.

Linda boiled the new potatoes until slightly tendered. She sliced them in half and sprinkled a mixture of spices on top. She put them into the oven to bake. Kelly was busy at the stove, asking Linda questions about the wok. She was to steam pea pods and zucchini. Linda had already steamed the baby carrots. She had made a wine sauce to give the vegetables flavor.

Linda and Kelly brought out two plates a piece and set one in front of a guest. After each person had a plate, the new partner's wife pleasantly asked for a salad.

"It will be served last. European style," Linda said. The woman smiled at Linda and looked around the table in awe.

Desert was nothing more than orange sherbet ice cream placed in a blender with fresh strawberries and bananas. It was served in desert glasses with diced strawberries on top and a little whip cream. Everyone raved over the appearance and taste of the meal. They sat around for another hour talking.

Linda and Kelly cleaned up the kitchen. They were free of the two little ones. Howard, Kelly's husband, was home babysitting. Linda thought Kelly wasn't so bad after all. Not once was she offended when Linda gave her tips on cooking. She talked to Linda casually as if they had known each other for years. Kelly was bubbling as she discussed plans for her dinner party.

"Your mother needs help. You need to check on her more often," Linda said as she put away a bowl.

Kelly's face turned sour. "Mother doesn't need help. At least not my help. I tried helping her, but she ignores me. Nothing is ever good enough," Kelly said. She turned her back to Linda.

"The Wright women are like that. Mother should be on a stricter diet. She's been eating like a pig since her last episode in the hospital. I know she needs help. I ignore her complaining and do whatever's necessary to make her comfortable," Linda said.

Kelly laughed a little. "Mother and Aunt Barbara are like twins. I really like talking to your mother."

"You talked to my mother?"

"Briefly. She heard me fussing at Howard. I'm so tired of him making plans and telling me at the last minute. Aunt Barbara told me that men are unorganized and to keep my emotions under control because it gives me the upperhand."

Linda had to brush it off. It would appear that Aunt Birdie would have told Kelly the same thing. According to Birdie, Carl didn't have a chance at winning had it not been for her aggressiveness in campaigning.

Linda and Kelly joined the others in the living room. Kelly had her purse. She kissed her father goodnight. She looked at her mother. "Do you need me to come over tomorrow?"

"I'm fine," Birdie answered.

Kelly looked disgusted. She shook her head. "I'll be over after church."

"Kelly, I'm fine."

"Great! Aundrea and I can watch you work. Maybe you can cook us something to eat," Kelly said sarcastically. She looked at Linda. Instinctively, they laughed. Kelly left.

"Malinda, how can I ever repay you?" Birdie asked. She yawned a little.

"You've already have. Your contacts are going to be a big help to me," Linda said.

Carl had his hat on. He was walking toward the door.

"Where are you going?" Birdie asked.

Carl didn't look around. "I need to pick up some papers at the office."

"This time of night?"

"I'll be back," Carl said and left.

Birdie tried not to look annoyed. Linda excused herself and went upstairs to bed.

"Carl is a shrewd man, Birdie. A person doesn't win public office by playing fair. Make sure he pays before the divorce. Women our age don't find secretary jobs easily," Barbara said.

"I'm even shrewder. Who do you think helped him win that public office?" Birdie said.

Chapter Seven

Lauren looked fearfully at John. He lifted the scattered newspaper and threw it at her. She turned around swiftly.

"What have I told you about handling my things? Get your retarded ass out of here before I beat the shit out of you!" he shouted.

Lauren ran to her room and slammed the door. She rocked in place, signing to herself. She moaned as she signed about being unhappy, but it came to an abrupt end when the door opened. She knew he had the belt and another whipping was in order. She only hoped her mother arrived soon because each whipping was getting longer and harder to endure. The licks seemed to never stop.

"Don't you slam another door in my house!" John yelled before lifting the belt.

Lauren covered her head as the licks landed on her body. She couldn't talk because her voice protected her face. She was surprised when the whipping ended quickly. He left her room. She was able to talk again.

"Mother, please help me," Lauren signed.

Her friend appeared again. She was the lady that shone brightly. She said her name was Angel and that they were play sisters. The lady offered her hand.

"Let's go! I know where you will be safe. We are going to Miss Stevens house," Angel said.

"Who is Miss Stevens?"

Angel giggled. "She's not Miss Stevens anymore. She's Mrs. Reed!"

"Auntie Linda?"

Angel nodded. They walked out of the house without being noticed.

Melanie waited at the airport for Lionel's plane to arrive. It was late. Lionel was attending a conference in Kansas City for a few days. It had been months since Melanie and Lauren had seen him. Although he talked to them on the phone often, she could not wait to see him.

Finally, the plane landed. Passengers appeared at the doorway. Melanie took breaths as she waited outside the glass area for him. He appeared quicker than expected. She waited for him to spot her. He did and smiled.

"Thanks for picking me up. I could have rented a car," Lionel said.

"I thought it would give us time to talk," Melanie said.

"How is Lauren?"

Melanie remained silent.

"What's wrong with Lauren? The last time I talked to her, she didn't have much to say as she normally does. I thought it was because I hadn't seen her since Christmas."

"She's fine. I was hoping that you could take her for the summer."

"How are things between you and John?"

"Lauren hasn't taken to him well. She gives him a difficult time. She needs to understand that you will always be a part of her life and that John is my husband and her father too. John and I need to spend some time alone."

Lionel was a little bothered with Melanie's statement about John being Lauren's father too. Lionel considered himself as Lauren's only father.

"I don't have a problem taking her for the summer, but it seems as if Lauren should be included in this time alone. Lauren has never given anyone a hard time," said a frustrated Lionel.

Although he had two children, Lauren was the easiest to bond with. His son Damon lived in the same city, but his ex-wife made visitation difficult. She did not want Damon to develop the same personality as his father, an adulterer.

"John doesn't like sharing you. He's working on isolating you from everyone. He was successful at breaking up your friendship with Linda and now it's your daughter," Lionel added. He finally got it off of his chest.

They were at Melanie's car. "By the way, where is Lauren? I wanted to take you two out to dinner," Lionel added.

"I can't continue to do things with you and Lauren. You can take her to dinner. She's at home with John."

Immediately, Lionel became uneasy. He got inside the car and hoped that his gut feelings were wrong.

Melanie walked inside the house. The look on John's face told her something was terribly wrong. She looked at him for an answer. He remained silent.

"Where is Lauren?" she asked slowly.

The first time John saw Lionel, he became jealous. Lionel looked nothing like what John had imagined. The younger man had too much confidence to enter his home. Lionel didn't like John either because he was obsessive and jealous of his friendship with Melanie. The relationship became closer since the death of Melanie's sister, Jennifer. It was a difficult period for everyone after the family secrets were exposed.

At first, Melanie was responsive to Lionel's offers of consolation. He visited as often as possible, especially since there was little hope in bonding with his son. All of a sudden, Melanie began dating an older gentleman with a strong financial background. Then a proposal followed six months after dating. Lionel never understood the quick proposal. Lionel didn't understand why Melanie accepted, knowing John didn't want children and after hearing about John, Lionel suspected that John didn't like children either.

"I've just gotten off the phone with the police. I think Lauren has run away," John answered.

Melanie raked her hair with her fingers. "How long has she been missing?" she demanded. John seemed perturbed by her attitude. He was ready to snap at her until Lionel caught his attention.

"*Why did she run away?*" Lionel barked. He waited for John to present the same indignant attitude with him. He was ready.

"Excuse me, but this is my house. Don't come in here starting shit!"

"I don't care whose house this is! My daughter is missing and I want to know why?"

John walked to Lionel and stood face to face. "Get out of my house!" John shouted.

The ringing doorbell brought a quick truce between the two men. Melanie invited the police officers in. Lionel listened as John explained how he sent Lauren to her room four hours ago because she was disobedient. Before he could go into detail about Lauren's behavior, the telephone rang. Melanie rushed to answered.

"Melanie, this is Keith. Lauren has just arrived. I can't get her to tell me why she's here. She keeps telling me that an angel or Miss Angel brought her," he said.

Melanie breathed in the tears. "We'll be there shortly," she said and hung up. She faced Lionel. "Lauren is at Linda's."

John walked out of the room without finishing the discussion with the police officers. Melanie explained to the officers that Lauren was safe. They asked a few more interrogating questions and then left. Melanie and Lionel rushed out of the house.

Melanie drove fast. There was silence as she traveled to Linda's house. Many thoughts popped into her head. The first one was what to say to Linda. Their last discussion was heated. No one raised their voice, but it was obvious that Linda would not visit again.

Lionel was furious. Every time he visited Lauren, it was always a fight. The first time he visited after Melanie's wedding, John had taken Melanie and Lauren to dinner and a movie, knowing Lionel was to pick Lauren up earlier that day. What infuriated Lionel most was Melanie's passive behavior concerning John. Now, his daughter had walked several miles to leave home. John had to have scared her away. Lionel wanted some answers.

"What's been going on? I don't want to hear any garbage about Lauren being difficult. You and John have been married over two years. It should be much better now," Lionel said.

Melanie didn't know if it was safe to discuss John's gambling addiction and how he went through her savings to feed the addiction. He traveled to Las Vegas frequently on her money. Had she not secured five thousand dollars from the sale of Linda's mother's boutique, she would be penniless, something she had already experienced. When they married, she had to use a large portion of her money to pay his debts.

"Things are a little difficult between me and John. We are having problems. That's why I'm asking you to take Lauren for the summer so that some things can be sorted out."

"I hope that you don't choose that no-good son-of-a-bitch over your daughter! I will take you to court," Lionel said without looking at Melanie.

Melanie parked the car in Linda's drive way. She turned off the engine. "You or no one else will take my daughter from me. Don't you ever tell me something like that again," Melanie said. Her eyes were shooting water and fire.

"I'm sorry...I'm just mad. I realize John is a successful business man, but it doesn't validate his scruples. I don't like John. He's obsessive, jealous..."

"Lionel, please! I don't want to get into it."

They sat quietly for several seconds. Melanie got out of the car first. Lionel followed. They went inside the house. Keith walked them into the family room where Lauren sat in a corner on the floor.

"She said something about a Miss Angel took her to Rosalyn's house. Rosalyn said Lauren was at her doorsteps and she wanted to come over here," Keith explained.

Melanie was concerned. She knew Rosalyn lived close to her. She did not know how Lauren knew how to get to Rosalyn's house. Melanie sat on the floor beside Lauren. She was signing to herself. Melanie knew that Lauren could hear, but voluntarily, Lauren became deaf. Melanie tapped Lauren on the shoulder. When Lauren turned around, she saw Lionel. She quickly removed herself from the floor and ran to him. He picked her up and hugged her tight.

"What's the matter Lauren?" Lionel asked.

Lauren began signing. Lionel stopped her small hands. Since her surgery, she was able to hear, but traumatic experiences created deafness.

"I want to go with you," Lauren muscled out in a nasaled tone. She hugged Lionel and buried her head on his shoulder.

"Did John hurt you?" Lionel asked. Lauren began to cry. "It's all right. Daddy's here. You want to visit me this summer?" Lauren nodded.

Melanie walked to Lauren. "How did you get to Rosalyn's house?"

"Miss Angel took me."

"Who is Miss Angel?"

"My friend. She said that I would be safe at Auntie Linda's."

"How does this Miss Angel look?"

"She's pretty. She has long hair. There's a mark on her head. She said she was hurt in a car accident," Lauren said while pointing to her forehead.

Melanie's mouth opened. There was something familiar about what Lauren was sharing. "Lauren, is Miss Angel real or make-believe?"

"She's real. She came the first time John spanked me. She said I would be safe at Miss Stevens, uh, Auntie Linda's. She's right. I do feel safe. Daddy's here."

Melanie took a deep breath. She turned around. Her head felt light. She felt warm. Something was consuming her. Her thoughts became jumbled. She was having a difficult time concentrating on what Lauren had shared. She felt herself slipping away.

Lionel watched as Melanie took deep breaths. He saw her close her eyes and her head bobbed up and down. He touched her face. She looked up smiling. Lionel felt strange. Lauren had just told them that an unknown person had taken her to Rosalyn's house and what was worse, John had been spanking her.

"Melanie," Lionel said softly. "Are you okay?"

"Of course, sweetie. Everything will be fine."

"John has been spanking Lauren. I thought I made it clear that John isn't to lay a hand on her. She can be disciplined other ways."

"I understand Charlie...uh, um, Lionel. I will take care of it. This time, it will be done the right way," Melanie said. Her thoughts were coming together and so was time. She looked at Lionel with a grin. "I will take care of John." Melanie reached for Lauren. She slowly went to her mother.

"My poor, poor baby. Mommie will buy you some ice cream. You want some ice cream?" Melanie cooed. Lauren nodded.

Melanie turned her attention to Keith. "I need to speak with Barbara...Aunt Barbara. Can I use your telephone?"

"Linda and Mother took a trip to Alabama. They are visiting relatives. They are in Nashville now. They will be home next Thursday."

"Aunt Barbara went home? I thought she would never go back. How is Linda?"

Keith thought Melanie's conversation was strange. Melanie started off upset but now it seemed as if it were business as usual. She asked of Linda as if the conflict between them did not exist. What was more strange, Lauren had ran away from home and it appeared that she had been abused in some way.

Keith tried to overlook the inconsistent behavior. He liked Melanie. He used to think that she was weak, but soon came to realize that he was wrong. She had a gentle strength that he admired. "Will you come to visit Linda next week?" he asked.

"Of course! It took me a very long time to come back. By the way, do you mind babysitting? I don't want to take Lauren back to the house for awhile and I need to get Lionel to the hotel."

"Lauren is always welcomed. I will keep her as long as you need me too."

Melanie smiled. She kissed Lauren on the forehead and put her down. She turned her attention to Lionel. "Are you ready to go to the hotel?" she asked with an inviting grin.

Lionel became uncomfortable. He knew what the smile meant prior to the birth of Lauren. Since their daughter's birth, he had not made love to her. Over the years, he had learned to control his behavior. Sex was taking a back seat in his relationships with women. It was too risky.

Still, her smile was confusing because she was married. She had to love her husband more than wanting him. She knew how he felt about her. They were just friends. They were once college sweethearts and nothing else. Lauren was the only connection between them. He decided not to continue to lie to himself. He could not find another woman that mentally stimulated him. With Melanie, it wasn't sex. It was something else that caused the attraction. He only hoped that years of practicing self-control was not put to the test because he was sure to fail.

Melanie came home very early the next morning. She slammed

the car door with force, hard enough to wake the neighbors. She entered the house as usual. She climbed the stairs to the bedroom. She was tired, but a bit jubilant.

When she entered the bedroom, John was waiting for her. She walked in, not looking at him. She removed a nightgown from the dresser drawer and went into the bathroom. John sat stunned from her behavior. Usually, she was cowardly when it came to him disciplining Lauren. She normally petted the child after whippings or any forms of discipline.

Melanie appeared from the bathroom. She walked to the bed with her head high. She was about to slip under the covers until John stopped her.

"Where have you been?" he asked.

"I had to take care of some business," she said with a smile.

John was furious. The response was what he usually said when he came home late. For her to say it with a smirk added fuel to his anger.

"Where is Lauren?" he asked.

"Lauren will be staying with her godparents until we settle our problems?" she answered without lowering her eyes or voice.

"How long is she going to be gone?" John asked firmly. He was trying desperately to gain control. He wondered how did he lose it?

"Lauren isn't coming back until we settle our problems," Melanie said forcefully.

"What are you talking about?"

"Our problems or is it your problems? You have just about cleaned out my savings account with your gambling. You hate children and you don't want to see me happy," Melanie said with a smile. She slipped under the covers.

Before John could slap her, she said, "And another thing, if you ever hurt my child again, I will kill you." Melanie turned on her side and went to sleep.

Chapter Eight

Melanie was on her way to have lunch with Lori, Estelle, and a few others. It was their typical monthly luncheon. She had missed the last three because of John. Either she was consoling an upset Lauren because of a spanking earlier in the morning or she had to nurse an obvious show of domestic violence. Today's meeting was important. They were discussing Lori's campaign and who would be the chapter's next president. Melanie's position as first vice president was a sure nomination for president. Although the elections were democratic, the small group was the heartbeat of the organization. The seven women called the shots. It was just a matter of formality.

Melanie usually arrived an hour earlier than everyone else because she and Lori generally talked alone. To her surprise, everyone was there early too. It was unusual. She quickly got out of her car and rushed to the door. A new face answered the door. Melanie stared hard at Annette. Then Melanie's expression softened when Annette grinned lightly.

When Melanie entered the house, lunch was already in progress. Everyone was cordial but Melanie wasn't. They started the meeting without her and they started an hour earlier. Eight women were in the room but the group was called "Seven Carats."

"Oh Melanie, I thought you weren't coming," Lori said with a smile. She looked at Annette to catch her expression. She was watching Lori the entire time. One corner of Annette's mouth turned into a grin when Lori looked at her. Then Annette narrowed her eyes at Melanie who was trying desperately to read the interaction between Lori and Annette.

Immediately, Melanie lost respect for Lori. No one ever came an hour early. Lori lied. It was the first time. It was easier for Melanie to accept being removed from the group because she didn't keep up, but now, she couldn't trust Lori. Melanie's posture straightened. She made eye contact with Annette again. Both women stared at one another. Neither offered the other a smile.

Melanie observed the group as they chatted about their husbands and children. No one said anything about the nomination for chapter president. Then the discussion became humorous. They discussed the ridiculous idea of Linda running for Regional Director. Annette offered the most comments. Everyone, except Melanie, roared with laughter. Annette's comments caught Melanie off guard. No matter how difficult things became between Annette and Linda, the pledge line of 1978 vowed to never let anything come between them when dealing with Lori and her crew.

"I don't think she has the support of her own mother," Estelle said trying to catch her breath.

"All she has is a bunch of old women who have lost their step. I can't wait until we take control, so that we can get those old bitches out of the way," Lori bragged.

Now they were talking indirectly about Barbara Stevens, the one who helped get Lori where she was. Although Lori didn't offer any comments about Barbara, the group did. Melanie stiffened.

Lori watched as Melanie withdrew from the group. Usually, she commented to show unity but not today. It nagged Lori to understand what Melanie was thinking. Even when they talked alone, Melanie had a special way of not showing all of her cards when it was a personal issue. Lori felt she owed a great deal to Melanie because she convinced the majority of the remaining younger sorors to leave the old chapter.

"Oh, enough of this gossip. Melanie, how about being the chapter's delegate at the conference?" Lori offered.

The rest of the group talked in agreement. Melanie knew instantly that she was being bought out. She was not getting the president nomination and it was probably her last luncheon. Lori was showing gratitude for her loyalty by giving her one vote at the convention.

Melanie had to strategically think her emotions and response within a matter of seconds. She had to put pride, hurt, anger and betrayal aside. Her eyebrows raised in surprise and her mouth dropped open.

"Thanks Lori! This is going to be great! Have you started planning the campaign?" Melanie asked with a soft smile. She had to throw in the campaign to see if Lori would continue to lie.

"We will meet sometime next month to discuss it in detail,"

Lori said slowly. The question was a tester to see if the water was safe. She knew Melanie very well. She created her. She made Melanie president of the undergraduate chapter.

Lying bitch, Melanie thought. She felt betrayed. She thought that she and Lori were good friends, especially after keeping Linda from holding any office in the new chapter the second year. Lori convinced Melanie that Linda may want to go back to the old chapter to be a part of her mother's politics, but Lori was wrong. Linda wanted to be with her best friend. Melanie knew she had made a big mistake when Linda left the new chapter and didn't do anything with the sorority until a year later.

Melanie's focus went to Annette who looked at her without smiling. Then she made the decision to resign from the group. "I may not be able to meet with you guys. Just let me know if I can do anything. You can always count on me," Melanie said grinning. She kept her focus on Annette. Melanie could not remove the phony expression from her face.

"I knew I could count on you," Lori said uneasily. She wondered if Melanie would stay loyal. She read the unspoken dialogue between Melanie and Annette. There had to be jealousy. That was what she wanted.

Melanie read Lori's comment to mean, *Thanks for being a good sport about us kicking your ass out of the group!*

It was going to be a battle, Melanie thought. May the best bitch win.

Melanie tried to relax before getting out of the car. Linda was home. They had not spoken in almost a year. Once, they were best friends like their mothers were. Barbara and Catherine did their best scheming and plotting as a team, in college. They became friends by being roommates. It gave them the opportunity to share everything. Nothing came between their friendship, not their husbands nor the one-hundred dollars that Barbara borrowed and never paid back. Now their daughters had become strangers.

The conflict between Melanie and Linda started with Melanie's marriage to John two years ago. John was a well-known minority general contractor in Kansas City. He was twelve years older than Melanie and had been married before. He was a high profile individual with many political contacts which enabled him to receive most of his jobs. His former wife divorced him because of domestic violence. John was able to convince Melanie that his former wife lied because there were no police records nor hospital records to support her charges. He claimed that she was angry because he was no longer in love with her.

John was the perfect gentleman to Melanie. He never became angry. He introduced her to his friends and clients. He was attentive to her. He accompanied her to every function she attended, and she in turn, supported him at dinner parties. She introduced him to the family. Everyone liked him, except William "Bill" Smith, Melanie's father. William was impressed with John's accomplishments, but it was the story about the ex-wife that concerned William. According to John, she was a woman who was quiet and meek in the beginning, but she turned out to be a paranoid liar. She bruised herself to convince her girlfriends that she was being abused.

William, a widower and divorced two times, had experience in not being in love long with his wives. He treated his wives far worst than what John's claims were, but William never physically abused any of the women. He spanked Melanie once and when he saw the crocodile tears in her big brown eyes, he never spanked her again.

John began isolating Melanie from her father. It wasn't difficult because William lived in Colorado. Next were the Stevens, Melanie's nonblood uncle and aunt. It wasn't very difficult because the couple traveled frequently, enjoying their retirement. John felt no threat from Gina, Melanie's cousin, because she lived in Chicago. But, it was extremely difficult driving a stake between Melanie, Linda and the sorority. If Linda called and Melanie wasn't there, she never received the messages, nor could she have a relaxing conversation with Linda when John was present. He constantly hassled her while she was on the phone.

One day, Linda confronted him about the undelivered messages. They got into a heated argument. Linda brought it to Melanie's attention. Melanie approached John about it and he became defensive. He made Linda out to be an instigator. He made it clear to Melanie that no one should come between their marriage and he left it at that. As far as the sorority, John made sure something was planned to keep her from being active.

Violence erupted the first time when John laid eyes on Lionel. He looked nothing like what Melanie described. Melanie usually took Lauren to the Stevens when Lionel came to visit. But one day, Lionel wanted to meet the person who was partially responsible for Lauren's development. Melanie hesitated but introduced Lionel to John. The older man saw something that Melanie didn't see, Lionel still liked her.

That evening, John became quiet. He didn't share the events of his day as usual with Melanie. They ate in silence. When she innocently asked what was wrong, John exploded.

"That man has seen Lauren many times before today. Why am I just meeting him?"

"What difference does it makes about when you meet him He is her father!"

It was something in the tone of Melanie's voice that released the anger. He reached across the table and slapped her hard. Melanie sucked in air. She couldn't say anything. She stood but he pushed her down. She sat down and stared at him. The blaze in her eyes made him leave the table.

Melanie rushed to the phone, but who could she call? She was a stranger with all of her friends. She thought about calling Aunt Barbara, but decided not too. She found a blanket in the linen closet and slept in the guest room. It was the beginning of the end.

After Melanie thought back to how she let her life change because of an abusive, jealous man, she rushed out of the car. She hummed to herself as thoughts of ignoring the most important people in her life flashed across her mind. She chuckled before ringing the doorbell. When the door opened, she smiled at Linda.

"So, did you bring back some cotton?" Melanie asked with a calculating grin.

Linda's expression was blank. She could not remember the last time her friend came to visit. She could remember her friend not saying anything when she complained about John. Later, Melanie began to defend his behavior. As Linda continued to complain, Melanie kept her distance. When Linda asked about Lauren spending the night to play with little Edward, the excuses were always shallow. But Linda had to think back to the most sensitive conversation she and her mother had:

"Malinda, consider yourself fortunate that you have parents at your disposal."

"You and dad have always been like parents to her."

"Bill was never the father to her like Edward is to you. And Bill has never given her the mother to be available to her like I have been to you. Melanie has never over stepped her boundaries when it came to you. She always knew that we did not belong to her."

"She took up for that bastard! I will never forgive her for that!"

Barbara closed her eyes. She understood her daughter's anger, but it wasn't the right time to not forgive. Malinda had always been protected. She never had to experience difficult times like Melanie. Barbara came to the conclusion that her daughter was too soft. If things did not go her way, she just wrote if off. She really never worked for anything, not even for a husband.

"Malinda, always remember this. In life, you will always need somebody. If you don't need help now, you will later. If you didn't pay the price for your luxuries, someone else did. When Melanie invites herself back into your life, receive her with open arms. Right now, she doesn't know where to turn."

Barbara stood. Her conversation with her selfish daughter was over. Catherine was her best friend. They had always planned for their daughters to be more than friends, more like sisters. That is why their names sounded like twins.

"When she comes to visit, she needs your help," Barbara concluded.

"I'll get Lauren," Linda said with a fake smile.

"Can I come in? I thought I would visit for awhile?"

Linda stopped smiling. "Keith tells me that Lauren had welts on her arms."

Melanie stopped grinning. She looked off to the side. "I was hoping that she could stay over here for awhile until I work some things out."

Linda stepped to the side. "What kind of relaxer do you have on your hair? It looks dry."

Melanie looked at the ground and smiled. "If I sat around the house all day, I wouldn't have an excuse for having shotty nails."

"They look pretty bad, don't they!"

Linda and Melanie small talked until Indie came into the room with a toy. Melanie smiled at her godchild and took the toy. Indie disappeared and brought two more items from her room and placed them in front of Melanie.

"How was your trip?" Melanie asked as she moved the toys to the side.

"It was the Clampetts and the Carringtons. The Beverly Hillbillies versus Dynasty. Mother was relaxed shopping at Wal-Mart, skinning fish and sitting on the front porch. Come to think of it, I liked the Clampetts better, too."

"Aunt Barbara told me a little about Titusville. I never thought she would go back."

Linda hardly heard her mother talk to anyone about her past. Linda's father only told her bits and pieces. "When did mother tell you about Titusville? Her family lives on the outskirt of town."

Melanie didn't know when she had heard about Titusville, but she knew. Melanie shook her head. "Years ago. I had always wanted to know more about my mother. It was equally good hearing about Aunt Barbara."

Linda decided to test the water. Her friend's visit was considered odd since her marriage. "How are things with you and John?"

Melanie did not want to discuss John and Lauren, but something was prompting her to talk. "I'm thinking about getting a divorce. He's not the man that I thought he was. I don't want to stay too long. Eventually, someone will get hurt."

"Statistics show that women and children are killed due to domestic violence."

Melanie released a hoarse laugh. "It won't be me or Lauren." Melanie laughed again. Then a big smile came across her face. "Is it true that you are running for Regional Director?"

Indie had just about emptied all of the contents from her bedroom in front of Melanie. Indie disappeared and came back with two of Linda's shoes. Linda looked at her ever busy daughter.

"Indie, I want you to put my shoes back?"

"Why?" Indie asked innocently.

Linda's mouth opened and her eyebrows raised. "Because I said so! Now put them back," Linda demanded and pointed to the door. Indie left with the shoes. "I have to put her in daycare soon. I heard Cheryl, the Alpha, has an excellent facility."

"I saw her the other day. She told me that she has computers and smaller classrooms. She's working towards an academy. She personally worked with Lauren after the surgery. She's good," Melanie said. She hesitated. "You haven't answered my question."

There was no way Linda could get around making a decision to run. At one time, she and Melanie would have discussed her campaign in details, but Linda didn't know whether to trust her. Linda had received many contacts from her mother's friend, but she wanted support from the college chapters, too. Many of her mother's friends had heard of Lori, as well.

Suddenly, there was a loud crash. Linda sprang from the sofa and rushed to Indie's room. Melanie ran in behind. Indie had a broom in her hand. When she saw her mother, she pointed to the top of her dresser and said, "Shoes!"

Linda looked at the broken music box on the floor. The four teddy bears were detached from the merry-go-round. It was the music box that Jennifer gave her for a baby shower gift for Camille. It was the one thing that connected the two. Linda closed her eyes and pursed her lips. She was ready to strike Indie when Lauren and little Edward entered the room.

Lauren bent down and picked up three of the teddy bears. "Can I have these, Auntie Linda?"

Melanie was ready to tell Lauren "no," but Linda said, "Yes."

Lauren rubbed the bears slowly. They were the most beautiful things she had seen. Linda had given her many gifts, but Lauren adored the bears. The bears beamed in her hands. "Thanks, Miss Stevens," Lauren finally said.

Linda looked strangely at Lauren. Only one person called her Miss Stevens. As long as Lauren talked, she had always called her Auntie Linda.

"Where did you get *Miss Stevens* from?" Linda asked Lauren.

"Miss Angel called you that," Lauren answered.

"Who is Miss Angel?" Linda asked.

"That's her make-believe friend. Lauren, you and Edward go in the other room," Melanie said. The two left. Melanie looked at

Indie.

"Git shoes!" Indie demanded, pointing to the dresser.

Melanie called Lauren back into the room to get Indie before Linda killed her. Lauren took Indie's hand and left. Melanie helped Linda pick up the broken box. Linda picked up the remaining bear.

"I'm getting tired of Indie. I'm ready to strangle her. Camille was nothing like her," Linda complained.

"Three-year-olds are very busy. It's time to put her in daycare. And besides, Camille died very young. It's time that you go back to work. Maybe running for Regional Director will keep you busy doing other things besides being a housewife."

"I don't know if I'm running. Looks like Lori has it wrapped up," Linda said. She looked at her friend for a response. Melanie was a strong supporter of Lori since the chapter split.

"I'm sure Aunt Barbara has plenty of contacts that can make it interesting," Melanie said.

"I want to do this on my own. I know I can. I did a lot of things for the new chapter that went unnoticed. Lori received my accolades. Everyone benefited from my hard work, except me," Linda said bitterly.

Melanie felt a little guilty. Linda had volunteered to be on all of her committees. Linda made a success of every project. It was very important because during Melanie's first year of marriage, she hardly did anything and she still won an office. If she had pushed it, she and Linda could have been first and second vice presidents.

Melanie extended her arms. She waited for Linda to accept her apology, but Linda didn't move. She could not accept the gesture.

"I'm sorry if I hurt you. If you want to be Regional Director, then I will help you," Melanie said.

"You belong to the new chapter. Aren't you helping Lori?"

Melanie laughed. When she laughed, it sounded unlike her. Even Linda noticed a slight change in Melanie's mannerism. Melanie noticed Linda staring strangely.

"We're friends, more like sisters. If you want me to help you then I will. And besides, fuck Lori."

Linda gasped slightly hearing Melanie's comment about Lori. Then Linda looked at her friend and grinned. It was like old times. Linda looked at the bear in her hand. She loved bears. They were considered her good-luck charms. It was time to let go of the sad past and embrace the future. She walked to Melanie and hugged her.

"Thanks, Angel."

"You haven't called me that in years."

"I have a list of contacts that mother's friends have given me. My aunt knows the mayor. She's working on a spread for the quarterly."

"Oh my! You are already ahead of me. When I get back from Atlanta, I will get started on some things that I've been thinking about."

"You're visiting Lisa?"

"Dad will be there. He has practically given up on visiting me. I'm going to surprise him. I didn't get a chance to see him when he came for a meeting. Even Aunt Barbara saw him and she was in the hospital. By the way, how is your mother?"

Linda shook her head. Her mother was so weak. She fought hard to maintain energy on the trip. The tigress with deep claws was slowing down.

"She's not the same. She's slowing down."

Melanie thought about how the group made fun of Aunt Barbara, insinuating that she has lost her step. To Melanie, Aunt Barbara will never lose her step.

"Maybe if she becomes involved in your campaign, it will give her something to do?"

"She has done enough by introducing me to her friends. I just want to do something on my own and get recognition for doing it."

"Politics can be quite aggressive. Are you willing to roll up your sleeves and do battle?"

"I've never had a fight before, but I think I'm ready."

The two were quiet for awhile. They heard little Edward yell at Indie and she in turn fussing back. Linda shook her head and sighed.

"So, how is Lisa? I know that you two haven't seen each other since the wedding."

"Lionel tells me that she and Cameron have separated."

"Oh? So, how is Lionel?" Linda grinned and waited anxiously for an answer.

"Great!" Melanie grinned back.

Chapter Nine

Lisa looked out of the window in her office still holding the receiver for several seconds after Cameron hung up. The separation had been difficult on him. He called her job every day to see if the baby was moving or if something was needed for the nursery. Lisa was determined to be alone as she soul searched.

It started with arguments about Celeste, Cameron's daughter. Lisa purposely made it difficult for the little girl to visit. Vivian, Celeste's mother, made it clear to Cameron that his wife was creating a chasm between him and Celeste. Cameron knew that Lisa was being unreasonable at times because there were days when they had nothing planned, but Lisa forbid the little girl to visit. Cameron found himself sneaking to visit his daughter. This began in the second year of their marriage. Cameron thought that Lisa longed for motherhood, so they decided to have a baby. It didn't happen until the fourth year of their marriage.

Lisa became secretive. She hardly discussed her whereabouts after work hours. She came home very late many times. Cameron constantly asked about her activities. Sometimes she answered but most days she said nothing.

One day she noticed her breasts no longer fit into her bra. Her lips were drying frequently. Her skin was drying too. It came to her. The last time she felt that way, she miscarried two weeks later.

After she received news from the doctor about the baby, she rushed home to tell Cameron. She prepared his favorite foods and waited for him. The wait lasted hours. She put up the food and went to bed.

When Cameron arrived home at midnight, Lisa was angry. She asked softly, "Where have you been? I cooked Lasagna."

He turned his head because he had been drinking. He stumbled around the room and then flopped into bed. Without looking at her he said, "I'm moving out this weekend."

Lisa made sure she wasn't home when he moved. She went to visit the old woman in Cartersville, Georgia who told the story that started the strange behavior. Lisa found a letter in a stack of papers her mother had left her. A woman named Miss Sweets wrote in cryptic writing to Mrs. Farrow that the twins of Mattie Mitchell were either dead or could not be found. They were given away to a Tom and Daisy Orville, an old white childless couple who were suppose to be the nicest people in town. They were suppose to be Christians. Miss Sweets' final statement was, Who are you? Have you been found?

According to Miss Sweets, it wasn't too difficult for the couple to accept the twin girls because they were so fair. They could pass for white. The couple did not treat the girls like their daughters. The two girls were primarily house workers for the couple.

At the age of fifteen, one was accused of murdering Tom Orville, but she escaped. It was later found out that the old man had sexually assaulted both girls. The twin who stayed behind was arrested but released from jail. She could not live in Covington anymore. She had to run for her life. It was always rumored that she was killed by the Klan.

Miss Sweets knew the truth about the girls. She was Miss Mattie's best friend. Also, she was a closet spirit woman from Louisiana who used roots in her earlier years. Miss Sweets could touch a person and speak the truth.

Lisa sat quietly that day in Miss Sweets' living room. Lisa had visited the woman once before. Lisa shook when Miss Sweets described the death of Tom Orville. She felt heated, as if she were there.

Tom Orville was forty-eight at the time of his death. He was a handyman by trade and a hunter by interest. He taught the girls to shoot and to skin game. At the age of ten, the first time the twins saw an animal killed, they became ill. When they had to handle a knife to help skin the animal, resentment built. The older they became, the better they became with the knife.

The girls slept in a room down the hall from Tom and Daisy. They had slept together since babies. At night, they rubbed each other's sore muscles from the hard work of the day. They talked each other to sleep at night. They were not denied an education because Daisy Orville taught them at home. She saw early how quickly the girls learned, especially Della. She was excellent in solving math problems and she could think quickly. She also read very well. They didn't have friends because they hardly left the house.

A few days after the girls' thirteenth birthday, Tom Orville saw Della hanging the wash. He walked outside the back door and stared at the young girl's body. As she bent forward lifting wet clothes, Tom stared harder. Della was his favorite. She had a beautiful smile and her eyes were not as suspicious as Deborah. Della had a gentleness while working. Deborah handled the knife with force and she was fearless while in the woods. But Della's softness appeared white to him.

Tom quietly walked up behind her. When she bent forward, she saw his boots. She quickly stood and smiled at him. He smiled back and continued to stare.

"Is there something you want?" Della asked in a pleasant southern tone.

Tom's chest heaved. "Fix me some bath water when you finish," he said and walked away.

Della heated the water and filled the tub. She announced to Tom that the water was ready. He told her to get some soap as he began to undress. She nervously left for the kitchen to get some soap. She saw Daisy Orville in the kitchen.

"Mr. Tom wants me to get him some soap," Della said.

"He's taking a bath now?" Daisy asked.

"Yes ma'am," Della said with a nod. She slowly removed a bar of soap from the pantry. She looked at the kitchen doorway for a few seconds. Daisy could sense something wrong.

"What's the matter, girl?" Daisy asked.

"Nothin'," Della said and left. She walked slowly to the back where the tub was. Tom was in the tub resting.

"Here's the soap," Della said and place the bar of soap on the floor.

"I can't get it. Bring it to me," Tom said without looking at her.

Della quickly entered the room and reached her arm out to him. He grabbed her wrist and placed a towel in her hand.

"I want you to wash my back," he said.

Della was still for a minute until he put her hand in the water to soap the towel. As he swished her hand around the water, he rubbed it on his penis. She stiffened. He continue forcing her hand between his legs until the rush came and left. He moaned a little and later told her to leave the room.

Ever so often, the girls had to bathe him. Daisy began asking questions and Tom silenced her. He later stopped talking to her and had the girls bathe him often. A year and a half later, Tom began to enter their room. He made Deborah leave. Della watched in fear as he approached the bed. She could feel her sister close by but it could not stop what happened next. His breath was foul and his husky older body was heavy. She felt the pain travel from her pelvis to her chest. She screamed loudly and he snapped at her to keep quiet.

Deborah's heart pounded as she heard her sister cry. Deborah jumped upon hearing the bedroom door of Tom and Daisy open. Daisy stood in the doorway. She saw Deborah standing next to the door crying. Soon the girls' door opened and Tom stumbled out. Daisy looked at him and rushed inside the bedroom. Tom left the house.

Deborah rushed to her sister and saw her in a fetal position. She was no longer crying. Deborah jumped again when Daisy entered the room.

"Clean her up. And don't say nothing to nobody," Daisy said angrily.

Deborah looked fearless at Daisy. The girl could not understand the anger and lack of compassion.

"Girl, don't look at me like that!" Daisy said with a sense of fear.

Deborah helped her sister from the bed and down to the room with the tub. Della sat in a chair and waited for her sister to finish the bath water. Deborah helped remove the blood stained night gown and helped her sister into the tub. She gently washed her back.

"If he do it to me, I'm gonna skin him like a rabbit. If he comes to you again, cut his throat," Deborah whispered in Della's ear.

Della began to cry again. Deborah rubbed her shoulders until she stopped crying.

"We should run away to Atlanta. They say color folks doin' good there," Deborah said.

"How we gonna take care of ourselves? We're only fifteen," Della said.

"Most folks think we's white," Deborah said.

"Not if you continue talking like that. They'll know right off we ain't."

"Why don't you want to leave? They ain't our momma and daddy. I bet they stole us from our real folks," Deborah said to cheer up her sister. It was one of their favorite games, pretending to be princesses who were stolen.

"How we gonna git to Atlanta? We ain't never been," Della said, feeling better. She got out of the tub. Deborah began to dry her off with the air dried towel.

"It's up the road. It ain't that far. We can live in the woods until we get there."

"What we're gonna do, Deborah?" Della said and began to cry.

"Shush. Don't let Miss Daisy hear you. Hold on to my knife. If he do it again, stick him in the neck," Deborah said and eased the knife out of her night gown pocket.

Della looked strangely at the knife. It was new. She wondered where her sister got the knife. Knowing Deborah, she probably stole it.

"Where you git that knife from?" Della asked accusingly.

Deborah's face was calm, but her eyes looked angry. "You too soft. You have to do whatever you can to git by. If you don't think about ya' self, who's gonna? I take care of you all the time. One day, ya gonna have to take care of me. When you do, you cain't be scared." She placed the knife in Della's hand.

Della gripped the knife and pulled out the blade. The shine from the blade held her attention for several minutes. Her sister's voice brought back her attention.

"Keep it with you all the time. You handle that thing better than me anyway. We got to stick together because when we git to Atlanta, we gonna need each other," Deborah preached.

Deborah brought Della a clean gown. Deborah could sense that her sister was not as weak as she appeared. Della was the Orvilles' favorite because she smiled a lot.

"Don't ever be scared to do what ya got to do! You hear me?" Deborah preached.

Della nodded her head and then went to their bedroom to change the sheets. Della thought to herself that her sister was right. She *was* too soft. She admired Deborah. She wasn't afraid of anything. Della wanted to be just like her. She was determine to become just like Deborah one day.

One afternoon, Tom was at home with the girls. Della was burning trash and Deborah was cleaning the house. He decided to approach Della again but it was Deborah. The only way he could tell the girl's apart was by the beauty mark above the upper lip. Deborah did not have one.

"Fix me some bath water," he said roughly.

Deborah threw down the rag and went to boil some water. At one time, she would have smiled, but she felt anger. She made the water extra hot. She removed the soap from the kitchen and waited in the back room for Tom Orville. He felt awkward being in the room with Deborah.

"Go on and leave," he said.

Deborah left the room and within minutes later, she heard him scream. She grinned and picked up the rag to finish cleaning. She heard him cursing and threatening her. Della walked inside the house.

"What's wrong?" Della asked low.

"I'm goin' to Atlanta," Deborah said.

"We need money. We got to think before we do something stupid."

"Well stay. I'm goin'!"

"They're goin' into town tomorrow. We can git as much stuff as we need and then we'll leave."

Deborah wasn't keen on the idea. But she decided to wait. She needed her sister. Della was better at talking and acting white.

The next day, the girls watched the couple drive off in the truck. They rushed back into the kitchen to gather food. They pulled items from the very rear of the pantry and filled two small sacks. They hid them under a barrel in the back.

That night, they talked over their plan. They were going to leave after the couple left for church the next morning. It would give them plenty time to get to Atlanta.

"Deborah, go out back with me. I gotta pee," Della said.

"Why didn't you go early?"

"Never mind. I'll go by myself."

Della got up to go to the outhouse in the back. As she straightened her gown, she saw the light from Tom Orville's truck pull into the yard. She froze. She heard the truck door slam. She waited a few minutes before coming out. She adjusted her gown. Her sister's knife fell out of her pocket. She picked it up and gripped it hard. She tiptoed into the house. She saw Tom Orville leaning against the wall near his bedroom. He seemed to have a difficult time standing. Then he staggered into their bedroom. Della became nervous. She walked swiftly to the room. The door was cracked open. She could hear her sister argue with Tom Orville.

Della eased into the doorway. She saw Tom Orville on top of her sister. She could hear her sister cry, "Stop!"

Della looked at the bedroom door of the couple. It remained closed. She figured Daisy Orville had learned to block out any thing from their bedroom since the first night.

Della entered the room slowly, gripping her sister's best friend in her hand. She saw the white man between her sister's leg. She heard her sister cry. It was her fault that her sister could not protect herself, so she had to do it. She gripped the knife and plunged it into Tom Orville's neck and jerked it out. He gurgled and slumped over Deborah. He splattered blood over her body. Her screamed pierced the night.

Della looked at her bloody hand and dropped the knife. "Come on Deborah, let's go," Della said in a shaky voice as she rushed to the dresser to remove some pants and a shirt.

"We caint! He's dead," Deborah said as she eased herself from beneath the limp body.

Della was confused. It was her sister's idea to leave and it was also her idea to cut Tom Orville if ever he tried harming them again. They debated quickly because a decision had to be made. Footsteps were coming toward the room.

When Daisy Orville entered the room, she immediately put her hands to her mouth. Her husband was lying in a pool of blood. She looked at the girls in shock.

"He tried to take me!" Deborah tried explaining.

Della climbed through the window and ran to the backyard and retrieved one of the sacks. She believed her sister would follow her so she left a sack. She waited at the place that they agreed would be a resting spot. She waited fifteen minutes for Deborah, but she was no where in sight. Della became nervous and took off running. She finally saw a house with a candle burning in the window. She banged on the door, Miss Sweets appeared. She recognized the girl instantly. They spoke without sharing words.

Miss Sweets stepped to the side and Della walked shyly into the house. Della looked around the house strangely. She wanted to tell the woman about the terrible ordeal, but she couldn't. Miss Sweets grabbed her wrist. Della became nervous because the grip was tight. She watched the woman close her eyes and nod.

Miss Sweets saw images of sexual abuse by both Tom and Daisy Orville. She saw Daisy touch the girls inappropriately when they were younger and then she saw Tom handling them like women. What was confusing to Miss Sweets was the image of seeing the same girl that was in front of her in tears at the Orvilles' house. It came to her that it was the other twin.

Miss Sweets walked into her bedroom and pulled out a bag and spoke over it. She brought the object to Della. "This will protect you. Git some rest 'cause it will be a long time before you will be able to sleep a'gin," Miss Sweets said. She fixed the sofa for Della.

The next night, Miss Sweets prepared Della to leave. Miss Sweets told her to head north to Missouri. She instructed the girl to take nothing for granted. There was no shame in doing what ever to survive.

"What's ya name?" Della asked.

"I'm a friend of your momma," Miss Sweets said.

"Who was she? Miss Daisy told us that she was dead," Della said hungrily.

Miss Sweets had to remember her promise to the spirits, never interfere with destiny. To tell the girl her name would cause trouble for both of them and Daisy Orville. "You have to go now. Don't look back! Your sister will be fine 'cause I'm gonna help her."

"How'd you know about my sister? I ain't said nothin' 'bout her," Della said.

Miss Sweets walked Della to the door and handed her the small sack. Della knew the woman was finished talking, so she left. As she walked down the dirt road, she felt stronger. The woman was right. She should feel no shame in doing what ever to survive.

Two days later, Miss Sweets visited Daisy Orville. She was always kind to colored people. It was why Mattie offered her the babies. Daisy Orville's door was opened so Miss Sweets entered the house. Daisy was alone in the kitchen.

"Hello Miss Daisy," Miss Sweets said.

Immediately, Daisy recognized her. She was the woman who helped her with a love potion to catch Tom Orville. She was also the woman who promised her that she would have children after the doctor said she couldn't. She was the woman that helped arranged the sale of the additional land that Tom bought.

"One of those girls killed my husband," Daisy said dryly.

"That's an innocent girl in jail. If you don't tell the truth, you will suffer to the end," Miss Sweets said and left.

She went to visit the other twin in jail. Miss Sweets had a special protection that day because normally, it would have been difficult to visit a black person who had killed a white person. Miss Sweets knew that the spirit of the girl's grandmother was with her.

Deborah had been beaten severely. She sat in a corner of the jail cell. Miss Sweets threw powder into the cell. The girl looked up. Miss Sweets handed her a swatch of cloth. Days later, Deborah was released but was warned to leave town. She went to Miss Sweets' house. They stayed in Covington for awhile but headed north of Atlanta to Cartersville. It was as far north as Miss Sweets wanted to travel.

According to Miss Sweets, Miss Mattie had been a high-stepper when she was younger. She teased and flirted with men. Some said she probably learned it from her mother who was Creole. Her name was Catherine Malveaux-Petterson. Miss Mattie's older sister, Louise, was a proper lady, a little like her grandmother. Louise married a teacher and lived up north. Mattie was the opposite. She liked being around men. Many men liked her but her eyes were fixed on one, Frank.

Frank was a dark man with curly hair. He was smart, an educated man. Mattie's, mother didn't like him because he was too dark. He didn't come from the right breed. Mattie was sent to Philadelphia to live with her sister to keep her from Frank. It was then she met Joe Mitchell, a porter on the train.

Joe was a hard working man. He worked hard to win Mattie's hand. She didn't love him, but it was time to get married. Mattie's mother approved because he was the right color. After they married and had two children, Carleton and Catherine, Mattie spent a month with her mother in Louisiana. Frank appeared one day out of nowhere. He was a doctor and married with three boys. As they talked, it was clear that they were still in love.

It was a warm July day, the day before Mattie was to go back home to Covington, Georgia. Little Carleton had gone fishing with his grandfather. Mattie spent the entire morning getting ready for a picnic. She dressed in a beautiful rose colored dress. She gathered up little Catherine and they headed for a creek far from the house.

Mattie spread a blanket and put the food on top. She waited patiently on Frank while Catherine skipped happily around trees. The little girl stopped suddenly after seeing a tall dark man. He smiled at her, but she eyed him suspiciously. When Mattie saw him. 'Over here,' she said with a smile. Frank joined her with a grin.

Little Catherine hid behind the trees and watch the two talk happily. It was the first time she saw her mother happy. Frank touched Mattie's face with a gentleness that Catherine had never seen before. The only thing her father did was yell and pushed on Mattie, which caused her to cry many times. But Frank was friendly and gentle. He laughed and smiled a lot. Catherine immediately liked him.

Catherine didn't understand what she saw minutes later but her mother was clinging onto Frank for dear life. They didn't let go of each other for a long time. Soon, Mattie quickly straightened her dress. She rubbed her hair and began fixing plates. She called for Catherine and they ate.

Mattie waited until dark before going home. She felt guilty. The few hours of pleasure could not remove the harshness of a brutal husband. One day with Frank took away years of pain. Mattie looked down at Catherine and said, 'Make sure you marry a nice man like Frank.' Catherine nodded.

Mattie walked up the steps to the door and froze after noticing a trinket at the front door. She banged on the door until her father opened it. Mattie panted as she pointed down to the trinket. Her father didn't know what it was. Soon her mother appeared. She saw Mattie pointing to the trinket. Miss Catherine knew what it was. It was a curse from Frank's wife. She knew roots.

"What have you done?" Miss Catherine whispered to Mattie.

Mattie put her hands to her mouth. She slowly looked up at her mother who slowly walked away. Mattie rushed from her mother's house with little Catherine to Sweetie's house because they were best friends and Sweetie knew roots.

Mattie pounded on Sweetie's door. Sweetie's husband opened it. Mattie pleaded with him to get Sweetie. Before he could, Sweetie came rushing to the door and begged Mattie to come inside.

"I can't, Sweetie. I got a curse. I brought a curse on my family," Mattie cried. Little Catherine held her mother's hand tightly.

Sweetie made her husband go into the house. "Mattie what happened?"

Mattie said nothing.

"Were you with Frank? You know his wife knows roots."

"Help me, Sweetie. You know roots too!"

"What kind of curse, Mattie?"

"It was some kind of trinket. I don't know...Can't you help me, Sweetie?"

Sweetie looked at little Catherine. She was a beautiful child, but Sweetie saw the child covered with blood. Sweetie closed her eyes and went back into the house. She came back with powders and something that looked like a very small broom. They hurried back to Mattie's parents' house. Sweetie began her ritual, throwing powders around the house and brushing around the door and around the house. She chanted and threw powder. Soon she was finished.

"Your momma's house is clean. But you can't go back inside," Sweetie said. She saw blood stains on Mattie's rose colored dress and Catherine was still covered with blood. Sweetie put her hands to her mouth.

"What's the matter, Sweetie? Isn't momma's house clean?"

"Mattie, you must leave here immediately. It's time to live the truth. It's time to be obedient. If you ever get scared, just call me."

Mattie knew that Sweetie saw something. Sweetie could not keep her eyes off of little Catherine. "Is something gonna happen to my baby?" Mattie asked trembling.

"She's going to be fine. Go Mattie," Sweetie said.

Two months later, Catherine Malveaux Peterson died. It was difficult for Mattie not to attend her mother's funeral. She didn't know if Frank's wife's curse was still following her, so she called on Sweetie. She said *Sweetie* so much that even little Catherine chanted her name. Everyday, Mattie said the name Sweetie until she appeared. Sweetie's husband died unexpectantly and she came to Georgia. Joe didn't like her. He said that she jooked too much and she was too close to Mattie. He didn't like that, so he banned Sweetie from their house.

The two women continued to visit in secret. Then Mattie became pregnant with the twins. Mattie was filled with happiness seeing two babies at one time. Joe became angry because Mattie was happy, so he made her give the babies away, claiming they were not his. They were the only ones with his eyes. On the day Mattie gave the babies away, the spirits came to visit her. They stayed with her every since.

One day, the spirits heard Mattie's cry for help. Three drunk white men came by the house. They drove their car into a ditch by Mattie's house. They asked Joe to help them. While Joe was outside helping them, Mattie was fixing lunch. One drunk man came inside to get some rags. He saw Mattie from behind. She turned around and smiled at him. He smiled back. Mattie stopped smiling and continued with lunch.

The man approached her from behind and whispered, *Hello Beautiful*, in her ear. Mattie eased away smiling. She turned around to offer him something to eat. He grinned and leaned over to answer her, but he fell on top of her. She tried helping him up, but he was heavy. He grinned and smacked a kiss at her. Joe saw it and became angry. He was so mad that he killed all three white me and then began hitting on Mattie. She got mad too and shot him in the leg. She was scared so she burned down the house with Joe in it. She took off with the children and drove the white men's car to Sweetie's house. Mattie didn't have to say anything because Sweetie knew the truth.

"You can't stay, Mattie. You have to cross water to remove the curse," Sweetie said.

Mattie cried. She clutched the pearl necklace around her neck, her mother's pearls. Mattie's hands became heated. She saw a beam of light around her children.

"The spirits sent help, Mattie," Sweetie said joyfully. She reached for Mattie's pearls. Mattie hesitated but removed them. Sweetie took the pearls to an alter and looked around the house wildly. She went outside to her rose bush and plucked one. She went back to the alter and chanted until the pearls beamed. Sweetie picked them up and gave them back to Mattie.

"Wear these always. They'll protect you," Sweetie said.

"What about the children? Will they be protected?" Mattie panted.

Sweetie looked at Carleton. His aura was unclear to her. Then Sweetie looked at Catherine. The little girl was still covered with blood, but the beam of light seemed to embrace her. To Sweetie, the little girl would be protected regardless of whatever happened to her. Sweetie couldn't tell this to Mattie.

"Your daughters and their daughters will be cursed until all unrest spirits are buried and that's only with love."

Mattie shook her head not understanding. "I must get my twins? I can't leave them behind."

"Leave them, Mattie. No one must know where you're going. Joe and three white men are dead. They gonna be looking for you."

"I can't leave them, Sweetie. They're my babies!"

"Miss Daisy promised to take good care of them. I'll watch them. You must go now. You'll only be safe as long as you're smart. Right now, you ain't smart. No one must know who you are, none of you's."

Mattie hugged Sweetie tightly. Sweetie whispered in Mattie's ear, "Your spirit will always be unrested until you find the love that was forbidden. Then you will be at peace."

Mattie looked sadly at her fatherless children. She didn't know how she was going to take care of them. She had no husband to support her. She had never given any thought to doing manual labor. Her mother only talked about a wife's duties. When Mattie looked into Catherine's big sad eyes she almost cried again. She had to pull herself together. She had to take care of her children. Mattie took Catherine by the hand. "Let's go children," she said.

Carleton grabbed Catherine's hand from Mattie. He looked horribly at his mother. "I'm to take care of Cathy. Daddy told me to," he said.

Sweetie shook her head. "No baby. Your grandmother told you that. She spoke it through your father."

Carleton ran out of the house. Sweetie looked at Mattie and said, "Joe will always hunt him. You shouldn't of done it, Mattie."

Mattie didn't want to hear it. There was nothing she could do about it. She took her children to Arkansas to stay with Joe's sister Pearl. Mattie lied to Pearl saying that a white man killed Joe and that she and the children had to flee. The white man burned the house down too. Carleton remained quiet as his mother lied. A few months later, Mattie left Arkansas and headed north to Missouri.

Lisa rubbed her eyes. She couldn't wait to leave the office. The baby made her more sluggish every day. She rubbed her small pregnant stomach and smiled after the baby gave her a rough kick.

"Boy or girl?"

Lisa swiveled around in her chair. She looked at the stranger curiously. "May I help you?"

The stranger sat down uninvited without losing eye contact. She crossed her shapely legs comfortably. She grinned at Lisa. "Boy or girl?"

"May I help you?" Lisa asked firmly. She was ready to call security. She didn't know if the person was a new employee at American Petroleum or one of Vivian's friends who had been harassing her.

The first time she complained to Cameron about women calling the house asking for him and that Vivian was probably behind it, he ignored her. He thought the same thing Vivian thought: Lisa was jealous of his relationship with his daughter. When Lisa complained about having the little girl over and how it gave Vivian an excuse to come by the house, Cameron became angry. The calls came frequently, ending with Lisa being called a bitch. Lisa put a block on the calls, but then there was the busted car window. Lisa stopped visitation and later Cameron moved out.

"Who are you and what do you want?" Lisa asked.

The stranger's smile faded. She made an intense stare at Lisa.

"I've been looking for you for a very long time. I'm surprised you don't know."

Lisa picked up the phone.

"I heard that you've been visiting my grandmother. Well, she's not my real grandmother, but she raised me after they found my mother dead in St. Louis. Grandma Sweetie is what I call her. Everyone calls her Miss Sweets. She called me and said that my cousin has come home," the stranger said.

Lisa remained silent, but closed her eyes when the baby kicked.

"My mother's name is Deborah Orville. She had a twin sister named Della Orville, who was your mother. According to my grandmother, she saw my mother being pushed through a window by her sister. It was hard to believe because I thought twins are suppose to be close. They stuck together through thick and thin. My mother went to St. Louis to find her sister. A month later, she was dead. She left and never came home. I was left with the weirdest bitch in Cartersville," the stranger continued.

Lisa rubbed her stomach because the baby moved more. She rubbed her eyes and took deep breaths. She rubbed her stomach more, trying to calm down the baby.

"Um, I hope it's a boy because the women in our family have fucked up."

Chapter Ten

Lisa let the telephone ring. She refused to answer another prank call. Since Cameron had left, the calls were becoming less frequent, but they had not stopped. Lisa had blocked ten telephone numbers, which included Vivian's number. Lisa saw the light on the answering machine. She hesitated before reviewing the message. She hit the button and heard Alicia's voice:

Hey Lisa. Just calling to see if the pregnancy is going well. Kyle and I want to visit this summer. I better get moving on the wedding plans. I can't convince him to elope. Give me a call.

Lisa shook her head. She never imagined Kyle and Alicia getting married. It took Alicia a long time to tell her that they were dating. Alicia knew that Kyle was a special friend to Jennifer, Lisa's best friend. Lisa hadn't mentioned Jennifer's or Kyle's names in the same conversation since the funeral.

Lisa understood Alicia's concerns about having a wedding ceremony. Alicia had a common background. She grew up poor. It was difficult for her to feel comfortable around people who were financially secured.

Kyle was from Minneapolis. He hardly dated black girls. He had an intense crush on Jennifer in college but after graduation, he began to put distance between their relationship. Another thing that made Alicia self-conscience was Kyle's middle-class background.

Alicia confided in Lisa about how embarrassed she was after

Kyle's first visit. Her mother cursed constantly, calling one of her brother's children "little fuckas." Her mother drank nonstop and her live-in boyfriend wasn't that much better. He sent Kyle to the refrigerator for beer constantly. He fussed at Kyle after sending him to the store for *The Best* beer. Kyle brought back a six pack of Heineken. The man called Kyle an ignorant nigga for not knowing that *The Best* beer was a store generic brand. He refused to pay Kyle for being dumb.

Alicia knew Kyle in college but she had never paid much attention to him. They saw each other on the airplane going to Chicago. Alicia attended a conference for daycare providers and Kyle attended meetings for information systems developers. Strangely, they sat side by side on the plane. Alicia recognized him and spoke. He returned her greeting dryly. Alicia ignored him and began reading her manuals.

A little boy in the seat behind Kyle moved about freely. The boy took an instant liking to Kyle and bothered him often. Kyle seemed irritated.

"So, you hate children." Alicia stated without looking at Kyle.

"I don't hate children, I'm trying to relax," Kyle responded.

"I didn't ask if you hated children, I'm telling you that you do!" Alicia said as she continued to flip through her manual.

Kyle blew air and closed his eyes.

Oddly, their meetings were in the same hotel. Alicia sat by herself in the hotel's crowded restaurant. Alicia's table was the only one available. Kyle decided not to go out for lunch, but he didn't want to sit at the same table with the rude woman. The waitress told him it was a thirty minute wait. Kyle had to do a presentation that afternoon so he swallowed his pride and courageously asked Alicia if he could join her. She frowned slightly and then nodded. Kyle sat down nervously.

They ate in silence. The waitress brought the check. Kyle paid the entire bill and left. Alicia frowned at him when he left without saying anything.

Later that evening, Alicia rushed to the business center room of the hotel to make copies for the next day's meeting. Kyle was making copies and humming a song that was playing on the radio. It was a country and western station. Kyle looked as if he enjoyed the music. When he saw Alicia, he sang louder and smiled.

"Will you be long?" Alicia asked politely.

Kyle nodded as he continued to sing, what appeared to be, his favorite song. When the song finished, Kyle repeated a chorus.

"You really know that song?" Alicia inquired.

"I like country music," Kyle answered.

"The only country and western group I like is Hootie and the Blowfish," Alicia said, trying to stir up conversation as she waited.

Kyle narrowed his eyes. "Hootie and the Blowfish isn't a country and western group."

"Well, they sound country to me," Alicia answered and turned her head.

Kyle looked at Alicia. She had been a bridesmaid in Lisa's and Cameron's wedding. She looked different now. She always had a nice shape but she didn't seem to behave as cool as she did in college. She hung around with loud girls, but she was always quiet. After she pledged her sorority, she became more feminine.

"It's all yours," Kyle announced as he gathered his copies.

Alicia had to remove Kyle's original from the copier before starting her project. Before she handed Kyle the paper, she noticed a few typographical errors. She also noticed that there was no heading at the top to identify columns.

"You may want to correct this. It has typing errors."

Kyle took the paper and sighed heavily. The department secretary had not corrected the mistakes that he circled. He cursed to himself.

"If you are going to present that, it should be reader friendly. You have no headings at the top and your categories look just like the rest of the text," Alicia suggested.

"I don't know how to put headings on the rest of the pages." Alicia shook her head.

"Since you have an eye for mistakes, do you mind reviewing this for me?"

"How much are you paying?"

"I bought you lunch today!"

"You had to pay for a seat. There was no place for you to sit," Alicia said jokingly.

"Are you the type of black woman that's always begging, looking for money," Kyle said with an attitude.

"No, I'm the type of black woman who was nice enough to speak to your rude butt on the airplane. You act like you don't know who I am. I went to school with you. We were also in Lisa's wedding together. Do you always act this ugly?"

Kyle was silent. Every time he saw someone from the wedding, it reminded him of Jennifer. It was difficult thinking about his best friend's wedding and his best friend's funeral.

"No, I don't always act ugly. Thanks for your critique."

Alicia remembered what Lisa told her about Kyle and Jennifer. Kyle's sad eyes made Alicia soften. "I know about you and Jennifer. I know that she was a friend of yours."

"She wasn't just a friend. She was more than that."

"If you want me to review your document, I will. You can pay me later," Alicia teased.

Kyle smile. "How about dinner? As small as you are, that's all I can afford."

Lisa decided to return Alicia's call later. Alicia was depending on her to be the matron-of-honor. She figured Lisa would deliver in plenty of time for the wedding.

Lisa wanted to talk to someone because she was thinking about Jennifer again. Lisa thought about calling Rochelle. She was in her last year of nursing school, and she wasn't sure if she wanted to be a nurse. She said that sick people made her sick.

The telephone rang again. Lisa decided to answer. "Hello," Lisa said roughly.

"Hello, Lisa. This is William. I will be attending a conference in Atlanta next week."

Lisa was silent.

"Lisa, are you alright?"

"I'm sorry. I'm surprised to hear from you."

"Why? I sense something is wrong. Is the baby okay?"

"The baby is fine. It's me and Cameron. We're separated."

"How long has it been?"

"It's been for quite some time. Do you need a ride from the airport?"

William was always impressed with Lisa's accommodating attitude. Although he wasn't the father that he should have been, his relationship with her had strengthened after the truth came out, and his relationship with Melanie had weakened.

"No, honey. I'll take a cab."

"It's expensive. I can pick you up."

William chuckled. "Okay. My flight arrives at 6:40 p.m. next Wednesday. Let me know if things change."

"No problem. I'll pick you up after work."

Lisa hung up and rubbed her stomach. The baby wasn't as busy as usual. She thought it was sleeping so she decided to take a nap, too.

As she relaxed in bed, she thought about the letter she had sent Gina a week ago. Lisa could not bring herself to tell Gina over the telephone about Paul; Gina's stepfather and Lisa's real father. Lisa was surprised that Gina had not called.

The ringing telephone broke Lisa's concentration. She picked it up.

"Hello, cuz. What's up!" the happy voice said.

Lisa froze. She wondered how did the person get her phone number since it wasn't listed?

"What do you want?" Lisa said impatiently.

"Is this how you treat family?"

"What do you want, Rhonda?"

"My grandmother wants to meet with us soon. She has some shit to tell us that the spirit has sent. Knowing Grandma Sweetie, the dead is talking to her again."

"When does she want us to visit?"

"You tell me what's good for you."

"My father is coming next week and I don't..."

"By the way, your husband is fine! Does he have a brother you can hook me up with?"

Lisa slammed down the phone. She could feel the baby move around from the excitement. First it was harassment from Vivian and her friends, now, it was from the new sick cousin. The telephone rang again. Lisa answered.

"Bitch, don't you *ever* hang up on me again. I'm trying to be nice, something I hardly ever do. If you don't want to see my grandmother then say so!" the angry voice shouted.

"Tell Miss Sweets, I'll give her a call. And another thing, you crazy-ass heffa, don't call my house talking shit to me. I'm going to ask you one more time. What do you want from me?" Lisa said between clenched teeth. She had to take a deep breath because the baby was getting more excited.

Rhonda laughed. "I was beginning to think you were soft," she said giggling. Lisa remained silent. "Grandma Sweetie said that your mother was smart."

Lisa held her silence. Rhonda took a deep breath. "All I want is to get to know you. I've been searching for you. We've only got each other," Rhonda concluded.

Lisa sat with a stone face, but then it softened. She smiled her biggest smile. "How old are you, little cousin?" she asked softly.

Rhonda became shy. "I'll be twenty-six this year."

"You are wrong about us being alone. We had three more cousins. One died in a car accident in '89. One is a little boy about nine-years-old, who lives in St. Louis and the big cousin of them all is two years older than me. She lives in Kansas City."

"How do you know all of that?"

"Didn't Miss Sweets tell you the family history?"

"She told me about my real grandmother, Mattie Mitchell, who brought a curse on the family. She had one son, Carleton, and three daughters, Catherine, Corine and Coretta. When the twins, Corine and Coretta, were given away, the white family renamed them Della and Deborah. Corine was named after Grandma Sweetie and Coretta was named after our great, great grandmother. Grandma Sweetie only knew about one other grandchild of Mattie Mitchell and that was you."

"Let me add to the family history. We have a boy cousin named Mitchell and an older cousin named Melanie."

"How did you get the chance to live with our grandmother?"

"All I know is Miss Mattie used to babysit me when my mother ran the streets. I didn't know that she was my real grandmother because she never told me. My mother died when I was twelve. I just stayed with the Miss Mattie until she died."

"How did she die?"

"In a car accident with our cousin Jennifer. You would have liked her."

"I've only been searching for you. I don't care about anybody else. We're the outsiders. No one gave away Melanie's mother."

Lisa felt the same way. Although she found out about Miss Mattie twins much later than Rhonda, Lisa felt angry after hearing Miss Sweets tell the story of the twins. Her mother never had a chance at life. No wonder she had very little directions. Lisa heard the signal for another call. She told Rhonda to hold.

"Hello Lisa, this is Melanie. How is the baby?"

Lisa shook. Her forehead felt warm. "Hi Angel...uh...Melanie, how are you?"

Melanie laughed. "Everyone is reverting back to college days. You are the second person who called me Angel. Look, I thought about visiting next week. I hear that dad will be in town. I thought Lauren and I would surprise him. It's been awhile since we've seen him."

"Sure. His plane is arriving next Wednesday evening. How is everyone?"

Melanie hesitated before lying. "Everyone and everything is fine. How is the baby and Cameron?"

"The baby is fine, but let me talk to you later. I have another call on the other end."

"I'll see you next week."

"Okay. See you then." Lisa clicked over to Rhonda. "That was our cousin, Melanie. She's coming to visit soon."

"What does she want?" Rhonda asked roughly.

"She's coming to town next week. Do you want to meet her?"

"Why should I?"

"I think you will like her. It took me awhile to like her, but she's cool."

"If you say so, then I'll meet her."

Lisa smiled to herself. It was perfect timing. Maybe she would present everyone with the truth. She had already sent Gina a copy of the court papers declaring Paul Smith as her father.

Lisa was getting cold feet. Not too long ago, she would have savored the idea of keeping the secret going. But something was cleansing her. She took the coward's way out by allowing Gina to tell the family. She didn't want anyone to know that she was deceitful.

Before Lisa said anything to Rhonda, the line signaled another call. When she clicked over, she knew immediately that she had made a mistake. It was another prank call. Lisa clicked back over to Rhonda. When she blew air, Rhonda knew something was wrong.

"What's the matter?"

"My husband's daughter's mother's friends have been fucking with me and I'm getting a little tired of it."

"Who is she?"

"Her name is Vivian Albright. She has some crazy friends. I don't know who they are, but I'm tired of it."

"Don't worry about it, cuz. Just concentrate on not stressing out. You have another life inside of you."

Lisa smiled. She was beginning to like her new family member. They had much more in common than the other member.

"We'll talk later. Oh, Cameron has a younger brother named Jason. He looks much better than Cameron. When he comes to Atlanta, I'll introduce you two."

The two women laughed.

Chapter Eleven

Gina's patience were wearing thin. Avery refused to talk. It wasn't like him to talk back to the teacher. He was only in the third grade. The academy he attended had a low tolerance for problem behavior. They called parents on the job if it was warranted.

"I'm going to ask one more time," Gina said.

"Momma, Avery bad. Ain't he," a little girl said.

"I'm not bad!" Avery yelled at her.

"Avery, stop yelling at your sister. Sidnee, stop saying ain't. Say isn't he. And Avery is not bad." Gina paused for a few seconds. "Avery go to your room until your father comes home."

Avery stormed out of the living room. Gina heard him crying. She decided to try it again. His behavior had been inconsistent since Thanksgiving. He was never disobedient at school. He liked his teacher. The whole thing puzzled Gina.

When Gina walked into the room, Avery quickly turned his head. She sat on the bed. "Avery, I want you to talk to me. I thought we were here," Gina said, taking two fingers and pointing them to her eyes.

Sidnee came into the room. Avery turned around. "Get out of here!" he yelled.

"It's my room too. Momma make him stop," Sidnee whined.

"I hate you!" Avery screamed at her.

Gina stood. She extended her hand to Sidnee, but she refused to go. "Let's go Sidnee," Gina said firmly. Sidnee slowly took Gina's hand. They left the room. They could still hear Avery complaining about hating Sidnee.

"Why Avery hate me?" five-year-old Sidnee asked.

"He doesn't hate you. He's upset right now," Gina said.

"He always say he hate me. He say he hope I die."

"He doesn't mean it. Help me set the table. Your father will be home soon."

Carlos was running late for dinner. Gina and Sidnee had eaten. Avery refused to come out of his room. Gina sat impatiently, hoping Carlos would arrive soon. It was getting closer to Sidnee's bed time and Gina was concerned about putting her in the same room with Avery. The family had outgrown the apartment. They didn't have money to move into a larger place because Carlos was working on his Ph.D. Even with loans, it was still expensive.

Carlos had to travel extensively to do research in order to complete his dissertation by the end of Fall. He was researching the black migration to the north. His focus was on the creation of urban ghettos. His travel proved valuable. He made several key contacts that lead him to organizations wanting him to give lectures. Many times, he was able to make dual purposes of the trips. He always went up the day before to do more interviews, surveys and observations.

Two years ago, his dissertation committee was not all in agreement with his progress on the topic. He concluded that the three white committee members were not in agreement with his views. Carlos intensified his studies so that he could prove to those members that he knew what he was talking about. He wanted to finish early because the family was in need of money. His plan was to defend his dissertation the following year.

Gina let out a sigh when she heard the key in the door. Carlos entered looking beat. Sidnee ran to him chanting "daddy, daddy." He picked her up and gave her his usual kiss. He put her down and she opened the flood gates, informing him of the events of the day. When she told him that Avery said he hated her, Carlos looked at Gina.

"I'll fix you a plate," Gina said and took off toward the kitchen.

"Is Avery in his room," Carlos grumbled.

Gina stopped in her tracks. "I want him to be left alone right now. You and I need to talk first," Gina said, giving Carlos her favorite *not in front of the children* look.

Carlos rubbed his eyes. "I'll put Sidnee in bed."

He picked her up and carried her to the room. She was still talking. Carlos gave an occasional "un-hun." Since her arrival, most of Carlos attention went to her. He was fascinated with her. She talked, walked and potty trained early. Carlos concluded, she was smart.

Avery was asleep on the floor. Carlos carefully stepped around him and put Sidnee in bed. He gave her another kiss.

"Good night, daddy," Sidnee whispered.

"Good night, sweets," Carlos said.

"Avery was bad today. He talked back to his teacher."

"Okay, Sidnee, you told me."

Carlos bent down and removed Avery from the floor. Avery moved around in Carlos' arms. Carlos hesitated before removing Avery's clothes. He was sleeping soundly. Carlos gently removed his clothes and slid him into bed. Carlos turned to Sidnee. She was wide eyed.

"Avery said he hate me," she whispered.

"He doesn't hate you. Good night, baby. Get some sleep."

Carlos left the room. He walked into the dining area. Gina had a plate on the table. It had been a long time since she fixed him a plate when he came home late. He usually reheated his own food because many times everyone was asleep. Every now and then, she got up to chat with him.

"What's happening with Avery?" Carlos asked, not looking at Gina as he ate.

"Mrs. Herring called. Avery was called on to recite his vocabulary. He said he forgot it. As she explained the importance of doing homework, he told her he didn't care." Gina sighed a little before continuing. "Mrs. Herring asked about Avery's relationship with his sister. It appears he talks a lot about Sidnee. Mrs. Herring is suggesting counseling."

Gina was hesitant about discussing counseling with Carlos. During the few sessions of their marriage counseling, she watched him breakdown as he confessed his anger toward his mother for causing his father to leave and not getting a basketball scholarship. He really didn't know why his father left, but still he blamed his mother. The guilt behind the confession caused him to not want to go back to counseling. He withdrew from Gina until the birth of Sidnee.

Although Carlos wasn't violent anymore, he became extremely quiet. Gina called Carla for help. They decided that Carlos was not going back to counseling. He felt too guilty about what he shared.

Gina's pregnancy with Sidnee was uncomfortable. The baby moved a lot. The little girl kept Gina up most nights. Sometimes, Carlos got up with her and turned on the television. Still he was quiet.

One day after coming home from a challenging day at work, Carlos received a letter from the University of Chicago. He was accepted into their history Ph.D. program. He ran up the stairs to the apartment. No one was home. Carlos waited patiently for an hour on Gina. She was very late coming home. He picked up the phone to call her job and saw the light flashing on their answering machine. The message said that Gina was at the hospital. The baby wasn't due until the end of February, but she came two weeks early. Carlos rushed to the hospital just in time to see little Sidnee Desiree come into the world. Carlos felt she waited for him before making her entrance. She was always considered his good luck charm.

"We need to get a bigger place. I don't like Avery saying that he hates his sister," Gina complained.

Carlos knew the apartment was too little, but there was not much they could do until he finished his studies. "I need one more year. We will be able to get a house and everything you have ever wanted."

"I don't want to lose Avery's spot in school because of unruly behavior. Maybe we can take a vacation this summer to spend time together as a family."

Carlos was irritated. "I can't take off. It will be over in a year."

Gina decided not to continue the discussion. She got up from the table. Carlos grabbed her arm before she walked away. "How are things at work?" Carlos eased her to the chair.

Gina kept her focus away. "Fine," she replied.

Carlos finished his meal in silence. He washed his plate and put it away. Gina was already in the bedroom. They undressed in silence. Gina reached for her gown, keeping her back turned toward him. He walked over and playfully grabbed the gown out of her hands. She tried unsuccessfully to get it back. She went to the dresser to get another one. Carlos stepped in front of her. She kept her eyes closed.

"I promise we will take a vacation next summer."

"Avery needs you now. You're hardly around."

"He's a growing boy. I was the same way."

"It's different. Avery has both parents."

"All I need is one more year and it will be over. I'll spend more time with Avery. Listen to me, he's okay."

Carlos stepped closer to Gina, trying to pull her closer to him. She didn't budge. She crossed her arms over her chest. For the past six months, she behaved shyly about making love. She was once an aggressive lover.

"What's up with all of this?" Carlos asked, extending his arms. Gina was silent. Carlos became impatient. He was becoming angry and fearful.

"At one time it was the beer. Next it was the fighting. I understood how you felt. What is it now?"

Gina kept her head turned. She was fighting to keep her emotions under control.

Carlos was considering the worst was happening. "You don't want me touching you. I need to know why?" he asked.

Gina didn't answer because she was choked.

Carlos braced himself. He asked low, "Is there another man?"

Gina swung around. She was flabbergasted. She forgot about her nude chest. "Why would you think I'm cheating on you?" she asked boiling.

Carlos defenses were down. He could only think about the last time, but this time, he wasn't drunk. "You don't want to make love anymore," he said and gave her back the gown. She snatched it out of his hands.

"Look at me! I'm fat!" she said between clenched teeth and tight lips.

Carlos blew relief. It was only the weight. She was ten pounds heavier since college. It didn't look bad. She was tall enough to carry the weight well.

Carlos decided to become playful. "You look fine. I like a woman with a little meat on her bones. I like grabbing a little butt." Carlos pinched Gina on the butt.

Gina was so frustrated with Carlos that she put on her gown. He stopped playing and kissed her on the forehead. "I'm going to do better," he said softly.

She shook her head. She felt as if she were being selfish. Carlos was putting the finishing touches on his dissertation. He hustled hard to bring in extra money. "Maybe I need to do more with the children," she said and walked to the bed. Carlos pulled her back.

"You've done enough. I need to manage my time better," he said and kissed her again on the forehead. "Can we have a little fun tonight?" he asked and lightly pinched her on the butt. Over the years, he had become a patient lover. It had become easier for Gina to respond to his touch.

Before he took his fun a little further, the telephone rang. Both looked at the telephone. Carlos picked up the receiver. He talked low and then not at all. He hung up the phone and sat on the bed. He put his head in his hands and then rubbed the back of his neck.

Gina watched his expression turn from pleasant to worry. "What's the matter?" she asked. She watched as Carlos rubbed his head with his hands. It seemed to take forever for him to answer.

"It's momma. She's in the hospital. It's her kidneys again," he said.

Gina sat down beside him. She grabbed his hand and began stroking it. Carlos had to clear his throat before speaking again. "I have to go home."

"What about your brothers?"

"Earl is back in prison and Junior is on crack."

Carlos' eyes pleaded with Gina for comfort. He was afraid. She put his hand to her lips and kissed it. "It's going to be alright."

"It's always a struggle. As soon as things go well, something else interferes."

Gina rubbed his hand against her face. "We have to have faith. It's the only thing that is going to get us through tough times."

Carlos nodded. He wasn't one for church. He never been one to take religion seriously. When he and Gina began counseling, he noticed that she would pray before they went to bed. He would leave her alone to spend time alone with her God. One time she was about to offer a prayer. She looked at him and extended her hand. He gave it to her slowly. Silently, she asked God for something. Carlos hoped that whatever his wife was asking for, she got. She released his hand and climbed into bed. He didn't know what she asked God for, but all he could remember that night was the best sex they had ever had.

Carlos enjoyment of the tender moment between him and Gina was interrupted when Avery cried out in his sleep. They sprang from the bed and rushed into his room. He was tossing and kicking wildly in bed. Carlos picked him up.

"Daddy's here," Carlos said, holding Avery firmly.

Avery opened his eyes and cried. Carlos rocked him. "You're having a nightmare," Carlos said.

"I don't like school," Avery cried.

Carlos looked at Gina. She had no idea of what would make Avery upset about school. Carlos sat on Avery's bed and faced Sidnee. She looked at Avery.

"Stop looking at me!" Avery yelled.

"Stop yelling at your sister. You understand?" Carlos said firmly. Avery didn't answer. He just cried. "What's happening at school?" Carlos asked.

"They were pushing on him," Avery whined.

"What are you talking about?"

"The Westside Blades were messing with us. They pushed Montez."

Carlos felt his chest tighten more when Avery cried again. "I'll take care of it," Carlos said.

When Gina saw anger rising on Carlos face, she removed Avery from his arms and began to rock him. Carlos walked out of the room.

"Momma can I get up?" Sidnee asked politely.

"No, sweetheart. Just lie still and go to sleep," Gina said.

Gina put Avery under the covers and sat on his bed until he went back to sleep. She eased off the bed and looked at a wide awake Sidnee. Gina sat on Sidnee's bed and listened to the curious little girl as she asked question after question. Gina remembered one of her mother's home remedies for restless children. She and Sidnee went into the kitchen for some warm milk. Gina put a pinch of Karo syrup in the milk. She and Sidnee sat at the dinette and sipped milk from coffee cups.

After they finished their make-believe coffee, Gina took Sidnee back into the bedroom and sat with her until she fell asleep. An hour had passed before Sidnee closed her eyes. Gina was exhausted. She walked into the master bedroom. Carlos was sitting on the side of the bed with his head in his hands. Gina took the initiative. It had been a long time since she was the aggressor. When she kissed him, he cleared his throat.

"We have to go to the academy and see what's going on," Carlos said.

Gina nodded. She pulled the covers back on her side and got in bed. Carlos slowly stretched out. What he was in the mood for had changed. He saw the familiar sight of Gina's back. She had tried but he turned her off.

Carlos rolled over and cuddled Gina in his arms. He kissed her on the neck. He could feel her smile. Everything was fine. He pulled her closer and closed his eyes.

Gina and Carlos sat stiff as they waited for the principal. The academy was a renovated building on the west side of Chicago. Only the paint and decor were new. The furnishings had been donated.

"Mrs. Cole will see you now," said a pleasant voice.

Carlos and Gina followed the woman through the door. Carlos' expression hardened as they approached the door opening. They greeted a short stout woman with a silver, short afro and raccoon circles around the eyes. The multicolor scarf added pizzazz to the tan skirt and loose jacket.

Mrs. Cole's greeting was cordial. She and Gina knew each other very well. Gina called constantly during Avery's first year of school. She attended every parent-teacher meeting and sold the most merchandise for fund raisers. Most teachers knew Mrs. Simmons, but no one had seen Mr. Simmons. He was a mystery.

Gina and Mrs. Cole talked for awhile. As Mrs. Cole asked questions, Gina responded with rehearsed lines. Carlos was ready to get down to business.

"Avery tells us that gang members are coming to the school assaulting students. We heard a third grader was beaten up. My son is afraid they're coming for him," Carlos said bluntly.

Mrs. Cole's eyebrows raised. She knew it wasn't going to be easy confronting the issue. A few parents had already contacted the school about their children receiving threats from the same gang.

"We are working on stronger security," she responded.

"Are these problem children on the premises?" Carlos asked sternly. Avery's safety wasn't the issue anymore. Breaking Mrs.

Cole's comfortable attitude was the challenge.

"These kids live somewhat close to the school. We are working on stronger protection. The police department has made other issues priority. We are thinking of an alternative solution."

Gina was satisfied with Mrs. Cole's answer, but Carlos appeared to have more frustration. "We are paying a steep tuition for my son to attend school here. We also work our butts off for school fund raisers. When do you think you can tell us about the other alternative?" Carlos rumbled.

Gina unconsciously gave Carlos a mean look. She was the one who toted around the candy sheets, calendars and magazine subscriptions. She was surprisingly offended at Carlos attempt to take credit for her hard work. When Gina saw Mrs. Cole's eyebrows narrow at her, she quickly brought her focus forward. She didn't want to give any indication of family strife.

"We are grateful for the hard work you and Mrs. Simmons do to help the academy keep down tuition costs. We are also fortunate to have a bright student like Avery attending the academy. It makes us proud that a student, such as Avery has our academy name on his transcript," Mrs. Cole said. She looked down before speaking again.

"I understand Mrs. Herring has recently discussed Avery's behavior with you. We hope everything is fine," Mrs. Cole said. She stared eye to eye with Carlos. He frowned, feeling trapped.

"We're working on it," he said.

"Our lunch hours have started. Mr. Simmons, why don't you stop by Avery's room and meet Mrs. Herring," Mrs. Cole said and stood. Gina and Carlos followed her out the door.

As Mrs. Cole walked down the hall, obedient students in uniforms greeted her with smiles and warm hellos. Carlos looked around suspiciously. He wondered if Mrs. Cole had anything up her sleeve. To Carlos, the woman didn't like him.

A group of third graders were leaving a room. They all sang a greeting to Mrs. Cole. She smiled as she spoke to them. Before they walked inside the room, Avery and another little boy walked out. Avery's eyes became large seeing his parents with the principal.

"Hello Avery. I thought your parents may want to come by to see you before leaving," Mrs. Cole said.

Avery looked at Carlos with mistrust. It was rare to see Carlos at school. Avery figured the worst. He was in trouble.

"Hello Montez," Gina said.

"Hello Mrs. Simmons," the little boy said.

"So this is Montez. I heard about those kids starting trouble. Are you okay?" Carlos asked.

Montez nodded at first and then said, "Yes sir."

"We're going to make sure that never happens again," Carlos

said with a smile. He extended his fist. Montez felt jumpy but smiled at Carlos. Montez took his small fist and tapped it lightly on top of Carlos fist. Avery pouted and walked away.

"Where are you going Avery?" Mrs. Cole asked.

Avery stopped. Without turning around, he said, "To lunch." He kept his back turned.

Carlos put his hands in his pockets. "We came to see you and Mrs. Herring. Will you please come back?" Carlos asked softly.

Avery turned around reluctantly and walked back slowly. Mrs. Cole directed Montez down the hall as she left. Gina, Carlos and Avery walked into the room. Carlos saw Mrs. Herring for the first time. At one time, his son talked constantly of Mrs. Herring. Carlos knew why. The teacher was no more than twenty-six-years old. She was chocolate color with big eyes and plump lips. When she smiled, her face glowed. She was medium height with a long waistline and a firm, round derriere. Carlos thought the woman was drop-dead gorgeous. He returned her smile.

Mrs. Herring praised Avery's work. She gently touched on the disobedient behavior in a soothing voice, treating it as normal. Not once did she call Avery disruptive or uncontrollable. She politely asked Avery did he have a problem understanding any of the assignments. Avery didn't look at anybody. He was silent, keeping his focus to the floor.

"Avery did you hear Mrs. Herring?" Carlos asked firmly.

Avery didn't look up. He began to cry. Mrs. Herring walked to her desk and removed a couple of tissues. She gently wiped Avery's face.

"We don't have to discuss it now. Why don't you join Montez for lunch?" Mrs. Herring said with a huge smile. Avery nodded and walked away sluggishly.

For the next ten minutes, Mrs. Herring talked about Avery's comments about his sister. She brought up family counseling. Carlos was silent but Gina remarked, "We need to talk to Avery. He's been tight lip about his feelings. I will give you a call."

"Avery is a good student. He has a few things to work out. Many times, children become a little jealous of their younger siblings because the attention is being shared. Avery is fortunate to have parents that care. Many of our children come from single parent homes. We encourage the mothers to allow their sons to participate in the Big Brother program. It's proven valuable," Mrs. Herring said.

They heard students in the hall. Gina and Carlos walked to the door with Mrs. Herring. "I'll see you at the sorority meeting," Mrs. Herring said to Gina.

"Don't tell me you're an Alpha!" Carlos teased.

"Of course! My husband is a Lambda."

"So am I!"

"Are you active?"

Before Carlos could answered, Gina blurted out, "*No!* I've been trying to get him active since he's been in Chicago."

"Let me inform you on what's going on. The Lambdas are gearing up to sponsor a basketball tournament this summer for ages seven to seventeen. I hope you can give your frat brothers a hand because they need help."

The two women looked at Carlos. He held up his hands. "Look ladies, I can't promise anything. I'll try."

The students filtered into the room. Montez and a couple other boys stared strangely at Carlos. He heard Montez whisper to the boys, "That's Avery's daddy. He's smooth."

Avery trailed in behind everyone. His parents were still invading his space. He tried walking around Gina. Carlos stepped into his path. "Your mother and sister have challenged us to a round of miniature golf. Losers have to pay for pizza. I hope you can still putt because I'm broke," Carlos said.

A smile broke at one corner of Avery's mouth. "They can't beat us. Sidnee is too little," he said.

"I see a forfeit coming," Gina said.

"Sidnee is too little. It won't be fair. We can help pay for the pizza," Avery said to Carlos.

"Like I said, I'm broke. How much money do you have?" Carlos asked.

"A lot! Four dollars."

Carlos held back the laughter. "Cool," he said and extended his fist.

It had been a long time since Carlos had extended the gesture. Avery rushed to returned the invitation. He took his small fist and tapped the top of Carlos' fist.

Chapter Twelve

Carlos removed shirts from the drawer slowly. His suitcase was almost full. When he turned his back, Gina put more underwear in the suitcase. Usually when Carlos traveled, it was mainly for one or two days. Now, he was unsure when he would return. The good news was, his mother's condition had stabilized and they found a donor, a young college student who broke her neck horseback riding. The girl died a few hours after the incident. It relieved Carlos because he was nervous about having surgery.

"Bring the children when you're able to take off. I want momma to see Sidnee. She's never seen her," Carlos said without looking at Gina who was not pleased with his request. She never got along with Carlos' mother. No matter what Gina bought Mrs. Simmons or kind words she offered, there was no love there.

"When do you want us to come?" Gina asked dryly.

Carlos struggled to close the suitcase. It was too full. "I know you and momma don't get along, but bring the kids to the house. You can stay at your mother's."

"I've tried to get along with your. . ."

"Momma has problems. She's always had problems."

Carlos closed the suitcase and set it in the living room. He took a long look at his car keys straddled on the cocktail table. It was going to be a long drive. A cold beer sounded good to him, but he quickly erased the thought. Upon his reconciliation with Gina, he promised not to drink. He took his eyes off the keys and went into the kitchen for a soda.

Before he could take a drink, he heard a familiar voice. "Daddy, you going to research?" Sidnee asked.

Carlos spun around quickly. He had just put her in bed a little over an hour ago. "Sidnee, what are you doing up?" Carlos asked firmly. It didn't matter how Carlos spoke to Sidnee. She usually ignored his attempts at discipline because he always softened.

"Why you research so much? Can we go to the circus?"

"Daddy research to earn a better living for his little Sidnee. We may not make it to the circus this time but next time we will. I promise."

"Can we get pizza when you get back?"

Before Carlos answered, Gina swooped down and picked up Sidnee. "It's time for bed, little lady," Gina said.

"She can stay up with me," Carlos said softly.

"Say good night, Sidnee," Gina said.

"Goodnight, daddy."

"Goodnight, sweets."

Gina rushed Sidnee under the covers. Sidnee wanted Gina to read a book. As Gina read, Sidnee asked questions. Gina refused to entertain them. It only added fuel to the little girl's energy level. Gina concentrated on reading. Sidnee finally closed her eyes. Gina sat on the bed for a few more minutes before moving. She tip-toed out of the room into the bedroom. Carlos was relaxed under the covers.

"You could have let her stay up. She's daddy's little girl," Carlos said, extending his arms to Gina. She took off her robe and got into bed on Carlos' side.

"She's becoming a disobedient little girl. You can't let her do everything she wants," Gina said and eased into Carlos' arms.

"Were you like Sidnee growing up?" Carlos asked. He rubbed his face on Gina's shoulders.

"The way my mother talks, I was more like Avery, quiet and shy." She lightly brushed the side of Carlos' face with her fingers. It always crumbled his stern expression.

"What kind of house do you want?" Carlos whispered into her ear. It tickled her, causing her to blush in the dark.

"I want a house with enough space for the children. I like brick houses," she answered, kissing him on the face. He moved her under him. He could feel her smiling. When she was happy, it always cut through the hardness.

"A brick house for my brick house," he said.

Carlos turned her face toward him and gently kissed the past. It caused her to quiver. As he rubbed his face against the almost nonexisting scar, she put her hand on his face. Both knew it would be a long time before seeing each other again. Tonight had to be special.

It was four o'clock the next morning. Carlos walked sluggishly into the children's bedroom to say goodbye. Usually he didn't. He wasn't gone more than three days at a time. When he turned on the lamp in between the bed, Sidnee woke up.

"Hi daddy," she chirped.

"How is daddy's girl?"

"You going to research?"

"I'm going to see your Grandma Dorothy. You want to see her?"

Sidnee nodded as she rubbed the sleep from her eyes. Carlos bent down and kissed her on the forehead. "Be a good girl," he said.

"Okay," Sidnee replied. She smiled at her hero. Before she could say anything else, Carlos kissed her again. If given the opportunity, Sidnee would offer a full conversation.

Carlos looked at a peaceful Avery. Carlos didn't want to wake him, but he wanted to say goodbye. He scooted onto Avery's bed. Avery shifted out of the way. Carlos removed the covers and picked Avery up. He frowned.

"I'm going to Kansas City to see your Grandma Dorothy."

Avery continued to rebel against the break in his rest. He frowned hard at Sidnee who was staring at him. "What you looking at?" Avery snarled.

Carlos turned Avery's face toward him. "I don't want you talking to your sister like that again. You here me?" Carlos snapped.

Normally, an attitude coming from Avery was grounds for a spanking. Avery nodded as he sat like a statue on his father's lap.

"Stop nodding your head and speak," Carlos grunted.

"Yes sir," Avery mumbled.

"I don't want you giving your mother or your teacher any trouble while I'm gone. Did you finish your homework?"

"Yes sir."

Carlos continued his intimidating stare at the young replica. It didn't matter. When Avery was in one of *his moods*; he was obedient, not humble. Carlos knew he had to do something quick before Avery became a problem. Carlos' jaws relaxed.

"What's going on, Avery?"

"She's always staring at me."

Carlos had no idea as to how to respond. "Are you going to join the basketball league?"

"I don't know how to play."

Carlos took a deep breath. How could his son not know how to play basketball? Carlos was the star player on his high school team. Avery had to know how to at least dribble the ball.

"I'll teach you. Your mother is going to bring you and Sidnee to Kansas City when school is out," Carlos said. He continued reading Avery's face, but it only reflected frustration.

Carlos put Avery under the covers and stood. "Remember

what I told you about your behavior," Carlos said, towering over Avery's bed. To the little boy, Carlos looked like a giant. No other classmate's father was as tall as his, at least the ones who had fathers.

"Yes sir."

Carlos started toward the door. "Daddy, can I get up?" Sidnee asked politely.

Carlos wanted to say, *yes*, but he knew Gina would have a fit. "Just lie down for a few minutes," Carlos said and turned off the light.

Carlos joined Gina at the dinette table. She had prepared breakfast. It had been months since she had cooked him breakfast. Carlos sat smiling. "Thanks, Gina," he said and gave her a kiss on the cheeks.

"It's a long drive to K.C. You sure you will be alright?" she asked, ignoring his appreciation. She still had a difficult time with compliments.

Carlos nodded as he bit into the turkey sausage and scooped up a heaping of eggs. He was starving. He looked graciously at the biscuits Gina made. It had been months since she had made biscuits. They were a little heavy with flour, but the idea that she baked them made them great.

"Are you going by Carla's and Dennis'?" Gina asked.

"I thought about stopping by your parents and Angel's house too. Lionel tells me that he's taking their daughter to Minneapolis this summer. Maybe I'll get a chance to catch him while he's at his conference."

"When is he taking Lauren?" Gina asked. She was surprised. Her last conversation with Melanie brought no clue that Lionel was coming to town.

"When school is out. I think Angel is going too."

"Why?" Gina asked, almost gasping.

Carlos knew he had said something he wasn't suppose to. He tried thinking of a acceptable answer. "It's Lauren's first time being gone by herself. Maybe Angel is making sure everything is fine." He poured syrup on the remaining two biscuits, trying not to look at Gina.

"I can't imagine Angel going away for the summer, leaving John. I know she and John are having problems. I think they are talking divorce," Gina exposed.

Carlos stopped eating for a few seconds. He didn't want his expression to bring more questions so he finished the last of his breakfast. He casually sipped his coffee. "How are things between Linda and Angel?" he asked.

"The same. It will be a year since they've spoken. When I called Edward on his birthday, Linda didn't seem to want to talk to me either. Someone has to give."

"Don't get in that mess!"

"I can't pretend nothing has happened. We're like sisters!"

"Things change when years pass. Even sisters change. Just don't become involved." Carlos finished his coffee. He put away the dishes.

"John insulted Linda and Angel defended him. He knows we're like sisters. He's jealous of anybody who takes up Angel's time. I don't care for him," Gina said.

Carlos came out of the kitchen. "I bet your friends said the same thing about me. If Angel loves John, then support her. Don't start taking sides."

"It was different with you. Everybody..."

"The only thing that is different is our names. Your friends still don't think we should be together."

Carlos knelt down at Gina's chair and hugged her. "When you get to Kansas City, we have to get a hotel room and finish where we left off," he said low.

"We don't have money for a hotel room!"

"I'll think of something." Carlos gave Gina a long kiss. They continued to kiss.

"We going to uh hotel?" Sidnee asked.

Gina quickly broke away from Carlos.

"Sidnee, what are you doing up?" Carlos asked.

"I'm not sleepy," Sidnee complained.

Carlos picked her up and put her back in bed. "Just lay still for a few more minutes," he said and rubbed his nose against her forehead. She giggled.

"Daddy can I. . ."

"Shush. Goodbye sweets."

"Goodbye daddy."

Carlos was less than twenty miles from Kansas City. He had stopped in St. Louis to visit a college friend. It had been five years since they had seen one another. Carlos came to the conclusion that he was changing. He and the friend had similar goals at one time. The friend was doing very well as a manager for a parcel delivery service. Carlos was a family man now. The friend bragged about not committing to any one woman. Carlos found the meeting repulsive.

Knots formed in Carlos' stomach upon entering the city limits of Kansas City. He and Gina had decided to stay away from Kansas City for a year during counseling. When he began his studies, it became five years.

Carlos took his time going to the hospital. He walked slowly to his mother's room. He had never been around her when she first became seriously ill five years ago. He had never seen a dialysis machine nor did he want to be around one.

When he walked into the room, his mother was watching the door in expectation of his arrival. Dorothy Simmons was not a soft woman. She had to work too hard with three boys. Carlos only knew by words when she was happy. If she wasn't cursing, she was happy.

"I thought you wouldn't get here until night. I guess you were speeding," she said. It was the only thing she knew to say.

Carlos walked closer to the swollen figure. The large veins in his mother's arms caused him to look away. He searched the room for an escape. He saw a chair on the other side. He decided to get it, hoping he could gather enough courage to look at her again. "I left Chicago at five thirty this morning. How are you feeling?"

"I'll be fine when I get out of here."

"The kids will be here in a few weeks."

"I probably won't recognize them. All I have is pictures."

Carlos decided to change the topic before it lead to Gina. "Do Earl and Junior know about your condition?"

"I wrote Earl a letter. I don't allow Junior around no-mo' since he took the TV two years ago. I'm concerned because I've been in the hospital for a week."

"I'll stay at the house until you get out of the hospital."

"Look in my pocketbook and get the key on the chain. I had the locks changed."

Carlos retrieved the key from the purse that was under his mother's leg. She always kept her purse near by, even when she slept. Carlos sat down to continue his visit. He didn't have much to say especially since they were not arguing or complaining.

"That gal's momma is my nurse," Dorothy said.

Carlos knew she was talking about Gina's mother, Marilyn Smith. Something was wrong with Dorothy's comment. Marilyn had stopped doing floor duties years ago. She was a top administrator. She had no reason to come to his mother's room.

"Are you sure it was Mrs. Smith?"

"I know that stuck up hussy when I see her. She only came by once, asking how I was doing."

Carlos decided not to further the discussion. Mr. and Mrs. Smith had been more than supportive of his studies. They paid Avery's tuition at the academy. When Carlos had to finance his first year in the Ph.D. program, Mr. and Mrs. Smith gave a large monetary gift the following Christmas.

Dorothy knew her son didn't want to visit long. She didn't mind. It was good having him home. He was the only one of the three she had ever trusted and supported. He was a survivor like herself. She had to work two jobs to take care of the family after her husband left.

When her oldest son became a problem, she wasted no time in

writing him off. He was too much like his father. All concentration was put on Carlos. He complained endlessly about responsibilities Dorothy had given him. She ignored him and gave no explanation.

Carlos was the star basketball player in high school. In his senior year, he began misbehaving. Dorothy acted quickly. She told the coach to put him off the team. It was the only way she knew how to respond. The coach talked Dorothy into letting Carlos stay on the team, but promised her that Carlos would sit out a few games.

Scouts from a few universities had their eyes on Carlos. When they found out about the reason for his lack of playing time, they turned their interest to other players. They figured Carlos may not be worth the investment.

Carlos was crushed after seeing his opportunity snatched away. He didn't speak to his mother for a very long time. The basketball coach encouraged him to go to Missouri State University.

Carlos chose not to tryout for the basketball team at Missouri State. His interests were on the same line as a young man who took time with him by helping him find an academic scholarship. When Dennis Williams took time to talk to Carlos, he became the big brother and father he never had.

"How's your schooling?"

Carlos blinked. His attention went to the owner of the tight jaws who was lying tense in bed. "I'm going to finish my dissertation early."

Dorothy did not know what a dissertation was. She just nodded. "Let me get some rest. I've been feeling tired lately."

"Are you okay?"

"I just need to get some sleep."

Carlos stood to leave. The whole visit wasn't more than an hour. "I'll call you when I get home," Carlos said.

Dorothy Simmons closed her eyes. Carlos left the room. Dorothy opened her eyes after hearing the door close quietly. She could rest comfortably in the hospital bed, knowing Carlos was at home, checking on her valuables. She felt relieved knowing he cared. She felt frustrated not knowing what a dissertation was. She blew out the tension. One day she would ask him when she didn't feel ashamed.

Carlos drove to the black newspaper to see his friend Ray Washington, an older gentleman who was Carlos' mentor. He was fifteen years Carlos senior. Ray had been a part of Carlos' life since he graduated from undergraduate.

Carlos walked into Ray's dank office unannounced. Ray was on the telephone. He grinned, showing a large gap in the front. He rushed off the phone to talk to Carlos.

"What's up, brother?" Ray asked slowly, giving Carlos the black power handshake. He dragged his words in a cool militant tone when he spoke. He used hand gestures slowly. His head tilted and turned each time a point was emphasized. He seemed to be stuck in the seventies.

"I came to see my mother. She's sick. What's been happening with you?"

"I'm just a brother trying to make a living. Sit down and rap to me."

Carlos chatted about his research. He went on continuously about his progress and discoveries. He searched Ray's face for approval. It was difficult because Ray's facial expression hardly ever changed. It kept within his motto "always keeping in control." Carlos paused for a few seconds.

"So what's happening with the family?" Ray asked.

"Everybody's fine. My daughter Sidnee is something else."

"What about Lil' Man?"

Carlos took an unconscious deep breath. "He's becoming a handful."

Ray folded his hands and stretched back in his chair. "Stay on him. We can't afford to lose another brother. Another thing, next time somebody ask you to rap, talk about your family first. It helps keep them number one in your life. Don't get me wrong! All of your research is important, but a man needs balance. Family is always important."

Carlos hung his head slightly. He never could do anything all the way right in the eyes of Ray. There was always something he missed doing.

"How long are you staying?" Ray asked.

"Two months. Gina is bringing the kids next month," Carlos said low.

"Cool. Bring them by the house."

"I will."

There was a couple of seconds of silence. Ray knew he had offended Carlos but didn't care. Carlos was a tough man. He could handle it. Carlos was like a son to him. A son he never had. Ray had three girls. He had hoped Carlos would become interested in the older one. But after meeting Gina, it all changed.

"I want to read what you've written so far. I know how white professors feel about black issues. There's a way of getting around the ones who are going to block you." Ray had a way of smoothing out misunderstandings.

"How?"

"By easing the blow. You can't blame everything on white America."

Carlos nodded. He didn't want Ray to read his work. It might not pass inspection. Carlos stood to leave.

"You're looking good. How much do you weigh?"

"One ninety. Since I stopped drinking beer, my weight stays down."

The two shook hands. Ray walked Carlos out the door and to his car. They talked some more about the dissertation. Carlos got into the car and drove to Dennis' and Carla's house.

When Carlos drove to Dennis' house, only Carla's car was in the driveway. Carlos hoped Dennis would come home soon. Since Carlos' reconciliation with Gina, he and Carla had barely spoken. Things had gotten better, but it was not the same.

He rang the doorbell and looked around the yard. The couple had recently done landscaping, probably Dennis. He enjoyed being a handy man. A little girl around eight-years-old opened the door. She stared at Carlos audaciously.

"Hello Tyler. Are your parents home?"

"Who are you?" she asked boldly.

"I'm Carlos. I guess you don't remember me."

"Mom-muh!" Tyler yelled.

She continued to stare suspiciously at Carlos. Soon Carla came to the door lightly fussing at Tyler about yelling. Carla saw Carlos and smiled. She invited him in. He gave her a hug.

"You took all of your hair off."

"So, you don't like it."

"It looks good. I've always liked short hair."

"Daddy don't like it," Tyler offered.

"I'm talking, Tyler. Go get Eric," Carla said.

Tyler walked away. Carlos and Carla talked for a little while until Eric came into the room with clothes falling off of his lanky body. He was the spitting image of Dennis. Eric stared at the stranger.

"This is Carlos," Carla said.

"Whuh-dup?" Eric said sluggishly. He extended his fist. Carlos tapped it and smiled inside. He never imagined Carla with a child that spoke slang.

"Now I want you to speak English," Carla said.

"Hey Carlos," Eric said.

"What's up?" Carlos asked.

"Same ole. Same ole. Moms and pops riding down on me. I can't do nothing."

"So it's like that."

"Yeah."

"How's school?"

"It's ah-ite."

"What have I told you about your grammar?" Carla scolded.

Eric rolled his eyes to the side. He was pleasant with his expression, but he had to let Carla know he disagreed.

"Feel like playing some Mortal Kombat?" Eric asked Carlos.

"I'll check you later," Carlos said.

"Peace," Eric said and held up his fist and left the room.

Carlos finally chuckled. Carla shook her head. Tyler continued to stare at Carlos. It caught his attention. "You don't remember me. Do you?" Carlos asked.

"Nope."

"Remember A-V?"

Tyler turned up her nose and shook her head.

"He'll be here next month," Carlos said. He and Carla began talking again. She asked him a series of questions about his research. Carlos was enthusiastic. He knew Carla understood because she was an owner of a Ph.D.

They heard the door open. Dennis walked in. When he saw Carlos, his face lit up. They did the fraternity secret handshake. "How is your mother?" Dennis asked.

"She's okay," Carlos said low.

Dennis walked into Eric's room immediately. "Let this be the last time I remind you about the trash can. Get up and take it to the back," Dennis said roughly. Eric walked slowly out of the room and outside.

"He's getting big. Last time I saw him, he was so high," Carlos said with his hand near his knees.

"If he doesn't get his attitude together, it may be the last time you see him," Dennis said and sat on the sofa. Tyler snuggled under his arm. He gave her a kiss on the forehead. When Eric walked into the house, Tyler snuggled closer to her daddy. Dennis gave Eric more things to do.

Carlos stopped talking for a minute to observe the interplay between father and son as well as father and daughter. The requests made of Eric were unnecessary. When Eric expressed his displeasure by frowning, Dennis reminded him who was in charge by giving his forceful expression. Tyler touched Dennis each time he talked to Eric. When Carlos and Dennis resumed their conversation, Tyler interrupted occasionally. Dennis patiently asked her to be quiet. Finally, Carla told Tyler to leave the room.

They sat down to dinner. Throughout the evening, Carla corrected Tyler's behavior. Dennis said nothing. Eric asked to leave the table. He looked at Dennis for an answer. Before Dennis responded, Carla told Eric and Tyler to go to their rooms.

"Thanks moms," Eric said happily and rushed away from the table.

"I want to see your homework before you go to bed," Dennis rumbled. Eric nodded and kept going.

"Daddy, can I stay at the table?" Tyler asked sweetly, half hiding behind her chair.

"I said go to your room or play with the computer until I come in," Carla said firmly.

The little girl pouted as she took off. Dennis shook her head roughly as she passed him. Tyler smiled.

"She's something else," Carlos said.

"Dennis has spoiled her rotten. I feel like whipping her butt at times," Carla said.

"She's a little girl. She doesn't understand a lot of things," Dennis said, trying to defend Tyler's behavior, but Carla held up her hand and continued complaining. She began clearing the table. She took out the Tupperware bowls and began filling them with leftovers.

"You still got that pool table?" Carlos asked Dennis.

"Let's shoot a round," Dennis answered.

The two men got up and took off toward the basement. Carla straightened her posture. "I thought you were going to start helping around the house," she said.

Carlos blinked. The comment from Carla was unexpected.

"I'll do the dishes later. Better yet, make Eric do them. He's old enough," Dennis answered, trying to keep his voice low. Carla walked back to the table and gathered the remaining dishes.

"I said I'll get them," Dennis said again, but Carla kept her back to him. Dennis beckoned Carlos to the basement steps. Carlos was uncomfortable. It was the first time he saw conflict in Dennis' marriage.

The basement was finished. It had wall to wall carpet. The pipes were covered with a lower ceiling. A large wine rack was attached on the wall behind the bar. The leather sofa and love seat and recliner still occupied the same space. The two walked into the game room.

"You've done a lot of work since the last time I was here," Carlos said.

"I needed to do something since we are going to sell it."

"When are you moving?"

"Hopefully soon. I need to get Eric out of this school district. His attitude is getting worse."

Carlos hesitated but decided to say it. "You ride him pretty hard. Maybe you need to ease up."

Carlos knew Dennis' personality would not allow slack. When Carlos latched onto Dennis in college, although they are only three years apart, Dennis took on a position of authority. When Carlos pledged Lambda, Dennis came back for Hell Week and showed Carlos no mercy.

"Carla says the same thing. Just because she doesn't believe in spanking, I'll whoop his ass. A young black male today is at greater risk than we were. I can't understand half the shit he's saying." Dennis racked the balls. He handed Carlos a cue stick.

Carlos did the break. A solid ball fell into one of the pockets. "Is the neighborhood getting bad?" he asked and tried for another solid ball but missed.

Dennis walked around the table to size up his shot. He stared intensely at the striped ball. "I want to move before it gets bad. If we sell now, I'm sure we can get a buyer who will pay at least twenty-five thousand more than what we paid."

"We need to stay in our neighborhoods. Young brothers and sisters need to see couples like you and Carla setting the right image. I'm surprised she's moving."

"She has no choice. This is my decision. I've allowed Carla to make a lot of decisions about major issues. I did that because I wanted a fifty-fifty relationship and to make up for past disappointments. I realized my fifty never got in and I can't change the past. I'm hardly stubborn. But when I am, Carla knows to back down."

Dennis stepped around the table to take aim at another striped ball. He missed the shot and stepped back. "You want a beer?" he asked.

Carlos became jumpy because he promised to stop drinking. The offer was too tempting. One beer should not cause a problem so he nodded. Dennis disappeared and came back with two Lowenbräus. Carlos felt his hands sweat when Dennis removed the cap and took a swallow.

Carlos looked at the bottle that was still waiting on the small table in the back. He tried to ignore it by gripping his cue stick tighter and concentrating on the solid ball near the corner pocket. He took a shot and missed.

"Man, how do you miss a shot like that?" Dennis teased. He took another swallow and put his bottle next to Carlos'. Dennis smoothly took small jabs at the striped ball near the same corner pocket. With precision, he tapped the side of the white ball, causing it to bump the striped ball on the opposite side. It fell into the pocket.

Carlos watched in admiration. Dennis was good at pool, basketball and chess. Everything he did was done to perfection. Carlos thought about himself. He worked hard at everything, even basketball which he was good at it. He had seen Dennis drunk a few times in college but never around Carla. Even when drunk, Dennis was in control. The first time Dennis saw Carlos drunk, he was a freshman talking loud. Dennis took him to the frat house and told him that if he could not control his drinking then don't bother pledging his fraternity.

Carlos felt he could control one beer. He walked to the table and picked up the bottle slowly. His hand shook slightly as he brought it to his mouth. "Your shot," Dennis called out. Carlos happily put the bottle down. He had to concentrate on hitting the solid ball at the right side pocket.

"How are things between you and Gina?" Dennis asked.

"Pretty good. She's complaining a lot about my research, claiming I don't spend enough time at home."

"What do you have? A year or two before finishing?"

"A year. She says I'm not at home enough and now money has become an issue."

"Carla complains about the same thing. I work my ass off trying to earn more commission so that *she* can open her practice. It took four years to get the larger accounts. Man, I don't understand."

"Now, Gina's complaining that she's fat!"

Dennis burst into laughter. "Thank God I've gone through that phase. Carla had us starving for two years because of the weight from Tyler. Had I known, I would have kept my pants zipped."

Carlos chuckled a little. "Sometimes I know when Gina's mad, but I don't understand. It's hard to figure her out at times."

"Read those women magazines. They'll tell you. Things like changing the topic or not answering your questions says: I'm mad at you because of something you did. But cutting off their hair or going to bed early so you won't get any play is: I'm mad at what you didn't do."

Carlos listened. He had read a few women magazines. He always skipped the articles about relationships. He didn't need it. He was married. "I just want to finish my dissertation, but we're struggling. Gina has good points."

"Women are smart. They all have good points. Stick to your guns. When a man gives up his role, it's hard to get it back, especially with strong women like Carla and Gina. They lose respect quickly."

Dennis called the eight ball in the left corner pocket. When Dennis brought the tip of the stick forward, Carlos absent-mindly picked up the beer and took a gulp. He coughed fervently. The taste was bitter. Dennis missed the shot.

"In most pool halls, you would get shot!" Dennis joked.

"Take it over," Carlos wheezed, trying to catch his breath. He put the bottle down. He was through with beer. He saw the eight ball fall into the left corner pocket. The game was over.

"Let me check this young brother's homework. He's good in math. I have to make up problems to keep his skills sharp. He gets mad, but I don't care," Dennis said.

They climbed the stairs, into the kitchen. The floor was mopped and the stove sparkled in the dark.

"I guess Carla decided to go to bed early," Dennis said and shook his head.

When Carlos made it to his mother's house, the toll from the trip kicked in. He rushed to call Gina. She was probably worried. He opened the door and instantly noticed the television missing. He turned on the lights and saw the house in a shamble. Someone had robbed his mother.

Carlos sat for a few minutes pondering over what to tell his mother. The television had always been her best friend. Her only worry in the hospital was being robbed. The news would keep her in the hospital longer. He decided to call Gina.

When Gina answered, the sound of her voice gave Carlos the impression that she had been waiting for his call. They talked briefly before Sidnee got on the telephone. She was always cheerful, telling him constantly how much she missed him and updating him on everything that went on. Carlos was warm inside as usual. Sidnee told him that she loved him. He missed home already. He asked Sidnee to get Avery. It took two minutes before he came. Carlos asked how was his day. It was fine. Avery did not volunteer information like Sidnee. Carlos asked him a few more questions before Gina got back on the phone.

"What's up with Avery?" Carlos asked.

"There're no problems in school. He's like this when you're gone."

"Carla cut her hair."

"I know."

"They remodeled their home."

"Carla told me."

"I miss you."

"How is your mother?"

"Moms fine. When are you coming to K.C.?"

"Next month. I'm getting ready for bed."

"It's still early."

There was no response from Gina.

"I'll talk to you in a couple of days," Carlos said and hung up. He rubbed the back of his head. Dennis was right. Gina was mad, but Carlos couldn't figure out if it was something he did or did not do. His focus went back to his mother. He picked up the phone again but hesitated. He decided not to tell. At least not right now.

Chapter Thirteen

Gina unfolded the document that was sent to her anonymously. The only clue she had was the postmark from St. Louis. She thought about calling Lisa but dismissed it quickly. The last discussion about Paul being Lisa's father was uncomfortable. Lisa called Gina and asked her to talk to Paul about donating blood toward her surgery.

Lisa received news from a college friend's mother that Paul Smith was her natural father. Years ago, Paul's brother, William "Bill" Smith, confided in him that he fathered Debra Arvell's child. Paul thought nothing more of it. He had agreed to a blood test mainly because William admitted paternity.

After Debra was announced dead, William upheld his parental responsibility to Lisa by paying child support without court intervention. He paid it to Miss Mattie because Lisa lived with her. She had been Lisa's baby sitter for years. Miss Mattie promised William that Lisa would not find out about him because he could not give her what she needed, which was his time. Both Paul and William were ignorant of the truth. Only Miss Mattie knew who fathered the child. She kept silent on the issue until her death. One phone call changed the course of how Miss Mattie treated the subject. She over heard a telephone conversation between Catherine and Debra discussing the issue. Miss Mattie silently agreed to be apart of their plan.

Debra called Miss Mattie a year later after abandoning Lisa at age twelve. Debra wanted to make sure that Lisa was okay and to share some news with Miss Mattie. Debra had talked to Catherine before the car accident, which took her life. They were in agreement that Bill Smith would pay for his mistreatment of

Catherine. The scheme was similar to the one concocted in college against Benny. Both women believed they would settle the score with the one person who caused havoc in their lives. Catherine was also set on exposing another secret, but died before it materialized.

William paid dearly. One time, Miss Mattie needed money, lots of money. She called William, but he could not afford her request. She kindly reminded him of the insurance money that he took without considering Catherine's other child who she was taking care of. William borrowed the money from his brother and never paid it back. It created a chasm between the two.

Gina finally had the courage to call Lisa. Before she picked up the phone, it rang. She rushed to answer. It was Carlos. He sounded sad. He explained the missing television. Now, with the missing television, his mother was sure not to heal properly. Her attitude may not allow it. Carlos also explained how she may need help after being released from the hospital. He was the only choice to help her. He did not want to stay in Kansas City. He had to finish his paper.

"Carlos, I don't care about how close you are to finishing your paper. Your mother is ill and you need to stay or make arrangements concerning her health," Gina fussed.

Carlos took a deep breath. "Gina, it's different with my mother. My mother has never been supportive of anything I wanted to do. She will probably decline my help anyway."

"Well, let her decline! Do you want your mother to die because you don't want to take the time to make sure she's okay?"

"Don't ever say that! I don't want you to ever say that again. I love my mother. Moms is different. She's hard and she's made me hard."

"I know you love your mother. If you didn't, you wouldn't have driven eight hours to see about her. It's time to let go of the crutch and move away from the path that your mother has walked."

Carlos was silent. All he could think about was the counseling sessions and him saying that he was angry at the person who took away his only opportunity to be someone important, a basketball star. Carlos began to breath hard.

"I'm sorry if I implied anything that is considered negative. I guess women are a little different when it comes to these things. When I get there, I will help you make arrangements for your mother," Gina apologized.

Carlos opened his mouth, but nothing came out. He rubbed his forehead. "My mother loved that television," he whispered.

"Your mother loves you more than that television."

"Thanks for being willing to help. I know how tough it is for you to do this."

"Now you see how much your mother loves you? She wanted you to marry somebody like Vanessa Williams," Gina teased for comfort.

Carlos chuckled a little. "I doubt if she will like Vanessa Williams either."

"I want you to call momma to see about some kind of home healthcare. Also, double check your mother's insurance to see how much of her hospital bills are covered."

Carlos blew air. It was overwhelming. "Okay, baby. I'll talk to you later." Carlos hung up.

Gina closed her eyes. She only hoped Dorothy Simmons hospital bills were manageable. Avery walked through the doors. Gina was surprised to see him inside so early. Usually, she had to call his friends' mothers to make Avery come home.

"This is a first! Did somebody make you leave?" Gina teased.

"Everybody's going to play basketball," Avery answered. He was headed toward his room.

"Why didn't you go? All you had to do was tell me where you were going."

"I don't know how to play basketball," Avery said pouting. Although the boys were very young, the Lambdas were starting a basketball league for the summer and the kids were getting geared up for it.

"Your father can teach you how to play."

"When? He's never here!"

"Come here Avery," Gina said softly.

Avery walked sluggishly to her. Gina grabbed him and hugged him. He squirmed a little. It caused her to smile.

"I remember when you used to want me to hug and kiss you," Gina said, kissing Avery on the forehead. He frowned slightly.

"Why is daddy gone so much? We never do nothing no more."

"Your father is working hard so that we can get a better place to live. He's almost finished. Later, we will be doing more things together. And it's *we never do anything anymore*. We have talked about your double negatives."

"Everybody else says double negatives."

"You are not like everybody else. Your parents care about how you speak. And by the way, how are you doing?"

Gina placed Avery beside her. His focus was on the floor.

"Have those gang members been at the school?"

Avery shook his head.

"What's the matter? Mrs. Herron wants you to be on her husband's basketball team for nine-year-olds. You should have fun this summer."

"I don't know how to play. People talk about me because I

don't like the Bulls."

Gina was almost breathless. Everybody in Chicago liked the Bulls. "What! *You* don't like the Bulls? Do you like Michael Jordan?" She forgot about her motherly talk.

"See, that's what I'm talking about! No, I don't like the Bulls and yes, I do like Michael Jordan. If you ask me, Pippen is the man, but nobody ever talks about him," Avery defended. He paused for a minute and counted his negatives. He realized he was clean and then he relaxed.

The phone rang again before Gina was able to fuss about Avery not liking the Bulls. She got up to answer. It was Carlos. He needed her mother's telephone number. Before he hung up, Gina thought of something cute.

"Did you know that your son doesn't like the Bulls?"

Avery's mouth dropped opened. He looked at his mother in disbelief. He could not believe his mother was making a big deal out of him not liking the Bulls. The only reason he didn't like the Bulls was because his father didn't like the Bulls. Avery even convinced his friend Montez to not like the Bulls. It wasn't difficult convincing him. Montez did not have a father active in his life so he adopted Avery's father. According to Carlos, Scottie Pippen was the heartbeat of the team but was overshadowed by Michael Jordan.

To Gina's surprise, Carlos didn't like the Bulls either. Gina began to fuss at him for not liking the Bulls. Carlos had to think of something quick because Gina would forget about the cost of the phone call and argue forever. She was a die-hard Bulls fan. Carlos never met a woman who loved sports more than he did. He made Gina put Avery on the phone. Avery took the phone and giggled.

"Don't let your mother fill your head with that Bulls junk. The Knicks has got to be the team to beat."

Avery grinned bigger. He looked at his mother and then laughed. Gina put her hands on her hips.

"I told her that Pippen was the man. Michael Jordan needs Scottie."

Carlos smiled. He felt the same way. "Women like the Bulls."

"My friends feel the same way, except Montez. He likes the Knicks too."

"Have those gang bangers been back at school?"

Avery paused. "I saw the police talking to three of them. They haven't been back."

"Good. Are you going to play ball this summer?"

Avery was becoming sadder. "I don't know how to play."

"Don't worry about it. Most boys your age don't play well."

"That's not true! One time, Montez made a basket."

"I'll teach you how to play. They have a 'Y in Kansas City

where brothers play ball. We'll go there when you get here. Okay?"

"Okay."

"Hang up the phone before your mother insults me by talking about the Bulls."

Avery said goodbye and quickly hung up the phone. He smiled at his mother, who looked at him suspiciously. "Daddy don't like the Bulls either," Avery said smartly.

Carlos was on his way to his mother's room. He saw Marilyn Smith talking to his mother's doctor. The man walked away. Carlos rushed to Marilyn.

"Is everything okay?" he asked.

"I was wondering how well your mother was responding to the new organ. Her condition has improved dramatically over the last few days. I guess your presence *has* made a difference."

"I don't know. She probably can't wait to get home."

"You will be surprised how a person's condition improves when they are visited by love ones."

Carlos just smiled. "I didn't think you worked the floor anymore. My mother said that you were her nurse."

Marilyn's forehead creased. Then she remembered coming to Dorothy's room to see if the doctor had made his rounds. Dorothy was in intensive care and had not opened her eyes since she was wheeled out of recovery.

"I didn't know your mother saw me. I wanted to make sure she was being attended to. I noticed that blacks were being overlooked when it came to organ donations. Organs from many blacks have been used to save white lives and I wanted to make sure your mother was not overlooked this time. She worked hard to get on the list and I don't want that hard work to go to waste."

Carlos face softened. He had always admired Marilyn. She was a woman that had taken a lot of punches figuratively and literally speaking. When Gina shared in counseling that her mother had been battered, she broke down crying. She did not want to follow in her mother's footsteps, but Carlos saw nothing wrong with Marilyn's footsteps.

"Thanks, Mrs. Smith."

Marilyn smiled again. Carlos was always formal with her. He was not her first choice for Gina, so she was not as relaxed with him like her husband. Paul immediately told Carlos to call him by his first name.

Marilyn learned to respect Carlos after seeing how hard he worked. She lost respect when he began fighting her daughter. But later, the respect came again when it appeared that Carlos stopped drinking beer and his behavior toward Gina was more gentle and loving.

"Carlos, you can call me, Marilyn."

"No ma'am. My mother would kill me!"

The two laughed. "Do you know how I can contact a home healthcare provider? I don't know how long I will be able to stay," Carlos said.

Marilyn was impressed to see that Carlos was trying to make arrangements concerning his mother's health. Most sons of sick parents didn't think on those routes.

"I'll see what I can do," Marilyn said and walked away.

Carlos was smiling as he entered his mother's room. But his joy was robbed from his mother's scowl.

"What's the matter momma?" Carlos asked.

"They keep asking me about my insurance."

"I don't want you worrying about insurance. I'm taking care of things."

Dorothy nodded her head. She wasn't sure if Carlos could handle everything. She had always felt that if she had girls, she would be better prepared for going home. Boys didn't handle business very well.

"Has Junior been by the house?" she asked.

Carlos could not think of the last time he lied to his mother. He was beaten severely for lying one time. "The television is gone," Carlos answered. He waited to see his mother's disapproval. But to his surprise, she just shook her head.

"I'd tried with Junior, but I guess I failed."

"Junior made the choice to take drugs. You had nothing to do with it."

"Earl is in jail and I don't know any of my grandkids but Avery. I don't know how he looks no mo'."

Carlos sat on his mother's bed and took her hand. "Gina is bringing the kids to Kansas City to visit for awhile."

Dorothy blew air. "That gal's coming to Kansas City?"

Carlos had to brace himself. He had always been a sponge for his mother's anger. The Smiths had been too generous to him. His mother could either be respectful to his wife or it may be the last time she saw her grandchildren.

"Momma, I don't mean any disrespect, but I want you to respect Gina. She's my wife and the mother of my children. I made sure that I picked a woman with your qualities as my wife."

"That gal ain't got my qualities!"

"Mrs. Smith's husband used to beat her like daddy beat you. Her husband left her for another woman like daddy left you. The only difference is Mrs. Smith wasn't afraid to trust again. She was able to hit the jackpot."

Dorothy's lips pursed. She never imagined Carlos to bring up his father. The family never talked about Lester Simmons since his departure. It was Carlos who tried defending her the last time her husband jumped on her. One day, Carlos tried hitting him with his small fists. Lester hit Carlos so hard that he knocked Carlos down and the boy didn't get up. Dorothy thought he had killed Carlos. Eventually, Lester left and never came back.

"That woman thinks she's high-and-mighty."

"She's just like you. Paul Smith is the only difference. When are they releasing you?" Carlos asked with finality. He was ready to close the discussion.

"I don't know. The doctor ain't said."

"I'll make sure another television is waiting for you," Carlos said with a smile.

"Boy, don't you go stealing! I don't won't nobody's junk up in my house!"

"No momma! It's ligit! It may not be as large as the old one, but it will be color."

Dorothy smiled inside. The Lord was watching over her like her pastor said. Her baby was home. She didn't know how long he was staying, but it didn't matter. She felt safe. "When you gonna finish that paper?"

Carlos' eyebrows raised. This was the first time his mother ever mentioned his dissertation. At first, Dorothy didn't know what a dissertation was, but she mentioned it to one of her black nurses. The woman gave Dorothy enough information to hold a small discussion on it.

"Next year," Carlos answered.

"You gonna be a doctor, right?"

"Yes ma'am. They are going to call me Dr. Simmons, momma. White America will have another black man with a Ph.D. to contend with."

Dorothy smiled. She had always told Shirley that Carlos was going to be important. He didn't need a basketball to do it either.

"Your paper is about black people, ain't it?"

"Of course! Who else am I going to write about?"

"I know you was mad 'cause I made you sit out on the basketball team. The only thing I could see was white men using you like a horse and then throwing you away when you couldn't work no mo'. But what you gonna git, cain't nobody throw away like a useless horse. They gotta pay you for your mind, not because you can throw a ball. Having white children reading 'bout you and talkin' 'bout you is power! Not if you can throw a ball," Dorothy said. She closed her eyes. Now the discussion was over.

Chapter Fourteen

Barbara sat quietly as Linda drove to Harrisburg. Linda received a letter from a member of Zeta Chi chapter stating that the school had suspended the chapter and was petitioning the national headquarters to do the same. When Linda told Barbara, she was surprised at her mother's care-less attitude. Barbara was quiet as Linda ranted and raved. Barbara only agreed to accompany Linda because it seemed important to her daughter.

"I have an idea on how to save the chapter," Linda shared.

Barbara sighed heavily. "Let's hear it."

Linda cleared her throat. "Instead of suspending the chapter, we can terminate the membership of those involved."

"The President was involved. The chapter leadership intimidated a young lady to the point that she stole. Now, all the members want to stick together. I am not supporting this rescue and I'm not getting Marilyn, Susan or JoAnn involved either."

"Why did you rescue when Jennifer was involved?"

"Because you asked me to. You did not ask me to do anything but accompany you on this trip. You have made it clear that you don't want my assistance."

"I didn't say that! I want to do this on my own. I want to come up with the ideas and plan of action. I know that I can do this."

"Okay. If you come up with a good idea, then I will support it."

"So, you didn't like my idea about terminating membership?"

"You did not listen. I told you that the members are sticking together on this. They should have reported this. And another thing, this chapter has not done a decent public service project in years. This is not what me, Catherine and Debra had in mind."

"This is the first time you have connected Debra Arvell to the chapter."

"Debra came up with the idea and Catherine groomed it. Debra has always been an integral part of starting the chapter. She completed the paperwork. She was good at that sort of thing."

After the group found out that Debra dressed up her paperwork to get accepted into Lincoln University and her tuition was mysteriously paid; they agreed that she should complete the paperwork to start the Missouri State chapter. The only problem was, she helped Ruby Lane complete the Alphas' paperwork for Missouri State too. The group became angry.

"Did you know all a long that Uncle Bill was Lisa's father?"

"I only suspected. No one confirmed it."

"Do you want to save the chapter?"

"I gave you my word. Come up with a good idea, and I will strongly consider it," Barbara said and fidgeted. She felt something lodged in-between the seat. She reached in the seat and pulled out one of the bears from the carousel. "What is this?" she asked.

Linda looked curiously at the bear she believed she had left at home. "Indie broke Camille's merry-go-round. That's one of the bears," Linda said.

Barbara held onto the bear. It was one of the few items Linda kept after Camille's death. The only other thing was the high-chair that Barbara bought.

Linda was at Morrison's Hall. She let Barbara out in front of the dorm so that she could find a parking space. As Barbara waited outside the dorm, she looked curiously at the students circulating the building. Times had changed so much since Linda attended the school. Boys were allowed to go inside the girls' dorms and into their rooms. The dress code was everything from showing skin to dressing sloppy. Barbara could sense that the trip was not going to be favorable.

Linda opened the door for Barbara. They made the trip to the second floor. The last time Linda was at Missouri State was for Jennifer's graduation. Everything had changed drastically. Linda never remembered boys allowed in the dorms. Morrison Hall appeared noisy to her.

Linda knocked on the chapter room door. Someone shouted, "Come in." Linda turned the knob slowly. She entered the room that was held sacred at one time. Everything seemed dark. The same furniture her parents donated was still there but was soiled with noticeable stains. The shield was in need of dusting and the same dry floral arrangements were there but many leaves were missing. Linda looked at her mother's face and became embarrassed.

"Hello, ladies. I'm Linda Stevens Reed and this is my mother,

Barbara Wright Stevens, a chapter founder. We came to hear your concerns."

The girls smiled. They straightened quickly but not in the manner of receiving a chapter founder. They did not offer Barbara or Linda a seat.

"Does anyone mind if I have a seat?" Barbara demanded.

One girl stood and offered Barbara her seat. Another offered a seat to Linda, but she refused. Barbara stared at the girl who gave up her seat. The young woman had a gold tooth. Barbara could not imagine an attractive person destroying her appearance with something as gaudy as a gold tooth.

Barbara continued to survey the room. She saw hair stacked high upon a few girls' heads. Some hairstyles were obviously after-five styles. The most unnerving observation was the dress code. Barbara had not seen so many stomachs and skin-tight dresses in her life.

Linda began her spiel on explaining what had happened and how they could help. After she finished, she caught a glimpse of her mother who looked at her with a frown.

The gold tooth spoke. She was the First Vice President and Dean of Pledges. She explained how a meeting was called with the Cherubs without her knowledge. It was only when she received a phone call from the police station that news regarding the girl stealing was known.

It was the continuing flash of the gold tooth that made Barbara irritated. "Do you ladies understand that there is no such thing as a pledge program? Therefore, there is no such thing as a Dean of Pledges?" Barbara snapped.

The gold tooth's eyes widened, but her mouth was slightly opened. Barbara could still see the gold tooth glistening. "What public service projects has this chapter performed this year?" Barbara continued. She was on a roll and Linda was thinking quickly about how to stop it.

The gold tooth mumbled about a Christmas party for a daycare. Barbara waited impatiently for the list of projects that the chapter submitted, claiming that they would perform. The gold tooth closed her mouth and shook her head. She turned her attention to her sorors. Barbara turned her attention to a girl who had a tattoo on her stomach. Barbara was furious.

"Can someone tell me about a project to teach illiterate adults? That is what's filed at Nationals. Maybe someone can explain how the dance concert with the Girl Scouts turned out."

A girl with curls piled high upon her head spoke. "Mrs. Wright..."

"It's Mrs. Stevens."

"Excuse me, but Mrs. Stevens, we didn't know we were suppose to do an adult literacy program or work with Girl

Scouts," the girl said. She shifted and someone bumped her head. Barbara looked on in horror because the girl's hair did not move. It was so stiff with hair spray that it appeared the girl who bumped the curls was injured.

The gold tooth looked at Barbara's expression. The woman was totally disappointed in them. The gold tooth had to say something. She was the next reigning officer. "Mrs. Stevens, we didn't know that Shontay put all of that on the form."

Barbara was able to get pass the glare of the gold tooth by hearing the name Shontay. "Who or what is a Shontay?" Barbara shrieked.

Linda knew it was time to step in. "Ladies, we need to speak to the president. We thought she would be here."

"I told Shontay that y'all was coming," a girl with an exposed stomach said.

Barbara stood. Hearing "y'all" and "was" in the same sentence was murder. She faced all of the girls and looked at them one by one. A few turned their heads in embarrassment. A couple lowered their heads. The gold tooth held her focus at Barbara. The girl tried to ease the tension by smiling. It was the wrong move.

"Why did you ladies join this sorority? Was it because of a fraternity member or did you think you could, uh, hang out with a group of cool sisters? Your reason should have been serving your community," Barbara said and walked to the door. Before she left she looked at the group of distraught girls.

"Kappa and class are synonymous. I'm hearing poor grammar. I see mutilated skin and hairstyles for the evening. And young lady, you are too pretty to have destroyed your appearance with a gold tooth. Malinda, I'm going to the Student Union," Barbara said, trying to keep her voice from cracking. She left the room.

The appearance in the room was not unusual for Linda. After doing the health fair and working on other projects, short and tight clothing, tattoos, stiff hairstyles and names like "Shontay" were not uncommon. Times were changing and her mother had a difficult time accepting it.

Linda looked at the gold tooth. The girl wiped her eyes. Linda walked over to her and removed a tissue from her purse. The girl shook her head but Linda insisted.

"My mother is in her sixties. At the time she pledged, a certain appearance was accepted and at the time I pledged, she didn't approve of our appearance either. There is no excuse for lying on your annual application," Linda concluded.

"Nobody knew that Shontay put that on the application," the gold tooth whimpered between tears. The rest of the girls began to cry.

"She had no right to talk to us like that!" one girl shouted.

Linda knew the girl was right but under no circumstances was anyone going to disrespect her mother. "You're right, she doesn't have the right to say any of those things, but no one is proud about what has happened. I need to know whether you ladies want to save the chapter."

"That's why we here!" the same angry girl shouted.

"Young lady, your grammar is poor. And please do not shout at me," Linda said without raising her voice and staring at the girl. She was taking time out of her schedule to help them and only a few showed for the meeting. Linda was angry.

"We all want to save the chapter," the girl said in a normal tone.

"Well, where is everybody? It only looks like ten of you want Zeta Chi to stay."

"Shontay and the rest are embarrassed about what happened. We told her and Nicole and the rest that a chapter founder was coming. We thought they would come regardless," one said.

"Okay, those of you who want to save the chapter, meet me and Mrs. Stevens at the Ramada Inn this evening at seven," Linda said.

The gold tooth shook her head. Linda walked over to the girl and put her arm around her. "You are a very pretty girl. You really didn't need to put that thing on your tooth. Nothing is permanent. If you want to remove it, let me know. Are you coming tonight?" Linda asked.

The girl put her hand to her mouth. "I can't," she muscled out.

Linda removed the girl's hand. The gold tooth was the one who wrote Linda, asking for her help. It was only after talking to the girl, Linda found out that she was not the president. The letter was well structured and was quite convincing.

"My mother only respects people who are brave. It's not your tooth. It's the hard work in convincing a white school to allow a black sisterhood to form on their campus. And now, that hard work is up for grabs. Are you coming?"

"Yes."

"Okay. I guess I will see everybody this evening. Those who don't come will probably have their membership revoked."

The girls gasped. Linda looked at the girls with confusion. They really didn't understand the seriousness of the issue. The sorority was mentioned in the local paper. It was an embarrassment.

Linda turned her attention to the gold tooth. "How did you get my address?"

"I called the Lee Summit Alumnae and left a message on the answering machine. Someone called back and gave me your address. She told me not to call but write you. She said Lee Summit was too busy to handle this and you would be better at resolving this."

Linda could only think of one person from the newly split chapter that arranged the meeting. "Will you guys walk me to the Union? We're still sisters," Linda said with a half smile.

The girls left the chapter room. On their departure from the dorm, a group of girls wearing oversized, navy blue warm-ups walked by. They were talking loudly. Linda waited for them to pass. "Who are they? Crips?" Linda asked, making fun of the Alphas.

The girls burst into laughter. "Those are the Alphas," the gold tooth said.

"Wait until I tell mother that the Alphas look like gang members."

The girls laughed again. They began to tell Linda about the campus gossip. All the fraternities, with the exception of the Gammas, had been kicked off the yard. Several Upsilons had babies and so on. Linda raised her eyebrows in surprise and made comments as warranted.

Barbara was standing at the back steps in the Student Union. She could still see the fight between Debra and Catherine. It had all been a misunderstanding. When Debra slapped Catherine, it was the break in the link. Everyone was shocked. They left Debra out in the cold.

They worked hard to get the school to meet with them and now a group of trashy looking girls were destroying their hard work. Barbara even thought about the picture on the chapter room wall. Although it was dust filled, it was still missing something. Debra's picture was left out. Every time girls who pledged Zeta Chi mentioned the founders, they never mentioned Debra's name. Barbara took it upon herself to share the information with Linda and Melanie.

The little bear that was lodged in the seat of Linda's car was in Barbara's pocket. It felt as if it were rubbing against her leg. She became irritated and removed it from her pocket. She looked at it. Barbara felt herself feeling feverish because the bear felt warm. She felt herself feeling light-headed because the bear glowed. She looked around for Malinda but all she saw was students dressed in oversized clothing and cursing. This was not the school she remembered. It wasn't filled with timid girls, wanting to become a part of a sophisticated sisterhood.

Barbara felt someone watching her. She turned around and was face-to-face with her daughter. Barbara could not speak. Everything in her was mute.

"Mother, I know these girls don't pass your inspection. I'm not impressed with what I see as well, but we must try to work with them," Linda said.

Barbara shook her head. Her eyes swelled with tears, but she could not let them fall.

"I know this is difficult for you, but times have changed. Nice girls have tattoos. Some wear the wrong hairstyles and one may have a gold tooth," Linda said.

"I don't want times to change. I want it to stay the way it was. Friendships were lost trying to make the best of Phi Kappa Psi," Barbara said. She put her hand to her mouth to protect the secret, the one that her daughter should never know. It was a fear of losing power. Of being the center of attention. It was nothing for Barbara to walk into a room and people take notice. The girls in the room hardly responded. They didn't notice her.

Linda noticed the same attitude with the other fussy older women. Something sacred had been soiled. The sisterhood had changed too much too fast. Now, they were willing to let the younger women have chapters of their own without being concerned about the gap that was being created.

Linda slowly took her mother's thin hands. Her mother's hands never calloused during her years of designing and sewing. Barbara Stevens always took care of herself. Linda noticed her mother only wore her wedding set, the original one. Her father bought her mother a larger diamond years later, but Barbara had not worn it in five years.

"I will handle this. When the chapter is saved, these girls will have earned it. I need your help to make it work. I am meeting with the Dean of Women tomorrow. It appears that different rules apply to the white Greeks," Linda said.

Barbara could see her daughter getting stronger. Linda could care less about saving the chapter. Something else was driving her. She was searching for something that was beyond Barbara's footsteps. Then it came to Barbara. Linda wanted recognition. She wanted to be the center of attention. Barbara smiled a little. It was time to step to the side gracefully.

"When you yell racism, you must have something very strong to support it besides words," Barbara suggested.

"Believe it or not, Tosha..."

Barbara looked strangely at Linda.

"The young lady with the gold tooth..."

Barbara sighed and closed her eyes.

"Tosha has news clippings of white Greeks doing worse and the school did nothing about it. She has clippings that go back two years. Tosha wants to be a lawyer, one to help black women."

"You can handle it. I don't want to be bothered," Barbara said with a wave of the hand.

"It is important that a chapter founder is present," Linda insisted.

Barbara's forehead creased. Her daughter was looking for

leverage and it was not to save the chapter. It came to Barbara. Linda was campaigning, but it was difficult to understand.

It was fifteen minutes before seven o'clock. A soft knock sounded on the door. Linda looked at Barbara. "We'll go to the lobby and talk," Linda said.

"Before you do, I want to meet Shontay," Barbara said without smiling.

Linda opened the door. Zeta Chi was standing in the hall. Their attire covered more of their bodies. Many of the girls looked embarrassed. Only Tosha smiled, flashing the gold tooth proudly. Linda invited them inside.

Barbara looked unimpressed at the group of girls. "Where is Shontay?" she asked.

Everyone looked to the back. A girl raised her hand.

"Step forward so that I can see the person who is trying to destroy my friends' hard work."

A short girl walked slowly to Barbara. Shontay refused to make eye contact. Barbara could not believe such a petite person could cause so much ruckus. Barbara started her speech. "As the leadership of this organization, I'm asking you to terminate your membership to save this chapter. Are you willing to do that?" Barbara demanded.

"Mrs. Reed said that if we showed, then our membership would not be terminated," one girl from the crowd offered.

Barbara eyed the girl with venom. "I don't think I was talking to you, unless you are Shontay." Barbara returned her focus to Shontay. "If you are willing to give up your diamonds, then everyone else can keep theirs. It's up to you."

Shontay closed her eyes. She sniffed and wiped away tears. "We were only playing," she whispered.

"You played the wrong game. Malinda, I'll accompany you to the meeting with the Dean of Women. Miss Shontay can give her answer at that time. If she says anything other than what I want to hear, then I will personally make sure that Zeta Chi is retired."

Chapter Fifteen

Linda took a deep breath. She began her speech to the Dean of Women. The small group presented news clippings of white Greeks vandalizing the school and abusing alcohol privileges in Panhellenic. There was a case where a white fraternity member was caught stealing a test. Although the paper did not mention that the boy was a member of a popular fraternity, the girls knew. The more evidence Linda presented, she realized that all the black fraternities were suspended immediately without any consideration.

The white woman sitting behind the large oak desk was a little uncomfortable, but was not willing to budge on the decision. It was time for Barbara to step in. She was appalled at the woman's lack of consideration to the inconsistency in applying school policies.

"Dean Gordon, I will not continue to waste any more of your time. It is obvious that something inappropriate was done, but I will not allow these young women to continue to be embarrassed by pleading with you."

"What do you mean Mrs. Stevens?"

"I will make three phone calls. One to the mayor of Kansas City, one to an anchor woman at a news station in Kansas City and one to an attorney. Out of the three, two are Kappa women. If you cannot see the injustice in your application of school policies, I know these three individuals will."

Although the black sororities' incidents were less in comparison to the white sororities, the black sororities delinquent acts received greater attention.

"Dean Gordon, I was the one who encouraged Trina to do what she did. I'm willing to terminate my membership to save the chapter," Shontay said with a strong voice.

Dean Gordon didn't seem pleased. Before she could say anything, Barbara interrupted. "I can see you stepping down as president, young lady, but you will always be a Kappa. This is what you call learning from the school of hard-knocks. If I have to call our national headquarters to get my point across, then I will, Dean Gordon. And by the way, why did the school deny these girls the right to have a graduate advisor from a Kansas City Alumnae?"

"Our policy states that a graduate advisor must be a faculty member of Missouri State University."

"If one of our own were monitoring these girls' actions, I doubt if there would have been any trouble."

The phrase "one of our own" left a bad taste in Dean Gordon's mouth. She was still ready to strike. "I believe Phi Kappa Psi wants what is best for their organization. If the national headquarters does not suspend this chapter than the school will not either. I must remind everyone that Missouri State does not tolerate illegal actions to become a member of a social group."

"Number one Dean Gordon, we are not a social group. I am requesting that this chapter be monitored by Kansas City Alumnae," Linda demanded.

"If Missouri State does not review its' policies on applying consistency in disciplinary actions, I will see to it that other entities will," Barbara announced.

"Phi Kappa Psi national headquarters has already contacted me and ensured me that a thorough investigation will take place. I must share that the parents of Trina Atkins are not pleased either," Dean Gordon commented.

"Whatever our national headquarters recommends, we will stand by it. I will talk to Miss Atkins' parents ," Barbara concluded.

Linda felt a small victory as she drove back to Kansas City. Her mother became the center of attention after their battle with Dean Gordon. The young women asked questions about pledging in the "old days." What Barbara shared made the girls ask for more. They wondered why did a great program such as the pledge mother/daughter stop? When Barbara explained how abusive pledging had become and the rising lawsuits, they simmered the questions.

Barbara announced that six were founding members of Zeta Chi, not five. No one had heard of Debra Arvell. When Barbara told how Debra was on two fraternity courts and made queen on one, the girls announced that she was "the bomb." Linda had to explain to Barbara that Debra was the best. It became sensitive when Shontay thanked Barbara for not taking away her membership. Barbara gave the girl no explanation. It was only seeing remorse that made Barbara change her mind. The girl hugged Barbara unexpectantly. The other girls hugged her too and cried. Barbara met Trina Atkins and talked with her. It was clear to the group that Barbara knew Trina's mother. Barbara promised Trina that she would have no police record.

Linda decided to break the ice. "Do you think Nationals will suspend the chapter?"

"It depends on what you have to say. You have put yourself out on a limb for these girls. I hope it is worth it."

Linda decided to change the topic. "Do you mind watching the kids for the next two weekends? I'm going to Indiana to visit Constance Wells and then Wilma Bradford in Chicago."

"Don't spend too much time with Constance. I doubt if she will support you."

"Why?"

"We hardly ever saw eye-to-eye on much. Try Agnes Richards. If you are convincing, then you can pull one of Indiana's Alumnaes. Lori will definitely pull the other one."

"Do you think Lori will win?"

There was silence for several seconds. Linda refused to allow her mother to not answer. Linda remained silent until Barbara spoke. "How badly do you want to win?"

Linda had to say it. "I think Lori is over rated. People have gravitated towards her because she has a lot of mouth."

"Lori is power hungry and smart. She has very little compassion for saving a chapter that will eventually get suspended. In other words, Lori will do anything to win."

"I don't have to do *anything* to win. I'm just as smart. Melanie and I were responsible for the strength behind Lee Summit, not Lori."

"Then let Melanie help you. I'm getting too old and I'm much too ill to travel up and down the road with you. It's time for you to make your own imprint."

"I did not ask you to help me campaign!"

"If you are trying to fool an old con, you better work harder on it. Most of the older women you are going to meet have been in this game for a long time. Don't be afraid to, uh, how can I say it without sounding ruthless? Don't be afraid to extend yourself."

Linda was pouting internally. Her mother was suppose to be her right arm without her having to ask. Now, Barbara Stevens was retiring.

"How did you know that Melanie is helping me?"

"She came over to talk. It's time for her to move on with her life, without John. Now, it's time for you two to become best friends again. Birdie wants you to give her a call."

Linda blew air. Although she was excited about the picture

with the mayor, she was exhausted. Campaigning was harder work than she had once thought.

"How come you and Aunt Birdie shut the door on the family? Sugah Doo, Aunt Rosie and Babe Brother are really nice people."

Barbara felt tempted to tell Linda the truth but decided not to. It took a long time to get over the abuse. Barbara never considered her action as shutting the door. She just stayed away. "My family came to my wedding, with the exception of Birdie. My home has been open to anyone who was willing to visit."

"You've never told me about them. For years, I thought you were an only child. You've only told me that your mother was dead."

"She is!"

"Mother, you know what I'm talking about!"

"And you know what I don't want to talk about," Barbara said and gave Linda a hard look.

Linda hesitated. Her mother was right. Linda could not fool an old con. "I just want to know about the person who gave you life. I want to know if she was a good cook? Could she sew? Was she shrewd? In other words, are you anything like her?"

Barbara smiled a little as she looked at the road. Many people thought Sugah Doo was like Effie Cole Wright, but Effie couldn't hurt anyone like Sugah Doo who was known for cutting people. Sugah Doo looked and was shaped like Effie.

Effie Cole set her sights on marrying the owner of the only jook joint in town. No one could catch Odie "Po Boy" Wright. Because Effie could sing so well, she had no problems accomplishing her goals. As Barbara thought about Linda's question, she could only compare herself to Effie Wright in two areas. Effie could cook and sew very well.

When Effie's husband went up the road to visit Miss Hotsy Roxie, Effie made sure the money stayed home when the man left. Miss Roxie gave "Po Boy" Wright a good time for almost free. When Po Boy came down with pneumonia, Effie took care of him. She was good to him, when she felt like it. She allowed Po Boy to call her name several times before seeing about him. Effie's sister, Mae, told Barbara that Effie was getting back at Po Boy for disrespecting her. Po Boy calling out to Effie was a way of him begging forgiveness.

"I can cook and sew like my mother but Birdie has her personality," Barbara finally answered. She was convinced that Birdie was just like Effie Wright. Birdie just couldn't cook and sew.

"So Effie Wright was pretty shrewd, huh?" Linda asked.

"In comparison to her day, she was very shrewd."

"So you are just like your mother?" Linda asked with a grin.

Barbara just smiled. She only hoped that Carl didn't get sick and need to rely on Birdie to nurse him to health. His chances of dying were greater.

"Do you feel like stopping by Melanie's?" Linda asked.

"Can't I go home? And besides, I didn't think you would want to go to John's house."

"It doesn't bother me anymore. Something strange has happened. Lauren called me Miss Stevens the other day. She has always called me Auntie Linda."

"And?"

"Jennifer was the only one who called me that. Thinking back to some of the discussions she and I had, she talked a lot about 'signs'."

"What are you talking about Malinda?"

"There is no way that Lauren knew to call me Miss Stevens. Since that day, I began feeling strange about not doing anything with my life."

"Your father and I have given you a head start. Keith has given you a safety net, just in case you fall. It is up to you to set an example for your daughter. She may not be so lucky."

"I don't need a nine-to-five or get stressed out from an undeserving manager to give Indie a good example.

"My friends offered their opinions about my boutique. They constantly told me that I had it made by marrying Edward. I didn't have to work. But, I had to have something to represent me, other than being a doctor's wife. I had to have something that I could fall back on in case my marriage to your father did not work."

Linda was quiet. The idea of her mother and father not together was never contemplated. She thought her mother had the boutique because it was her dream not because she had to work.

"You don't think I'm setting a good example for Indie?"

"You are a wonderful mother to both children. What you are is bored! You and your girlfriends, in college, played games together. You enjoyed it. Now, everyone has their own game and you don't fit in anymore. You are taking a giant step by running for Regional Director. It can be fun, but it has to be your game. Comprehend?"

"A little."

"Do it because you want to, not because of me."

Linda began driving to her parents' house.

"We're not going to Melanie's?" Barbara asked.

"I'm taking you home. You need to get some rest," Linda said as she pulled into her parents' driveway.

"You are a very smart woman. Your grandmother was smart. Your aunts are smarter. And of course, your mother is the smartest. Make sure you put forth your best effort in this race.

Allow it to consume you because that is what it's going to take to win. This is not about beating Lori, it's about winning. Comprehend?"

Linda smiled and nodded. "Do you mind checking out a daycare for Indie? It's suppose to be very good."

"Just because I'm not campaigning doesn't mean I can run your errands."

Linda was used to Barbara's off-beat behavior. She and Indie had become friends since their girls' trip. After witnessing the actions of Birdie's granddaughter, Barbara bragged about Indie more.

"I need another opinion about this place."

"Fine. Are you and Keith coming over Sunday?"

"Keith will probably come. I need to work on some things."

Barbara caught herself before commenting. She had just told Linda to let the race consume her. It appeared that it had already begun. Barbara got out of the car. Linda's motor was still running when she popped the hood to the trunk. Barbara opened the car door and got out. Linda got out to retrieve the luggage. She began walking toward the door. Barbara noticed the engine was still running.

"You forgot to turn off the car," Barbara said as she caught up with Linda.

"I'm not staying. I've got some things to do," Linda said and kept going. Barbara stopped.

"You are not dropping me off at the front door! You will come inside and visit your father. You don't have that much to do," Barbara complained.

Linda took a deep breath and sat the luggage down. She obediently walked back to the car to turn off the engine. She joined her mother at the front door. Barbara struggled to find her keys. Linda removed hers and opened the door. Before they stepped inside, Linda turned her attention to her mother.

"Thanks for coming along. I wanted those girls to meet you. I thought it would inspire them to do something. If Zeta Chi is saved, it will be because those girls worked their butts off trying. I got some ideas that I'm going to share with Melanie. I think I can handle it from here," Linda said. She gave Barbara a hug. She hardly ever expressed intimacy with her mother, only making sure that she was comfortable during her illness and afterward.

Barbara patted Linda on the back and nodded. She felt that her daughter was ready. It was time to let go. Not only did Barbara want Linda to win, she wanted Linda to beat the hell out of Lori for calling her an "old bitch" who had lost her step. Barbara also knew that Linda was still going to need a little help in doing it.

Chapter Sixteen

Lisa sat quietly as Miss Sweets finished her story. It was nothing like the last two visits when Miss Sweets filled in several missing links within a matter of hours. Lisa's whole life was completed in one morning and one afternoon. The only thing Miss Sweets talked about on this visit was her hunger for children and how Rhonda was a blessing to her.

Lisa had difficulty believing Rhonda could be a blessing to anyone. The young woman was crude and had a mean streak. One day, Lisa decided to go shopping with Rhonda. As Rhonda approached a parking space, someone pulled into the space quickly. Lisa thought the woman saw Rhonda approaching the space, but the anxious shopper ignored protocol and offended Rhonda. The lady would find out later that her car was keyed severely on the passenger side.

Lisa saw something different in Rhonda as she interacted with Miss Sweets. Rhonda was at the eighty-six-year-old woman's beck and call. Rhonda sat on the floor and massaged Miss Sweets' feet. The old woman smiled as Rhonda hummed while she stroked her feet gently. Rhonda replaced the socks on the feet and got up to wash her hands.

Miss Sweets opened her eyes and smiled at Lisa. "She's a sweet girl," Miss Sweets said in a weak voice.

Lisa looked unbelieving. Miss Sweets beckoned for Lisa. She obediently waddled to Miss Sweets. The old woman reached for Lisa's arm. When she touched the wrist watch, she saw the future.

Miss Sweets released Lisa's arm slowly. Miss Sweets took

several deep breaths. A blur vision came to her mind. "Three spirits are looking for peace. All three are looking for love, the love they were denied. Everyone must be very careful because if they ain't, they will make the same mistake as these spirits. Their souls will always be confused."

"Grandma Sweetie, you still talking spirit stuff to Lisa?" Rhonda asked with a smile. She handed the woman a glass of lemonade.

"I'm lucky to have this gal around. She's always checking on me. I told her momma that I was gonna make sure she grew up right."

"I'm gonna leave now. Don't get offended if she falls asleep on you, Lisa. She's just taking her beauty rest," Rhonda said and grabbed her purse. She kissed Miss Sweets on the forehead and left.

Miss Sweets looked at Lisa with a gentle smile. "You may not think she's good, but she is. She spent a lot of money looking for you. I couldn't quite see where you was but she found you. I hope you welcome her. She's innocent. She never done nothing to nobody unless they wronged her or whoever she loves."

Just like Miss Mattie, Miss Sweets knew everything. Talks about spirits was not unusual for Lisa. Miss Mattie talked about them all of the time.

"Miss Sweets, what were you saying about three spirits?"

"Huh?"

"You were telling me that three spirits were looking for peace and that everyone must be careful."

"Well, I guess they better be!"

Lisa was getting a little agitated. The first time she talked to Miss Sweets, the old woman spoke with strength. Later in the conversation, she became disjointed. Lisa didn't know if she could get Miss Sweets to clarify her statement.

"Miss Sweets, do you know who these spirits belong to?"

Miss Sweets began to nod off. Lisa decided to let the old woman rest. Lisa checked the house before leaving. It was something that she had always done before leaving Miss Mattie's house.

Lisa went into the kitchen to make sure everything was put away. Then she went into Miss Sweets' bedroom to prepare the bed for the old woman. Lisa pulled back the covers and fluffed the pillows. She left to get Miss Sweets. When Lisa made it back to the living room, Miss Sweets was awake.

"I got your bed ready for you to lie down," Lisa said.

Miss Sweets looked up strangely. She recognized the spirit that was named after her. Soon, the other two will appear. The spirits needed to be guided back to the proper realm. Miss Sweets was too old to clean spirits away. She only hoped that the three individuals had enough strength to do the right thing.

Miss Sweets stood. She walked slowly to her bedroom. Lisa helped her into bed. Miss Sweets took three deep breaths. "Corine, be a good gal. You know you was named after me. I'd never hurt anybody," Miss Sweets said and closed her eyes.

Lisa tucked the covers around Miss Sweets. Lisa left the bedroom and walked through the living room. Before she turned off the lamp, her focus went to the coffee table. A pocket knife was lying next to a candy bowl. Lisa hadn't noticed the knife before. She picked it up to look at it. She thought maybe the knife belonged to Rhonda. She seemed like the type that would carry a knife. Lisa didn't want Miss Sweets to wake up and see the weapon on the table, so she put the knife in her purse and left.

Lisa had just walked inside her house when the telephone rang. She took her time to answer it. She slowly picked it up and spoke. Cameron was on the other end.

"I've tried calling you all day. I thought that you were in the hospital."

"I'm not due for another six weeks. I've been visiting my grandmother's friend. What's up?"

"Vivian had a flat. She started out to pick up Celeste from a friend's house and her tire was flat. She was able to catch me before I left."

Lisa did not care if Vivian had a flat or was involved in a car accident. Vivian always needed Cameron for something and he seemed to be available each time.

"Why couldn't she call Triple A? She's always calling you and you're always responding. Let her know that the next time she calls me, I'm pressing charges. My phone calls are being monitored."

"She needed me to pick up Celeste! I'm not going to argue about Vivian."

"Fine. Goodbye!" Lisa slammed the phone down. Within seconds, the phone rang again. The answering machine picked up. Lisa heard Cameron asking her to pick up. Lisa waited a few seconds before answering abrasively.

"As long as Celeste is involved, I need to help Vivian. I will never ignore my responsibilities to Celeste."

"We've known each other for a very long time. When I tell you that Vivian has a serious problem, I know what I'm talking about. She has harassed me for the last time."

"I've talked to her about those phone calls, but of course, she denies it. Have you received any calls lately?"

Lisa had to think. The calling and hanging up had lessened. She had only received one call within a two week span and Rhonda apologized for being the culprit.

"I just want Vivian to know that I'm pressing charges if it gets traced to her."

A few seconds of silence passed.

"How is the baby?" Cameron asked.

"It's a little jumpy at times. The doctor says it's normal."

"I want to come home."

A few more seconds of silence escaped.

"I want us to be a family. We can work it out."

"You have moved out twice. I don't want to come home and find you gone again. If you want your freedom, then file for a divorce."

"I don't want to fight about Vivian. You don't want me doing anything to ensure my daughter's welfare."

"Vivian is using Celeste to get to you. Don't you see that she succeeded in breaking us up?"

"I don't want Vivian. And I don't want to lose you. We've been through too much."

"Something is seriously wrong with her. I think she's mentally unstable."

"I want to hear you complain about gaining too much weight. I want to talk about the baby keeping you up at nights. I want to discuss his daycare."

"*His?* How do you know it's a boy?"

"A son is all I've been thinking about. And besides, you're not the type to have a girl. You're too mean!"

Lisa was about to get excited but stopped. She smiled. Cameron had teased her about being a tomboy and telling her that she would birth three boys like his mother.

"If you think I'm mean, you ought to meet my cousin."

"I didn't know you had a cousin."

"I met her a few weeks ago. My mother had a twin sister and that sister had a daughter. My cousin has been looking for me since she graduated from college," Lisa bragged.

"If she's that mean, I don't want to meet her!" Cameron teased.

"I'm going to introduce her to Jason."

"No way! I don't want my brother being hen pecked by some mean woman. Are you hungry?"

"I haven't had much of an appetite."

"How about if I grab a bite to eat and come over? I can stop by Blockbuster's and rent a movie."

Lisa was hesitant but agreed. She hung up. She began to move around happily. Although she and Cameron talked daily, it had been quite some time since she had seen him. The phone rang again. This time it was Rhonda.

"What are you doing?" Rhonda asked.

"I'm waiting for Cameron to come over."

"Is it okay if I came over too?"

"I thought you were going out tonight."

"Ain't nothing in the clubs."

Lisa wanted to say "no," but Rhonda seemed to be a lonely person. Lisa met a few of Rhonda's friends. Rhonda was proud as she introduced Lisa, who worked for American Petroleum and lived in Dunwoody. The friends appeared impressed. One lived in Bankhead, one lived in College Park and one lived in the city of Atlanta. They had fairly nice shapes and fake hair. They were very basic women, who seemed nice. All three had a child a piece. They seemed to scheme their way through life.

"I know you want to be with your man, so I'll chill out over here," Rhonda said, not being offended.

"You can come over. You can meet Cameron."

"I've already seen him."

"Now, you can meet him. I've told him about you."

Rhonda perked up. "Really? What did he say?"

"He can't wait to introduce you to his brother."

"Ho', stop lying! You know he didn't say that."

"What have I told you about calling me names? It may be fine with your friends, but I don't play like that."

"I'm just playing!"

"I don't play like that!"

"Okay! It's all good."

"It's time that you stop speaking slang. If you want to meet a decent man, he's not looking for someone who sounds like she didn't finish high school."

"I have a college degree, just like you."

"Prove it!"

"You were an economics major, right?"

"Yes."

"Economics is built upon three concepts: scarcity, cost and marginal analysis. I don't remember half the shit I learned about it because I was an accounting major. As long as my assets equal liabilities plus working capital, I'm straight! Sorry, I'm balanced."

"Have you taken the CPA exam?"

"Once. I only passed one part, so I stopped."

"You should never quit."

"I may try it again."

"Why do you hang out with Tomika, Nee Nee and Falita? They're younger than you anyway."

"I like people who I can trust. Those sisters don't change their stripes, so it's easy to predict their behavior. If I treat them right, they treat me right. We got each other's backs. When I was trying to get through my last year at Georgia State, they hooked me up with enough food stamps to last three months. I don't have to go out of my way to be their friend. I just have to be on the up and up."

"Where did you meet them?"

"We worked together during the time I was in school. I encouraged Nee Nee to get her GED. I encouraged Tomika to go to cosmetology school. As you can see, girlfriend can do some hair. As far as Falita, I talked her into leaving the biggest ho' in Atlanta. It was hard, but she's got another man and he treats her good, even if he is old as hell."

"Besides hooking you up with food stamps in college, what have they done for you?"

"Nee Nee makes me feel like the smartest sister in the world. Tomika makes me look like the finest sister in the world, for free. Falita tells me I'm the most together sister in the world. They all pump my ego."

"What happens when you outgrow them?"

"I will have left Atlanta by then. Grandma Sweetie tells me that I won't be here for long. I will stay as long as she's alive."

"By the way, I got your knife."

"What knife?"

"There was a pocket knife left on Miss Sweets' coffee table."

"I don't have a pocket knife."

"Do you think it was her knife?"

"Grandma don't have nothing but butter and butcher knives."

"I thought it belonged to you."

"I don't carry a knife. I have mace, just in case a brother wants to act a fool."

The two women chuckled. Cameron knocked on the door.

"I have to open the door for Cameron," Lisa said.

"Okay, I'll see y'all later."

Lisa took her time opening the door. Cameron was smiling with a bouquet of flowers in one arm and a bag from Applebees in the other. Lisa invited him inside. He walked through the door and immediately walked into the kitchen. Lisa followed him. Cameron removed two plates and a vase from the cabinet. Lisa filled the vase with water and began snipping the flowers.

Cameron stole peeks at Lisa. The last time he saw her, she was four months pregnant and not that big. Now she was in her eighth month and her stomach looked like a basketball. To him, she glowed with the pregnancy. Her skin looked healthy. Her fingernails were longer. Her face was a little fuller. She was the most beautiful pregnant woman he had ever seen.

Lisa finished snipping the flowers and placed them in the vase. Before she could lift the vase, Cameron stepped behind her put his arms around her. His hand began to massage her stomach. He waited for the baby to kick, but was disappointed.

"Is he sleep?"

"No. He's moving."

"So, you agree. It's a boy." Cameron kissed Lisa on top of the head. He picked up the vase and put it on the mantle. He went back for the plates. Lisa sat on the sofa. Cameron positioned the plates on the coffee table. He sat on the floor as usual.

"What movie did you get?" Lisa asked.

"Kickboxer with Jean-Claude Van Damme."

Lisa rolled her eyes. Cameron was a karate movie freak. He was a Van Damme fanatic. Lisa began eating the ribs from Applebees while Cameron put in the tape. As the movie began, Rhonda knocked on the door.

"Are you expecting anyone?" Cameron asked.

"That's my cousin," Lisa answered.

Cameron got up to open the door. Rhonda smiled at him. She spoke and entered without an invitation. She walked into the living room and got comfortable. Cameron came into the living room.

"Cameron, this is my cousin, Rhonda," Lisa said.

"Hey Cameron, nice meeting you!" Rhonda said happily.

"Nice meeting you, too, Rhonda. So, your mother and Lisa's mother were twins?"

"Yeah. That's something, isn't it?"

"How did you find Lisa?"

"My grandmother's last contact was St. Louis. I searched through the telephone company and received no luck. But, the spirit gave my grandmother a sign. Lisa called her, due to a letter her mother had left."

Cameron gave Lisa a long look. First it was the unexplained money to put down on the house. Next, came the strange behavior toward Celeste. Now, a letter from a mother who had been dead twenty years ago. Still, Lisa had no discussion on any of the subjects.

"What y'all watching?" Rhonda asked.

"Kickboxer," Cameron answered.

"With Jean-Claude Van *Damme*? Ahhhh, that's my man! Woo he's fine!"

Cameron silently started the movie. Strangely, he enjoyed hearing Rhonda commenting on the movie. Even if Rhonda constantly called Van Damme the most gorgeous white man in the world, Cameron was glad she liked karate movies.

Cameron tried making a physical connection between Lisa and Rhonda. Their eyes were similar. Rhonda was a little darker and had a more muscular build than Lisa. It was something about Rhonda's roughness that reminded Cameron of Lisa in their freshman year in college. It made them innocent in a special way.

When the movie was over, Cameron nor Rhonda made an effort to leave. They chatted about hating the traffic in Atlanta.

"Rhonda, what do you do for a living?" Cameron asked.

"I'm a bookkeeper for a consulting firm. I like to call myself an accountant since I pay the bills, do the billing and maintain the books."

"Sounds like an accountant to me. Do you have a degree?"

"Can't you tell?"

Cameron wanted badly to say, *not really!* Maybe it was because she was young. She looked very young.

"Usually, people with degrees in accounting are accountants."

"These Negroes I work for are cheap and stupid. They have the audacity to call themselves consultants. I have to leave within the next six months."

"Why?" Cameron asked.

"They ain't got no money! Their clientele has dropped off over the last year and a half. They spend money like it grows on trees."

"Have you tried discussing it with them?" Cameron continued.

"Hell yeah! But they don't listen to me. They think I'm young and dumb."

"Maybe it's the way you are explaining it."

"What are you trying to say?"

"You have a unique way of putting things. You have to speak a certain language to be heard, regardless of being young."

"I speak English like they do. Come straight nigga!"

"Let's start with calling me Cameron. You seem to be very bright, But if you are working with business people, then you need to speak business language. If you want me to come straight, then I will. You don't sound like you have a degree."

The room was quiet for a few minutes. "What do you do, Cameron?" Rhonda asked.

"I'm an engineer," Cameron said without bragging.

"Electrical, mechanical, chemical, industrial or domestic?"

"Electrical."

"Where did you attend? Georgia Tech, MIT, Case Western or Cal Tech?"

Cameron looked closely at the person whom he misread. "I attended the University of Rolla?"

"Missouri?"

"Yes."

"Um. Let me get moving. Lisa, I'll check you out later."

Rhonda got up and walked to the door. Lisa and Cameron followed her. Cameron walked Rhonda to her car while Lisa waited at the door. Before Rhonda opened the door, she looked at Cameron. "Either you are good at lying or you really don't remember me," she said.

Cameron looked closely at Rhonda. He still could not make a connection. "Who are you?" he finally asked.

"A couple of summers ago, you and some buddies came to Wonderland one night. You each tipped me twenty dollars."

Cameron's face dropped. He remembered. The Betas'

convention was in town and several Betas from Missouri State attended. Instead of going to the crowded clubs, Cameron, Brad and Tony decided on Wonderland, Atlanta's most popular black strip club.

The three had been drinking heavily. They, along with several others, barked and whistled at the dancers. It wasn't until a muscle-tight dancer came out that Cameron's full attention went to the stage. When she spun around, Cameron noticed her eyes first. He took his attention to long shapely legs on a short torso.

Rhonda danced with precision. She spinned and did splits. What was unique about her show was the fact that she did no dirty acts. She touched her body playfully as she danced. When she rotated her hips, muscles in her stomach rippled. The men did not go wild over her show like the other dancers.

It took Cameron, Brad and Tony to see something that the others didn't. They each took out their wallets and pulled out twenties. They approached the stage waving the money.

"Forget it man, she's like intermission. She won't let you touch her. I guess she's been dancing here too long," a regular said.

Cameron ignored the man. His look became very intense. He flashed the twenty again, but Rhonda ignored him. He was slightly offended.

"Bring that tight ass over here!" Cameron shouted.

Rhonda danced over. She struck a pose by putting her arms over her head. Cameron reached over to put the money inside the front of her G-string, but Rhonda pivoted and stuck her tight ass in Cameron's face.

Tony and Brad roared with laughter and placed their twenties at the side of Rhonda's G-string. Cameron didn't find it humorous because he was drunk. He reached around her and shoved the money inside the front. Rhonda turned around and gave him an angry look. She danced away.

Later that year, Rhonda recognized him when she made her first attempt to visit Lisa at American Petroleum. She saw the two leave the building during lunch hour. It took her almost another year to gather the courage to visit Lisa again.

Cameron smiled at Rhonda. "I remember. Wonderland, three years ago," he said low.

"I see we hang out at the same places," Rhonda said.

"Believe it or not, that was my first and last time going. You still dance there?"

"After you pushed that twenty in the front of my shit, I figured that was the last time a man was going to disrespect me when I danced."

"I apologize. I'm not really like that. Me and my friends were really drunk."

Rhonda's attention went to the porch where Lisa was waiting for Cameron. "Your wife is waiting for you. If I ever catch you fuckin' around on her, you and the bitch will pay," Rhonda said with venom.

It was the tone of Rhonda's voice that sent chills through Cameron. "I may not have been a good boyfriend, but I'm a very good husband."

"A real man wouldn't leave a pregnant woman."

Cameron thought, if he had known Lisa was pregnant, he would not have left either. "Drive home safely," Cameron said.

"How old is your brother?" Rhonda inquired as she got into the car.

"You may be a little too much for him."

"You mean I'm not good enough for him. Is he an engineer too?"

"He has your situation. People call him a car mechanic, but the work that he does, I call him a mechanical engineer."

"I'm a little different. I have a degree," Rhonda said and shut the door. She started the car and left.

Cameron shook his head as he approached Lisa. Her arms were folded across her chest. He kissed her on the forehead and opened the door. They went inside the house and talked for awhile.

Cameron stayed another hour. He pulled Lisa into his arms. He rubbed her stomach, hoping to feel the baby kick.

"I think he's resting right now," Lisa said.

"I must feel him," Cameron said and continued to rub Lisa's small pregnant stomach. "Are you the right weight?"

"If I get any bigger, I'll explode!"

"I read somewhere that low birth weight babies can develop problems."

"This baby eats too much to be underweight," Lisa said for comfort. If she let Cameron have his way, she would have taken every test imaginable to make sure the baby was fine.

Finally, Cameron felt something jab Lisa from the inside. He jumped. Then he felt two thumps on the stomach. "Is that him kicking?" asked an excited Cameron. Lisa nodded. Cameron sat her on top of his lap and kissed her on the lips. Lisa pulled away.

"Don't make me pay for being happy," Cameron whispered.

Before Lisa responded, Cameron's pager sounded. Lisa knew who it was without looking. She removed herself from Cameron's lap. He hesitated before using the phone.

Cameron listened as Vivian complained that another tire was flat. She was on her way out and noticed the back of her car sitting low. "Call Triple A and tell them it's a possibility that your tire needs air. That's what was wrong with the other one," Cameron said low. Vivian became angry and slammed down the phone. Cameron blew relief. He went back to the sofa where Lisa was sitting.

"Rhonda is something else!" Cameron said and put Lisa back on his lap.

"She's nice but a little rough."

"And you want to introduce her to Jason? She will probably scare him to death."

"Jason is a renegade. He just doesn't talk like he's from the hood."

Cameron had to agree. Jason, the natural straight-A student, surprised everyone when he dropped out of college. He wanted to become a certified mechanic. It all came from receiving Lionel's handed down Impala. Jason asked his father for a few thousand dollars to do repairs. Jason was a natural at fixing things. When he was little, he was always taking something a part, just to see how it worked. His father saw potential, but everyone else just yelled at him.

Charles Johnson hesitated but gave the young man the money to replace the motor, carburetor and transmission. Charles wanted to see how well Jason could manage the project. After a few frustrating months, Jason completed his task, along with a paint job. Jason works as an assistant service manger at an Acura dealership in Minneapolis. He's becoming restless because he wants to do much more than work on cars.

"I know you, of all people, are not trying to pass Jason off as some great catch?" Lisa fussed.

"Rhonda is a step up from what he's been dating. At least she has a degree."

"If she had three kids and was on Welfare, she would still be a step up."

Cameron gave Lisa a peck on the lips. She started to fuss playfully, but he gave her a long kiss.

"I'm coming home," he said.

Chapter Seventeen

Everyone was quiet as Cameron drove back from Louisiana. Miss Sweets said she wanted to be buried back home where her spirit could find peace. She hardly knew anyone in Georgia. She only stayed because of Rhonda. Miss Sweets felt that Georgia was a better home for the child. Rhonda and her mother had never settled anywhere after Rhonda's father went to D.C. and never sent for them as promised.

Cameron had crossed the Georgia border. He was hungry. He had not eaten anything and he believed Lisa was hungry too. He saw an exit for Cracker Barrel. "You all want to stop and get something to eat?" he asked. Lisa was in agreement but Rhonda said nothing.

Cameron pulled into the Cracker Barrel parking lot. He parked the car and got out. Lisa struggled to get out. She was about to close the door, but noticed that Rhonda had not moved.

"Go on in. We'll be there," Lisa told Cameron. He left the two women in the car. Lisa sat in the back seat with Rhonda.

"You can get something. I'm not hungry," Rhonda said.

"I can't leave you out here by yourself. I know this has to be hard on you," Lisa said.

No sooner when the words left Lisa's mouth, Rhonda burst into tears. She had not cried, even after going to check on Miss Sweets and finding her in bed the same way Lisa left her.

"She said that I was a perfect child. I was no trouble to nobody. She was the only person that loved me. She really cared about me," Rhonda sniffed between tears.

"I care about you," Lisa said.

"She said she liked it when I rubbed her feet. Her feet were so messed up, but I didn't care. Nobody liked us because we didn't go to church. Man, I tell you, people can be some ugly mothafuckas, especially church people."

Lisa put her arms around Rhonda. She thought back to Miss Mattie and how she liked when Lisa brushed her hair. Lisa thought back to the days when kids teased her about Miss Mattie. They called the old woman crazy.

"Grandma Mattie was like Miss Sweets."

"They were suppose to be best friends."

"I can believe it."

"Now, I ain't got nobody. I'm all alone."

"You got me. You can come by my house whenever you like. And I still want you to meet Melanie."

"She don't want to meet me."

"When I tell her everything I know, she will want to meet you. She's not a bad person. She's a little stuck-up, but I promise, you will like her eventually."

Rhonda wiped her face with her hands. Lisa went inside her purse and had no luck in finding a tissue. She took her hands and wiped Rhonda's face. Rhonda took Lisa's hand and smelled it. Miss Sweets told her that once she smelled a certain scent on a person, she will be able to determine whether or not they were connected. Rhonda was disappointed because she couldn't smell a certain scent on Lisa.

Lisa said nothing as Rhonda rubbed on her hand and sniffed it. Lisa felt that whatever made Rhonda feel better, she was willing to do it.

Lisa took one of Rhonda's hand and rubbed it. She brought the hand to her face to kiss it and noticed it smelled like flowers. Lisa frowned as she smelled Rhonda's hand again.

"What's wrong?" Rhonda asked.

"What kind of perfume are you wearing?"

Rhonda's forehead creased as she tried to think of a perfume she was wearing but then she smiled. She wasn't wearing any.

"I'm not wearing any perfume. You're smelling me. Grandma Sweetie said you belong to a person if you can smell a certain scent. What do you smell?"

Lisa put Rhonda's hand up to her nose again. "It smells like flowers."

"Grandma Sweetie said that our great grandmother Catherine Malveaux Peterson was a lover of flowers. When Grandma Sweetie cleaned her house, she used roses."

Lisa grinned at Rhonda. So much of Miss Mattie was coming into her memory. She grinned wider when Cameron came to the car. "We better go inside and keep him company before he has a fit," Lisa said and giggled.

Rhonda still had Lisa's hand. Rhonda laughed and brought Lisa's hand to her nose. She smelled the flowers. Rhonda kept Lisa's hand to her nose and took a long sniff.

"Okay cuz."

"Guess what? Cameron's brother will be visiting soon."

Rhonda shook her head. "I don't think I want to meet him."

"Why not? He's nice."

Cameron knocked on the window. Lisa opened the door and asked him to give them a few more minutes. Rhonda stared blankly at Cameron as he walked away. Lisa noticed Rhonda's expression.

"Did Cameron say something to you?"

"It's cool. I've got a man."

"You deserve a better man. Jason is cool. He's nothing like his brothers. He's not a stuffed shirt. Everybody thought he was crazy when he dropped out of college."

"When you tell him about me, make sure you tell him that I used to dance at a strip club."

Lisa was quiet for a few seconds. She motioned Rhonda to get out. They walked to the door of Cracker Barrel. "If you want Jason to know that, then you can tell him yourself. He doesn't have to know everything about you," Lisa said.

"Cameron already knows," Rhonda said.

Lisa stopped. "How?"

"I told him," Rhonda lied quickly. She opened the door. "I don't like secrets. People find out anyway," she said and waited for Lisa to enter. Lisa walked through the door. They joined Cameron at the table.

As they ate, Rhonda kept her focus on Lisa. They talked about men. Cameron cleared his throat occasionally. The two women laughed every time.

"Did Lisa tell you that Jason is coming to Atlanta in a couple of weeks?" Cameron threw in.

"Um, hum. I know you don't want me to meet him," Rhonda said.

"My brother isn't good enough for you?" Cameron asked with a sly look.

"Okay, give me the four-one-one on homeboy," Rhonda said.

"He makes a decent salary and he's not abusive to women," Cameron said.

"So, what's wrong with him?" Rhonda inquired.

Cameron wiped his mouth with the napkin. His posture became straight. He stared Rhonda in the eyes. "He's a recovering drug addict," he said.

"Shit! I knew it was too good to be true," Rhonda said.

"He's been clean for three years," Lisa added.

"Coke or crack?" Rhonda asked.

"He was a heavy pot user and snorted cocaine. When my parents divorced, he took it pretty hard. No one was around to give him the support he needed so he turned to drugs. He never had a strong male image to guide him. My father was never around for any of us," Cameron said. The expression on his face reflected anger.

"What's your problem? Who guided you or are you perfect?" Rhonda asked.

"I have difficulty facing problems. Sometimes I shut down or I runaway. I'm getting better because I understand what's important," Cameron confessed. His expression did not change.

"And what's that?"

"Number one is my wife. Number two is my child and number three is my mother. Everyone else has to earn the remaining numbers," Cameron said.

"No man has ever been honest with me, not even when I catch them in the act. When you tell your brother about me, make sure you tell him that I danced in a strip club," Rhonda said.

"You can tell him what you believe is important. The reason I've told you about his addiction is because he doesn't have a problem talking about it. It's in his past," Cameron said.

"Is that his only problem?" Rhonda asked with a smirk.

"He's a smoker," Lisa said.

"How long is he staying?" Rhonda asked.

Lisa looked at Cameron for an answer.

"A week," Cameron answered. "Oh, he'll be twenty-nine soon. Is that too old for you?" Cameron asked teasingly.

"I was afraid he was too young," Rhonda said laughing.

"My girlfriends in St. Louis are giving me a baby shower the weekend after Jason leaves. You want to come along?" Lisa asked.

Rhonda's face lit up. The only time she had been out of Georgia was to attend Miss Sweets funeral. Even when she was searching for Lisa, she paid for information to find her.

"Hey, that's cool. When are y'all leaving and coming back? Do I need to take time off work?" Rhonda asked in the same breath.

"We're leaving Friday morning and coming back Monday morning," Lisa said.

"Okay. Now when is your father and cousin coming?" Rhonda asked.

"Wednesday," Lisa answered.

Cameron looked strangely at Lisa. "Melanie is Lisa's step-sister," Cameron said.

"I thought you said she was our cousin," Rhonda said.

"We'll talk later Cameron," Lisa said. It was time to come clean. William was coming to town and it was time that he knew the truth as well.

* * *

Lisa waited anxiously for Melanie's plane. Everything was going well. Melanie's flight was arriving two hours earlier than William's flight. He changed his departure at the last minute. Lisa thought it was best to tell Melanie the family secrets first. She would probably be thrilled not being sisters, but how will she take to Rhonda. Lisa saw passengers walk through the gate. Then she saw Melanie with Lauren. Lisa waved to them. Lauren took off running to Lisa.

"Hi Auntie Lisa," Lauren said and signed.

"Hi Lauren. How is my favorite girl?" Lisa asked joyfully. Lauren began signing.

"Lauren, I want you to talk to Lisa," Melanie said, slightly forcefully. If she did not remind Lauren to talk, she wouldn't.

"I have something for you," Lauren said and opened her Barbie back-pack. She pulled out one of the bears from the carousel. She handed it to Lisa who looked at it strangely. The bear felt heated in her hand.

"Thank you, Lauren," Lisa said. She turned her attention to Melanie. "William's flight is scheduled to arrive in an hour. I thought that we could talk," Lisa said.

Melanie could sense that something was wrong. They walked to William's gate to wait for his plane. They sat away from the crowd. Melanie asked Lauren to play across from her and Lisa. Lauren walked away obediently.

"How is Cameron?" Melanie asked.

"He wants to move back. I told him I needed time to think about it. Either he learns to work out problems or it's going to be a divorce," Lisa said.

"Is everything going well with the pregnancy?"

Lisa nodded. She handed Melanie a document and then looked out the window. Melanie read the paper. She looked at Lauren, who played with her Barbies happily. Then she looked at Lisa. "Does Paul know?" Melanie asked.

"He should. He took the test."

"Does dad know?"

Lisa shook her head. She refused to look at Melanie.

"Are you going to tell him?"

"I have too. It's not fair to him."

Lisa and Melanie sat in silence for a few minutes. They watched how Lauren set up shop with the Barbies. She had them sitting side by side. She occasionally moved their hands as if they were signing to one another.

"Is telling dad what's bothering you?"

"The whole truth is bothering me," Lisa said and looked at Melanie. "Miss Mattie was my real grandmother and my mother was your mother's sister along with my mother's twin."

Melanie looked at Lisa unbelievingly. She was never told of

anyone other than an uncle.

"Where did you get this information?" Melanie asked slowly.

"I met Miss Mattie's best friend from Louisiana. She told me how Miss Mattie left the twins to a white couple because her husband made her give them away. Miss Mattie had to leave them because she killed her husband. Miss Sweets said that she had no choice because the law would have known what she had done," Lisa said. She released a big sigh.

"Where is this best friend?"

"She's dead. We buried her last Saturday in Louisiana."

Melanie did not want to believe it. She needed proof. It took a long time to accept Lisa as her sister.

"Did she show you any proof?" Melanie inquired.

Lisa became bothered with Melanie's attitude. "I wanted to tell you the truth. You don't have to believe me," Lisa said with an attitude. She stood to stretch her legs. She was ready to walk away.

"I didn't mean to question the integrity of your information. It's all shocking. Maybe you should wait before talking to dad. You probably need to talk to Uncle Paul first."

"Why? Paul's done nothing for me. William paid for my education and everything else. He needs to know his brother is a bastard."

"Okay. Tell him. I thought it would be simpler to tell Uncle Paul first."

Lauren walked over to Melanie with a bear. "Here mommie. This is your good luck charm. Take it," Lauren said. Melanie took the bear and put it into her purse.

William's flight arrived five minutes early. Lisa hung back as Melanie and Lauren waited for him to walk through the gate. When William appeared, Melanie called him. He looked to his left and saw a surprise. He rushed to her and hugged her. He had not seen her in two years.

"Hello kitten. What are you doing here?" William said happily.

"Lauren and I came down to surprise you," Melanie said.

William looked at Lauren. She smiled, but she did not approach William. He had hardly shown acceptance toward her. She only knew him as granddad William, which meant nothing to her. Granddad Charles was much nicer.

"Hello Lauren. How are you?" William asked with a genuine smile.

"Hello Granddad William," Lauren said politely.

"Where is Lisa? Did she let you pick me up?" William asked Melanie as he bubbled with excitement.

"She's over there," Melanie said and pointed to the chairs.

When William spotted Lisa, she waved at him. William beckoned her to come to him. Lisa took her time coming.

"Hello, William," Lisa said.

William smiled and spoke. His reaction to Lisa was nothing like Melanie's. Since the exposure of the secret, he was relaxed dealing with Lisa. He had always appreciated her hospitality when he visited or called.

The group walked slowly to the parking lot. Lauren held Lisa's hand as they went to the car. Melanie and William talked the entire time as Lisa drove to William's hotel. He and Melanie were in the back. Lauren sat up front.

"Auntie Lisa, when will you have your baby?" Lauren asked.

"In another six weeks," Lisa answered.

"What is it?" Lauren continued.

"I don't know. What do you think it is?"

"I hope it's a girl like me!"

Lisa smiled and pulled into the Hyatt. The attendants came out to help William with his luggage. "Why don't we go out to eat? It won't take me long to check in," William said.

"Cameron was off today. He barbecued. I thought maybe we could go to my house to eat," Lisa offered.

William paused for a minute. The last time he talked to Lisa, she told him that she and Cameron were separated again. William nodded and walked to the hotel door.

"You can go in with William. I'll watch Lauren," Lisa said. She believed that Melanie may want to tell William the new found information.

"I will only get in his way. He'll be out in a few minutes," Melanie said.

Lisa drove the car away from the door. She looked in the rearview mirror. Melanie was looking at her. "You can tell dad about Uncle Paul. I'm not saying a word about it," Melanie said.

"I didn't expect you to," Lisa said.

"Yeah. Right," Melanie said with a grin. She felt different. It was as if she could read Lisa's thoughts. "I will not treat this cousin any different than how I will treat you after you discuss this issue with dad. It seems as if you have me pegged wrong," Melanie said. She could sense Lisa was about to mention the newly found cousin.

Lisa stared at Melanie who sat in the back grinning. Lauren turned around. "Mommie, you still have your good luck charm?" she asked.

"Sure baby. Here it is," Melanie said and pulled the bear from her purse. The heat from the bear was draining her, but she fought to keep her focus on Lisa. "Is it okay if Lauren and I stay with you?" Melanie asked.

"I expected you to," Lisa answered.

"Do you know anything about taxes for small businesses?" Melanie asked.

"I'm only familiar with individual taxes. You can ask Rhonda," Lisa said. She saw how Melanie looked curiously. Lisa hesitated. "She's my cousin."

"Don't you mean our cousin?"

William arrived at the car. He smiled at everyone. "I'm ready to eat some Atlanta barbecue," he said. Lisa drove off.

When Cameron saw Lauren, he picked her up and gave her a big hug. He hugged Melanie next. William was the usual. He was professionally pleasant. It was a tense situation when Melanie met Rhonda. Cameron and Lisa almost held their breath until Melanie spoke to Rhonda. Even Rhonda was stiff. Lisa just said, "Melanie, this is my cousin Rhonda." Melanie was very pleasant to the outcast cousin. William looked confused. As long as he had known Debra, she never talked about family.

Everyone small talked during dinner. Afterwards they went on the patio. Lisa took a deep breath. "William, can I talk to you in private?" All eyes focused on William.

"Sure honey. Where do you want to go?"

"Let's go inside."

William and Lisa left the group. They went into the living room. William waited for Lisa to sit, but she didn't. She kept her back toward him. William sat and waited patiently. Lisa went to the coffee table and removed the paper. She handed it to William. Once he took it, she turned her back and watched as her childhood flashed in front of her. She could see her mother reading fairy tales to her. She could see her mother teaching her the difficult words, making a game out of it. The only man she could see was Henry, the one her mother attacked with a pocket knife.

Lisa turned around. William was looking at her without an expression. Lisa could not determine if it were good or bad. She decided to bring an end to the false responsibilities William had to her.

"Someone sent some papers to me. That was in the bunch. I wanted to tell you on the phone so that you didn't feel that you had to visit me, but I couldn't. I told Angel. I haven't told Paul," Lisa said and took a deep breath. She wanted to apologize to William for her mother, but she couldn't. She knew no words to say. Her whole life had been built on deception. She couldn't blame her mother for the things that she did because Debra Arvell never had a chance at a good start.

Lisa looked up at the ceiling. Tears filled her eyes. She tried to keep them from falling. They refused to obey. She wiped her eyes. "Rhonda is my mother's twin sister's daughter. Miss Mattie was my real grandmother. She was forced to give away her set of twins. Me and Rhonda are Angel's real cousins."

William rubbed the back of his neck. For so many years, he paid for a child that wasn't his. At times, he paid a great deal. Then he thought back to the last thing Debra told him, *"You selfish bastard, you are going to pay for treating me this way."* William's face felt heated but then he smiled. Debra was the smartest woman he knew. There would always be a part of her that he would love.

"I don't know if my mother knew the truth before she died," Lisa said, breaking William's concentration. He believed that Debra knew the truth and was ready to do whatever was necessary to make him or Paul pay. William knew he used her as a sounding board when things went sour between him and Catherine. He also made promises to Debra that he could not keep. The only promise he kept was to uphold his responsibility as the father to Lisa. It was only for the sake of paying support.

"I promised your mother that I would take care of you. Although I wasn't the father you wanted, I made sure you received a good education at Hillside. I wanted you to be prepared to earn a living, independent of anyone. I think that is what she wanted," William said. He felt as if he made peace with Debra.

"If you don't mind, Cameron will take you back to the hotel," Lisa said and began to waddle out of the room. William walked behind her.

"This doesn't change the way I feel about you. If you ever need me, don't hesitate to call me," he said.

Lisa stopped. She nodded and then kept walking. William released a deep sigh. It served no purpose breaking ties with Lisa. She was an adult and probably needed very little now. But the information about Miss Mattie and three daughters was unnerving. William decided to go back to the hotel.

William walked back to the patio. Rhonda and Melanie were having a serious discussion. Melanie looked up at William. "You're ready to go?" she asked.

"My meetings are starting early tomorrow. Cameron, Lisa said that you are taking me back to the hotel," William said. Cameron left to get the car keys.

"Are you free Saturday? I thought we could spend some time together," Melanie said.

"I'll be on the golf course in the morning, but I should be free after one o'clock," William said.

Cameron came back with the keys. He and William left. Once they got into the car, William's pleasant attitude dissipated. "I don't like becoming involved in anyone's personal affairs, but if you're going to leave, then stay gone. Don't treat this marriage as a revolving door," William said without looking at Cameron.

"We are working out our problems," Cameron said defensively.

"I think *you* need to work out *your* problems. If you don't want to be married then put an end to it," William said, just as defensively.

"Is this coming from you or Lisa?" Cameron asked.

"I've been married three times. I think I'm qualified to speak for myself," William answered.

"What makes you so caring all of a sudden? You're not her real father anyway," Cameron said in the heat of anger. When the words left his mouth, he apologized to William.

"You're right, I'm not. Good or bad, I'm the only father she knows. I've been consistent. I didn't pop in or out," William said. He had never imagined defending himself as Lisa's father. It was something in her expression that evening that hit his soul.

Cameron refused to respond to William's allegation. He started the car and drove off.

Melanie, Lauren and Rhonda came inside the house. Rhonda called out to Lisa. They heard a faint noise come from the master bedroom. They went inside and saw Lisa lying on the bed crying. Rhonda stood at the door while Melanie approached the bed.

"Did dad say something mean?" Melanie asked.

Lisa shook her head.

"What's wrong?" Melanie continued.

"I need to get some rest. You and Lauren can take the bedroom upstairs near the bathroom. Rhonda if you want to stay, you can take the room down the hall from them," Lisa said.

Melanie rubbed Lisa's shoulders for a few minutes before getting up to leave. Lauren held the remaining bear out to Rhonda. "Here, Auntie Rhonda. You can have my last good luck charm," Lauren said sincerely.

"I will always keep it with me," Rhonda said and smiled.

"Good. You're suppose too," Lauren said.

Melanie took Lauren by the hand and left. Rhonda walked over to the bed and faced Lisa. Rhonda sat on the bed and took Lisa's hand to see if she could still smell the flowers. The fragrance was still there.

"I don't know about Melanie. Girlfriend is something else," Rhonda said. She released Lisa's hand.

"What happened?" Lisa asked.

Rhonda stretched out on the bed and turned to face Lisa. "She asked me about taxes. The type of questions she asked tells me that either she lied on her taxes or she is getting ready to screw over somebody," Rhonda shared. Lisa took a deep breath because the baby was moving. She knew that it was not going to be a restful sleep.

"What's happening with your father?" Rhonda asked.

"I told him the truth. He's not my real father. His brother is."

"What! This sounds like a soap opera."

"You can say that again."

"Does his brother know about you?"

Something was taking over Lisa. She wasn't as sympathetic as earlier when talking to Rhonda. At one time, she hated William, even if he had shown an interest after the secret became known. Now, she felt sorry for him. It was Paul whom she hated. "That bastard knows about me," Lisa said in a raspy tone.

"Do you know where he is?" Rhonda asked, looking innocently at Lisa.

"He lives in Kansas City. I know his whole damn family," Lisa said. The tears had dried up.

Rhonda noticed that Lisa was cursing. It really didn't bother her, but it was unusual to hear the person who told her to watch her language using the same language. "If I ever find my father, I'm gonna spit in that son-of-a-bitch's face. He promised my momma that he was gonna send for us. That nigga went to D.C. and that was it," Rhonda said.

Lisa thought spitting in Paul's face wasn't good enough for him neglecting her. She wanted to spit in the whole family's face, including Gina's. "Kansas City is only four and a half hours away from St. Louis. I think I will pay him a visit when we go to the baby shower," Lisa said.

"I'll go with you, just in case the nigga wants to start some shit," Rhonda said and smile at Lisa. She returned the smile. Lisa thought Rhonda was right. They were the outsiders. Melanie didn't have to fight for anything.

Lisa looked into Rhonda's hungry eyes. They looked lonely, searching for something that could never be obtained by people like them. "You miss Miss Sweets?" Lisa asked softly. Rhonda nodded. Her eyes began to fill with tears.

"It's going to be okay. I want you to remember something. When Jason comes to town, no matter how horny you feel, don't sleep with that brother," Lisa warned.

"If he ain't paying my bills, you don't have to worry about me sleeping with him ever," Rhonda said. She and Lisa made eye contact. They laughed out loud.

"Miss Sweets said something about three spirits being unrested. Do you know what she's talking about?" Lisa asked.

"She says that people usually confess their sins before dying. It releases their souls. Those who don't, their spirit won't leave until the act they committed is resolved by the person they have possessed. If that person goes through with the same act, that spirit continues to hang around. But, if the person is put into a situation to perform the same act, and they don't do it, it's suppose to release the spirit and they go off to never-never land or some shit like that."

"What spirits are still hanging around?"

"Well, Miss Mattie became a Christian and confessed all of her sins. She admitted to killing her husband but never asked for forgiveness. She didn't think she did anything wrong. Also, she had the opportunity to tell the twins the truth but didn't. She allowed them to search the earth looking for her love. And, your mother never confessed to killing that white fucka. She also held on to a secret."

"Did my mother really kill your mother?" Lisa asked.

"Sorta. Miss Sweets saw my mother being pushed away. She fell to her death."

Rhonda relaxed as if she were finished. Lisa only counted two spirits. "What about spirit number three?" Lisa asked.

"Spirit number three is strange. It has something to do with obsession and the Prodigal Son. Instead of her being happy that her sister escaped without harm, she was angry because she stayed behind."

"Is that it?"

"Yep."

"Do you believe that we're possessed?"

"I've learned to take Grandma Sweetie's spirits as I need them."

Chapter Eighteen

Melanie was on the plane thinking about the conversation she
had with William. She shared with him the abusive incidents with
John. She watched as her father became internally angry. He
remained silent until she laid out her plans. William's only
response was, "If you think it's the best move for you and Lauren,
then I'll help you."

"Mommie, you still have your good luck charm?" Lauren
asked.

"Yes, baby. It's in my purse," Melanie answered in
exasperation.

"I taught Auntie Rhonda sign language," Lauren announced.

Melanie thought about Rhonda. Had it not been for the
amount of information Rhonda shared, Melanie would have
ignored her. The only thing Melanie liked about Rhonda was her
physique. Although Melanie was in between a size six and eight,
she had always yearned for a tight, dancer style body like
Rhonda's.

When the plane landed, Melanie gathered Lauren to leave. As
Melanie retrieved her garment bag, her peripheral focus went to
the gentleman standing at her left. It was John. Lauren saw him
too and gripped Melanie's hand.

"Why didn't you tell me that you were going out of town?" he
demanded.

"I needed to get away for awhile," she answered. Her garment
bag was on her shoulder and Lauren's grip was removing the
circulation from her hand. When they were outside, Melanie tried

desperately to remember where she parked her car.

"Where did you go?" John demanded.

"Since you've been waiting for me, you know that the plane arrived from Atlanta," Melanie said smartly. She was about to step off the curve when John slapped her. She lost her balance and fell. John looked around quickly to see if there were any witnesses. As he surveyed the scene, Melanie took off with Lauren. They raced to the parking garage. Melanie looked around wildly for her car. She spotted it in the middle of the row that they were standing in. They walked quickly to their safe haven.

Melanie fumbled with the keys. They fell to the ground. Before she picked them up, she saw Lauren signing to herself, "I'm unhappy." Melanie snatched the keys from the ground and opened the doors.

Once inside, both panted. Melanie brushed her hair from her face. She reached for Lauren. "You want to go to Auntie Linda's?" Melanie cooed. Lauren clapped. It had been years since Lauren clapped when she was happy. Melanie had no time to analyze Lauren's behavior. She started the car and drove away.

There were no cars parked in Linda's driveway. Melanie thought they were parked inside both garages. She and Lauren rushed to the front door. Melanie rang the doorbell. There was no answer. Then she banged on the door. Still, no answer.

"Shit," Melanie said out loud.

"Let's go to Auntie Barbara's," Lauren suggested.

They jumped back into the car and headed for the Stevens'. Keith's car was in the driveway. Lauren clapped. They rushed out of the car and practically ran to the door. Linda's father opened the door. His expression became brighter.

"I was about to give up on seeing you," Edward said and extended his arms. Melanie walked to him and gave him a big hug. "Hello, Lauren," Edward said as he held Melanie. Lauren signed her greeting.

"You don't feel like talking?" Edward asked pleasantly.

"Lauren, I want you to speak to Uncle Edward," Melanie said out of breath.

"Hello, Uncle Edward," Lauren said shyly.

Edward bent forward and gave her a hug. They walked into the family room where Barbara was relaxing in a recliner. Keith was watching television. Indie and little Edward were playing with toys on the floor. Barbara saw Melanie and smiled. It was like old times, having everyone over on Sunday.

"Malinda is on the phone. How was your trip?" Barbara asked cordially. She looked strangely at Lauren who refused to move from the doorway opening. Lauren had yet to acknowledge her, which was unusual. Any time Lauren saw little Edward, they would immediately play together.

Melanie tried to get an answer together. She didn't want her voice to break or show excitement. She blew out air and smiled. "Dad is doing fine," she answered.

It didn't take Barbara long to understand what had happened. Melanie and Lauren looked like two refugees. "Come here Lauren and give me a hug," Barbara said with a smile. Lauren walked slowly to Barbara and hugged her lightly. Usually, the little girl would hug Barbara so tight that it took her breath away.

"What's the matter, Lauren?" Barbara asked.

Lauren looked at Melanie. Then she looked at Keith. She looked around the room and began to sign, "I want my father."

Barbara looked at Melanie for an answer. She turned her head away. Barbara sat upright in her chair. "Keith, will you take the children to the kitchen and give them some fruit that's in the refrigerator?" Barbara asked.

Keith obediently removed the children from the room. Edward came in to sit.

"Edward, I need to talk to Melanie alone," Barbara said while looking at Melanie. Edward followed the others out. Barbara waited for Melanie to talk but she became stubborn and remained silent.

"You want to talk about it?" Barbara asked firmly.

"John came to the airport complaining. It's nothing."

"What happened to your face?" Barbara continued. The hand print was becoming noticeable.

"I don't want to talk about it!" Melanie said rather loudly.

"You need to go to the police and press charges."

"I don't want to talk about it!" Melanie said louder.

"This isn't a person who becomes violent after drinking. This is a violent, dangerous man. And another thing, you lower your voice when talking to me."

Linda walked into the room in time to see her mother and Melanie square off. Before Linda could say anything, Barbara spoke first. "I need to talk to Melanie alone," she said without losing eye contact with Melanie.

"Mother, I need..."

"Did you hear what I said?" Barbara asked slowly with her eyes shooting fire. Linda walked out of the room and Barbara's attention returned to Melanie. "This is not about you. This is about your daughter and the example *you* are setting for her. I don't ever want to see that child behave that way again," Barbara said angrily and walked away.

Melanie looked around the room wildly. She was insulted by Barbara's insinuation. Never did she imagine ending up with an abusive husband. She wanted to leave, but she had no place to go. She knew she could stay almost anywhere, but it was embarrassing and humiliating. She decided to let Lauren stay with Linda and she would go home. When she turned around, Linda was standing in her path.

"Mother is getting old and senile," Linda said.

"I don't know what to do," Melanie whispered.

"I've always minded my own business, but I need to say this. You have never loved John. He arrived in time while you were grieving over Jennifer. This man is dangerous. I know someone who knows his ex-wife. The reason she never had children is because she miscarried. I heard that he put her in the hospital once."

"I can believe it now."

"I have plenty of room. You can stay with me until the divorce becomes final."

Melanie looked questionably at Linda. "Mother and I talked," Linda confessed. Melanie shook her head. Linda had to restore her mother's confidence. "I told her that I wanted us to work together on my campaign. I told her that I didn't feel comfortable going over to John's house," Linda continued.

"How were your trips?" Melanie asked.

"The chapter is up for suspension."

Melanie looked curiously at her. Linda was a little confused. "Didn't you tell them to contact me for help?" Linda asked.

"What are you talking about?"

"The chapter's vice president wrote me and explained how the chapter was up for suspension. She said that she contacted Lee Summit Alumnae. Someone told her that they were too busy to help them and to write me and ask for help. I thought it was you."

"What's happening with the chapter?"

"A cherub was intimidated into stealing. The school caught whim of it from the newspaper and now it's under national scrutiny. You should have seen some of the sorors. They looked like video sluts and one had a gold tooth. Mother was appalled."

"I can imagine. No one checks on undergraduate chapters anymore. They are raising themselves."

"Some are pretty sharp. The soror with the gold tooth was smart, but I couldn't overlook that gaudy piece of artwork in her mouth. She has got to get that thing removed."

"What about your other trips?"

"I hope that we don't get fussy and negative when we get old. It took everything in me to keep from choking the breath out of one old broad. She was nice, but she complained too much. I should complete my visits by the end of the month."

"How many chapters will be represented at the conference?"

"Ninety graduate chapters and forty undergraduates."

"Lori has sent campaign information to a lot of undergraduate chapters. Do you think you can visit a few? If you make contact with some, they can convince some others to vote at the conference. They are not as politically rooted as the graduate chapters. I think you can pull a large number of the grads because of Aunt Barbara."

"I want them to vote for me because I convinced them."

"What about me?"

"Because we convinced them, okay? We can do it! We built Lee Summit."

"This is a little different. The voters expect us to tap dance for their support."

"I want you to review my bio and the other material I want to send for the quarterly. I need a second opinion."

They walked into the family room. Indie and Lauren were on the floor playing with Barbie dolls. Lauren looked up at Melanie and smiled.

"You feel much better?" Melanie asked with a smile. Lauren shook her fist for "yes." Melanie decided not to make her talk.

Linda handed Melanie a folder. Melanie looked at the information inside. It was good, but it was missing the punch to make people take noticed. Even the letter from the mayor wasn't making a good contribution.

"Linda, why are you doing this?" Melanie asked.

Linda had to concentrate on her response. "At first, I looked at it as something to do. The more time I spend with the older sorors, I realize a gap is forming. They really don't want it, but they don't want to contend with restless younger women who haven't paid their dues. After visiting the chapter, it's getting worse. I want to bridge the gap. There needs to be respect at every level."

Melanie smiled. She heard what she was searching for. "Let's build a theme around bridging the gap. We are going to take it from where you split with the old chapter and then we will expand on your projects with the new. We will take you back to the old chapter and the projects you have worked on."

Linda was becoming more in tune with her mission. She finally realized that it was what she was trying to accomplish; although, it started as a bruised ego.

"Do you remember the conversations with the women you visited?" Melanie asked.

Linda nodded.

"Get their permission to quote them. Using dialogue between you and high profile Kappas will surely pull many of the graduate chapters."

"How do you know that they are high profile?"

"How did you meet them?"

"A friend of Mother's."

"Aunt Barbara is not going to give you names of people who

will not amount to much for this campaign."

Linda's expression was changing. She was still riding on her mother's coattail. "This is about me, not Mother," she said with a frown.

"Wrong! Don't get too sensitive about it. This is about Aunt Barbara too. You are representing her whether you want to or not. She has made too many strides for you to treat this campaign lightly. Lori would kill to be in your position."

"I don't want people to think I'm going to be the same person. I'm not like my mother."

"You can't fill her shoes, Linda. She's knows that. What she is doing is opening the door. It's up to you to walk through."

"I'm not trying to fill her shoes!"

Melanie knew Linda was lying. It was Linda's fear of disapproval from Barbara that kept her from exerting herself outside the comfort zone of being with friends.

"Aunt Barbara is excited about your campaign. She doesn't know what you are doing, but she expects you to do your best. You know how she is. The excitement is in the surprise."

"Do you mind helping me rewrite my campaign page for the quarterly?"

"Why don't I write it and fax it to you? Make what ever changes you want and fax it back."

"I need to take the kids home. Are you sure you don't want to come?"

"I'm sure. I want to work on this layout and I want to talk to Aunt Barbara."

"Do you know who had the chapter write me?"

"Only the recording secretary retrieves messages. It appears we have an ear working for us on the inside. Maybe she is fed up with the Melanie bashing."

"Are they bashing you?"

"Just a couple."

"I don't want her doing anything to jeopardize her opportunity to move up the ranks. I know how badly she wants to be in Lori's circle. She turned out to be a friend after all."

"We took a pledge and besides, she's not doing anything wrong. She's right! They are too busy. I'll have this finished in a few days." Melanie beckoned for Lauren who had just entered the room. Melanie extended her arms. "You are going to stay with Auntie Linda until I get us a place to stay. It's going to be you and me again," Melanie said with a smile.

"What about daddy?"

"You're going to Minneapolis this summer. You and daddy are going to have a great time together."

"Are you coming too?"

"I have to work. Don't worry, you're going to have fun!"

Linda gathered the children and left. Melanie went upstairs to Barbara's bedroom. She didn't know what to say, but a talk was needed. She lightly knocked on the door.

"Come in," Barbara said.

Melanie walked into Barbara's palace. Barbara's bedroom was designed for her. Edward didn't mind. He had an extensive library on the first floor that he called his own.

Melanie sat at on the small, plush, cream sofa in the center of the room. Barbara was reading in her rocker. Not once did she look at Melanie.

"I felt that we needed to talk," Melanie said bravely. Barbara continued reading. "I'm a good mother to Lauren," Melanie said and sighed heavily.

"I've never said that you weren't," Barbara said. Her focus was still in her book.

"I'm setting the best example I can for her. You make me out as this horrible person for making a mistake. I'm not perfect. I can't stop John for being an idiot! This marriage is taking it's toll on me too."

Barbara put down her book. She removed her reading glasses. "If you had no where to go then I can say I understand. Marilyn is one of the bravest people I know. She left with nothing but Gina, the boys and the clothes on their backs. She started with nothing because she was too proud and too embarrassed to ask for help."

"The only person I can be is myself. I've only had myself for years."

"That's not true! I've been there for you and so has Marilyn, Susan and JoAnn."

"It wasn't the same! I couldn't have you the way I wanted. You belonged to Linda. I didn't have the smart, intelligent Catherine Smith to set the example that you're talking about. God took her from me and it wasn't fair," Melanie cried.

"Come here," Barbara said.

"Linda has felt threatened for years because of me. All she has ever wanted was your open approval and so do I."

"Come here," Barbara said again.

"You don't know how happy I was when you told me that you wanted to present my designs. I was only seventeen. Having Barbara Stevens say 'I approve' is close to impossible. But to tell me that I'm not setting a good example for my daughter is unfair. Aunt Marilyn may be brave, but she was no angel," Melanie said between tears.

"Come here, Melanie," Barbara said with finality. Melanie stood next to the rocker. Barbara stood up. "All of us have made mistakes. To live sixty years and not be able to speak from experience is living in vain. I've never lived in vain. What I'm telling you is not being judgmental, but to share from experience."

"John showed up at the airport! He hit me in front of people!"

"You have already moved five thousand dollars into one of my accounts. I have given you the name of an excellent attorney. The problem is you are wrestling with the embarrassment of a failed marriage. Your mother was stuck there too."

Melanie remembered reading the part in her mother's diary about fear of divorcing Bill. He had already left, but she had hoped he would come back. Then Melanie thought about Miss Mattie. According to Catherine's diary, Melanie picked up an estranged relationship between Miss Mattie and her husband. It wasn't clear to Melanie what happened, but it appeared that Miss Mattie felt no sadness when her husband died.

"I have an appointment with the attorney on Thursday. Hopefully the process won't take long."

"Being a mother is a trial and error role that no one has successfully written a book on. I promised your mother that I would raise you like my daughter if anything ever happened to her. You are not taking anything away from Malinda. Her personality will not allow closeness."

"I've read mom's diary hundreds of time. Each time, I hurt," Melanie said and cried again. Barbara took her into her arms and hugged her tight.

"I hurt too. Catherine was my best friend. A tragedy is something you never get over."

"The older I get, the more I lose memory of her. I've just found out that Debra Arvell was mom's real sister. Miss Mattie had a set of twins that were given away to a white couple."

Barbara became very still. She remembered Debra telling her that her mother gave her and a sister away to a white couple and how mean the couple were to them. Debra searched for the identity of the mother who gave her away and was unsuccessful. She felt that her mother was in Missouri because an old woman led her there. She could have gone anywhere but the woman told her to go to Missouri.

"How did you find out about Debra and Catherine?"

"Lisa told me."

"You need to talk to Carleton and see if he knows about this. Maybe Lisa is the missing link to the family that you have always wanted," Barbara said unfairly. Her feelings were hurt because Melanie did not see her as a substitute mother.

"You, Linda and Uncle Ed have always been family to me. I enjoyed moments with Uncle Ed more than being with my own father. You are the only mother I have ever known," Melanie said tearfully. She never wanted Aunt Barbara out of her life.

Barbara walked Melanie back to the sofa. They sat. "A divorce can be very messy. Even if you want nothing but your freedom, it can be emotionally draining. John made it difficult for the last wife and he will make it equally difficult for you."

"I'm ready to do whatever is necessary. I've already began looking for an apartment."

"Honey listen. He can make it very uncomfortable for you. You must move as much money from his bank account so that you can start over in another city."

"What? Another city?"

"John is mentally unstable. He stalked his last wife until he met you. Unfortunately, I found this information out recently. You can't stay in Kansas City."

Melanie's focus was to the floor. She never imagined leaving a job that she liked and friends who have been with her since college. The mere idea of where to go was overwhelming. She looked up at Barbara. "Where should I go?" she asked.

Barbara was at a lost for words. She was able to give the younger woman advice throughout her young life, but she could not think of anything at the moment.

"We'll talk about it later. I need to make some calls," she said. She needed time to think of a plan.

"I think Linda is becoming more aggressive about the race," Melanie said to change the topic.

"Gloria told me that she has visited several of our comrades. They were impressed with her because she had a personal touch. After being introduced, not once did she mention to them about voting for her. She talked about their ailments, proper dieting, exercising and them writing books about their lives. She cooked for Connie Brown, whom I could never stand. Bless her heart, she recently had hip surgery. Now, these old hussies want to steal my daughter," Barbara said in a fussy way but with enthusiasm.

"I suggested the theme 'Bridging the Gap.' Do you have any ideas?"

"That's excellent! Talk her into having...a Bridge party. We'll have card tables around the room so that graduate chapters can sit and talk with undergraduates. Malinda can visit each table and share her ideas on bridging any differences. Or, we can set it up like a talk show and Malinda can answer questions or have Nationals answer questions. Why don't you contact several undergraduate chapters to see what's on their minds. I'm getting too old to hear young women complain."

A smile spread widely across Melanie's face. Barbara was campaigning. Barbara wanted to prepare the older women on what could be said during the campaign. Barbara always wanted to have several plans in case one didn't turn out right.

"Do you think the undergraduates will attend a Bridge party? It might seem out of their league."

"The Bridge party is for me and my friends. You girls can do the Oprah Show."

Chapter Nineteen

Melanie had turned off her computer and was cleaning off her desk for the weekend. She said good bye to the man working security. "You need an escort to your car?" he asked. Melanie declined as usual. Although the Youth Center wasn't in the best neighborhood, Melanie knew many of the children who lived around the center.

When she inserted her key into the lock, she felt a hand grab her wrist. She jumped and saw John. He gripped her wrist tighter. She tried desperately to free herself but was unsuccessful.

"When are you coming home?" he asked.

Melanie did not respond. She continued to wrestle with his grip. He let go of her wrist. "I asked you a question," he said.

"I'm not coming home," Melanie said without confidence.

"When you do come, don't bother coming inside. The locks have been changed and your shit will be in the yard," he said, breathing in her face.

"Mrs. Brooks, are you all right?" a neighborhood youngster asked.

When Melanie turned around, she was facing three of her regular attendees. They knew she was in trouble. John backed off and walked to his car. He drove off.

Melanie's face was flushed. She wanted to thank the three but couldn't. She rubbed her face with her hand. She had to get away.

"Mrs. Brooks, next time he come around, me and my boys gonna take care of him," one youngster said.

Melanie wanted to say *thank you*, but wasn't allowed to. They were trying to teach the youths how to settle problems without violence. She could not disrespect their offer by telling them no.

"I doubt if he comes back. I think he knows I have help," Melanie said with a smile.

"Mrs. Brooks, why he gonna dis you on your job?" one youngster asked.

"He's a sick person. I want you guys to have a safe weekend, you hear?" Melanie said maternally.

"Yes ma'am," the three said. The oldest one wasn't satisfied. "You be safe Mrs. Brooks," he said.

"I will. See you three Tuesday. Thanks for escorting me to my car," Melanie said. She got inside her car and began to shake. She had to remove her things from the house. The only person she could think of helping her was Carlos. She knew he was in town. She drove off to Linda's house to call him.

Melanie was on the phone talking to Gina. They talked thirty minutes before Melanie shared the news about the abuse. Gina was quiet. Melanie continued about retrieving her things from the house.

"I'll call Carlos. He's probably at Carla's house," Gina said.

"I don't want to involve him in this. I don't want John to do something crazy," Melanie lied.

"Carlos can handle it. I'll be in town at the end of June for two weeks. I need to talk to you about something," Gina said.

Melanie had an idea about what Gina wanted to talk about. It was about Paul. Melanie did not want to discuss it. "I'll be staying at Aunt Barbara's," Melanie said.

"I'll have Carlos call you over there."

"I'm at Linda's right now."

"Oh! I hear she's running for Regional Director. Do you think she will win?"

"Aunt Barbara will make sure of it," Melanie said very low.

"Don't say anymore! I know she wants no help from Aunt Barbara."

"Aunt Barbara knows too, but she doesn't want Linda to embarrass her. She can't stand the idea of Linda losing. She's taking this race personally. Lori called her an old bitch," Melanie continued low.

"I thought Lori worshipped her. Aunt Barbara has too many friends for Lori to make a costly mistake like that. I can't imagine Lori doing something so stupid like running her mouth openly."

"She's slipping, I guess. How is Sidnee?"

"Your goddaughter talks continuously. I wish you could take her for a couple of weeks."

"When I get situated, I'll keep her for two weeks."

"Don't worry about keeping her. We need to work on getting

your things. I'll call Carla. Stay by the phone."

"Thanks Gina."

Melanie hung up and sighed a sign of relief. It was just a matter of minutes before she received help. Her attention was drawn to Lauren.

"Mommie, dinner's ready," Lauren said.

Melanie walked into the kitchen. Linda had prepared the table for four. She had a highchair for Indie. It was a simple meal for Linda: spaghetti, salad and garlic bread. Melanie was ready to eat.

The telephone rang in the middle of their meal. It was Carlos. He and Dennis were ready to go over to Melanie's house. She quickly finished her meal and prepared to leave.

"Mommie, where is your bear?" Lauren asked.

Melanie blew air and pulled the bear from her purse. She decided to keep it there because Lauren constantly asked about it. It didn't take much effort to keep the bear with her since it was so important to her daughter. Melanie asked Linda for a set of luggage.

"I can come along. Mother can keep the kids," Linda offered.

"I don't want Lauren to think anything strange. Carlos and Dennis are helping me. I'll be fine," Melanie said and waited in the living room for Carlos and Dennis.

The two men arrived twenty minutes later in separate cars. It had been four years since Carlos had seen Melanie and Linda. When he walked inside the house, he hugged Melanie hard. She wanted to cry but controlled herself.

"Is Lauren okay?" Carlos asked softly.

"Yes. You haven't seen her in awhile," Melanie said and called Lauren. The little girl walked into the room. She didn't recognize Carlos or Dennis.

"Lauren, this is your Uncle Carlos," Melanie said.

"Hello Uncle Carlos," Lauren said with a smile. She liked him because he smiled like her father. She knew the man was helping her mother.

"Hi Lauren. You're getting big," Carlos added for small talk. Linda walked into the room. Carlos hugged her. They chatted briefly.

"This is Carla's husband Dennis," Carlos said.

"We haven't been away from school that long. Hi Dennis. How are you?" Linda asked.

"Hi ladies. I'm doing fine," Dennis answered.

"I guess we can go," Melanie said.

They left the house in three different cars. If it took all night to retrieve her things Melanie was prepared to do it.

They parked the cars in front of the house. John's car was gone. Melanie did not see her things on the lawn. She didn't know what to expect. She got out of the car and talked to Carlos. They went to the door. Melanie decided to try her key in the lock. It worked. She was still unsure about everything. She was ready to disable the alarm, but it wasn't set. John hardly ever set the alarm.

"I don't know what's going on, but I need to move my things," Melanie said to the men. They looked at her strangely. Gina told Carlos that John had threatened Melanie about changing the locks and throwing her things out on the lawn.

Melanie rushed to the master bedroom. She removed another set of her luggage from the closet and packed quickly. Everything John had given her stayed behind. She went to the dresser. She tossed lingerie and underwear into another suitcase. She cleaned out the drawers. She went to the night stand to get her mother's diary. When she pulled the drawer opened, a gun rested on top of the diary. Melanie didn't remember a gun in the house. She decided to take it in case John decided to do something stupid.

The men took the luggage to the car. Melanie packed Lauren's things in Linda's luggage. Carlos startled her by giving her two boxes. Melanie put as many of Lauren's toys inside the boxes. She became emotional over the things she was leaving behind. She became nervous when she heard John's voice. She heard him come up the stairs.

"Are you leaving?" he asked calmly. Carlos and Dennis were behind him.

"You told me to get my things. I thought you had changed the locks?" she asked.

"What are you talking about?" he asked curiously.

"You know what I'm talking about. I guess you won't have a problem with me getting the rest of my things tomorrow," she said.

"If you want to move out, then take everything you want," John said and left Lauren's room.

"If I get a truck, will you guys help me tomorrow?" Melanie asked nervously.

"Sure," Carlos said.

John remained quiet as Melanie removed the furniture in Lauren's bedroom. Carlos and Dennis were finished breaking down the furniture and placing it into the truck. Melanie carefully wrapped the china she kept from Miss Mattie's house. The china was a wedding gift from Miss Mattie to Melanie's mother, Catherine. It was the only important thing in the kitchen. She took pots and pans but left everything else. She had removed the majority of her personal things the day before. Whatever wasn't placed on the truck would get left behind.

"I think we've got just about everything," Carlos said. Dennis was outside rearranging the truck.

Melanie marked the box of china and instructed Carlos to place it on the truck. She searched her mind for anything she could have missed. All important documents, memorabilia, clothing and furniture were on the truck or already gone. Melanie took one last look at the house she had begun to decorate. At one time, it was the most pleasant place to relax after work. Later, it became four walls of anger and abuse. She had no problem leaving it for the last time.

Before Melanie walked out the door. John took her hand gently. "I still love you despite our differences. I might not have handled things the right way," he said.

Melanie didn't know what to make of the change in his behavior. It was like the earlier years. He was attentive and gentle. She wondered if he could be the same again.

"I hope that you reconsider before filing for a divorce," John said sincerely. He walked away slowly.

Melanie wanted to run and hug him. She had always hoped things would get better. She began questioning whether moving out so soon was the best move. It could possibly work. Carlos turned out to be a good husband. Maybe, John needed someone who believed in him. He never had that.

"Are you ready to go?" Carlos asked softly. Melanie hesitated before nodding.

"It's going to be all right," Carlos added for comfort.

"I don't know if I'm doing the right thing," Melanie confided.

"I don't know what happened, but give it some time to work itself out," Carlos said. He and Melanie left the house and drove to the storage facility.

Carlos and Dennis worked nonstop at unloading the truck and placing its contents carefully in the storage space. Melanie began to feel different. Her thoughts were on planning her exit from Kansas City. Then she thought about the many slaps across the face and hard shoves she had endured. Her mind traveled to the whippings Lauren had suffered. No longer was she thinking about getting back together with John. She wanted to get back *at* him.

"We're finished, sis," Carlos said and stretched. Melanie gave him a big hug. He hugged her tighter. "See I told you it was going to be alright," he said.

"Thanks Dennis. I don't know what I would have done without you two," she said.

"I had an option of doing yard work, car pooling the kids or helping you. I think I made a good choice," Dennis said with a huge smile.

"How is Carla?"

"We're working hard on getting her own practice started. She's been invited around the country to give lectures on youth development. It's time for her to spread her wings and leave the school system," Dennis said.

"Maybe she can do something at the Youth Center. We could use an expert to help us develop more meaningful programs. By the way, can you guys convince your fraternity to do something for the Center. I've approached all Greeks to do a program this summer. Everyone has committed except the Lambdas," Melanie said with a grin.

"It might be too late to convince the organization, but Carlos is going to be here for a while. Maybe a few of us can do something," Dennis said.

"Is anyone doing a basketball tournament? It doesn't have to be big, just organized. Is there someone I can talk to, to get a schedule started?" Carlos asked. He saw the excitement on Melanie's and Dennis' face.

"You can talk to me. I'm the Director. I'll give you a call on Tuesday with open dates," Melanie said.

"I guess we better start practicing, Dennis. It's been a few years," Carlos said.

"I still play every now and then. You need to get into shape," Dennis said laughing.

"Okay, dude. Let's get this truck back so we can see who is in shape," Carlos said.

Linda flipped a page in her notebook. She looked at Melanie, who stared at the girls unceasing. The one with the gold tooth robbed her attention the entire session. The girl caught Melanie staring at her. Melanie never bothered to refocus her attention.

"Do you have any suggestions?" Linda asked Melanie.

The girls' attention were intense. They were told that Melanie Brooks was the one who would evaluate the plan.

Melanie could not help looking at the gold tooth. "First, you must remove that gold tooth," Melanie said without sensitivity. The girl's focus went off in a distance. "Please, don't get upset. You want to be a lawyer, don't you? What judge is going to take you seriously with that gold flashing in their face?" Melanie said softly.

"We can discuss it later," Linda said with emphasis.

"No, we are going to discuss it now. We are talking about these girls serving as hostesses at the President's reception. I know of a dentist who can remove that thing," Melanie continued.

"David?" Linda asked without looking at Melanie. She nodded.

"No one asked her if she wanted it removed," one girl said defensively. She had been uncomfortable about the entire meeting. She didn't like the two women telling them what to do.

"It's not an option," Melanie said firmly. She eyed the girl suspiciously. Everyone seemed enthused about saving the chapter, except her. She complained that it was going to be too much work.

Linda saw what was beginning to develop, a struggle. She was not going to put anymore effort into saving Zeta Chi if the remaining members of Zeta Chi were not interested.

"I want to make something very clear. We have an excellent plan of action to save the chapter. I will not waste anymore time if I don't get a consensus. Either we are all in agreement or no deal," Linda announced.

She walked over to the girl. Without looking at her, she said, "Are you in or out? Please make your decision quickly," Linda said.

The girl looked around the room for eye support. She received none, not even from the gold tooth. "Why we got to do so much?" she complained.

"It's, why do we have to do so much. Either you are with us or not," Melanie said. She was losing patience.

"Why you frontin' me?" the girl said angrily.

"Leave my house," Linda said softly to the girl. Linda looked at the other girls. "Those who do not like what I have just laid out can also leave," she said and looked at the complainer. She was still sitting. "Maybe I didn't speak clearly," Linda said.

The girl looked as if she were ready to cry. "I rode with D'Andrea," she protested.

"D'Andrea, please take your friend home," Linda said.

D'Andrea rose slowly and grabbed her purse. "We are expecting you back in thirty minutes," Linda added. D'Andrea and the belligerent friend left quietly.

"I want to hear right now if I have your support for these programs," Linda said.

"I don't mind helping the elderly or serving the homeless, but I have a problem working with people with AIDS," one brave girl said. Many agreed with her. Linda came to the conclusion that she might be stretching her goals.

"Why don't we put that program on the back burner and focus on the other four. Once we make a commitment to do this, there can be no excuse for not following through. You must show up on time and give one-hundred percent," Linda preached.

"We will take the results of your work and submit it to Nationals. I doubt if they turn down your hard work. The important players will be at the President reception. It will give them an opportunity to meet all of you," Melanie said. She began to relax.

The gold tooth hand raised slowly. Linda recognized her to speak. "I won't be able to participate in the President reception. I don't have the money to remove this gold. It cost too much. When I graduate, I'll have it removed then," she said softly.

"How much money do you have?" Linda asked.

"I should have two-hundred dollars by the end of the month."

"How much do you have now?" Melanie asked.

"A hundred and fifty."

"David will remove it for two-hundred dollars. He can bill you the fifty dollars later," Melanie said.

The girl looked at her unbelieving.

"Trust me. He's a friend of ours," Melanie said.

The girl looked at Linda for a stamp of approval.

"Dr. Howard is a very special friend," Linda said with a smile. The girl relaxed. "We must divide into four groups. With a show of hands, who wants to work at the daycare?" Linda asked. Every hand raised.

Linda called off the other projects. Nobody wanted to work with the elderly or the homeless.

"You guys are lazy. You want the easy project. Ladies, we need some of you to take on the more difficult task of working with the homeless. How about it Tosha?" Melanie asked with an inviting smile. She figured the gold tooth would not be as noticeable with the homeless as it would at Cheryl's daycare. Melanie did not want Cheryl to see a Kappa with a gold tooth.

Tosha smiled with her lip covering the gold. "Okay. Make Erika help me," Tosha said jokingly.

"Okay Erika, you have been nominated," Melanie said happily.

Erika complained ferociously but, Melanie ignored her. She felt an attitude of preference. She searched the room for other untouchables. She selected another girl whose hairstyle was unfitting for the time of day. Linda saw immediately what Melanie was doing and suggested that the girls pull a number for the project. The education majors were given first choice for the daycare. The social service majors were encouraged to work with the elderly.

D'Andrea made it back from her trip. She saw everyone in a happy mood. She looked a little discontent.

"What's the matter?" Melanie asked.

"Kenya really wants to do this. She's upset at what has happened to the chapter," D'Andrea said.

"She has no respect for older sorors. We can't afford her saying something inappropriate to high level sorors. She has to learn how to control her anger," Linda said.

"Tell Kenya she can redeem herself if she works with the homeless," Melanie said, ready to burst into laughter. Linda wondered what was happening to her friend. She was never one to show favoritism.

"Let's eat lunch," Linda announced.

Everyone started toward the kitchen. The girls walked happily into Linda's kitchen, commenting on how "cold" her house was.

Linda looked at Melanie for an answer.

"Cold means good," Melanie said with a giggle.

"I know what *cold* means. What's up with you?" Linda asked with a slight giggle.

" I don't know. I have been feeling this way for a while now."

"Are you going to talk David into removing that thing for two-hundred dollars? I really don't know him that well. He's Keith's friend."

"I still have his number. Aunt Marilyn want those who are volunteering for the hospital to be there at eight o'clock sharp. She said if any of them don't show or is late once, she won't give them a clean bill," Melanie said.

"Do you think they will do this for six weeks without a problem?" Linda asked.

"They have too," Melanie said and then paused. "Lori knows that you are saving the chapter. She's wondering why they didn't ask Lee Summit. I told her that I didn't know. That is when she told me that there has been a change of plan. The chapter president will be the voting delegate."

Linda's mouth dropped. She searched Melanie's face for an emotion. There were none. Her friend was an outcast because of her. It made Linda angry. "I'm sorry. I would never imagine Lori going back on her word."

"It's okay. After the conference, I'm going inactive."

"Don't do that! Come back to the old chapter. The sorors are a little fussy, but they can be fun."

"I'm leaving Kansas City after the conference."

"What? Why?"

"I have to."

"What about Lauren? Keith and I are her godparents. How are we going to be there when she needs us?"

"I have to leave because of John. I have a feeling if I don't, someone will get hurt."

Linda could not believe her best friend was leaving. The idea of Melanie out of her sight was unthinkable. Even during the time she cut visitation ties because of John, she was able to see Lauren.

"What about mother? You two have always been close."

"She gave me her blessing."

Linda did not understand. Her mother would never bless Melanie out of her life. "I don't believe you!" Linda snapped.

"John has been beating me for a long time. His ex-wife is deaf in one ear because of a blow to the head. This happened after the separation."

Linda choked when she tried speaking. She swallowed hard. "We are the only family you know," she said in a shaky voice.

"It was difficult for Aunt Barbara too. She doesn't want what happened to John's ex-wife to happen to me. I have her blessing."

"Where are you going?"

"Where ever I go, we will always be family. Lauren will always know you, Keith, Uncle Edward and Aunt Barbara. I think I have imposed on the Stevens for enough years."

"That's not true! Don't ever say that again!"

"It is true. It's time to develop another family."

Linda walked away. How could Melanie say such a mean thing? Although there was small friction about Melanie's attachment to Barbara, it never came in the way of their friendship. The statement ate at Linda's core.

"I'm not saying it to be mean. I'm being honest," Melanie said as Linda climbed the stairs, forgetting about her guests. Melanie decided to join the loud talking girls in the kitchen. She figured Linda would come down after she freshened her face.

Chapter Twenty

Cameron waited for Jason's plane to arrive. He was edgy. He was losing optimism about moving back in with Lisa. She made it clear that she was fed up with his inability to face problems and his immediate response to Vivian's requests. He was getting tired of Vivian too. She called constantly. It had very little to do with Celeste. The last phone call was a complaint about someone breaking one of her car windows. They didn't take anything but the damage had been done.

Cameron was also concerned about whether he would have a good relationship with the baby, especially if things became worse between him and Lisa. He never imagined fathering children that were scattered everywhere.

Jason walked through the gate with his outdoors carryon. Cameron smiled at his younger brother. Jason was taller than him and was fairly lean. He had broad shoulders and a small waist. His long torso was carried by strong legs. He didn't smile as much as the other brothers. When he did, his teeth hardly showed and his smile always looked mischievous. He wore a ponytail. He had long soft sideburns which connected to a very light beard and mustache. It kicked him out of the clean look that his brothers had. It didn't matter. Jason always considered himself as the "black sheep."

"Hey brother, what's up?" Cameron asked with a huge smile. It had been two years since he had seen Jason. He seemed to have gotten a little bigger.

Jason gave his mystic smile. "Hey Ron, I guess Atlanta is up. Where's Lisa?"

"She's meeting us at the restaurant. Looks like you're filling out. You've been pumping iron?" Cameron asked for the sake of conversation.

"Just a little. I don't want to get too big. Mom wants to know when the baby is due. She's been fussing about not knowing anything about you," Jason said in a mellow baritone voice. His voice was not as deep as Lionel. When Jason talked, it was slow. All of his movements seemed deliberate.

"I thought she knew. I'll give her a call," Cameron said as they walked to the car.

Jason caught him up on all the news from Minneapolis. It gave Cameron a connection to home since he had been away for four years.

Jason put his luggage in the trunk and squeezed into the car. He tried adjusting the seat, but it was as far back as it would go. He casually brought his knees up a little and hoped that the ride was not long. Nothing seemed to fit him. It seemed as if he never fitted properly into anything or anywhere. He never complained. He always found a means to adjust.

Lisa and Rhonda were waiting at the *Cheesecake Factory* for Cameron and Jason. They sat and talked about Miss Sweets, Miss Mattie and Melanie. During the process of closing out Miss Sweets final business, Rhonda found a letter Miss Mattie had written that dated back to the late thirties. She thanked Miss Sweets for taking care of the land. Also, she promised Miss Sweets that she would disappear and for her to look after the twins. The information made Rhonda feel a twinge bit better about Miss Mattie and Lisa felt a great deal stronger about her first notion that Miss Mattie had no choice in the matter.

Rhonda and Lisa were becoming closer. When Lisa gave Rhonda a key to her house, it was like her moving in. She was always over to visit but she never spent a night. She waited on Lisa hand and foot, telling her that she would make sure that Lisa would never need anything from anybody as long as she was around. Lisa picked up that Rhonda was used to caring for people and not use to anyone caring for her.

"Tell me some more about Jason," Rhonda said anxiously.

"Jason is a casual brother. He isn't into impressing people. He's respectful but he has lived according to his rules. He's never been involved in, what I call, a serious relationship. He's smart, so don't try to play him stupid just because he doesn't talk much. He's different, sorta unique," Lisa said.

"What do you mean?"

"Uniqueness turns him on. The women he has dated were not what you call the norm, but it was something about them that he liked," Lisa said. She saw the concerned look on Rhonda's face.

"Is he into white girls?" Rhonda asked with a frown.

Rhonda was smart, Lisa thought. It should prove to be a good match. "He's dated both. He has to instantly like what he meets," Lisa said.

She could see Rhonda getting a little nervous. She was treating the evening as a date. When Lisa saw Rhonda in the slinky, black, short-sleeve mock top with the matching hip pants and a thin, sliver chain at the hips, she believed that Jason would take an instant liking to Rhonda. The only problem, Rhonda wasn't wearing a bra. Lisa didn't know if it would turn Jason off.

"How does he dress?" Rhonda continued.

Before Lisa could answer, Cameron and Jason entered the restaurant. "See for yourself," Lisa answered.

Jason had on a starched, white, cotton shirt with sleeves rolled up, over his elbows. It was opened three buttons down and tucked neatly into stone-washed jeans. His brown, cowboy boots put him into the unique category. It was the start of summer.

Rhonda looked quickly at the two men as they approached her and Lisa. She gave Lisa a horrified looked. She thought going braless may not have been a good idea. Lisa told her to be herself and braless was it. Her breasts were so round and firm that bras added extra clothing, which she didn't like.

Cameron bent forward and kissed Lisa on the cheek. "How is the baby?" he whispered.

"He's fine," Lisa whispered back.

Jason looked at Lisa and smiled. This time he showed his teeth. They were beautiful, but he always hid them. "Hey sis, how are you?" he asked in a slow and deliberate tone.

"I'm ready to explode. Jason, this is my cousin, Rhonda," Lisa said with a huge grin.

"Hello Rhonda. Nice to meet you," Jason said.

Rhonda clasped her hands together. To her, Jason was beautiful. He looked like he came out of a magazine. It was something different about him. He didn't carry the arrogance that many attractive men she had met did. "Hi Jason. Welcome to Atlanta," Rhonda said with an genuine smile.

"Are you from Atlanta?" Jason asked with a pleasant face.

"Um, hum," Rhonda said, nodding her head. She refused to make eye contact.

"I finally meet a real Georgia peach!" Jason said with a smile, showing his teeth. It made Rhonda blush. She looked at Lisa.

"I guess we can tell them that our party is here," Lisa said as she tried standing. Jason helped her up. They walked to the counter. Since it was a Wednesday evening, the restaurant wasn't too crowded. It wasn't a long wait for them to get a table outside. It was nice outside.

As they ate, Cameron did most of the talking. He asked Jason about the dealership where he worked. They were having problems with merchandise theft.

"What kind of inventory system do y'all have? I bet the person filling the order is in on it," Rhonda said for conversation. She didn't have much to say earlier.

Jason turned his attention to her. He looked at her with a serious expression. Rhonda didn't know if he was offended or in agreement by what she had said.

"That's what I told the regional manager. I'm thinking they are suspecting me," Jason said.

"Why? You're the assistant manager. You don't do inventory," Cameron said, slightly concerned. The whole family was concerned when they found out about Jason using drugs.

Jason took a deep breath before speaking. "They know about me going through rehab. Why not suspect me? They think I'm a thief anyway," Jason said. His eyebrows creased inward.

"Have you ever taken anything from them before?" Rhonda asked bluntly. Lisa felt like sliding under the table and Cameron felt like yelling at her.

Jason looked at her with a mischievous grin. "I guess you can say that I have," he announced. He watched the look of disappointment surface on Cameron's face. Lisa just frowned. "When my girlfriends brought their cars in, I only charged them for labor. The other guys did it too, so I saw no harm in doing it. That's when I truly realized that brothers had a different standard," Jason said with a grin. He took out a pack of cigarettes and removed one. "Does anyone mind if I smoke?" he asked as he leaned back into his chair.

"I need to use the restroom," Lisa said as she struggled to get up.

"I'll go with you," Rhonda said and shot up out of her chair.

"Girl talk?" Jason teased. He slumped in his chair and lit a cigarette. He took a long drag before looking at Rhonda.

"This will give you time to finish your cigarette. We don't like cigarette smoke," said a sassy Rhonda. She saw Jason grin at her. She turned around and rushed to catch up with Lisa.

Jason watched Rhonda strut away. He sucked on his bottom lip before taking another drag. "That babe's got a nice ass. She doesn't have fat anywhere," he said to Cameron.

"I don't know if you are blind, but those tits are slammin'," Cameron said. He was a breast and leg man; Jason liked a tight butt; and Lionel liked big eyes and full lips.

Jason gave a hoarse laugh. "So, you're not dead."

"I can look. I just can't touch," Cameron said with a smile.

"Not me. I have to feel free. I wonder if that babe's honey is sweet," Jason said as he stared in the direction that Rhonda walked.

Rhonda played with her hair until Lisa finished using the toilet. When Lisa waddled out of the stall, Rhonda was grinning from ear to ear. "Boyfriend is fine. He looks way better than Cameron," Rhonda said gleaming.

Lisa began washing her hands. "Just don't sleep with him. He's used to women offering free goods. All the Johnson men have charming personalities and they expect it to work for them," Lisa said. She wiped her hands.

"I see why," Rhonda said with hands on hips.

Lisa put her hands on Rhonda's shoulders and looked her in the eyes. "He won't insist on it, it usually just happens. He has never been serious about anybody. He's very nice and will treat you good as long as he's with you. Women still call him, begging him to go out with them," Lisa preached.

"He's that good?" Rhonda asked with an attitude.

"This is not a joke. I think he can probably be interested in you, but you got to play it right. Make him earn anything you give him. You don't have to be tough with him because he doesn't like tough women. Be firm when telling him *no thanks*," Lisa said. She slowly removed her hands from Rhonda's shoulders. They left to join the men.

When they made it back, Rhonda asked about the check. The men had taken care of it. Rhonda thanked them and gathered her purse to leave.

"Leaving so soon?" Jason asked.

"I'm not on vacation. I have to work tomorrow," Rhonda replied.

Jason thought about being playful. "I like your top. It fits you nicely," he said with a grin.

"Thank you. I stay in shape to make sure that all of my tops fit nicely," Rhonda said with a bigger grin.

"Why don't you hang out a little longer?" Jason asked politely.

"No thanks," Rhonda said firmly. "Like I said, I have to work tomorrow. If you want me to show you around the city, give me a call," Rhonda said just as polite and left.

Jason removed a carton of orange juice from the refrigerator. He had fixed himself breakfast. Before he sat down to eat, Lisa came into the kitchen.

"I would have fixed you breakfast. I didn't know what time you were getting up," Jason said.

"Don't worry about it. I usually eat my heaviest at lunch. What do you have up for the day?" Lisa asked.

"I thought about taking Rhonda out for lunch. She's taking me to the laser show at Stone Mountain this evening. Later, we're suppose to go to a reggae club," Jason said and filled his mouth with pancakes.

"Sounds like fun. I'm surprised she's going to lunch. She usually doesn't take breaks," Lisa said.

Jason stopped eating. "She doesn't take lunch? I wanted to surprise her," he said surprisingly.

"She works for a small firm. She manages the office."

"She works hard. I guess she makes a lot of money."

"She works hard. I doubt if she makes the kind of money she's worth."

"None of us do. Do you think she will go to lunch with us?"

"Us? I'm not going to be a third wheel."

"Why not? I want to talk to you about something."

Lisa had a certain closeness with Jason. He always called her "sis." Surprisingly, he listened to what she had to say. He treated Lionel's ex-wife the same way, but after the divorce, Stacy wasn't available to him.

"What's going on?" Lisa asked as she cut open a bagel.

"Are you and Ron getting a divorce?"

Lisa stopped for a few seconds. "We're trying to work out a few things."

"I've never seen him so depressed. He talks about you and the baby all the time."

"It's going to work out. What's going on with you? Are you still seeing Courtney?"

Jason gave a mystic grin. He had moved in with Courtney six months ago. Things had turned sour. When Lisa met her, she didn't like her. "I see her every now and then. Why don't you like her? Is it because she's white?"

"I don't like her because she uses drugs. All she talked about was doing videos or meeting Prince. You need to date women who have brains. I don't know how good she is in bed, but it seems like she's got you wrapped around her fingers."

Jason finished his breakfast. He smiled at Lisa. "She doesn't use drugs anymore. And, it isn't about sex. She enjoys doing different things. She's different."

"When are you going to do more than work on cars? You should be designing automobiles, not fixing them," Lisa said and sat her plate on the table.

Jason thought back to the conversation with his father. He said the same thing. Jason was close to his father. They had conversations about new technology and investing money.

"I'm going back to school this Fall. I'm going to live with dad until I get my degree."

"Have you discussed this with Cameron?"

"Do I need too? I know he's still angry about dad leaving mom, but what can we do about it? It happened so long ago. I need to move on with my life and so does he. It makes me sick, knowing you are living alone. He's doing the same thing dad did."

"That's why I'm giving him time to think about this marriage. This will be the last time he moves out without divorce papers. I don't want him setting a bad example for his son."

"You're having a boy?" asked an excited Jason.

Lisa had a smirk on her face.

"Come on! Tell me!" Jason prodded.

Lisa remained silent. Jason got up. He knelt down beside Lisa and put his arms around her and the chair. "I'm saving myself for a woman like you. She has to be smart enough to make tough decisions and pretty enough to be pregnant," Jason said and planted a kiss on Lisa's cheek. Jason was very affectionate with Lisa. He treated her like a delicate doll.

The telephone rang. Jason answered it. Cameron was on the other end. Jason brought the cordless phone to Lisa. Before Lisa began talking, she asked Jason to wash her car. He complied.

Jason and Lisa arrived at Rhonda's job at noon. The office was small with fairly modern furniture. Rhonda sat in the front. She was surprised to see them. Lisa was surprised to see Rhonda's semi-professional appearance. She had on a short skirt and a nice blouse. The panty hose and pumps made her look professional. When Jason placed the small bouquet of flowers, that he bought at the grocery store, on Rhonda's desk, she became speechless. No one had ever given her flowers. She became instantly embarrassed because she didn't have a vase.

"I thought you might need this," Lisa said and pulled a vase from a bag.

Seeing Rhonda excited about something as simple as a cheap bouquet of flowers gave Jason a thrill. He watched her rush the flowers and vase into the bathroom. His eyebrows raised as he looked around the office. From the looks of it, Rhonda was the only employee outside the three consultants.

Rhonda appeared with the flowers in the vase. She placed them at the front of her desk. She was speechless, but she had to thank Jason for the flowers. "Thanks, Jason. What are y'all doing here?"

"What are you doing for lunch?" Jason asked politely.

"As you can see, I have to answer the phones and do everything else."

"Can't you break away for an hour? I'm dying to try some real Atlanta food," Jason said charmingly.

Rhonda had to think hard and quick. She hardly ever took lunch because she was afraid to ask the consultants if she could. She was always needed to do something around the office. She had worked there two years and had only taken one week of vacation. It was taken as long weekends. When she requested time off for the trip to St. Louis, she was given a hard time.

Rhonda decided to walk and talk with authority, something Lisa preached about often. According to Lisa, if one didn't demand respect, they never received it. Rhonda left the room to tell one of the consultants that she was going to lunch. It took awhile for her to return. When she did, she was smiling.

"Where are we going?" Rhonda ask as she retrieved her purse.

"What do you suggest?" Jason asked.

"Let's go to *Hodges*. You have a taste for oxtails?" Rhonda asked.

She watched Jason frown in horror. He paused between chuckles as he rubbed the back of his neck.

"Have you ever tried oxtails?" Rhonda asked and held the door open for him.

"*Noooo*," Jason answered.

"Trust me on this," Rhonda said and walked out the door.

Rhonda piled a quilt and a small cooler in the trunk of the car. Jason stood to the side until she finished. "I hope the next time, you will let me help you," he said to her.

"I'm so used to doing things by myself, I forgot about you," Rhonda said with a grin.

As Jason drove to Stone Mountain Park, he admired the greenery on the way to the park. He commented often as he tried driving the speed limit. No one on Highway 78 was doing the speed limit but him. He liked the pace of fast moving cars, so he joined them. Soon he was at the park's gate and waited his turn in line to enter. He noticed that an annual pass was twenty-five dollars. When it was his turn, he looked at Rhonda. "Do you have a park pass?"

She shook her head. Jason handed the man twenty-five dollars. The man gave Jason an annual sticker for the car and some pamphlets. Jason handed it all to Rhonda and drove through. She looked at the sticker and then at Jason with appreciation. She directed him to the parking lot.

Jason removed the quilt and the small cooler from the trunk. They walked to the open space on the lawn which faced the mountain. A group of white people brought a very large tarp to spread on the grass. Rhonda instructed Jason to double the quilt and lay it outside the tarp.

"I don't think they would mind if we sat on their tarp. I would hate to get this quilt dirty," Jason said.

Rhonda was ready to complain, but Jason asked the white group if he and Rhonda could join them. They were very pleasant when they agreed. Jason spread the quilt and extended his hand to Rhonda. She looked strangely at the white group as she eased her short skirt to the ground. Jason got a good view of very brown lean legs. He sat on the outside of her.

Rhonda found herself staring at Jason's legs. He was outfitted in Eddie Bauer khaki, knee-length shorts and a soft yellow polo shirt. His legs were sturdy, not muscular. Rhonda stopped staring at Jason's legs and instructed him to remove two bottles from the cooler. He did and frowned at them.

"What's ginger beer?" he asked.

"You ain't had ginger beer before? Where have you been? Try it!"

Jason removed the cap and took a swallow. He coughed from the potency of the beverage. It was a heavy, malt flavored gingerale. After he finished coughing and wiping tears from his eyes, he looked at Rhonda laughing at him. She had a genuine smile. The only connection she had to Lisa were her eyes. They weren't hazel, but they had the almond shape and were larger. They made her seem older than her baby face. She was darker than Lisa and her face was round with full lips. She reminded him of a younger version of a model he had seen in an Ebony magazine. The model looked exotic to him.

"Why didn't you warn me? This stuff is potent," he said. They talked until the show began.

As the lasers hit the side of the mountain, Rhonda looked in awe. She was captivated by the cartoon characters in the show. Jason felt a certain innocence about her, but he knew that she wasn't. His attention went to a teenage couple that was standing close to them. Jason looked at the boy and could tell it was the couple's first date. They were standing almost two feet a part. The boy did most of the talking. The girl seemed a little irritated from standing. She frowned a little.

"Why don't you two join us? There's enough room," Jason offered.

The young people looked at one another. Jason scooted over toward Rhonda and shifted her between his legs. The young couple eased onto the quilt.

"I had to save you, man. Your girl was ready to leave you standing," Jason said jokingly as he eased Rhonda closer to him. The boy grinned shyly at Jason.

"The next time he comes unprepared, leave him, girlfriend," Rhonda said to the girl who giggled. She put her hand to her mouth and looked at her date with a smile.

Jason put his arms around Rhonda and occasionally whispered in her ears, causing her to giggle. Soon, they could smell marijuana in the air. It made Jason a little jittery, especially around the young couple.

"You guys know what's burning?" Jason asked the teenagers. They nodded shyly.

"Do you guys smoke pot?" he asked sternly.

The the young couple's eyes widened. "No sir!" the boy said firmly.

"Don't start! It only leads to worse things. It makes you feel good for only a short time. Then you have to keep spending money to keep feeling good for a short time. You later realize that there is nothing you can buy that will make you feel good. It has to come from within. You know what I'm talking about?" Jason continued with the boy. He always felt that young black boys were primary targets for drugs.

"Yes, sir. I understand what you're saying," the boy said.

"What about you?" Jason asked of the girl.

"I don't use drugs," she said with wide eyes.

"Don't ever start. You guys want a ginger beer?" Jason asked with authority.

The boy looked concerned. They had just finished a brief discussion on drugs and now the man was offering him a beer. He looked at his date and she was smiling.

"I ain't never had a beer," the boy said.

Jason smiled at him. "This is not a real beer. It's ..." Before Jason could finish, the girl jumped in. "It taste like gingerale," she said.

"Tell 'em, girlfriend. Educate him," Rhonda said and handed the couple a ginger beer a piece. She took one out for herself and took a swallow. Jason asked for some. She tried taking out another bottle, but he stopped her.

"Let me have some of yours," he said low. His hand was on her stomach. He could tell she was braless. The idea alone made him excited.

Rhonda reached her bottle back to him and reminded herself that nothing was going to happen. Jason took a swallow and gave the bottle back to Rhonda. She slowly wrapped her lips around the bottle as if kissing Jason.

Soon, they saw the horses of the confederate generals ride off the mountain and the show was over. Jason had the boy carry the cooler while he carried the quilt. He and Rhonda walked ahead of the teenagers.

"Do you think they will be smoking pot at the reggae club? I don't want to be around it," Jason told Rhonda.

"I have a better idea. Let's go back to my apartment," she said. Jason smiled.

The ringing telephone awakened Lisa. She answered sluggishly. It was Rhonda. She seemed vibrant. She talked to Lisa briefly before asking to speak to Jason.

"I think he's still sleeping. He came in late from the club," Lisa said with a yawn.

"We didn't go to the club. We came back to my place," Rhonda said. There were seconds of silence. "I gave boyfriend the best manicure and pedicure he has ever had. He tried pulling his smooth game, but I did what you said. I kept my clothes on," Rhonda said happily.

Lisa struggled out of bed to wake up Jason. When she entered the room, she saw his nude body dangling out of the full size bed. He was lying on his stomach. Lisa backed away from the door and called him. She heard him moan to her. She walked toward the door talking to him. He quickly wrapped a sheet around himself. Lisa appeared at the door. Jason's hair was all over his head and his eyes were half closed.

"Rhonda's on the phone," Lisa said.

"Oh shit! We're suppose to go horseback riding today. What time is it?"

"It's after eight."

"And she's on the phone?"

"She's a little different," Lisa said, believing Rhonda was playing a game with Jason. She had scored the first point and was ready to win the match.

Jason rolled over to the phone. When he picked it up, he smiled. "How is my Georgia peach?" he asked seductively.

Lisa left the room feeling relieved. She went into the kitchen to get something to eat. Before she could reach for a pot, she felt a sharp pain which caused her to stop. She sat down and took deep breaths. She felt comfortable again. She decided to call Cameron to visit her in case she went into labor. She wasn't due for another four weeks and she still had the trip to St. Louis and Kansas City to make.

Jason dragged himself into the kitchen. He saw Lisa rubbing her stomach. "What's the matter, sis?" he asked frowning.

"I felt a sharp pain."

"Maybe I need to stay here."

"I'll be alright. I'll call Cameron to sit with me. How was the laser show and the reggae club?"

"The laser show was great. We went to Rhonda's place afterwards and chilled. She gave me a manicure and pedicure," Jason said and extended his hands.

"What happened to the reggae club?"

"I'm glad we chilled at her place. We got to know each other a little better. She's pretty smart in a very honest way. She told me that the pedicure would make me sleep better and she was right. I can hardly get up."

"What are the plans for today?"

"I told her that since I'm in Georgia, I will do what the Georgians do. When she comes to the Twin Cities, she will do what the Twin Citians do. We're going horseback riding and barbecuing today. Tomorrow, we're going fishing and then we're going to listen to the ball game on the radio. She said that she and her grandmother fished together when she was younger. It should be interesting."

"She's not a true city girl. Where she grew up is kind of rural."

"That's what makes it interesting. She told me that she lived in Atlanta since college. When she danced at a strip club, she found out that city people lied with a straight face. She wanted to dance, but they wanted her to do more."

"Does it bother you that she danced in a strip club?"

"She said she only danced there and nothing else. She's a nice person. We all have done things that we are not proud of."

Jason removed milk and eggs from the refrigerator. He took a bowl out of the cabinet and began to combine the ingredients. His attitude was very casual.

Chapter Twenty-One

Marilyn had just hung up the phone from talking to Gina. The news was disturbing. It was really true. Paul was Lisa's father. Debra had confronted her about it years ago, but when Marilyn asked Paul about it, he denied it. He claimed that Bill was the father. Paul took the blood test to clear the air. Nothing came back but a letter from Debra saying, "Honor your responsibilities to our daughter." After word about Debra's death, Paul never mentioned the child again.

Marilyn wanted desperately to discuss the issue with Paul. So many thoughts consumed her. She wanted to believe that Paul knew nothing of the truth. He loved children. He spent an enormous amount of time with her children. He disciplined them without second thought. They were his children, he reminded her. The idea of him ignoring Lisa was unbelievable. If he did, it shed a different light on the man she loved in college and for most of her adult years.

Marilyn's phone rang again. This time, she had visitors. In walked five young women from Zeta Chi chapter. Barbara tried to prepare her for what she believe would be a shock. Only one girl fit the description of what Barbara described.

The girls remained standing. Marilyn stared at the stack of curls on one girl's head. Marilyn wondered if the girl thought she looked attractive with a dressy hairstyle that had a blond streak in the bangs. When the girls began to shift a little, Marilyn invited them to sit.

"It's a pleasure to meet you Mrs. Smith. You are the second chapter founder we have met," one said pleasantly.

"Thank you," Marilyn said.

The girls waited on instructions, but Marilyn could not get past the blond streak. When did they start letting girls like her into the organization? How did the young woman expect to work in the hospital with that hairstyle?

"Linda Reed said that you would brief us on what is needed," one girl said.

Marilyn had to gather her senses. It was time to focus on her job. "According to your project plan, your objective is to develop sensitivity toward those physically incapacitated. Are any of you nursing majors?" Marilyn asked. She saw one hand raise.

"Let's get something straight. This project is serious. You will be around sick and terminally ill patients. Your attitude must reflect comfort. I will not have anyone turning up their noses or having a bad attitude. You are to be on time and dressed out in a hospital smock. All dangling earrings, heavy makeup and extreme hairstyles are to stay outside of this hospital," said a stern Marilyn. The young women's eyes became large.

"Does anyone care to back out? Do it now. If anyone does not show during these six weeks, I will not sign off on the project. In this hospital, patients are counting on us to be here everyday," Marilyn said.

"What time are we to be here and where do we report?" the nursing major asked.

"I will see three of you at seven o'clock in the morning in my office. The other three can report at one o'clock in the afternoon. You will only work four hours," Marilyn answered. The pleasant looks from the girls were gone. Marilyn realized it might be because of her.

"I'm glad to see that you all are working hard to restore Zeta Chi. As a founder, I want to make sure that community service still ranks number one. I know the quality of your performance will surpass the nursing students," Marilyn said.

"Mrs. Smith, back in the old days when you pledged, what types of projects did you do," the dangling earrings asked earnestly.

Marilyn had to recuperate from hearing the term "old days." She cleared her throat and thought hard about what the sorority did. It was hardly a comparison to what the list of projects Linda shared with her.

"During that time, we worked hard at civil issues. Blacks were being heavily discriminated against. We made sure that education was available via free tutoring or working with our churches," Marilyn said. She wondered how it compared to working with the homeless, the elderly and the physically ill.

"Hey, that's deep. My mother said that Blacks didn't have serious problems with homelessness and making sure the elderly were taken care of. Black people took in their parents and grandparents. I guess our generation don't care," the heavy makeup wearer said.

"Many values have been lost or compromised. Your generation learned it from another generation. Don't ever think this problem is your generation's fault and you have to fix it alone. We all share some responsibility. I hope what ever you ladies learn during this period will be used to help teach someone else," Marilyn said.

Her attitude was changing toward the girls. She had to admit to her own bias toward their age. After hearing herself talk, she decided to practice her sermon. It was time to stop avoiding and start participating.

"Thanks for your time, Mrs. Smith. I have to get my mother's car back. I told her that I needed it for two hours. My time is almost up. I don't want her to think I was hanging out with my friends," the stacked hairstyle said.

"I can call her, if you like. I understand how she feels," Marilyn said with a smile.

The girl gave Marilyn the telephone number. After Marilyn announced to the girl that she could keep the car for an additional hour, all the girls blew relief. They had rode together. Once Marilyn got off the phone, they bombarded her with questions about the pledge mother/daughter program. They wondered if something like it could ever be restored.

Marilyn chatted about what she remembered. She didn't tell the girls that it wasn't a pleasant experience for her, but her attitude was positive. She found a digestible way of telling the girls that pledging will never happen again.

Marilyn decided to take the girls on a tour of the hospital. As she walked down the hall, she saw the familiar sight of Mrs. Hawkins. She was a very old woman who checked in often for general care. A different family member brought her every time. This time, a young man around college age was with her. He seemed antsy to leave.

Marilyn watched as the young man eased away from the woman's wheelchair. Before he could leave, one of the young women called out to him. He turned around. He knew all of them. He returned to the desk with a smile. To his misfortune, the girls looked at him angrily.

"Where are you going?" the stacked hairstyle snapped. She had her hands on her hips. The others followed suit and put their hands on their hips.

"Uh, I was dropping off my great grandmother," he muttered. He wiped his hand across his nose.

"Drop her off? Aren't you going to see that she gets to her room?" the dangling earrings fussed. The young man looked guilty.

"You ain't suppose to treat old people like that. I bet she wiped your nasty behind when you were little," the heavy makeup wearer said.

"I was going to check on her later," the young man sputtered.

"Yeah, right. Mrs. Smith, this is Julius. He don't have no respect for old people," the heavy makeup wearer said. She was perturbed with the young man.

Marilyn was getting more agitated from hearing the young women use the word "old." It was difficult seeing herself aging. The young women were trying to be polite, but she was having difficulty accepting it.

"Young man, it would be nice if you made sure that your great grand mother was settled. It wouldn't hurt to hang around for a couple of hours," Marilyn said pleasantly.

The young man nodded and looked at the girls. Their verdict was still guilty.

The nurse at the desk gave the young man the room number. Before he could grab the wheelchair, the stacked hairstyle did. "Go on and go! We'll take care of her," she said and rushed the old woman off. The other girls quickly followed behind.

Marilyn cringed as she saw the young women race Mrs. Hawkins down the hall. The old woman's leg dangled off the foot support. Marilyn was happy to see the young women wanting to help, but they had to learn procedures before taking matters into their own hands.

Marilyn rushed up behind them. "Wait a minute!" she shouted.

The girls stopped on a dime with eight cents change. Marilyn was out of breath and at the looks of Mrs. Hawkins, so was she. The girls looked innocently at Marilyn. She wanted to scream at them, but their looks softened her attempt at discipline.

"Make sure she's properly in her chair before taking off. Check to make sure her feet are secured," Marilyn said, somewhat in a pleasant tone.

The dangling earrings placed Mrs. Hawkins foot on the metal base. She bent forward to ask Mrs. Hawkins if she was okay. The old woman's mouth was opened. Nothing came out.

"Take your time pushing her. She can't afford to get excited," Marilyn said.

The girls continued their journey at a slower pace while talking the entire time. Marilyn took a deep breath. It was difficult to discern if it was easier to work with eager beavers as opposed to attitudes.

After the nurse and the young man entered the room, Marilyn decided to check on Carlos' mother. She was scheduled to be released in a few days. The doctors were amazed at Dorothy

Simmons' recuperation. They didn't think she would take to the new organ so well.

When Marilyn reached the room, Carlos was leaving. He was happy to see Marilyn. "Momma is doing fine. The doctor says she can leave in a few days," he said.

"Good. I have an agency for you to contact about home healthcare. I also have something else that might work in addition to the home healthcare," Marilyn said.

"Thanks. Momma was a little worried that I might not be able to handle things. I guess sons aren't as responsible as daughters," Carlos said with a boyish grin.

"I think you have done a wonderful job in getting information," Marilyn responded.

"Actually, it was Gina's idea to ask you. I didn't have a clue."

"You are still doing a wonderful job. Your mother appreciates it greatly."

Carlos was a little shy about continuing a conversation that would convict him. He decided to change the topic. "Gina and the kids will be here this weekend. She's staying for two weeks."

"I talked to her earlier today. She tells me that Avery did very well this school year. He's playing basketball this summer."

"I'm suppose to teach him how to play basketball when he gets here. He pulled this school year out barely. His behavior has been a little difficult lately," Carlos shared. He wanted to get Marilyn's opinion. He had already talked to Dennis about Avery. According to Dennis, it was a male thing. It was difficult discussing it with his mother because it was like the old days when she fussed constantly and blamed him for everything.

"Every child is different. I had to learn by trial and error with Gina and the boys. Usually, when children act out, something is wrong."

"We have asked him what was the matter and he says 'nothing'. I don't know what else to do."

"Children don't tell you the problem, they just behave in a way to get your attention. Once you spend time with him, he will tell you. You have to be smart enough to listen."

"Was Aaron and Ronnie different than Gina?"

"Not really. When they wanted my attention, they behaved equally stressful. The problem comes when they carry resentment."

"Are any of them carrying resentment?"

"If they are, they have covered it well. I have done battle with Gina for years. We have called a truce now. Ronnie visits every holiday and Mother's day. He will always be closer to Paul. And Aaron will always be my baby," Marilyn said with a smile.

"Didn't they understand that you worked hard for them? Every thing you sacrificed was because of them?"

"Children don't understand long term plans very well. They don't see sacrifices as something out of the ordinary. When they become adults, they understand. When they become parents, they appreciate. The sacrifices and long term plans must stay intact. What you do is give as much of yourself now as you possibly can. Parenthood was never meant to be convenient."

Carlos nodded. He had to figure out how he was going to juggle his dissertation and Avery. The last thing he wanted was resentment. Marilyn had made some good points. No matter how much he praised Marilyn, Gina still had something negative to add. Although Marilyn did not deserve a clean bill, she wasn't that bad, Carlos thought.

"Thanks Mrs. Smith. I'll see you this weekend when Gina arrives."

"You can call me Marilyn."

Carlos shook his head. A woman like Marilyn Smith deserved respect. Carlos walked away smiling.

Marilyn hesitated before walking into Dorothy Simmons' room. It was no secret about how Dorothy felt about Marilyn. No matter what Marilyn did, Dorothy did not cut her any slack.

"Hello Dorothy. I hear that you will be going home soon," Marilyn said. She wasn't overly friendly, just pleasant.

Dorothy turned to face Marilyn. It was hard for Dorothy to believe that Marilyn was a battered wife. The woman looked and behaved as if men had waited on her hand and foot. It was equally difficult for Dorothy to accept that Marilyn pulled the strings on getting the organ, especially after making things so hard for Marilyn and her daughter.

"I want to thank you for getting me that kidney," Dorothy said nervously. She practically owed Marilyn her life.

"This hospital has given a new definition to racism. You had worked too hard not to get that organ. I wasn't going to let it slip through the cracks."

"It's hard when you doing thangs by yourself. Carlos trying to be helpful."

"You gave him a scare. He didn't think it was going to turn out well. I had to remind him that you are a strong woman. Now he's relieved and happy."

"He didn't tell me that he was scared!"

"He didn't want to alarm you. He's fine now. He's making arrangements for your home healthcare."

"He probably won't get it right."

"Surprisingly, he just got through discussing it with me in the hall. Once you're released, everything should be in place."

"I'll believe it when I see it. Thangs would probably go better if'n I had girls."

"Don't be too sure about that! Sometimes girls can be just as questionable," Marilyn said softly, trying to make a connection with Dorothy. Marilyn didn't want any problems when Gina and the grandchildren arrived.

"Gina don't seem unstable to me," Dorothy said.

"She's not unstable, but we have our battles about things. Sometimes she listens and sometimes she doesn't. I decided to let go and let her do things her way."

"Ain't that the truth! Children never listen. It took Carlos being thirty-some-years-old to do something for himself. I tried talking him into it early. First, he thought I didn't want him to play ball. Then he thought I didn't want him to married Gina. I wanted him to do thangs with his life first and then settle down. Now he strugglin' and carin' on."

Marilyn had to be very careful in dissecting Dorothy's comment. The statement gave no credit to Gina who had done more to influence Carlos' direction than his mother. Marilyn decided to end the discussion before someone became offended.

"Experience can be the best teacher. It will make both of them stronger."

"Ain't that the truth!"

When Paul came home, Marilyn was sitting in the living room. She hardly sat there unless she had visitors. The scene alone made Paul stop and talk.

"How was work?" he asked.

Marilyn was not in the mood for small talk. She wasn't in the mood for condemnation either. She didn't want to discuss something that happened years ago. Debra Arvell had been dead for, what many people believed to be, years. When Barbara called after Lisa's wedding, the news was a blow to Marilyn. She didn't want to believe that Debra was alive the entire time, keeping a low profile. It wasn't until she, Barbara, JoAnn and Susan performed the last rites at Debra's funeral when they found out that she had lived many years after they believed she was dead.

"Carlos' mother should be home by this weekend. Gina and the children will be here as well," Marilyn said without looking at Paul.

"What's the matter?" Paul asked. It didn't take much for him to know that his wife was upset.

Marilyn debated whether or not to discuss the issue. Gina was upset and wanted answers. Marilyn convinced her to wait and discuss it face to face with Paul.

"Before Gina comes, I want to discuss something with you."

Paul searched Marilyn's face for an answer. She started a statement and left it hanging in the air for a couple of minutes. He decided to sit down beside her and listen patiently. He only hoped that Gina wasn't having marital problems. He gently took

Marilyn's hand.

"Gina received some documents in the mail. They were copies of court papers stating that you are the father of Debra's daughter."

Marilyn wanted her hand back but Paul would not release it. He could not believe what he had heard. Although Debra called him and sent him a letter stating he was the father to her daughter, he never believed it or at least he chose not to believe it.

"When did this happen?"

"What difference does it make? Are you that girl's father?" Marilyn asked with watered eyes. When she first asked Paul, he denied it and later claimed his brother Bill was the father. Marilyn wanted to give him another chance.

Paul gripped Marilyn's hand tighter. He had always hid his fears and hurts from Marilyn. Being the oldest of four, he was not allowed the freedom like Bill and his younger brother. Neither had responsibilities like him. Bill helped take care of their sister for a few years until she died. He didn't give up his dream of graduating from college like Paul did. Paul never forgave Bill for not helping with their mother. Later came the money. Bill never paid back the five thousand dollars he borrowed.

"I never received anything from the blood tests. How was I to know that I'm her father?"

"I want to ask one more time. Did you know that you were her father?"

The answer should have been easy, but Paul had to think. Debra never lied to him. The one time they had sex in school, she flat out told him that she liked his brother and that she expected Paul to buy one of her books for class if they were going to do it. She waited for the money before they did it. It was a business transaction. No other girl treated him that way.

When Paul met up with Debra later, again, she told the truth. She wasn't looking to settle down with a maintenance man. He would have to do better with his life. Once she saw that he was doing better, she said that she would consider marrying him. She treated him better too.

"I didn't want to believe it. She was having an affair with Bill at the same time. When I found out, I was hurt. My life was in shambles. I wanted to leave all bad memories behind."

"You let Bill care for that child all these years?"

Paul wanted to blurt out "yes." It was time that Bill took responsibility for something. Paul figured indirectly, he took care of Debra's daughter. He was always helping Bill.

"Me and Bill took care of the child." Paul released Marilyn's hand and began to exit the room.

"I know this is difficult for you, but Gina wants to discuss it with you too. When she asked you a few years ago, you denied it.

She wants to make sure you told the truth. Lisa is very special to her," Marilyn said in a shaky voice. Her daughter was upset. Marilyn had to convince Gina that she knew nothing about it. Things had gotten better between the two over the years.

"Gina and I will talk. I'll eat out," Paul said without looking at Marilyn.

"I've already cooked."

"I'll eat it tomorrow."

"You don't like leftovers."

Paul finally turned around. He could not determine the extent of Marilyn's concern.

"What I don't like is wondering why my wife is more concerned about my brother taking care of a child that he could have fathered too. I will eat leftovers if I have to."

Before Paul left the room, Marilyn said, "Bill and I have always been friends, nothing more."

"Bill had too many women friends," Paul said and left the room.

Chapter Twenty-Two

It was Sunday. Gina was on Interstate 70 West. She stopped in St. Louis to visit a few college friends and to spend Saturday night. Everyone came over Marie's house so that she could visit all at one time. As usual, Sidnee received all the attention. Avery kept quiet as the women fussed about how cute and smart Sidnee was. Gina slowly eased herself to Avery as he sat quietly.

"Momma, we there yet?" Sidnee asked.

Gina decided to ignore the question. It had been ten minutes since she had heard the same question. Gina hoped dearly that Sidnee would drift off to sleep. The little girl was wired up from the attention she had received earlier.

"Is daddy in Kan-City?"

"Baby, sing the Barney song for momma," Gina finally said. She had to hold her temper because she still had two hours to drive. Listening to the Barney song was even worse. Gina hated Barney.

Sidnee sang the Barney song. She added extra verses to help keep herself busy. The more she sang, the more Gina became irritated. She didn't understand what children saw in the purple dinosaur. He was big and stupid looking.

"It's your turn," Sidnee said to Gina. Instead of singing, Gina popped in a cassette. The car was filled with the sounds of Luther Vandross.

Gina felt a little guilty from ignoring Sidnee. The little girl talked entirely too much. Avery was nothing like her. He was hardheaded when he was Sidnee's age, but he didn't ramble half as much.

Soon Sidnee was asleep. Gina was able to concentrate on the trip. She would unload the luggage at her parents' house first. Next, she would talk to Paul. Gina rehearsed the opening statement for a week. Each time she said it, she became more nervous about what the answer would be. The other problem was trying to believe her mother. Gina wasn't settled on the answer she gave her. Gina knew that her mother and the rest of the group were angry with Debra Arvell.

The next thing that had Gina unsettled was Lisa coming to St. Louis for the baby shower. They had not talked in months. Gina was convinced that Lisa was the one who sent the documents. Although the package had a St. Louis post mark, she knew it was from her. The sorors were very excited about the shower because there had not been to a baby shower in two years.

It had been over four years since Gina's last visit to Kansas City. The city was becoming almost unfamiliar. After making the more familiar turns, she was driving up her parents' driveway. She saw her two brothers' cars. Everyone was expecting her but Carlos. He was probably at his mother's house.

Gina slowly got out the car. Before she could shut the door, Sidnee woke up. "We here?" she asked groggy.

Gina didn't say anything. She unsnapped Sidnee and removed her from the carseat. The little girl looked around strangely. All of a sudden, the front door opened and out walked Aaron and Ronnie. The smiled slightly as they approached the car. They were happy to see her, but they treated her at arms length. Because Gina was the oldest, she chastised them badly when they were growing up. She was more like a mother/sister.

"Hey Sidnee! You're getting big," Aaron said.

"Who you?" Sidnee asked.

"That's your Uncle Aaron," Gina answered. She gave the garment bag to Ronnie.

"Where's Avery?" Ronnie asked as he adjusted the garment bag on his shoulder.

Gina looked inside the car and saw Avery sitting, still pouting. "Come on out, Avery," Gina said.

Avery took his time getting out. He looked at his two uncles. They were tall but not big like his father. They seem different too. They seemed to have an interest in him.

"What's up Avery? Give me some," Aaron said and extended his fist.

Avery slowly took his fist and tapped Aaron's fist. "You want to meet your cousins?" Aaron continued. Avery nodded his head.

"Avery, stop nodding," Gina chastised. She handed a suitcase and carryon bag to Aaron. He took it obediently.

"You a mean momma! I bet you beat Avery everyday," Aaron said laughing. He looked at Avery and winked. Avery smiled a little.

"Boy, take my things in the house. How does it feel to be a father?" Gina asked Aaron.

His son was born two months ago. He and Ronnie had a son a piece. Both were married. Aaron recently married the girl who had his baby. They lived together a year before the baby was born. Two weeks ago, they said their vows in front of the Justice of the Peace. Gina missed Ronnie's wedding because she had just delivered Sidnee. It seemed that he held a grudge against Gina for not attending.

Aaron looked at Gina with a big grin. "It feels good. My boy looks just like me. He's got my nose, my eyes and my mouth," Aaron said as they walked up the steps.

"How's Katrina?"

"She's fine. She's losing the weight already."

"Don't make an issue about her weight! It takes time for a woman to lose weight after a baby."

"It didn't take Simone a long time to lose her weight," Ronnie said defensively.

Gina stopped and looked at the brother who caused her mother grief while she was in college. "Every woman is different. Simone was skinny from the beginning. She may not have a weight problem."

"You use to be skinny. What happened?" Ronnie continued. He was about to open the door when Gina stopped him.

"Don't start any trouble," Gina said slightly low. Ronnie knew not to push it and Aaron was ready to go inside. "What's your problem?" Gina demanded of him.

"I don't have a problem," Ronnie said defensively.

For the first time, Ronnie didn't wait for Gina to have the last word. He walked inside the house. The rest of the group followed behind.

Gina could smell food. It had been a long time since she had eaten her mother's cooking. She went into the kitchen followed by Sidnee and Avery. Ronnie's and Aaron's wives were in the kitchen with Marilyn.

"Hi momma," Gina said.

Marilyn smiled. It had been four years since she had seen her daughter and grandchildren. It was two months after Sidnee was born. "Hello Gina. Hello Avery," Marilyn said grinning her biggest grin. She extended her arms.

"Hi grandma," Avery said and hugged Marilyn.

Marilyn looked curiously at Sidnee. The little girl was the spitting image of Carlos. Sidnee returned the curious look. She leaned against Gina's leg.

"Well Miss Sidnee, I finally get a chance to see you again. Give your grandmother a hug," Marilyn said slightly uncomfortable.

She didn't understand her feelings. It was something about Sidnee that she could not connect with.

Sidnee continued to lean against Gina's leg. She looked around the kitchen.

"Sidnee, didn't you hear your grandmother? Give her a hug," Gina said, slightly surprised at Sidnee's behavior. Usually, the little girl had no problem socializing. She talked constantly.

Sidnee whined a little.

"I know you are not whining! I can't keep you quiet half the time and now you won't talk," Gina said. She was a little embarrassed.

"By the time she leaves, we'll be friends," Marilyn said with a smile.

Gina began chatting with her sister-in-laws and cooing her nephews. Sidnee kept behind her, not removing from her place at Gina's leg.

After Gina finished her conversation, she began helping Marilyn with dinner. The in-laws remained seated. Gina took the initiative and began giving assignments. The young women handed the children over to their fathers and assisted with dinner.

Before the food was placed on the table, Paul entered the room. He spoke to Gina and picked up Avery. Paul tickled Avery's stomach. Then Paul extended his arms to Sidnee. She didn't refuse, but she didn't move. Paul slowly picked her up and spoke softly to her. Sidnee finally said something.

The scene between Paul and Sidnee brought back old memories to Gina. He was a very gentle man and never raised his voice. If ever Paul was disappointed in them, the expression on his face was punishment enough. It didn't stop him from disciplining them. He had a way different than Marilyn.

Paul walked over to Gina with Sidnee in his arms. "She looks like you," he said. He put his arm around Gina. She wanted to cry. She had so many negative thoughts about Paul. After being in his arms, all bad thoughts had dissipated.

Gina smiled at Sidnee who had her fingers in her mouth. "Carlos says she looks like him," Gina said.

"In his dreams," Paul said. He put Sidnee down and looked at Gina. "You have a minute before dinner?"

It was time, Gina said to herself. All she wanted from Paul was for him to say that he didn't know about Lisa's birth. It would make everything right. She would call Lisa and they could talk.

As they walked into a room that Paul called his personal office, he became nervous. He wondered how to begin the conversation. Gina was the most difficult out of the three children to win over. And when he did, she was the most loving toward him. Ronnie had always longed for his real father and Aaron was just the baby.

They sat on the small sofa. Gina kept her focus on the floor. She refused to allow Paul to see her expression if the news was not what she wanted to hear.

"Your mother tells me that you received some documents in the mail, declaring me the father of Debra Arvell's daughter," Paul said bravely. He waited for Gina to respond. He wanted her to say whatever was bothering her, but she remained silent.

"I would like to hear how you feel. I know Debra's daughter is special to you."

"When I met Lisa, she was very defensive. She protected her feelings and hurts. Her mother pretty much neglected her and her father refused to acknowledge her. She searched a long time to find the mystery man. When she found Uncle Bill, she was angry but somewhat happy. All she ever wanted was a family."

"I was going to marry her mother at one time. When I found out that she was seeing Bill, I walked out of her life. I didn't want an explanation or to hear from her. She told me that she was pregnant but I didn't care because I didn't trust her."

Gina's heart was racing. She could not believe that Paul would abandon any child. All she could remember were times he proudly introduced them as his children.

"It's hard for me to hear that you walked away from your responsibility to Lisa and allowed Uncle Bill to take the blame. I don't know the man that you have just described. I don't think I want to know him either."

"If I'm honest with you, will you still be my little Gina-Weena?" Paul asked in a shaky voice. Saying "Gina-Weena" always brought a grin on Gina's face but not now.

"I want you to be honest with me," Gina said firmly.

"Will you still be my little Gina-Weena?"

"I will always be your little Gina-Weena, Paul!" Gina snapped. She had a strong suspicion about what Paul was about to say.

"When Debra told me that she was pregnant, I fought with the notion of marrying her and taking care of her and the child. When Bill told me later on that he had fathered Debra's child and needed money to give to her, I was relieved because I had ignored her. But deep down inside, I felt that the little girl was mine. I gave Bill a few thousand dollars to give to Debra. It sounded as if she was blackmailing him."

"If you felt that she was yours, then why didn't you take care of her?"

"When Debra approached your mother about the child..."

"Momma knew about Lisa?"

"Not the way you're putting it. Debra told Marilyn that I was the father of her child. Marilyn confronted me and I denied it. I told her that it was Bill's child and left it at that. When I was asked to give a blood test for paternity, I did. If it came back negative, I could stop feeling guilty. If it came back positive, I could act like I didn't know. In either case, I had the perfect excuse but I never received the results from the test."

Paul felt a sense of relief. He refused to tell Gina that Debra wrote him a letter after the test, telling him to honor his responsibility to their daughter. Guilt began to sink in. When Bill confided in him that he was secretly taking care of Debra's daughter, Paul allowed him to because Bill hardly ever stayed consistent with responsibilities. Paul was married to Marilyn and finally happy. He was slowly letting go of the anger against his brother for not coming home when their mother needed him.

"Are you going to tell Uncle Bill?" Gina asked, breaking Paul's concentration.

"We're going to talk."

Marilyn walked into the room. "Why don't you two talk later. Dinner is getting cold," she said and left the room. Gina and Paul removed themselves from the sofa and walked into the dining room.

Paul told everyone to join hands as he blessed the food. He thanked God for his family. He thanked God for an understanding wife. He thanked God for watching over his daughter and allowing her to grow into a strong independent woman. He thanked God for Bill.

The boys thought nothing of Paul's blessing. They thought he was happy to see Gina. She was always his favorite. Gina felt good thinking that Paul was thanking God for being a father to Lisa in his absence and Uncle Bill for being a guardian angel for her. Marilyn's heart sunk. She knew then that Paul knew the truth all the time.

Gina was in the family room watching television when Carlos came into the house. Avery was in the family room with Gina. Sidnee immediately ran to Carlos. He picked her up and showered her with kisses. She caught him up on everything from leaving Chicago to eating ham with cherries on top. Carlos enjoyed Sidnee's chatter.

When Carlos walked into the family room, Avery smiled at him. Carlos put Sidnee down and picked up Avery. He tossed Avery over his shoulder to hear him laugh. Carlos pretended to drop Avery. It always made him scream with joy.

After playing with Avery, Carlos approached the sofa. He leaned forward and kissed Gina slowly on the mouth. He rubbed the side of his face against her face. If the children weren't in the room, he would have touched her breasts. The thoughts alone made him feel warm inside.

"How is your mother?" Gina asked softly.

"She's at home resting. I thought about taking the kids over there later this evening," Carlos said. He stroked Gina's neck. When he felt her tighten, he asked, "What's the matter?"

"Besides missing you, nothing," she said seductively.

"Instead of getting that hotel room, I thought about tying momma up and sticking her in the closet. We can take care of things in my bedroom," Carlos whispered and sat down.

"Daddy, can we go to McDonalds?" Sidnee asked.

Gina whispered to Carlos, "Why don't we throw her in the closet with your mother."

Carlos smiled and put Sidnee on his lap. "You want to visit your Grandma Dorothy?" Sidnee nodded. Carlos put her down. He put his arm around Gina and played with her hair. He kissed her on the lips again. He could feel himself getting hard. He wondered where could he make love to his wife? They needed to be alone. He had something that he wanted to share with her.

"When are you visiting Carla?" Carlos asked.

"Probably tomorrow. I need to get some rest," Gina said with a yawn.

"Their house looks great! Dennis landscaped the yard and finished the basement."

"Carla says they're moving to a larger house. I thought their house was large enough for them."

"It is! They've got three bedrooms on the first floor and another bedroom in the basement. Dennis doesn't like the neighborhood anymore."

"Carla didn't say anything about it getting bad. Do they have gangs?"

"Dennis wants to keep a tight grip on Eric. He feels the neighborhood is influencing Eric's attitude."

"Carla hasn't complained about Eric's behavior. What's wrong?"

"It's not the neighborhood, it's Dennis. When I visited them, I noticed Dennis came down hard on Eric."

Just then, Avery walked over to the pair and asked Carlos to help him with a puzzle.

"Not now, Avery. Your mother and I are talking," Carlos said slightly irritated. Avery walked away and began putting together the puzzle.

"Anyway, Dennis either ignored Eric or gave him any and everything to do. Tyler, on the other hand, got away with murder, except when it came to Carla."

Sidnee approached them with a headless doll. She asked Carlos to put the head back on the body. Carlos sat her on his lap and began mashing the doll's head onto the neck. "Anything Tyler wanted, Dennis would have given it to her if Carla hadn't stepped in," Carlos said. He finished his task. He gave the doll back to

Sidnee and stood her on the floor.

"Tyler is something else," Carlos said and stretched. He looked at Gina and noticed she was frowning. Her arms were folded. "What's the matter?" he asked.

"So what you're saying is you and Dennis treat your children alike."

"Huh?"

"You and Dennis show favoritism toward girls."

"I don't show favoritism towards Sidnee!" Carlos said in surprised. Gina motioned him to lower his voice. He looked suspiciously at the children and then at Gina.

"I treat each child equally," Carlos said low. He could not believe Gina accused him of showing favorites.

"When Avery asked you to help him with the puzzle, you sent him away because we were talking. But when Sidnee brought over that damn doll that she's always beating up, you spent time with the little brat," Gina said low. Not once did she let her expression ease up.

"It's easier for Avery to play alone with the puzzle than for Sidnee to play with a headless doll," Carlos said breathless.

"You chose to give your time to Sidnee than to Avery."

"That's not true! Avery doesn't need a lot of attention."

"That's what you think. Have you wondered why he gets so angry at her?"

Carlos let out a huff. He wanted Gina to take back every word she had said. From her expression, his chances of winning the lottery were greater. "I don't show favorites when it comes to the children," he said, concentrating on each word.

"Okay. Get your butt off of this sofa and give equal time to each child."

Carlos shook his head, but Gina kept staring. He reluctantly dragged himself from the sofa and walked over to Avery who had six pieces of the dinosaur puzzle together. He was pondering over a puzzle piece until he saw Carlos lower his body next to him.

"I don't know where this piece go," Avery complained as he held up sharp teeth to Carlos' face.

"Let's see how this thing is suppose to look," Carlos said as he looked at the box. It was a Jurassic Park puzzle. Carlos couldn't imagine Avery liking something so scary. As he focused on the image of the T-Rex, Sidnee sat beside him and began picking up puzzle pieces.

"Put them down!" Avery shouted.

"I want to play," Sidnee said pouting.

"This is my puzzle!" Avery said loudly.

It had been a long time since Carlos spent time with the children. He didn't know how to diffuse the disagreement. He looked at Gina who refused to acknowledge his presence. Carlos let out a deep breath and said very softly, "Sidnee, why don't you play with your doll and let Avery have his puzzle pieces."

"I don't want to play with her. Her head's broke," Sidnee whimpered. She held the puzzle pieces hostaged in her lap.

Carlos looked at the doll that was headless again. "Sidnee, how did you take her head off? I just got through fixing it," he said with his voice rising. He picked up the doll.

Sidnee's eyes swelled with tears. Her chest began to expand noticeably. She began to sniff. Then her lips turned down and the tears began to fall.

"Come on, Sidnee. Don't cry," Carlos said heart broken.

"I don't have nothing to play with," Sidnee said as she rubbed her fists into her tear filled eyes.

"It's 'I don't have anything to play with'," Avery taunted. Sidnee cried harder.

"That's enough, Avery," Carlos said sternly. "Come on, Sidnee. Give daddy the puzzle," Carlos said and extended his hand.

Sidnee slowly handed over the pieces and cried harder. She buried her face into the carpet. Carlos thought it was foolish to make a big deal over a puzzle. He was about to suggest that they play together until he saw the expression on Gina's face.

"Sidnee, if you stop crying, daddy will buy you some ice cream," Carlos counter-offered sweetly.

"Oh no you won't! Sidnee, get up," Gina said firmly. Sidnee didn't move, but the volume of her bawling lower. "Sidnee did you hear me?" Gina asked firmly. Carlos became a little nervous. He had only seen Gina spank Sidnee once and an argument followed afterwards.

"I am going to count to three," Gina said forcefully. Sidnee took her time removing herself from the floor. She continued to cry dry tears.

"Gina, why don't we..." Carlos was interrupted by Gina's stern expression.

"Why don't we what?" Gina snapped.

Carlos decided to release the request and finish putting together the T-Rex. It was simpler. He saw Gina walking Sidnee out of the room.

"Look daddy!" Avery said and showed Carlos the teeth to the T-Rex. Avery placed it next to the piece Carlos had just put down. Carlos let the excitement on Avery's face replace the sadness on Sidnee's face.

Carlos gathered the children and packed them into the car. Gina walked them out to the car. "I'll visit your mother later this week," Gina said.

"Take your time. I don't want you to feel forced."

"You really have missed me! Are you staying at your

mother's?"

Carlos nodded reluctantly. He had to stay with his mother until she got better. Maybe he would be able to go back to Chicago the same time with Gina. The last time they were apart for more than a few days, they were separated, contemplating divorce.

Carlos gave Gina a quick kiss and got into the car. He backed the car down the driveway and onto the street. He gave Gina a wave and drove off.

Gina walked into the house sluggishly. She was exhausted. She wanted to stretch out on her old bed with Carlos beside her. Something about the trip home made her want to move back to Kansas City. Although Kansas City was smaller than Chicago, she began to consider raising her children in a safer environment. The gangs in Chicago were getting worse. It was getting to the point that the once quiet neighborhood they lived in was getting dangerous.

"Why don't you lie down for a while?" Marilyn said.

"I could use some rest before the kids get back."

"A mother's job is never done. She's on duty twenty-four hours a day. She dreams about her children in her sleep."

"I wasn't prepared for this. Avery is stubborn. Spanking him doesn't get the results I'm looking for. And Sidnee is another story. Carlos has spoiled her rotten. She wants my attention all of the time."

"No woman is truly prepared for motherhood. Each child is different. You have to try different methods until you're successful."

"How do I know that I'm successful at this time? They keep my nerves in knots!"

"Paul told me that I had done a good job with you all at the time we had married. I looked at him as if he didn't have any brains. He said that I had worked double-overtime on two shifts for too many years and now I needed help."

"Momma, children were different then."

"Oh? You had a smart mouth and Ronnie was stubborn. Spanking you didn't get the results I was looking for and punishing Ronnie was useless. Paul had another way of handling problems. He helped a great deal."

They were in the family room. Gina began picking up toys. Marilyn began helping on instinct.

"How are you holding up financially?" Marilyn asked.

Gina wouldn't look at her mother or answer the question. She continued with the chore of cleaning.

"I prefer if you told me it's none of my business instead of ignoring me. I can't wait until Sidnee does the same thing to you."

"I don't like talking about money. We are living as tight as we can. Carlos and I appreciate your help with Avery's school. He's really learning a lot without the stress the other children in our neighborhood are experiencing."

"Once Carlos finishes, it will get better. He tells me that he has another year. Twelve months is not a long time. It will ease up."

"Avery needs Carlos now. His attitude can change drastically by then."

"The children can stay here for the summer so that you can get a breather."

"I have everything under control!"

"My sisters and I use to visit my grandmother for the summer. Although we chopped cotton and worked like hell, I realized later that it gave my mother a rest. It's time for black women to stop being super women. We need help."

"We didn't stay with grandmomma for the summer! You dealt with us all of the time."

"Your grandmother was willing, but I wasn't. The Black Power movement changed my life forever. My views about religion had changed. I didn't believe in staying in church all day long or everyday of the week. Therefore, sending you to your grandmother was not an option. I didn't give my mother the chance to be like Big Momma and I didn't get the relief like my mother got."

"Momma, I don't know about Sidnee staying here for the summer. She's shy."

"Sidnee will be alright. If it gets too difficult, I'll send her home. I know you are concerned about your baby, but I'm concerned about my baby now."

Marilyn saw Gina wipe her eyes as she searched the room for more toys. She had put them all away. There was nothing more to distract her from facing her mother, so she continued wiping her eyes.

"This may sound like a stupid question, but do you need money?"

"Carlos will have a fit if I took money from you."

"A woman's pride is different from a man's. We know how to make things right. You will save on daycare costs this summer, so it's...an excuse."

Gina saw another side of her mother, a schemer. Marilyn had presented herself as a strong woman for so many years. She never behaved as if she needed anything from anybody. Gina remembered heated discussions between her mother and Aunt Barbara about Marilyn having a strong, dominating personality. According to Aunt Barbara, if Marilyn kept it up, Gina would never find a husband. According to her mother, Gina didn't need a husband.

"Momma, this doesn't sound like you."

"I tried to keep you from making the same mistakes that I

have made. I wanted you to take advantage of the power women should have. I have to understand that you are different than me. A husband is very important to you."

"I can live without a husband," Gina said defensively. Her mother's comment caught her off guard.

"I know you can but a husband is important. You understand that better than I did at your age. Women can do everything by ourselves, all alone. The question is: Should we? No, because we need help," Marilyn said on her soap box.

For the first time ever, Gina and Marilyn were girlfriends.

"I didn't bring a lot of clothes for the kids," Gina said.

"Sidnee seems like a shopper. I can break the ice by taking her shopping when the time comes."

Gina smiled at the thought of her mother and Sidnee shopping. Gina and Marilyn never had a *girl's* day out. "Ronnie seems to have an attitude. What's wrong?"

Marilyn had to clear her throat. Gina did not understand that Ronnie was angry at her for not attending his wedding. "Why don't you ask him?"

"I did but he didn't say anything."

"He's a little angry that you didn't come to his wedding."

Gina paused. She was surprised. She had just delivered Sidnee. Ronnie should have understood. "I couldn't come. I had just delivered Sidnee."

"I know."

"I can't believe he's mad! Aaron never made an issue of me not being at his wedding."

"Ronnie has always held you in a high position. He understands, but he's just angry that you couldn't come."

"That's plain stupid!"

"The problem is, you never apologized for not coming nor did you talk to him about it. You just assumed that it was okay by sending a gift."

"Why should I apologize for having a baby? He should understand that."

"I never understood why you were so angry at me for so many years. You should have understood that I had to work so that you could live in a decent house and go to a good school."

"Momma, that's different. We hardly talked nor did we do things together."

"When I came home from taking care of sick people, I couldn't talk. I walked the floors and gave more than one-hundred percent. I gave sick people more of me than my own children. I felt guilty, but I knew my children understood that it couldn't be helped."

Gina was silent. She remembered Marilyn coming home exhausted. All she wanted to do was eat and go to bed. Only when Gina became a mother did she fully understand. Gina nodded. "I'll talk to him."

"Good. He only wants to hear you say that you would have come but you couldn't."

Paul entered the room. He was smoking a pipe. He looked at Gina nervously and asked, "Do you think Lisa wants to meet me?"

What a stupid question, Gina thought. Of course Lisa wanted to meet him. She's been searching for him all of her life. For some reason, Gina became jealous. Was it because Paul had a blood daughter or because Lisa offered competition now?

"She's expecting a baby soon. You are about to be a grandfather," Gina said, trying to sound agreeable.

"I'm already a grandfather. I have three tough grandsons and one beautiful granddaughter," Paul said.

"Okay, you have experience. But this baby is going to be your *real* grandbaby."

"Ronnie, Jr., Aaron, Jr., Avery and Sidnee *are* my real grandchildren. I can add three more to the bunch, if you and Carlos are willing," Paul said, instantly picking up on Gina's discomfort.

Gina laughed. "We have given you enough grandchildren. I'll let the younger ones fill up the house."

Carlos made it back with Avery and Sidnee. The children ran into the family room. They were happy.

"Momma, Momma, Grandma Dorothy sick," Sidnee announced.

"Daddy's gonna take me to play basketball," Avery added.

"Now your grandfather can really play basketball. I averaged thirty points per game in college," Paul bragged.

"You bragging about thirty points in college? I averaged thirty-five in high school," Carlos said and tossed his hands into the air as if making a basket.

"How was your free throw? If it was below eighty, don't talk," Paul said and took a puff from his pipe.

"Seventy-five was my lowest! I heard about your games at Lincoln. Why didn't you go pro? You sounded better than the Good Doctor."

"Nobody was scouting at Lincoln. And besides, basketball served its purpose in college."

Carlos agreed in silence. He could have had an opportunity at UCLA and probably could have gone pro. Then he thought about what his mother said. He was needed somewhere else. He probably may not have been the man he had turned out to be.

Avery looked in awe at his father and grandfather. They were better than Michael Jordan and probably better than Scottie Pippen.

Chapter Twenty-Three

Linda sat in a gown on Indie's bed until she fell asleep. It wasn't usually necessary because Indie went to bed early and woke up early. The daycare report for the day stated that Indie was not as active as usual. She hung close to the teacher. The instructor believed that Indie wasn't feeling well. Since the addition of five teacher's aides, thanks to Zeta Chi, Indie received an abundance of attention. Because she was not shy or selective, it was easy for the young women to woo over Linda's daughter.

When Linda picked up Indie from the daycare, she was a little sluggish. She picked at her dinner and she whined during the evening. Linda gave her children's Tylenol and a bath. When Linda put her in bed, she wanted to sit in Linda's lap. The behavior was unusual because Indie was very independent.

Linda went into the study and began to go over her to-do list. She rubbed her eyes. She had been running nonstop for four weeks. She was burnt out from mailing campaign information and checking on the younger women and their efforts to save the chapter. All reports seemed to be good except for Marilyn's. There was a problem. One girl did not show or call.

The conference was days away. All eyes were on Kansas City. For the first time in years, five past chapter presidents were going to be in attendance. Kansas City Alumni was the hosting chapter. Lee Summit tried it's best to participate as hostess, but the older women had it wrapped up before the chapter split. Linda was responsible for organizing the President's reception. The menu was set. Linda went through the ordeal to get Melanie to make seven garments that the younger women could wear for the occasion.

Everything went into working with the younger women to save the chapter. Linda stopped visiting the list of contacts to focus on Zeta Chi. She felt a stronger responsibility to the young women who now depended on her. At this time, being regional director was being shoved to the rear. She was being bombarded with calls from younger sorors of Zeta Chi. Some called just to talk. Linda thought back to her college years. She would have never given anyone, outside her circle of friends, the time of day.

Keith walked into the study. He had come home thirty minutes earlier than expected from delivering a baby. "How's Indie?" he asked.

"She finally went to sleep. She acted like a big baby."

"Sweetheart, she's a baby."

"She wanted to sit in my lap until she fell asleep. She hardly does that."

"Is she running a fever?"

"No, I gave her some Tylenol anyway."

"How's the campaign coming?"

"It's harder than I thought. Some people are easy to talk to but others are difficult to penetrate. I think Lori can do a better job at working with people like them. I heard she has the support of some of the women I have visited."

"Are you giving up?"

"I'm being realistic. Aunt Birdie has given me tips on being diplomatic but sometimes I don't care about some of the complaints."

"What are the complaints?"

"Everything from not being heard to not enough attention to black women issues. I can't solve every problem."

"You're not suppose to. Do what you feel is important. Don't make promises that you don't intend to keep. By all means, take note of the issues you have been campaigning on and keep reiterating. You are standing for a particular issue. Don't stray from it to win votes."

Linda was about to get up from the sofa when Keith stopped her. He pulled her very close to him. He kissed her on the ear. Linda blew air.

"Everyone gets a little of you and I can't have any," Keith said very softly.

"I'm just tired."

"I know you are but I'm wondering if you are tired of me."

Linda looked surprised at Keith. "What are you talking about?"

"I think you know what I'm talking about. It's been weeks or shall I say months."

"It's not you. It's been me."

"A man knows when his wife is not interested anymore."

"Keith, you should know that I love you."

"You're right. I should know, but I don't. I'll leave you to your planning." Keith walked out of the room. Linda looked in amazement. She never imagined having a conversation as the one that had just ended. Any other time, she would let a conversation of misunderstanding go. Usually, Keith allowed her to have her way. Not now. He left the room without saying they would discuss it later. Linda decided to finish the conversation.

When Linda entered the bedroom, she saw the bear from the carousel on the night stand. She didn't know how it got there. It was usually in her purse. Lauren harassed her so much about keeping it with her that Linda felt the only way to ease the little girl's discomfort was to put it in her purse. Why was it out? She didn't have a clue. None of the children had ever ventured into her purse.

"Keith, you want to talk about it?"

"I don't know what I should talk about. I think I've made my point clear."

Linda sat on the bed. She saw Keith turn on his side. "Don't turn your back to me," she said. Keith hesitantly turned back around and sat up. His expression was not understanding. He looked is if she had disturbed his rest.

"What is it that keeps you arms length from your family?" he asked.

"I'm not arms length from my family. I've been attentive to everyone's need."

"Being a wife and a mother is a job, but it should not be performed only as needed. It should be something that you breath and sleep."

Linda became angry. Never had anyone questioned her actions in either role. "I am not a robot. I love my children! And how dare you say that?"

"Because these roles are difficult for you. You are complaining that Indie acted like a baby. My God, she is a baby! Since Camille died, everything has become difficult. Why are you running for regional director? What is it that you're looking for?"

Linda turned away swiftly. She struggled to get out of bed. Keith grabbed her arm. She jerked her arm hard, frowning at him as she struggled.

"It wasn't your fault. Camille died from a common death that afflicts children her age. There was nothing you could do."

"Let me go Keith!" Linda yelled.

"If you want me and the children out of your life, you are going to have to leave. I will not let you ignore us in our presence."

Linda's struggle became less. Keith refused to let her arm go.

"How dare you tell me that I don't love my children?" Linda

said hoarsely. She looked at the little bear as it grinned at her.

"I didn't say you didn't love the children. You are afraid of losing them. Your mother told me that she felt the same way when she lost the twin. She always wished that she was more attentive to your needs as you grew. It was easier to give you what was enough, not what was needed. I want our children to get what is needed."

Keith fought hard to keep his emotions under control. He didn't have to fight with Linda anymore. She relinquished the battle.

"I want to see you kiss Indie. I want to see you embrace Edward. I want you to make love to me again."

"I can't!" Linda cried.

"Yes you can. They are your flesh and blood and I've been your friend since age eighteen. I've taken a lot of your bratty behavior and I've loved every minute of it. All I want from you is to try."

Linda was limp in Keith's arm. She was thinking about Indie being sick. She was an active little girl, even when she had a cold. Then the thought of Camille came to her. The baby smiled at her when she waved bye-bye on her way out the door. Camille usually giggled when Linda wave bye-bye. That night, Camille just smiled. It dawned on her that Camille's behavior was different that night. Her mother's friends told her that she would know if something was wrong with her child. It took close to six years after Camille's death to understand that something was different about her child.

Camille's death was a struggle for everyone. Barbara began drinking again, Linda quit her job and Keith worked long hours to forget his little girl that was the victim to SIDs. He often felt guilty that maybe he ignored his wife in the process. Everything seemed fine when Edward Steven Reed was born.

"It's my fault for ignoring you after Camille's death. I used the hospital to escape. I didn't know what to offer you after she died. I should have been there to help you through it instead of believing you were fine," Keith said.

"I am fine. I need to check on Indie," Linda said between tears.

"She's fine. It's probably a virus that's going around the daycare," Keith said. He cuddled Linda in his arms. He kissed the top of her head. He knew if he continued to focus his attention on her, he would not be able to stop himself. Tonight, he wasn't able to draw back if she said no. He slipped under the covers with her in his arms. He squeezed her tight.

"I'm okay, Keith."

"You might be okay, but I'm not. I need attention, appreciation...love. I know sex, by itself, isn't love, but it's an indication that you're still interested," Keith said with pleading eyes.

"I will always love you," Linda responded.

"If I I touch you like this, will you kiss me on the forehead," Keith said as he lightly ran his fingers up Linda's back. She smiled and Keith did it again. Linda kissed him on the forehead.

"If I touch you like this, will you kiss me on the cheek," Keith said softly as he took the back of his hand and caressed Linda's stomach. She lightly kissed him on the cheek.

"If I kissed you right here," Keith said and nibbled down Linda's chest to her breast, "will you make love to me." Keith nibbled lightly on Linda's nipples. He could feel her relax in his arms. He carefully scooted her underneath him. He stopped nibbling and looked down at her. "If you tell me to stop, I won't take you to Aruba," Keith said with the left side of his mouth rising to a grin.

Linda touched the side of his face. His light beard tickled her hand. She took her pointer finger and lowered his bottom lip. Then she took her finger and slipped it under his chin. She brought his face to hers and kissed him.

Keith pecked lightly on Linda's face. He watched as she closed her eyes. He raised her gown over her hips and stroked the inside of her thighs. Linda released a deep sigh. Keith stretched over Linda. He whispered in her ear, "If you want to run for regional director then give it your best shot. Do it because you want to. Your mother doesn't care one way or the other. You have her respect."

Keith lowered his body. He could feel Linda receiving him. He could sense he had his wife's attention. He felt in control over the moment. It was a matter of taking off work to go to Aruba. He had promised her two years ago. Maybe after the conference. It would serve as a treat especially if the election turned out to be what she was feeling.

Linda struggled to get out of bed. Keith allowed her to sleep in, but she couldn't. She had a full day ahead of her. She thought about staying home with Indie. Little Edward was at her mother's so Linda's concentration was on Indie.

Linda put on a robe and walked into the kitchen. Keith was cooking breakfast. He gave her a kiss on the cheek and turned over a pancake.

"Where's Indie?" Linda asked.

"She's still sleeping," Keith answered.

Linda knew instantly that something was wrong. She left the kitchen immediately and rushed into Indie's room. The little girl was asleep. Linda's hand shook as she touched Indie. The little girl was burning with fever.

"Keith!" Linda shouted.

Indie woke up. She was listless. She reached her arms toward

Linda and whined. Linda instinctively picked her up. Indie felt like fire.

Keith rushed into the room. He looked worried.

"She has a fever!" Linda rushed to say.

"Calm down. She's going to be fine," Keith said and picked up Indie. She refused to look at him. She whined for Linda.

"I'm taking her to the emergency room," Linda said. She took Indie out of Keith's arms.

Before she could take Indie out of the room, Keith stopped her. "Take her temperature; give her some more Tylenol and sponge her down. If her fever doesn't break, then take her to the doctor," Keith said.

"What? The doctor? She needs to go to the hospital," Linda said.

Keith knew that Linda wasn't thinking. She had nursed the children through colds and fevers when they were cutting teeth. Their children were in good health. But, it wasn't winter and they weren't cutting teeth. The scene was new to Linda.

"Please listen to me. She's going to be fine. Give her Tylenol, sponge her down and give her some juice. If that doesn't work, then we will take her to the hospital," Keith relented.

"Boo-boo, mommie," Indie cried.

Linda rushed Indie to the bathroom and sat her on the toilet stool. It was obvious that Indie had diarrhea. She cried as she held the sides of the stool.

"Indie, be a big girl for mommie," Linda said.

"Remember, she's a little girl," Keith said.

"Keith, please!"

Keith left the bathroom. He continued with breakfast. A few minutes later, he heard water running in the tub. He then heard the medicine cabinet door shut. He felt a small victory.

Thirty minutes later, Linda appeared with Indie in her arms. Indie kept her head on Linda's shoulder.

"Give her to me so that you can eat," Keith said.

"I'm not hungry."

"I hope it's not because of my cooking."

Linda went to the refrigerator and took out a bottle of cranberry juice. She poured some in Indie's favorite cup. Linda sat down with Indie and offered the cup. Indie turned her head. Linda waited until Indie turned her head around and put the cup to her mouth. Indie took a drink and rested her head on Linda's chest.

Keith got up to answer the ringing telephone. He brought the cordless phone to Linda. Melanie was on the line.

"I wanted to let you know the last dress is finished. I didn't realize how much I missed designing. The girls look great in them," Melanie said.

"Thanks for pitching in."

"The only problem I had was getting the last girl's fitting in. I'm working with Carlos on his basketball tournament. He has really come a long way. He is much more relaxed and patient now. He's talking about moving back to Kansas City."

"I doubt very seriously if Gina would consider moving back. She's in a position at International Foods with flexibility."

"Carlos seems to think she will go for it. By the way, she's in town. She wants to come by to visit you."

"Tell that hussy to call me. How dare she come to town and not tell me? Have you seen her?"

"Not yet. When Aunt Barbara called Aunt Marilyn, Gina answered the phone. Even Aunt Barbara fussed at her."

"Mother has been driving me crazy about the open forum. I can't seem to concentrate on campaigning anymore. I heard that a few chapters from mother's contacts are supporting Lori. She didn't bother to visit them like I did."

"I hear you're doing well with the undergraduates. They count as votes."

"I've hardly done anything with the undergraduates. How did you hear that?"

"Zeta Chi has become popular with many undergraduate chapters. They attend step-shows to support other undergraduate sorors. When they give their big weekend party, they usually receive a large turnout from other chapters. I think they have been doing a little campaigning on the side."

Linda paused. Then she smiled a little. Indie looked at her and returned the smile. She thought Linda was smiling at her. Linda smacked a kiss on Indie's forehead.

"Are you still there?" Melanie asked.

"Yes. My baby-poo is sick."

"What's wrong with her?"

"Keith said some kid at the daycare gave her a virus. He should know. He's a doctor," Linda said and winked at Keith.

Keith stopped eating. He told Linda that it was possible that a child at the daycare could have passed a virus. Linda only listened to her mother when the children had colds or were teething.

"I talked to David two days ago. The gold tooth-buster came through," Melanie said.

"Have you seen Tosha?"

"No, but David said she smiled constantly after looking at her new cap. He felt good about helping the little darling so he's donating the cost to charity."

"I haven't seen David since Jennifer's funeral. How is he?"

"He's getting married in September. Don't worry, you will get an invitation."

"How is the divorce coming along?"

"I thought it would be easy because I want to get rid of John as soon as I can but it's not. We are scheduled to go to court in two weeks. He wants to make sure he protects his assets, as if I want anything from him."

"Is Lauren doing okay with Lionel?"

"She couldn't be happier. Like a typical man, she spends her time with his mother. He's sending her home for a week because he has to travel. I thought about letting her stay with his mother, but I really miss her."

"How is Mother? Is she sticking to her diet?"

"She has been a busy body lately. She's very excited about the conference."

"It's only a conference. She acts as if it's the convention."

"If mom were alive, I know she would be happy if I were running for Regional Director. Aunt Barbara wants to see you walk away a winner."

"I don't think I'm going to win."

"Your spread in the quarterly was fantastic. The quote from the mayor was awesome. Even Lori is sweating. She didn't think you would come out fighting. That is why she is working harder with the older women."

"That's why some of them are supporting her."

"Where did you hear that from?"

"Mrs. Massey and Mrs. Bircher told me that they heard she made contact with some of the sorors of alumnaes that I had visited. The women said that they were impressed with her."

"What does being impressed with someone have to do with votes?"

"Would you vote for someone that you were impressed with?"

"Those same women were impressed with you. I say it's an equal battle. Make sure you visit the undergraduates' step-show. Your presence is going to be important. Aunt Barbara is having a Bridge party. She wants you to drop by. You don't have to stay long. She wants her other-side-of-the-tracks friends to meet you. To my understanding, they were a secret society. They only come together when one needs help."

"Are they gutter women? I didn't think mother knew any."

"They call themselves The Other Side of the Tracks friends. It's twelve of them. They were all poor women who worked hard to pledge Kappa. They always held on to the one thing they enjoyed as a whole."

"And what is that?"

"I don't know. She won't tell me. I think it has something to do with cards. She says that when one needs help, they always have a Bridge party."

"I have never seen mother play cards and I don't think she

knows how to play Bridge. What in the world is she doing?"

"I don't know. It must be some sort of party. All of them are coming. Matter of fact, some are members of alumnaes in the central region.

"Some of mother's contacts turned out to be a bust. I don't think they have the pull like mother think they do."

"So you think Aunt Barbara is an old bitch who has lost her step?"

"What?"

"I wasn't going to say anything, but Lori called Aunt Barbara an old bitch who has lost her step."

"She called my mother a bitch who has lost her step?"

"No, an old bitch, with gray hair and a cane, who has lost her step."

Linda paused for a second. Indie reached for the cup of juice. Linda handed it to her, but Indie wanted Linda to feed it to her. Linda sighed and held the cup for Indie.

"When and what time does mother want me to stop by?" Linda asked.

"Friday night around eight. You can go to the step-show early to meet the sorors and then stop by the house."

Linda was finished talking. She handed the phone to Keith. She watched how Indie became a baby again. She behaved helpless which was unusual for her. She always wanted to do things for herself.

"If you don't mind, could you make reservations to Aruba near the end of August. It should give me time to reroute my patients," Keith said and kissed Indie on the forehead. The telephone rang again. Keith answered it. It was Gina. Keith handed the phone to Linda and kissed her on the lips. She smiled at him as he left the room.

Chapter Twenty-Four

Linda and Melanie were at Bartles Hall. They saw dozens of young women standing outside the building with Phi Kappa Psi T-shirts. Linda had to relax. She hated crowds. She hardly attended dances while in college. She barely attended the ones the Kappas gave.

The two women walked inside the building. Many more young women and men were inside talking very loud.

"We're suppose to meet Tosha and Shontay near the entrance," Melanie said.

"Is Lori coming too?"

"I heard that she wasn't but she knows that you're coming."

"How did she know that?"

"I believe someone from the old chapter told her."

"Why would they do that?"

"She was trying to get tickets to the President's reception. As she talked about the conference schedule, someone shared information about you being at the step-show."

Linda did not know how to take the information. It appeared that no one from the old chapter would water her chances at winning. Melanie's next statement caught her off guard.

"After talking to several undergraduates, they think the graduate fees are too high. You have a remedy?"

Linda had to think for a few seconds. After working in the health fairs, if people didn't get something free, they wanted another alternative.

"Maybe fees for those coming out of college can be paid in installments for the first three years after college. It can give them an opportunity to participate and not be stressed by the cost. By age twenty-five, they should be able to get a fairly decent job and pay the fees like everyone else."

"It's an excellent idea. One more thing, be as comfortable with them as possible. They also think older sorors treat them like children."

"Most of them are!"

"I know but try and act like they aren't. Just don't get too relaxed with them. A certain level of respect has to be present."

"I can't relax now, so I doubt if I will call any of them *girlfriend*."

A large group of girls approached them. Linda gave a genuine smile when she saw Tosha smiling. The young woman was already attractive and the removal of the gold tooth gave her a softer look.

"Hi Linda and Melanie. I want y'all to meet some sorors from UMKC, KU, Mizzou, Rolla, UMSL and Lincoln," Tosha said. She would not stop smiling.

Melanie and Linda spoke to the young women. Linda surveyed the girls and relaxed immediately. They had conservative hairstyles and wore pearl earrings.

"Are you ladies ready to step?" Linda asked.

"I don't know about the sorors from Mizzou but Lincoln is ready," one girl said.

The group began to disagree softly about who were better steppers. As Linda and Melanie enjoyed the exchange of opinions, Shontay came with more girls. She introduced the other girls to Linda and Melanie. They were from the University of Chicago, Drake University, University of Iowa, Ohio State, Oklahoma State and Indiana State. The young women were not as conservative as the others, but there weren't a lot of wild hairstyles or exposed bodies. The young women were just as nice as the other ones.

"I haven't seen a good step-show since I left college. It will be interesting to see the new styles of performance," Linda said.

"Are you staying for the whole show?" Tosha asked.

"I have to leave before ten o'clock. I need to pick up my daughter," Linda answered.

"You should see her little girl. She is so cute. I want a little girl just like her," a girl from Zeta Chi said.

"Make sure you are ready. My daughter takes up a lot of my time. My husband helps a great deal. It's good to have a spouse to help you because children can get on your nerves," Linda said in a joking as well as parental way.

"I'm studying to be a pediatrician. I don't have time to think about children or a husband," one girl said.

"I'm waiting until I'm thirty. By that time, my business should be established," another one said.

"What kind of business do you want?" Linda asked.

"I want my own marketing consulting firm."

"Don't get discouraged if it takes longer than age thirty. Some businesses take more time to get established. Don't lose focus on that dream either. I have always wanted my own catering business. Now since I'm a mother, it will take a little more time."

"She's catering the President's reception. We're in it!" a girl from Zeta Chi shouted.

"You should see the dresses Melanie designed for us. They are in there!" another Zeta Chi member said.

"Melanie is a fashion designer. You should see her portfolio. I hope someday, she will go back to designing. Some popular dresses I see today are similar to what she designed when she was in college," Linda shared.

All of the girls looked at her. They made requests for dresses for next year's balls. Melanie discreetly looked at Linda with disapproval. Linda ignored her playfully like she had done when they were in high school flirting with boys. If a boy wanted Melanie's attention, she tried making excuses to leave but Linda ignored her.

"If any of you are getting married soon, Linda can do your reception for a reasonable cost," Melanie said. She refused to look at Linda who was about to faint because the girls' attention were on her.

"Melanie and I play like this. I'm not cheap, ladies," Linda said.

Surprisingly, the girls laughed, but still asked questions. She eventually turned the conversation around to campaigning.

"Is everyone considering going active after college?" Linda asked.

Some girls mumbled about the fees, some complained about lack of respect for their ages and others commented about not feeling welcomed. The last comment caught Linda by surprise.

"Why do you feel that way?" Linda asked one of the girls.

"No one ever talks to us. We can't get national officials, regional directors, or national officers to come to founders' day activities at our school."

"Have you ever invited them within a reasonable time?" Linda continued.

"One time, we wrote nationals a year early and asked for a representative to come to our school."

Other Kappas came to the crowd that had formed around Linda. They came to see what was happening. When they heard that Linda Reed, a campaign candidate, was present, they hung around.

"We have gotten representation from nationals, but the older sorors always talk down to us," one said.

"Nationals only go to large universities. Although we are a small school, we should still be looked at like the alumnaes or larger schools."

"There is no excuse for being ignored. I hope you understand that the regional representative position was created to put into place someone, with similar interests, who could hear your concerns and take them back to nationals."

"Is it possible to get a national official to come to Drake University?"

Linda wanted to tell the girl the truth. With the hundreds of chapters the sorority had, it was impossible for nationals to make an appearance at every chapter upon demand.

"I suggest before everyone goes back to their chapters, exchange numbers. It would be easier for each state to request nationals presence instead of each chapter. All undergraduate chapters in Missouri should ask that a national representative meet at, uh, Drake University. Make sure you have a working agenda for the person who is coming to meet with you. You will be surprised that working together as a united body brings about better results than standing alone as a chapter. Remember, we are all sisters," Linda preached.

Melanie smiled as her friend caught the attention of the younger women. They nodded in agreement as Linda spoke.

A girl stepped close to Linda. "Hello Mrs. Reed, my name is Jessica Patterson. I'm running for regional representative."

The girl's appearance took Linda's breath away. She was very brown with long hair. She wasn't fat but she wasn't thin. She seemed fairly shy. The girl reminded her of Jennifer. It took a few seconds before Linda could speak.

"Ms. Patterson, were you listening to the concerns mentioned?" Linda asked.

"Yes ma'am. I agree with you, but the regional representative doesn't have a lot of money to travel. Also, school work has to be considered too. I was hoping that a recommendation for a travel budget, outside of traveling to nationals, be considered."

Linda found herself wanting to be connected with the young woman. She wanted everyone to see them as a team.

"Ms. Patterson, a budget that you mentioned will mean an increase in fees. Are you ladies willing to pay more for what Ms. Patterson has recommended?"

Most of the girls agreed. As they talked about the recommendation, the conversation steered to problems with school. Some universities threaten to suspend chapters on little grounds of abuse. Shontay shared how Linda was helping to save Zeta Chi from suspension. They bombarded her with questions. Not once did Linda say she wanted the girls' vote.

Melanie saw Lori first. Melanie had to gather her composure

because now it was obvious whom she supported. As Lori and three women approached the crowd, Melanie stepped closer to Linda. They made eye contact with each other and then stared face to face with Lori.

Linda had a mischievous grin. It wasn't difficult squaring off with Lori when it came to presence. It was only difficult in campaigning. Lori was smart and cunning.

When Melanie looked at Lori, there was no smile. She stared at the person who embarrassed her in front of people who respected her. Melanie's expression was filled with malice. Her look made Lori look away.

"Hello ladies. My name is Lori Bass-Collins. I'm running for regional director. How is everyone?" Lori said cheerfully.

The girls spoke low as they greeted Lori. The tone of Lori's voice sounded rehearsed. Her smile was plastered on her face. She looked over them and not at them.

"I thought I would stop by to see some good stepping. What schools do we have represented?" Lori continued cheerfully.

A few girls shouted out their schools.

"Well alright for UMKC and KU!" Lori said like a cheerleader.

The doors opened. The students left to get ready to perform. The six women looked at one another in silence.

"So Melanie, how are you?" Lori asked. The cheerfulness was gone.

"Linda, we had better get inside. We have reserved seats," Melanie said while looking at Lori. Then she looked at Annette with raised eyebrows. A smile formed slightly at the corner of Annette's mouth. Melanie looked at Lori first, then Estelle, but she refused to look at Sharon. She walked away with a look of malice.

Before Linda walked away, she looked at Annette. "It's good seeing you," Linda said pleasantly and walked away.

"I think the girls did a great job campaigning. I could tell they were excited by your little speech," Melanie said. She and Linda were close to Linda's parents' home.

"How do you think they felt about Lori?" Linda asked. She turned down her parents' street and noticed several cars parked in her parents' driveway and around the house.

"She sounded exactly the way Aunt Barbara said that she would, rehearsed. Young people like for people to be real with them. I guess Aunt Barbara's guests are here," Melanie said. She got out of the car. Her own car was blocked in by the visitors. Linda looked around curiously. She only noticed Marilyn's car.

"It's a matter of four days, now. I think I'm going to take a long rest after this is over," Linda said and opened the door to the house. Her father was in the study. Her mother was in the basement with strange voices. Linda figured that Lauren, Indie and Edward were asleep. Barbara did not allow them to stay up past eight o'clock. It was nine o'clock.

Linda walked through the kitchen to get to the basement. The kitchen table was filled with empty and half-filled plates. She and Melanie walked down the kitchen steps to the basement. The noise volume increased. Linda saw three card tables with four women sitting at each. All the women looked out of place. Some had delicate features. The one shuffling cards at one table looked like an experienced card player. The diamonds on her fingers were contradictory. Many held the cards in their hands as if someone would steal a peek. The only things missing were cigarettes dangling from their mouths and beer bottles.

Barbara looked at Linda and then at the cards in her hand. "How was the step-show?" Barbara asked.

"Isn't that something the young women do?" a stranger asked Linda.

"We left the show early and to answer your question, yes," Linda said to the stranger.

"Why did you play that queen? You saw me lead with the ace," one woman fussed softly at her partner as another shuffled the cards.

"So, how is the Bridge game coming along?" Linda asked earnestly.

Several looked at her strangely before looking at Barbara. She decided to introduce Linda and Melanie to the group. The women turned down their cards and gave Linda their attention. She said nothing to them.

"Maybe we should be a little more cordial to our guests," one joked.

"I'm sorry. Enjoy yourselves, ladies. I don't play Bridge," Linda said.

"We're playing Whist, as in Bid Whist," one corrected.

"I don't play Bid Whist either. I've only played Spades. Nice meeting everyone. Have fun," Linda said and turned around to leave.

"Would you like to learn?" one asked kindly. She and a couple of others were a few years younger than the group. All eyes were on Linda. She knew when people had another agenda. She didn't know what was on the group's agenda.

"How about you, young lady?" a fairly older one asked Melanie who also knew something was up.

"I'm bidding four uptown," said a woman at Barbara's table.

"I pass," the one next to her said.

"Six downtown," Barbara bidded.

The woman sitting next to her was surprised. "Okay, what's the trump?"

"Diamonds, of course. Partner, when was the last time you've been to Boston?" Barbara asked and tossed over the kitty. She replaced the cards and tossed the queen of diamonds on the table.

Linda saw her mother toss cards onto the table and her partner gathered them to make books. She became startled by the woman's request again. She insisted on teaching her the game. Linda walked slowly to the table. One woman gave Linda her seat and brought over another chair and sat it next to Linda. One woman gave her chair to Melanie and walked up the steps.

"We have been playing cards together for years. The first thing to remember is it's a game. You never play with people who are not in the same league. Are you following me?" the woman asked Linda as she dealt the unshuffled deck of cards.

"Not really. I'm a beginner and you guys have been playing for years. Are we getting ready to play?" asked a shrewd Linda. She jumped after hearing shrills from her mother's table.

"It would be unfair to play with you. We're teaching you. Since you know how to play Spades, it won't be that difficult teaching you Bid Whist," the woman said and dealt the entire deck.

Linda picked up her cards and looked at them carefully. She had a lot of hearts, one joker, two spades, one diamond and no clubs.

"From your expression, you look confused," the woman said.

"I am."

The woman next to Linda leaned close to her to look at her cards. Linda brought her cards close to her body and looked at the woman.

"You don't trust me?" the woman asked with a grin.

"Why are you looking at my cards?" Linda asked.

"We are going to teach you how to play. She has to know what's in your hand in order to help you," another woman said.

"Whose side is she on?" Linda asked curiously.

"If she's helping you, I would think she's on your side. I don't know how well you learn, but it's quicker if someone shows you instead of one of us talking you through it. We don't have a lot of time," the first one said.

Linda showed the woman her cards. The woman smiled. "This is so appropriate," she said.

The other women began bidding. It was Linda's turn. She looked at the woman sitting next to her. "Tell them you are bidding six low," she said.

"Six low," Linda said.

"What is the trump?" one woman asked.

The woman next to Linda pointed to the hearts. Linda called

out hearts. One woman cursed. Linda turned over the kitty and one more heart and the other joker turned over. The woman instructed Linda to pick up the kitty and selected the cards that would replace it. Linda had all hearts, two jokers and the ace of diamonds.

Under the woman's instructions, Linda tossed the cards onto the table. Her partner gathered the books. Linda realized that nobody could make a book because she controlled the game. She smiled as she tossed the last card onto the table.

"Do you know what a Boston is?" one woman asked. Linda shook her head. "It's when you win the game by making all of the books."

"On your first time playing, you won the game by a landslide. You won with hearts," another said.

"What does winning with hearts suppose to mean?" Linda asked.

"It means nothing in Bid Whist, but it means everything in this campaign. I read your spread in the quarterly. Not only do we need someone whose focus is community service, but one who recognizes the need to strengthen cohesiveness in the sisterhood. I'm Clara Adams," the woman said.

Linda was surprised. Clara Adams was the First Vice President. She introduced Linda to the other women around the table who were presidents of the Chicago, Oklahoma City and Indianapolis Alumnaes.

"As long as we are not playing in the same league, we can help you win," Clara said with a smile.

"It's an honor to meet you," Linda said.

"Oh tsk! Does your mother have any bourbon?" Clara asked.

"I could use a gin and tonic about now," one said.

"A glass of white wine for me," another said.

Winning did not seem to come easy. Linda realized the women expected her to wait on them. She looked at the woman who had not ordered.

"Nothing for me. I don't drink," she said.

It became clear to Linda what favors were. She wanted to win the election but not at the cost of taking care of a bunch of old women.

"Is this what is expected of me if I win?" Linda asked the one who helped her with the cards.

"What are you talking about, hun?" she answered.

Linda came to the conclusion that the old hens were very smart. She also knew her mother would not introduce her to anyone who would harm her down the road. She got up to fill the requests. Her parents had a bar in the other room. It had been off limits for awhile. It appeared that her mother could comfortably sit around people who drank without much difficulty.

Melanie had finished her card game too. She looked as if she were ready to go. She made eye contact with Linda.

"Melanie, sweetie, could you bring Mrs. Randall a glass of white wine?" Barbara asked with a smile.

Linda almost frowned at her mother, but Barbara continued to smile. Linda's focus went to Melanie. She looked as if she were ready to choke someone. Linda decided that the old women were not going to get the best of them.

"Anybody else need anything before we leave?" Linda announced.

All the women replied, "Not at this moment."

Melanie and Linda walked quickly out the card room and into the room which had the bar. Linda search the shelves for the bourbon. She took out a bottle of Chardonnay from a small refrigerator.

"You won't believe what one old girl told me. Her husband tried prolonging the divorce because of alimony. She said she did what the Godfather did. She held a gun to him and said that either his signature or brains would be on the paper. Everyone at the table laughed at it. I found out it was a toy pistol, but the old girls thought it was funny, especially Aunt Marilyn," Melanie said.

Linda almost lost her breath. "She wasn't serious, was she?"

"I don't know. One told me that she moved in the middle of the night to Chicago. She placed an ad in an obscure newspaper in Kansas City, asking the whereabouts of her estranged husband. Since no one read the paper, no one responded. She was able to be free of the asshole within a matter of a few months."

"I guess they were trying to give you some advice. No wonder they call themselves 'Friends From the Other Side of the Tracks'. My table of biddies are trying to make me pay for their vote. It's not going to happen."

"Let's hurry so I can take Lauren home."

"Has John been by the apartment?"

"Lauren said that she saw him while riding her bike. I have to make my move soon. He won't agree to something quick. I made it clear that I didn't want anything from him."

Linda and Melanie heard Barbara asking what was taking so long. Linda was about to get mad until Melanie laughed. Linda looked at her for an answer.

"Can't you see what they are doing? One hen told me to keep under control at all times. They are probably wondering if you will snap under pressure or do something unpleasant. They are testing you," Melanie said.

A scowl came across Linda's face. Her mother and her friends were very secretive. Once they developed a circle, it was hard to penetrate.

"I have an idea. Let's behave as if we want to hang around.

Mother doesn't like for me to be around her when she's entertaining."

The two women walked the drinks into the other room. They showed no emotions as they sat the drinks in front of the women.

"Mother, I made a Boston," Linda said proudly.

"That's great, honey. It's called running a Boston. How did it feel?"

"It felt better than sex!"

All the women, with the exception of Barbara, roared with laughter. Clara Adams laughed the hardest.

"Aren't the young women having a step-show?" Barbara asked to divert the attention from Linda's statement.

"It's probably over by now," Melanie answered.

"I think the young women usually have a dance or something, don't they?" said the woman who told Melanie about threatening her ex-husband with a toy pistol.

"Un-un," Linda said while shaking her head.

"They are doing *something*," Barbara emphasized.

Linda heard a truce. "Mother, thanks for keeping the kids. I'll get them."

"Thanks for keeping Lauren, Aunt Barbara," Melanie added.

"Let them sleep. You can pick them up in the morning. Maybe you need to try out some new moves, especially if playing cards is better than sex," Barbara said to Linda and looked at her cards. The women laughed again.

Linda approached the steps. Before she began to climb them, she looked at Clara Adams and asked, "The deck was stacked, wasn't it?"

"Feel fortunate it wasn't stacked against you."

Chapter Twenty-Five

Rhonda sat on the floor rubbing Lisa's feet. She talked about Jason. He called only once since he had left Atlanta. They talked for two hours and then he rushed off the phone. He gave no explanation but said that he would talk to her later.

"Why don't you give him a call?" Lisa said.

"I would but I don't have his telephone number. He said he was moving soon and he was getting a new number."

Lisa closed her eyes. It felt as if the baby was doing a handstand in her womb. She was excited but nervous. The talk of labor pains and delivery pains had her slightly frightened but not as frightened as telling Rhonda that Jason lived with a woman. Another dilemma was telling Rhonda that Cameron was moving back home. Rhonda had made herself at home. She had often told Lisa that she was going to take care of her and the baby. As far as she was concerned, Cameron could stay gone.

"If Jason doesn't call again, leave him alone. He's not stable when it comes to commitments," Lisa said.

"I know you said that he's a love 'em and leave 'em type, but it was smooth with him. We talked about things that hurt us and what we want to do with our lives. He seemed for real! He don't trip off of shit like long hair and who your parents are. He's tight."

Lisa knew the real test with Jason was making a decision. He was drifting. He talked a little about regretting dropping out of school. He shared a few other things with her. Usually, he didn't say anything he didn't mean. If he didn't want to continue seeing a woman, he would say, "It's time for space."

"What is it about Jason that you like?" Lisa asked. She hoped Rhonda would talk about how handsome he looked so she could put things in perspective.

"When I told him that I danced in a strip club, he smiled and asked, 'Will you dance for me one day?' I cursed him out because I thought he was trying to get into the panties. He had never been to a strip club. He thought only prostitutes stripped. I told him that I only danced. I didn't make the money like Nee Nee and Falita. Niggas didn't pay enough money to rub my ass."

"What did he share with you?"

"He said that everyone thought he was sweet and innocent until he started smoking pot. It started when he was fourteen. He never understood why his folks didn't get along. He said something about a half-sister and everybody calling his father an asshole. He never felt that way and felt guilty because he never sided with his mother. He was wondering if he hated women."

"Don't tell me he thinks he's gay!"

"No! He gets along with his father have a special relationship. He admires his father, but he doesn't want to cheat like his father did. He sorta wants to be like him but not a ho'."

"Out of the three of them, Jason is probably the most honest and the least like his father. Lionel had an extramarital affair and Cameron has difficulty facing problems and runs from them."

"How does Lionel look? He can't look better than Jason."

"He and Jason look similar, but Lionel is darker. He used to date Melanie in college."

"Our cousin Melanie?"

"Um, hum. He's Lauren's father."

"What? Is this some kind of soap opera?"

"Girl, if you only knew!"

Rhonda finished her foot massage. Lisa thanked her and got off the sofa. She waddled to her bedroom. Rhonda was right behind her. They got into bed. It wasn't an unusual scene. Rhonda had visited Lisa every night to keep her company. Lisa had taken the place of Grandma Sweetie. Rhonda would talk Lisa to sleep. Once Lisa was asleep, Rhonda would get up and quietly leave.

Lisa was tired, but the baby wouldn't let her sleep. She began to ponder over how to tell Rhonda that Cameron was moving back.

"Are you ready to visit St. Louis?" Lisa asked.

"Somebody told me that St. Louis is rough."

"You're talking about East St. Louis, Illinois. It's across the river. St. Louis is smaller and older than Atlanta. It sits on the Mississippi River. I like the riverfront. They have a lot of clubs with live music."

"Now I see why Miss Mattie moved to St. Louis. She had to cross a body of water to remove the curse."

Lisa became warm. Every time they brought up something

Miss Sweets told them, it made her feel different. "Do you think we're cursed?"

"It's not a curse to have your momma's spirit around."

"My mother killed two people."

"That really bothers you. Don't it?"

"I can understand her killing the white man but not her sister."

Rhonda decided to tell the truth. The first time she talked about her mother's death, she wanted Lisa to feel guilty. "Grandma Sweetie said the spirit gave her a vision that my momma found your mother. Instead of being happy that her sister escaped the law in Georgia, my mother was angry and jealous that your mother moved on with her life. The only vision Grandma Sweetie saw was them being in the hallway in a project. They were arguing and then my mother cut her sister with a knife. Your mother pushed her out of the way but the windows were broken out. My mother fell to her death."

"My mother was cut by her sister?"

Rhonda nodded out of embarrassment. She was too little to remember her mother. Once she began her search for Lisa, she demanded that Miss Sweets tell her the truth.

Rhonda did not want to continue the discussion so she decided to change the topic. "Do you have a suitcase I can borrow?"

"Sure. By the way, Cameron is moving back tomorrow."

Rhonda looked intensely at Lisa. She had taken care of her so why would she want Cameron, someone who would probably move out again? She didn't want to share her cousin with anyone. They were just alike.

"Why are you letting him move back? What if he moves out again?"

"We've been talking a lot more now than ever. He didn't understand what I was going through because I wasn't as honest with him as I could have been. He knows this is his last shot. Besides, I want him to witness the birth of his son."

"I thought you were having a girl."

"It's a boy."

Rhonda decided not to talk Lisa to sleep. She was hurt. She was going to be an outsider again. She got out of bed.

"Where are you going?" Lisa asked.

"I'm going home."

"It's late. Stay in the guest room."

"I need to get home," Rhonda said and picked up the key ring that she made with the bear that Lauren had given her. She walked to the doorway.

"You don't like Cameron, do you?"

"He thinks he's so much. I would never leave you and I'm only your cousin."

"He's not really like that and being my cousin means more than the way you're putting it. I'm glad that you found me. I would never leave you either."

"When you bring the suitcase over, just blow the horn. I'll come down to get it."

"I think Jason is going to call you soon."

"I don't care! I got a man."

"Has Ace ever hit you?"

"If he ever does, he better keep running. I don't play that shit. My momma and Miss Sweets never hit me. They didn't have to."

"What else did Jason tell you. I want to know," Lisa said and shifted back so that Rhonda could lay next to her.

No matter how much Rhonda disliked the idea of Cameron moving back, it was hard to turn down an invitation to talk Lisa to sleep. She plopped her body close to Lisa. She didn't look at her as she shared how Jason's girlfriend in college had an abortion. The girl never asked Jason how he felt or if he wanted the baby. He was so hurt by it that he dropped out of college.

"Jason told you that?" Lisa asked.

"We were talking about the things that hurt us most. I told him how I waved goodbye to my mother one day and never saw her again. I hate getting close to people because they always seem to leave. Grandma Sweetie is the last hurt."

"Was the abortion or his parents' divorce the most painful."

"I think the abortion was. He really liked that girl. It was as if she didn't want a part of him. Personally, I think girlfriend wanted to do more with her life. Jason doesn't appear to be the type to make long term plans. She probably didn't know if he would be a good father."

"He's going back to school in the Fall."

"He told me! He's a smart brother."

"Does he want to get married?"

"I didn't ask. When I saw that he was sounding down and out, I lit some candles and gave him a pedicure. He was a little uncomfortable because brother had some toes that looked pretty scary. His feet looked good in the sandals, but when I got a closer look, I almost freaked out. He chilled when I began to rub them."

"Why do you like rubbing people's feet?"

"A foot massage relaxes the body better than any body massage. It's called reflexology. When you touch certain pressure points, it can get rid of headaches and any other pains."

"Holistic medicine seems to be the thing now. Maybe you should think about doing something like that. You seem to be good at it. Every time you rub my feet, I always feel great. You have a magic touch."

"My momma used to rub me all the time. Grandma Sweetie

said that's how I got my strong body. Momma stretched my muscles and made them flexible. I can do dance movements that take dancers years to master."

"My mother taught me how to cook. She was gone so much that it came in handy. I could cook by the time I was ten-years-old. When I lived with Miss Mattie, she helped put the finishing touches on what my mother showed me."

"Miss Mattie was something else, wasn't she? She killed her husband and escaped the law, just like your momma."

"It took me a long time to forgive my mother for leaving me with Miss Mattie. After hearing about her past, I can't be angry anymore. You should feel the same way about your mother."

"I was never really mad at her. When Grandma Sweetie talked about her, it was always good."

"I want you to be my baby's godmother."

"Get out of here! Really?"

"Of course. If something ever happens to me, I know you will make sure that he gets a lot of love."

"Have you told Cameron?"

"He wants Jason to be the godfather. At first he wanted his good friend Kyle to be the godfather, but Jason is a better choice."

"Thanks, Lisa. I can't wait to meet your friends in St. Louis."

"I think you are going to really like Rochelle. She's down to earth. The other ones are cool too. Rochelle is just a little different."

"Does your father know we're coming to visit?"

"Hell no! I want him to be just as surprised to see me, as I was to find out about him."

"All of this traveling won't hurt the baby, will it?"

"I'm not due for another three weeks. I feel fine."

Lisa was outside Rhonda's apartment. She gave the horn two quick blows. Rhonda was supposed to meet her at the car to get the suitcase. Lisa waited a few minutes before blowing the horn again. She could see Rhonda's lights on in her apartment and her car was in the parking lot. Lisa grudgingly got out of the car with the suitcase and climbed the steps to Rhonda's apartment. Before she knocked on the door, she could hear Rhonda yelling. Then she heard a slap and Rhonda screaming.

Lisa shook. When she touched her face, it felt warm. She closed her eyes to catch her bearings. She opened them and focused on the doorknob. She turned it and entered the apartment. She could hear Rhonda crying in the bedroom. The apartment became dark. Lisa wanted to leave and call the police. She reached into her purse for her cellular phone, but she pulled out the bear that Lauren had given her. The bear seemed to grin at her. She put it inside of her purse and continued feeling for the phone. Instead, she pulled out the pocket knife that she took from Miss Sweets' house.

Lisa stared at the knife for a few seconds. Then she flipped the blade out like an experienced user. The handle of the knife rested in her palm. When she heard Rhonda cry out, "Please don't do it," it caused Lisa to react on impulse. She hid behind the door and watched Rhonda's boyfriend mount her, cursing her, telling her that he 'wanted some'.

When Rhonda screamed, Lisa rushed into the room. The room was dark to her and the figure on top of Rhonda looked white. Lisa swiftly threw her arms around the man's neck and placed the blade at his throat. He stopped. Lisa pressed the blade further into his skin, causing blood to trickle at the side of the knife. She didn't feel the pressure of the baby or swollen feet. She felt anger. She wanted to kill him.

Ace was still. The force of the arm did not feel like a weak woman. Lisa felt herself fight between plunging the knife into his throat and stopping her purse from banging against her leg. The movement of her purse took her concentration off of cutting Ace's throat.

"Rhonda, hurry up and put on some clothes. I want you to get out of here," Lisa said roughly. Rhonda moved slowly. "Hurry up and leave," Lisa shouted.

Rhonda continued to move slowly. It was her apartment so where was she going? She wanted Ace to leave. "Where am I going? I live here," Rhonda protested.

Lisa eased the blade away from Ace's throat and stepped back. She continued to back away. She dropped the knife and broke into something of a run. She ran out of Rhonda's apartment and down the steps. She hid in some bushes at the side of the building. Her heart was beating fast. She tried waiting patiently until Ace left. Finally, she could see him get into his car and drive off fast. Then she heard Rhonda calling her name.

When Lisa saw the car turn out of the parking lot, she felt safe. She slowly came out of the bushes and waddled to the steps. She took her time climbing to the top. Rhonda was there waiting with the knife in her hand. The anger in her face made Lisa pause.

"You dropped this damn thing and left me in there with that crazy bastard," Rhonda said in a hoarse voice.

Lisa had difficulty placing Rhonda's voice. It didn't sound like her. It sounded older and extremely angry. Lisa tried thinking of a way out.

"Why did you leave me?" Rhonda shouted.

"I told you to leave, but you took your time," Lisa answered in a shaky voice.

Rhonda seemed to be getting stronger. She had a smirk on her face. "This is your knife. Take it," Rhonda said, jabbing the knife at Lisa. "Take it. You are much better with it than I am," Rhonda continued. Her eyes looked glassy. She swung the knife at Lisa who ducked in time from being cut in the face.

It came to Lisa about Miss Sweets' vision of the three spirits. It was the same scene that caused the twin to die. "Rhonda, stop it! Put that thing down," Lisa snapped.

Before Lisa could say anything else, a door swung open. An angry resident yelled at them to quiet down. When Lisa turned to look at the man, Rhonda nicked her on the arm with the knife. Lisa looked at the blood oozing from the cut, and then she looked at Rhonda. She was ready to apologize, but Lisa backhanded her, catching her at the side of the face. The knife flipped out of Rhonda's hand and the contents in Lisa's purse spilled. The bear rolled in front of Lisa.

Rhonda was standing at the top of the flight of steps. She saw the knife lying next to Lisa's bear. She thought it was her bear and wondered where were the keys that were attached. She bent forward to pick it up and realized it was Lisa's bear. Lauren had given her one too. Rhonda picked it up along with the knife. She was about to hand both items to Lisa, but was given a hard shove causing her to tumble sideways down the steps. Luckily, she grabbed a bar in the handrailing. It caused her to stop. She dropped the knife and gripped the bar and bear tightly. She panted and then cried.

Lisa's body shook. Everything became bright again. She saw Rhonda lying on the steps crying. Lisa realized that she injured Rhonda. Lisa left the contents of her purse on the ground and waddled down the steps as fast as she could. Rhonda's face was between the railings. She held onto the bear.

Lisa didn't say anything but hugged Rhonda.

"I searched so long for you and you do some shit like leave me with that crazy fool," Rhonda cried.

"I told you to leave. He looked as if he was going to hurt me too. Why didn't you leave with me?"

"I was scared I didn't know what to do. You left the knife."

"Why did you cut me with that thing?"

"I didn't mean too. I was getting ready to apologize but you slapped me and pushed me down the steps."

"I thought you were going to cut me again."

"I would never hurt you."

The two women cried. The scent of flowers became stronger.

"Hurry up and get your things. Does Ace have a key to your apartment?"

Rhonda shook her head. She slowly picked herself up. She handed the bear to Lisa. They walked slowly up the stairs and picked up the contents of Lisa's purse from the ground. They went inside the apartment and Lisa called Cameron. She told him that she needed him to change the lock on Rhonda's door.

Rhonda was in her bedroom packing clothes. She already knew what she wanted to take to St. Louis.

"Do you think Ace is going to jump on you again?" Lisa asked.

"He's just jealous. He's not a stalker. Someone saw me and Jason together. He thinks I'm fuckin' around on him."

"You need to move from this apartment. I don't trust him. You can stay with me and Cameron until you get another place."

"I appreciate your offer, but I'll be okay," Rhonda said and continued the task of packing. The more she put into the suitcase, the happier she became. It didn't matter if Ace came back. If protection was needed, she had to do what Miss Sweets instructed her to do, gouge out his eyes.

Lisa sat. She felt more uncomfortable. She felt like walking but the baby's pressure made it difficult to stand. She sat and looked around Rhonda's apartment. It was scarcely furnished. She had a dinette set, sofa, coffee table, stereo and television set. Surprisingly, Rhonda was a very neat person.

Rhonda entered the room with a suitcase and an overnight bag. She looked ready to go. She saw Lisa trying to relax.

"You want me to rub your feet?"

Lisa shook her head. The offer was nice, but she was too uncomfortable. She hoped that Cameron would come soon.

"How did you get into Georgia State? It seems as if tuition would keep you from attending," Lisa said.

"Some woman my mother and Grandma Sweetie knew gave me money for my college education. I never met her, I talked to her on the phone twice. She said that I reminded her of her daughter who was taken away from her. To my understanding, she attended her daughter's graduation unnoticed."

"This woman just popped up out of the blue?"

"I guess. I remembered she talked to Grandma Sweetie for a long time one day. Then Grandma Sweetie handed me the phone. This woman told me that she knew my mother and that she wanted to do something nice for me since I had a hard life like her daughter. Then she gave me some advice."

"What was it?"

"She said I was smart and to always play it cool with men because they didn't like smart women. When men are sleeping, women are thinking. She also warned me to never open the door to strangers. She said it was a metaphor and I would use it when the time was right."

"When did she tell you that?" The statements were very familiar to Lisa.

"I think I was about sixteen. Grandma Sweetie said that lady

married a rich man and that she had money to give away.
Grandma Sweetie never took a hand out before, so this lady was
special."

"When did you last talk to her?"

"It was my junior year in college. Grandma Sweetie said she
died in a car accident. That's why I danced in that strip club.
Grandma Sweetie needed money and I did too."

"Did she ever say anything about her daughter?"

"She said something about her graduating summa cum laude
and being president of her sorority and how proud she was of her.
She told me that I could do the same thing. By that time, I had
too many B's and I didn't want to pledge Kappa."

Lisa wiped tears from her face. She knew Rhonda had talked
to her mother. Lisa wondered why her mother never came back?
She never gave her mother any trouble. She longed to lay next to
her in bed as she hummed her to sleep.

"Did she ever say why her daughter was taken away?"

"I don't remember too much. The only thing Grandma Sweetie
said was she couldn't see her daughter again. What's the matter?"

Lisa shook her head. It was time for the conversation to end. It
was also time to release the last bit of anger toward the person
she knew as Debra Arvell.

Cameron knocked hard on the door. Rhonda went to answer
it. When she opened the door, Cameron looked angry. Rhonda
became uncomfortable.

"Are you okay?" he asked frowning.

"Yeah."

"Have you called the police?" Cameron asked as he walked
inside with a bag from Home Depot.

"I don't need to call the police. He won't bother me again."

Cameron stopped removing items from the bag. He looked at
Rhonda. "You can't take any chances with a man who will beat
you. I'll change your lock, but you need to move."

"My lease ain't up until the end of August. I can't afford to
break my lease!"

"Does this guy know where you work?"

Rhonda shook her head.

"Good. You can stay with me and Lisa," Cameron said and
started removing the old lock from the door.

Rhonda turned sideways and made eye contact with Lisa. The
tears had been wiped away. A happy glow took its place.

"I can help take care of the baby," Rhonda said happily.

Lisa grinned. Rhonda was just like Miss Sweets. She was not
accepting a hand out either.

Chapter Twenty-Six

Cameron was near Ky Dam. The scenery of the water was relaxing as he crossed over the bridge. He enjoyed driving the Suburban on long trips. He looked in his rear view mirror at Rhonda. She looked relaxed. She stared out of the window in a daze. The water had her attention.

Cameron looked quickly at Lisa. She, too, seemed dazed at the water. Both women stared at the river hypnotized.

"You two love water, huh?" Cameron asked for the sake of conversation.

Lisa looked back at Rhonda. Their mothers' spirits were gone. They didn't know if it was the sake of water or not making the same mistake their mothers had made. The two women felt a sense of relief. They didn't know if it were good.

"A few frat brothers are coming to the shower," Cameron stated.

"Who's coming?" Lisa asked.

"Tony, Brad, Clifton and Drew."

"Is Brad coming to see Tina?"

"I think he's ready to settle down now. He's hoping for another chance."

"I guess Tony is coming to see if Alicia is really getting married. He had his chance."

"Kyle might be there."

"I still can't believe he's marrying Alicia! They don't go together."

"I need to know the four-one-one on these people. Y'all gossiping and I don't know who y'all gossiping about," Rhonda said.

"I'll let Lisa tell you the scoop. I'm staying out of it," Cameron said.

"All of us went to college together. Brad and Tony were two of the biggest playboys on campus and..."

"They weren't playboys!" Cameron interrupted.

"Anyway, when you see them, you'll know what I'm talking about," Lisa told Rhonda.

"They're tight, huh?" Rhonda asked.

"Very tight! Kyle was the biggest nerd in school and he's marrying my shippee," Lisa continued.

"What's a shippee?"

"A shipmate. She pledged Alpha with me. Girlfriend was super cool in college. She's moments away from a Ph.D."

"Are your friends down to earth?" Rhonda asked.

"Most of them are. Some are a little quiet."

"What kind of person is Rochelle?"

"Loud!" Cameron commented.

"She's down to earth, too. You are going to like her," Lisa said and hit Cameron on the arm.

"Are we going out tonight?" Rhonda continued.

"Everybody is going to the riverfront. I'm staying in," Lisa said.

"Is the Arch near the riverfront?" Rhonda asked. Her adrenaline was flowing.

"Yes. One day, we're going to the Ozarks. You will like it. It's quiet and relaxing," Lisa said with a smile.

"Can we get tickets to the ball game? I want to see Ozzie Smith play in person. The man still got it going on, even if he is getting old," Rhonda said. Lisa raised her hand for a high-five. Rhonda gave it a firm tap.

"What do you know about Ozzie Smith?" Cameron asked teasingly.

"The man has won more golden gloves than you have fingers. He's the best shortstop in the history of baseball. I know about baseball."

"There might be a home game Sunday. I'll get tickets," Cameron offered.

"What about Saturday evening? Aren't we going to Kansas City on Sunday?"

Cameron looked over at Lisa. She refused to look at him.

"What's happening in Kansas City?" Cameron asked aloud.

Rhonda realized she made a mistake. When she and Lisa talked, the visit to Kansas City was not treated as a secret. It was part of the trip.

"I wanted to see Kansas City, so Lisa was trying to squeeze it in," Rhonda lied.

"Is that true?" Cameron asked and looked at Lisa again.

"I'm going to see Paul," Lisa answered.

"When were you going to tell me?"

"It's not a big deal!"

"Yes it is! You're not suppose to take this trip. Why would you want to risk going further than St. Louis?"

"I want to see him, okay?"

"I thought William made it clear that nothing had changed."

"You don't understand what it's like not knowing your parents. You've been in a comfortable position all of your life. What have you struggled for?"

Cameron did not want to argue about his blessings and Lisa's lack of. It used to be a favorite argument in their early years of dating. He could not let the statement go by without bringing closure to an opinion that was incorrect.

"Just because I didn't grow up with kids teasing me or not having parents around doesn't mean I have not struggled. You had Miss Mattie who was a better mother than you could have ever hoped for."

"Don't say anything negative about my mother!"

"I'm not saying anything negative about your mother. You have to appreciate what you were given. You seem to water down everything Miss Mattie has done for you."

Lisa's focus was straight ahead. She was so angry with Cameron that her body temperature was rising in the air conditioned car.

"Who are you taking to Kansas City with you, Rhonda?"

Lisa said nothing.

"I told you years ago that I would take you to see your father and I would stand beside you when you tell him everything you have wanted to say. I will not allow you to put yourself and the baby in danger just to tell off some bastard."

"I'm going regardless," Lisa said very low.

Cameron sighed. "What time do you want to go?"

"You don't have to go, Cameron. I'll go with her," Rhonda said.

"No, I need to keep my promise."

Everyone was quiet as Cameron drove into Illinois. Lisa felt happier, knowing she was two hours away from home. The first thing she wanted to do was visit Miss Mattie's grave to pay respect. It would be the perfect time for Rhonda to feel the presence of the powerful little figure that never showed any signs of weakness. Lisa wanted to visit Jennifer's grave too. Maybe seeing the tombstone would release the guilt of her friend's death. The last item on the list was to visit Carleton. He had to fill in the missing pieces to the twins existence.

Cameron hit a pothole on Highway 64. Lisa felt the pressure of the baby getting heavier.

"These streets are raggedly. Are St. Louis' streets raggedly?"

Rhonda asked.

"The Midwest gets a lot of bad weather in the winter. It makes it difficult to keep the streets smooth, especially if you are not willing to pay the taxes to do so. I'm from Minneapolis. Our streets are much smoother than these streets and we get worse weather," Cameron said.

"Before we go to Alicia's, I want to see my grandmother's and Jennifer's graves. I talked to Carleton and he said that I could visit him too," Lisa said.

"I was going to suggest it," Cameron said.

"Does Carleton know about me?" Rhonda asked.

"Yes. He wants to meet you. I told him about the letters my mother and Miss Mattie sent Miss Sweets. He wants to see them too," Lisa answered.

"What time is the baby shower?" Cameron asked.

"Tomorrow at four. It should give the last minute shoppers time to get gifts," Lisa said with a laugh.

"What time are we going out tonight?" Rhonda asked.

"I don't know. St. Louis shuts down early. I think Rochelle is having something at her place afterwards," Lisa responded.

Lisa tried adjusting herself in the seat. Her back was uncomfortable. She shut her eyes to relax for awhile. For the last two nights, she couldn't sleep. She didn't know if it was the baby or Cameron wanting to hold her in his arms.

"How much longer do we have?" Rhonda asked.

"About another hour. Are you excited?" Cameron asked.

"Yeah! I'm going to see my real grandmother's grave, visit my uncle and meet Lisa's friends. This trip is going to be something."

"I talked to Jason at work yesterday. I told him that you were staying with us for awhile."

Cameron waited for Rhonda to say something, but she was silent. She did not bother to look up. She was polishing her nails.

"He's trying to get settled. He's moving in with my father," Cameron added in defense of Jason.

"Oh," Rhonda said, still keeping her focus on her nails.

"He might come back to Atlanta. He had a nice time when he was there."

"He was good company," Rhonda said cordially.

"Are you angry at him?"

"Why should I be? He's not my man!"

"Do you like him?"

"Why are you asking me these questions?"

"I take that as a *yes*."

"You act like you know everything!"

"You don't like me. Do you?"

"I don't like the way you treat me."

"And how is that?"

"Like I'm stupid!"

"I think you are *very* smart. I may not agree with how you talk, but you are a very bright young woman."

"What's wrong with the way I talk? I don't use correct English?"

"You are a little abrasive. Sometimes that can scare men away."

"I have to be myself. I'm not trying to impress anybody."

"Never think you are the best that you can be. You can always be better. You were smart enough to stop stripping and you are smart enough to do whatever is necessary to improve yourself."

Rhonda looked out of the window. The top of the Arch was in view.

"That's the top of the Arch. It's now a matter of minutes before we hit more potholes," Cameron announced.

As they crossed over the Mississippi River, Lisa woke up. The familiar surrounding of St. Louis' riverfront came to view. She sat up.

"Can we stop to get something to eat?" Rhonda asked.

"Where do you suggest, Lisa?" Cameron asked.

"If you have a taste for Chinese, we can go to the Silk Rose in the Central West End," Lisa answered.

Cameron drove to the restaurant. He got out of the car and stretched. Lisa and Rhonda were still in the car.

"Cameron was talking a lot of stuff," Rhonda said.

"He was trying to tell you that Jason likes you. He's wrong when he said that you are scaring Jason. For some reason, you scare him," Lisa said and got out of the car. Rhonda followed.

It was hot and humid. Rhonda and Cameron fanned as Lisa stared at Miss Mattie's headstone. It had flowers lying beside it, fresh flowers. Lisa remembered how she did not have time to grieve because the old women of the church rejoiced about Matilda Clairmont going home to Glory.

Lisa felt a swish around her. The old feeling of the angels was back. Lisa knew Miss Mattie was with her. But once they crossed the river heading back to Atlanta, it would probably leave. Lisa smiled. It was time to see Jennifer's grave.

Cameron drove further into the cemetery. They piled out of the car and walked to Jennifer's grave. She wasn't that far from Catherine's site. As Lisa looked at the headstone, the name appeared brighter. Fresh flowers were at her headstone too. Thoughts of conversations in college surfaced. The one Lisa remembered most was Jennifer asking if she were a virgin. The conversation reminded her of Jennifer's innocence and honesty. Something about being at Jennifer's grave gave Lisa a sense of life.

"Where is your mother's grave?" Rhonda asked.

Lisa had to think hard. She didn't visit her mother's grave site often. She had made a stop before leaving St. Louis after the wedding to put fresh flowers on it. She had the location written down on paper. She searched her purse for it. She couldn't find it. It was very strange because she made sure she had it before leaving Atlanta. Then she remembered, it was in her wallet. She pulled out her wallet and handed the paper to Cameron. They had to go to another cemetery.

Lisa made Cameron stop at a grocery store to buy flowers. On their way inside, they saw Margo leaving the store. Lisa recognized her first.

"Hi Margo," Lisa said smiling.

Margo looked at Lisa hard and then smiled. She gave her a big hug. "Oh my goodness, Lisa! You look so cute pregnant. How are you?"

"I'm ready to deliver," Lisa answered.

"Hello, Margo," Cameron said.

Margo gave him a hug too. "I had heard you two were having a baby. What brings you to St. Louis?"

"I'm having a baby shower tomorrow. Instead of making everyone come to Atlanta, I decided to come home. How have you been?"

"I'm getting married in September."

"Who is the lucky guy? Peter?" Cameron asked.

Margo's face turned sour. "No way! I met a nice guy about two years ago. I'm ready to settle down and he is too. Matter of fact, I saw J.D. in this same store. He and his wife have a little girl. Do you know what you're having?"

"A boy. This is my cousin Rhonda," Lisa said to Margo.

The two women spoke. Rhonda noticed how polite and pleasant Margo was in extending her hand to her.

Margo and Lisa exchanged telephone numbers. Margo left. The trio went to the floral department to pick up a bouquet. When Lisa turned around, she was facing her line sister Trish. She was always a large girl, but she had gained at least fifteen more pounds since Lisa last saw her. The two women squealed with delight and hugged each other hard.

They rambled about who was coming to the shower. Before Lisa allowed Trish to go any further, she introduced her to Rhonda. Trish behaved as if she knew Rhonda for years. It helped ease Rhonda's uncomfortable feeling about being in a new place.

"Some of us are meeting at Alicia's tonight around nine. Everybody else will be at the shower tomorrow," Trish said.

"Okay. Don't tell Alicia I'm here. She's not expecting me until later," Lisa said. She hugged Trish again before she left.

"Is this is a reunion?" Rhonda asked as she looked in Trish's direction.

"She's my line sister. Trish was one of the nicest ones on line."

Cameron paid for the flowers and left the grocery store. Lisa felt uplifted after seeing Margo and Trish. She was looking forward to visiting her mother's grave site.

When Cameron drove through the cemetery opening, Lisa felt empty. She tried thinking of happy thoughts as they drove closer to the site. They got out of the car and walked to a desolated grave. It was so different than the last time she had visited. The grass was much better maintained last time. Lisa decided that when she got back to Atlanta, she had to do something about the upkeep of her mother's grave.

"Why does it say *Debra Arvell?* Her name was Della," Rhonda said.

"She went by that name for years," Lisa answered.

"It's suppose to be Orville not Arvell," Rhonda corrected.

"I guess she changed her name like Miss Mattie did because the law was looking for her. She was very young when she ran away," Lisa said and placed the bouquet of flowers at the headstone.

Lisa didn't feel any sense of life from the grave. It felt different from Miss Mattie's and Jennifer's grave. Their spirits were present at their site, her mother's wasn't.

"Let's leave and go to Carleton's house," Lisa said.

They returned to the car and drove off. Cameron was getting more concerned about Lisa. She struggled to walk and was moving even slower. "Before I go to Carleton's house, I need to know if you're okay," Cameron said.

"The baby is getting heavier. It slows me down," Lisa answered.

"When we get to Alicia's, I'll give you a massage. You need to finish taking the squaw vine tea I gave you. It's suppose to help with labor pains," Rhonda said.

Lisa thought about the taste of the tea that Rhonda concocted. She made her drink it twice a day. She didn't want to hurt Rhonda's feeling by not taking it. It was suppose to be something that Miss Sweets gave her mother when she delivered her.

It was four o'clock when they arrived at Carleton's house. He was at home. He had retired last year from the post office. Lisa struggled to get out of the car. She felt a surge of energy as she walked closer to the door. She rang the doorbell and waited for Carleton to answer.

"Hello, Mr. Peterson. I'm Lisa," Lisa said. She had called him Mr. Peterson for as long as she had known Jennifer. To call him something different didn't feel comfortable.

"Come in," Carleton said.

The group walked inside the house. They followed Carleton to the living room. Cameron and Rhonda sat, but Lisa walked to the fireplace. Jennifer's picture was sitting in the middle. She had taken the picture in their senior year in college.

"Rhonda, this is Jennifer," Lisa said.

Rhonda got up to take a closer look at the picture. The woman reminded her of Melanie's daughter Lauren.

"She's pretty," Rhonda said.

"Mr. Peterson, do you have any pictures of Miss Mattie. Rhonda would like to see her. All of my pictures are packed away in boxes," Lisa said.

Rhonda was not so keen on seeing Miss Mattie. She wanted to see Lisa's mother. Every time she asked Lisa about a picture of her mother, Lisa told her that all of her pictures, except her wedding album, were boxed up.

Carleton returned with an old photo album and loose pictures. He pointed to Miss Mattie on a few pictures. Rhonda stared at the tiny person. She reminded her of Miss Sweets. Carleton proudly displayed Catherine's and Jennifer's pictures. Carleton removed an old picture from the stack.

"This is a college picture of Catherine. I think this is your mother. It looks just like Debra," Carleton said.

Rhonda moved in quickly to see the picture. For the first time, she saw her missing link. The woman looked a lot like the two pictures she had of her mother.

Lisa looked at the picture. She had never seen any college pictures of her mother. Catherine stood close to Debra. They had on very nice clothes. After seeing the picture of the two together, Lisa could see that they were related.

"How much do you know about the twins?" Lisa asked Carleton.

"The only thing I remember is momma giving birth to two little girls. They were around for awhile and then I didn't see them anymore. Momma cried a lot. When I asked her about them, she said that they had died."

"Can you tell me about my mother and father?" Lisa continued.

"I knew Debra from being Catherine's friend. I thought she was very pretty. She flirted a lot. I asked her out once, but she said it was something about me that she didn't find attractive to date. Her and Catherine fell out about some secrets or something. They didn't talk for a long time. Before Catherine died, they were on speaking terms again.

"Several years after you were born, Debra told me that she was looking for Bill's brother Paul. She said that he was your father and that she needed some money. She wanted me to help her find him.

"Some months later, I heard that Debra was dead. I didn't know how she died or nothing. Right after momma died, someone told me that Debra always wanted her body to be shipped to Georgia so I helped make the arrangements."

"Who told you that?" Lisa asked.

"Her sorority sister, Barbara Stevens."

"My mother's real name was Della Orville. She was one of the twins that Miss Mattie gave away. This is Rhonda. Deborah Orville is her mother. We were hoping to get more information about our mothers' past," Lisa explained.

"Before momma died, I asked about the two baby girls. She said that daddy made her give them away because he didn't think they were his. Momma claimed that they were," Carleton continued.

"Do you remember a Miss Sweets?" Lisa asked.

Carleton's forehead creased. Then it came to him. "I believe she was that lady that came to stay with us for awhile. She helped momma deliver the twins."

Lisa wanted to hear more, but Carleton's information was limited. After listening to Rhonda talk about the woman that contributed to her college education, Lisa was convinced that the woman who helped Rhonda was her mother. According to Lisa's calculations, her mother didn't die when she was twelve-years-old. She had to have died some time in the late eighties. Lisa was also convinced that her mother shared the news of her sister's death with Miss Sweets. No way could Miss Sweets see the image of Rhonda's mother falling. The type of spiritualism Miss Sweets engaged in, required her touching a person in order to see. The real Deborah Orville had been buried.

"I stopped by Jennifer's grave," Lisa said.

"I went out there yesterday to put flowers on hers' and momma's graves," Carleton shared.

"I was hoping you could give us more information about the twins," Lisa said.

"I don't know anymore. I'm surprised to hear that they were alive. Sometime, it's best to let things go. Everything is not meant to be told. You and Rhonda are family and y'all are always welcomed in my house," Carleton said. He stood and extended his arms to Lisa. She struggled to stand. He helped her up and hugged her. Carleton turned to Rhonda and extended his arms. She was apprehensive but complied. He gave her a tight hug.

"Mr. Peterson, Lisa needs to rest. She's been riding for nine hours. We have to go," Cameron said.

Carleton did not want his two nieces to leave. He was ready to offer his home but decided not to. He walked them to the door and outside to the car. He waved at them as they drove off.

Lisa relaxed a little. There was only one person who could tell her the truth surrounding her mother's death. It was the person who gave her the ceremonial cloth. Since she was going to Kansas City on Sunday, she was going to make one more visit.

Cameron was ten miles from Alicia's townhouse complex in Florissant. St. Louis' traffic was nothing like Atlanta's. It was the start of rush hour and they were moving at normal speed. When Cameron drove in front of Alicia's building, Lisa winced.

"What's wrong?" he asked nervously.

"My stomach tightened," she answered.

"You're not going to Kansas City," Cameron said angrily. He stared at Lisa, daring her to make an issue of it. She was quiet. "This trip is too much for you. I'm calling your doctor to see if you can fly back," he said.

"I'm not due until another two weeks," Lisa said.

"Babies come when they want to," Cameron said.

"Sometimes the uterus gives them their eviction notice," Rhonda said.

Cameron looked back at Rhonda to shut up. She returned his look with her guard up. Cameron drove the car in front of Alicia's townhouse. Everyone sat still.

"Cameron, get the things out of the car," Lisa said.

Cameron got out and left Lisa and Rhonda inside. "I want you to rent a car. You and I are going to Kansas City," Lisa said.

"Are you sure? I don't want to be in any shit," Rhonda said.

Cameron opened the door for Lisa. She used his arm for support to get out of the car. Before she made it to Alicia's front door, it had opened. Alicia rushed out and gave her a big hug. Before she let go, she whispered, "Kyle and I postponed the wedding."

Chapter Twenty-Seven

Lisa struggled to move the large box. Cameron quickly placed it close to her. She had already opened several gifts. Rochelle bought her a car seat. Crystal and Tina went in on a stroller. Trish bought undershirts and two receiving blankets. April bought a baby monitor and other people bought mobiles, clothes, crib sheets and baby toiletries. Lisa even received gifts from Maria and Iris, which were mailed to Alicia's home.

Lisa read the card on the box. It was from Alicia. When she opened it, everyone oohed and ahhed. It was a diaper genie.

"I knew it had to have something to do with Alpha Theta Lambda. Alpha Genie and diaper genie. You heffas make me sick," Rochelle complained.

Everyone laughed, but Rhonda laughed the hardest. She and Rochelle hit it off well upon meeting at Rochelle's apartment. When Rhonda put on a short, fitted dress and high heel strappy sandals to go out, Rochelle complained that she was trying to steal all of the men and to stay her cute ass at home. Rhonda immediately took a liking to her.

They went to a Latin club and danced until it closed. They stayed up the entire night talking. Rhonda told Rochelle that she danced in a strip club. She looked at Rochelle for a response. Rochelle told her if she had her body, she would strip too. It eased every discomfort about being on the outside. Rhonda also shared her feelings about Jason. When Rochelle told her that all of the men in his family were "hoes," Rhonda became more concerned about Cameron.

A knock sounded on the door. Alicia opened the door and Brad, Clifton, Drew and Tony came in with unwrapped gifts. They chanted at Cameron. He was bubbling with excitement. Clifton and Drew lived in St. Louis; Tony lived in Kansas City; and Brad lived in Overland Park, Kansas. Alicia shushed at them to keep the noise down.

The new guests kissed Lisa on the cheek and handed her the boxes. She smiled at the gifts. They made sure that Beta Gamma Delta symbols were on the boxes.

"Couldn't y'all have wrapped the gifts?" Rochelle complained.

Brad walked over to her and gave her a tight hug. He whispered in her ear, "It's alright. I know you need a man." He released Rochelle and grinned. His light beard almost hid his only dimple. When he looked at Tina, his smile was more genuine.

"Hello, Tina," he said.

She returned the smile and spoke. She didn't expect to see him. It had been two years since they had last seen each other. She had not dated anyone since. They sat down and enjoyed the shower.

After Lisa opened the last gift, they ate cake and talked. They began to make plans to go to the riverfront. Rhonda became excited. She rushed over to Lisa. "I'm going with them. What time did you want to head out for Kansas City tomorrow?" she whispered.

"Did you get the car?" Lisa asked.

Rhonda nodded.

"Let's leave around ten. I don't won't Cameron to get suspicious."

Rhonda nodded again.

"Are you having a good time?" Lisa asked.

Rhonda nodded hard and grinned. "Rochelle is tight! I can't wait 'til she comes to Atlanta. She said when she finishes nursing school, she might move to Atlanta."

"Don't Tony and Brad look like playboys?" Lisa asked teasingly.

"Those brothers are too cute. What's wrong with Alicia and Tina? I'll take them," Rhonda said low.

"Have a good time," Lisa said.

"I'll make some more tea before I leave," Rhonda said and headed toward the kitchen.

Lisa's stomach turned as she thought about the squaw vine tea. She had been drinking it for a week. According to Miss Sweets, squaw vine and red raspberry tea was to ease labor pains.

Lisa saw how happy Cameron was as he talked to his friends. He talked the entire week about the plans he had for his son. He was more excited about the birth of the baby than she was. She hoped that he was ready to become a father.

Several Alphas sat around Lisa and talked to her. She was overwhelmed with attention. Janet had finally come around. They talked about how she was setup during the pledge period and that she needed to leave the horrible meaning of her pledge name in the past. Only one Genie from the line of '80 could not be found. That was Evelyn. Her drug problem was so bad that she hardly recognized anyone whom she attended school with.

Rhonda brought over a cup of tea. The sorors began teasing her.

"Look out, Tina Turner! This girl's got legs," Paula teased.

"Is she going out with us? I hope not because I want to catch," Crystal's sister teased.

Rhonda was overjoyed from the attention. According to every woman in the room, she was beautiful. She had gorgeous legs, a fantastic shape and beautiful skin. She never looked at herself that way. Her body was naturally shaped, so it wasn't something she worked hard at. She received many compliments from the men in Atlanta, never from women. After dancing at Wonderland, she never took a man's compliment seriously.

Rochelle left Alicia with the men. She joined the group of women. "Alright, stop the Alpha talk. I'm here," Rochelle said.

"It's fine with us. You know we're cousin sorors with the Kappas," Crystal said.

"What are y'all talking about anyway?" Rochelle asked.

"College," Tina answered.

"Can we talk about goals and careers?" Rochelle continued.

"How is nursing school?" Tina asked.

"I'll be finished next spring."

"No offense, but I am surprised that you are in nursing school. Do you like taking care of sick people?" Anne asked.

"My focus is physical therapy. I want to help people recover from accidents or injuries."

"I remember when Jennifer said that you were going to make an excellent nurse," Crystal said.

Everyone was silent for a few seconds. "That was my girl. She was my favorite shippee. She was a really sharp sister. I hated that she died so young," Rochelle said.

"She left us with something powerful, but we were too young to understand. After Sean beat her up, she was able to show him up without malice," Crystal said.

"What did she do?" Rhonda asked.

"She beat Sean in an election and became the first female president of the Association of Black Collegiates. When she gave her speech, she didn't bash him. She was cool. She just told people to look at this bastard without saying it," Trish said.

"She's our cousin too," Rhonda said.

Everyone looked at Lisa. She struggled to get up. It was time to lie down. She didn't want to discuss family secrets, especially with the group in front of her.

"I'm going to lie down for awhile. The trip has finally caught up with me," she said.

Everyone hugged her. She waddled to the men. Cameron put his arm around her. She told him that she was going to lie down. She bid good-night to the group and retired to the guest bedroom. She wanted to be alone as she thought about her trip to Kansas City the next day.

Rochelle and Rhonda arrived at Alicia's home at 9:30 a.m Sunday. Lisa was ready to leave. It was difficult convincing Cameron that they were going to brunch at the art museum. He talked about tagging along. The women convinced him that it was an all girls' trip.

Rochelle drove off and onto Interstate 270 to connect with Interstate 70 West. Rhonda explained to Lisa about Rochelle coming along. Rhonda didn't have a major credit card to rent a car. Lisa showed her displeasure by staring angrily at her.

They were silent until Rochelle spoke. "Lisa, we go back a long way. I remember the times you talked about meeting your father. I want to help."

Lisa remained quiet. Rochelle decided to change the topic. She asked about the pregnancy. Lisa gave brief answers. Rochelle continued to talk until Rhonda said something about Brad and Tina dancing cozy together at the club.

"That brother needs to get his act together before she wakes up and smells the coffee. He's sweet but he ain't that sweet for her to sit around and wait," Rochelle said.

"So what's the four-one-one on Tony?" Rhonda asked.

"He really likes Alicia, but he's intimidated by her getting a Ph.D. Now, she's marrying the weirdest looking brother in the world. I don't know what is Tony's problem. Hell, she only wants to be a professional, educated babysitter," Rochelle continued. Rhonda burst into laughter.

"Rochelle, cool it! Alicia has worked hard to get where she is. I don't want you saying anything to her when she tells you that the wedding is postponed," Lisa said.

"Why is she postponing the wedding?"

"Don't tell her that I told you, but Kyle thinks he's moving too fast. He needs more time like every other sorry man in this world," Lisa said.

Rochelle became quiet. Although she and Alicia fussed constantly, she would never wish anything like that on her. "Was he like this in college? I didn't know him that well."

"Jennifer liked him. He ignored the hell out of her. I tried giving him the excuse of being bashful but that isn't his problem. Cameron says Kyle really likes white women. Cameron couldn't believe that he would ask a person like Alicia to marry him."

"I was wondering what was up. She hardly ever talked about our dresses. I paid my deposit."

"Can you imagine the money she has spent? She was suppose to help Cheryl with the accreditation on her academy. She was suppose to move to Kansas City in September. Right now she's too embarrassed to talk to anyone."

"So when does he want to get married?"

"I really don't think he wants to. I have a funny feeling he's running out on her."

"If they don't get married, that bastard better pay me back my deposit"

"If I was her, I would kick it with Tony. The man is sexy fine," Rhonda said.

"Tony needs to get more umph to his career. He's dragging his feet," Rochelle said.

"What does he do?" Rhonda asked.

"He's a manager at UPS."

"What's wrong with that!"

"When I talked to him last night, he bent my ear about wanting more out of life, but he didn't have any goals. Alicia has always had goals. She knew she needed to be an expert in her field in order to move ahead. I doubt if Tony is the one for her."

"You never know. She is still planning to move to Kansas City to help Cheryl with the accreditation. Maybe, she will get a better opportunity to know Kyle and who knows? She might get a chance to understand Tony a little better," Lisa said.

Rochelle was close to Columbia, Missouri when Lisa winced. "What's the matter?" Rochelle asked.

"My stomach feels like it's tightening."

"Have you felt like this earlier?"

"Not really. My back has been killing me."

"Have you passed the mucus plug?"

"I'm not in labor."

"When are you due?"

"In two weeks."

"Maybe it's false labor. I wouldn't think your doctor would allow you to travel so close to your due date."

Lisa was silent. She felt guilty. She had been on bed rest since her eighth month. The doctor was concerned about her going into labor early. After the myomectomy, she told Lisa that she was concerned about her having children and carrying until full term. Her uterus may not allow it.

Lisa took deep breaths. She let her head rest on the seat. She only wanted to think about laying eyes on Paul Smith. She rehearsed her speech over and over. She had to remove most of the cussing. It sounded too juvenile.

"I think we should go back," Rochelle said.

"By the time you turn around, we could be in Kansas City. I will rent a car and drive myself. I don't need anyone blocking my plans," Lisa fussed.

"I don't want you going into labor," Rochelle said.

"Aren't you studying to be a nurse?" Rhonda teased.

"Yeah but I did *not* like my maternity course. I've seen enough twats to last me a life time," Rochelle said nervously. She had a strange feeling that Lisa was going into labor. She decided to get some gas.

Rochelle encouraged Lisa to use the restroom. As Lisa went to get the key, Rochelle hurried to the pay phone and made a collect call to Alicia. Rochelle's heart raced while waiting for Cameron to come to the phone. When she broke the news that they were on their way to Kansas City and Lisa was probably in labor, Cameron exploded. Rochelle hung up quickly, thinking Lisa was on her way out of the restroom. She quickly paid for the gas and sat inside the car.

Lisa finally appeared. She walked slowly to the car. She asked Rhonda to switch places with her so that she could lie down on the back seat. Rhonda sat in the front. She and Rochelle sat stiff. They looked at one another.

"What's the matter?" Lisa asked.

"Nothing," Rochelle said and continued driving.

Rochelle was thirty minutes outside of Kansas City. Lisa sat up. "I hear you are planning to move to Atlanta when you're finished," Lisa said.

"I just want to leave St. Louis. I haven't made up my mind as to where I want to go."

"When are you coming to visit?" Lisa continued.

"I have a break in the middle of August before the Fall semester begins."

"Great! Me and the baby should be on schedule by then. You mind stopping at a gas station. I need to use the restroom."

Rochelle stopped at another gas station. When Lisa disappeared, Rochelle called Alicia again. Cameron had left about two hours ago. According to Alicia, he was so angry that it took twenty minutes to find his car keys which were lying on the dresser.

"How is Lisa?" Alicia asked.

"Strange! I really think she's in labor. She's not carrying on like the women in the maternity ward at Barnes."

"Cameron was cussing. I have never heard him cuss before."

"Shit! Now she's going to be mad at me."

"You should have told him the truth. Suppose she has the

baby on the road."

"We're here now."

Lisa came out of the restroom. Rochelle smiled as she talked. "Okay Rosalyn, I hope I get a chance to see you. I know it's last minute."

"Is she standing there?" Alicia asked.

"Yeah. Goodbye," Rochelle said grinning and hung up.

"How is Rosalyn?" Lisa asked as they walked back to the car.

"They were getting ready to go to church."

Rochelle was close to the Smith's residence. Lisa took deep breaths. She tried working herself up to get angry. Nothing happened. When Rochelle turned onto the street, Lisa became nervous. Her hands shook. She put them on her face.

Rochelle parked the car in front of a big house with two garages. The lawn was freshly cut. Bushes sculpted the front of the house. The driveway was long. They waited for Lisa to make the first move. Her focus was on the car's ceiling. She closed her eyes to keep the tears from falling. All she could think about was the man inside offering all of his attention and finances to children that did not belong to him.

Rochelle started the engine. "Where are you going?" Lisa asked. Her voice shook.

"I'm not going to let you walk up the driveway. You are going to get curb service," Rochelle said and zoomed the car up the driveway. A car was already there. Rochelle put the car in park and got out. Rhonda got out and opened Lisa's door to help her out.

Rhonda grabbed Lisa's hand as they walked to the front door. Lisa continued practicing her speech. This time, she added a few cuss words. She rubbed at the nagging charley horse that bothered her the entire morning.

Rochelle rang the doorbell. They waited patiently for someone to answer. Finally, the door opened. Lisa laid eyes on the person who had been a mystery all of her life.

When Paul saw her, he knew immediately who she was. He rehearsed a speech, too, but did not expect to say it until they agreed to meet.

"Come in," Paul said.

Lisa wouldn't move. She opened her mouth but nothing came out. She looked at the beautiful brick walls, nicely trimmed bushes and the black lacquered door. She looked at the plush carpet under Paul's feet. All she could think about was a tiny apartment with hard floors and roaches. The only relief was going to Miss Mattie's house for the best meals she had ever eaten.

"Aren't you coming in?" Paul asked.

When she was younger, an invitation as the one offered was the one thing she had hoped for. She imagined running into the arms of her father and him telling her that he had searched long and hard for her. She only remembered seeing those scenes in the movies. Lisa's eyes swelled with tears.

Paul did not know what else to do. The scene was extremely awkward for him. He thought his invitation was kind. He thought about the scene over the last few days. He rehearsed his apology and excuse. The tears in the young woman's eyes reminded him of the last conversation with Debra. The big difference was she didn't cry. She was hurt.

Before Paul began his spiel, Marilyn came to the door. Once she laid eyes on Lisa, she froze. She stood next to Paul. Seeing Marilyn stand close to Paul made Lisa want to leave. She turned around, but Rhonda stopped her.

"I had so much to say. I had so many questions to ask. I don't know why I'm here," Lisa mumbled.

"It's hard talking to you through the door. Please, come into the house," Paul said.

"Why? So you can show me what I missed?" Lisa asked crying.

"I want to talk to you," Paul said softly.

"Go inside, Lisa," Rochelle said.

"*No!* She doesn't need him," Rhonda snapped.

"Young lady, please keep your voice down," Marilyn said.

"Who in the hell are you talking too?" Rhonda continued.

"Rhonda, be quiet. You're not helping her," Rochelle said, staring at Rhonda. She wanted to say something again, but Rochelle motioned her to hush.

"I would like for you to come inside and relax for awhile. There are many things I would like to say too. You don't have to stay long," Paul said gently.

Rochelle assisted Lisa inside the house. Lisa remembered coming inside the house once. She came to visit Gina for advice. Paul was not home at the time. She remembered a beautiful house with nice furniture. Flowers and ruffles trimmed Gina's bedroom. It was made for an only girl.

Lisa walked into the living room. Gina came from her bedroom. She saw Lisa. Immediately, guilt took over. She refused to hide. It was difficult for her to take sides. She had to sit with Paul to help him through the discussion.

"Hi Lisa," Gina said.

Instead of speaking, Lisa stared at Gina. How could she not call after receiving the information? She knew it was from her. All she had to do was give advice as promised from the pledge mother creed.

Gina sat down in a chair. Before she got comfortable, Paul asked her to leave the room. Gina looked at him strangely. She slowly walked out of the room. Paul looked at Rochelle and Rhonda and politely asked if they would leave the room too.

Rochelle moved quickly, but Rhonda took her time.

Once alone, Paul looked around the room. He could not think of one thing to start the conversation because he forgot his speech. He decided to speak from his heart. As he told the story about dating Debra Arvell while doing maintenance work in a project, Lisa wiped her eyes. Her reaction made him choke.

He continued with the truth about Debra seeing him and Bill at the same time. His brother owned up to the responsibility because Debra told him that he was the father too. It was later when Debra claimed that he was the father. He took the blood test and never received the results until a few days ago.

Lisa couldn't say anything because her stomach tightened again and her back was aching. She felt a great deal of pressure pressing down. She had to go to the bathroom quickly. She got up slowly to find the bathroom. She struggled to sit on the toilet seat. She felt something thick escaping her. It was pinkish in color. It took several minutes to clean up. She held on to the wall because the pressure of the baby made it difficult to stand. She felt her stomach began to tighten. There was nothing she could do to brace herself for the pain. She cried out.

It came to her. She was in labor. She didn't think that labor would make it difficult to stand. She became nervous. She only thought about the preconceived notion of being in Atlanta delivering her baby. Cameron was suppose to be at her bedside telling her to breath or to push. At that moment, fluid ran down her legs. She panted. She could feel the tightening and pressure happening again. She opened her mouth but nothing came out.

Rhonda sat still. Her stomach felt tense. She looked around the room. Lisa had yet to come out of the rooom with Paul. When Rhonda's stomach twitched, she knew the spirits were telling her that her cousin was in labor. She stood quickly.

"Has anyone seen Lisa?" Rhonda asked.

"She's with Paul," Gina answered.

"They're talking," Rochelle added.

Rhonda could not relax. She rushed into the living room and saw Paul alone. "Where's Lisa?" she asked

"She went to the bathroom," Paul said.

Rhonda quickly rushed to the bathroom and called for Lisa. No sounds came from within. "Lisa, are you okay?" Rhonda asked loudly.

"Tell Rochelle I passed the plug and my water broke," Lisa managed to say. She heard Rhonda shouting for Rochelle and people rushing to the bathroom trying to open the door. She had a difficult time concentrating on the knob. Her body behaved on a cue from another source. Once she opened the door, Rhonda rushed in first. Lisa leaned on her cousin for support.

"Lisa, are you in labor?" Rochelle asked.

Lisa took deep breaths. She could not talk to anyone. She wanted to cradle. A few minutes later, the tightening occurred again. She grabbed her stomach, hoping it would ease the pressure and pain of her pelvis.

"When was the last contraction?" Marilyn ordered.

"A few minutes ago," Lisa whispered.

"Can you tell me how many minutes ago?" Marilyn continued.

Before Lisa could respond, she felt it again. She panted as her back gripped with pressure. She closed her eyes and called on Grandma Mattie. Miss Mattie always told her to call her if ever in need.

Rhonda held Lisa's hand and began to cry. There was nothing she could do to help her cousin. The squaw vine tea was to help ease the labor pain. It didn't appear that it had done anything.

"I can't tell how far apart the contractions are coming. Let's get her to the hospital," Marilyn commanded.

As Lisa left the bathroom, her legs buckled because she could feel the contraction again. Paul immediately picked her up. Lisa looked at him with teary eyes.

"I'm so sorry. I wished I had known the truth," Paul whispered as he walked her out of the bathroom.

"Gina, get a blanket. I want to see how far she has dilated. I think this baby is coming faster than expected," Marilyn said.

Paul continued holding Lisa. She only weighed one hundred and thirty pounds. He felt her shake, bracing herself for the next contraction. He held her tighter.

Gina spread the blanket on the floor. Paul placed Lisa carefully on the floor. Gina looked at Paul and then away. Marilyn went to work to remove Lisa's underwear. Everyone turned their heads, fearing what would come out.

"Gina, dial nine-one-one," Marilyn said. She believed Lisa would probably deliver within the next five hours.

Marilyn saw Lisa shake. She did not cry nor did she scream. She was tough like her mother. Marilyn began stroking Lisa's hand. She coached her into taking deep breaths. It was difficult for Marilyn to determine if Lisa was having contractions. She was relaxed. Rhonda was crying at her feet while massaging them. Lisa opened her eyes and continued to take deep breaths. Although the pain came and went, it was manageable.

There was a knock on the door. Gina rushed to answer. Instead of being the paramedics, it was Cameron. His face was flushed with anger. He entered the house without speaking. He had driven close to ninety miles an hour to get there. Once he arrived, he had to call Alicia for directions to Gina's house. That took awhile because they had to call Cheryl who lived in Kansas City.

Cameron saw Lisa lying on the floor. He rushed down to her. He couldn't fuss or talk. He sat next to her and held her hand.

A knock sounded on the door again. This time, it was the paramedics. They came inside with a bed. Rhonda stood off to the side as they worked with Lisa. Cameron looked at Rhonda for an explanation.

"She wanted to come. She said that she was going to drive by herself," Rhonda said angrily.

Cameron swallowed. It was time to see the birth of his son. He was excited about it days earlier, but now he was nervous.

Chapter Twenty-Eight

"**P**ush," the doctor told Lisa. She beared down hard. She took deep breaths. She was in pain, but not like she imagined she would be. She gave a final push and felt the release of the load that she carried for months. She cried and laughed at the same time. Immediately, she wanted to see the baby. She wanted her baby in her arms. She wanted to feel him next to her chest.

The doctor and nurse were tending to the new born. He finally let out a cry. Lisa cried along with him. She weakly stretched out her arms for him.

"Just a second, Lisa. They're cleaning him up," Cameron said nervously. His face was flushed. His eyes were watered. He took deep breaths.

"What's the matter with him? Check to make sure he has his fingers and toes," Lisa said exhausted.

"He's fine. He has all of his fingers and toes," the doctor said and handed the bundle to Lisa.

She looked at her baby. He was wrinkled and red. He squirmed in the wrap. Lisa brought him closer to hear him breath. She wanted him to cry again. Finally, he made a noise. She laughed and offered him to Cameron. He declined.

"What's the matter?" she asked.

Cameron opened his mouth and then shook his head. He could not express the emotions of seeing pain on Lisa's face for the first time ever, or the doctor cutting his wife without the help of the epidural to release the baby. Every thought made Cameron think about not being helpful to his wife as she gave birth to their son. He also thought about not being present as Vivian went through the same trauma.

"Aren't you going to hold him?" Lisa asked. The joy on her face was slowly diminishing.

Cameron slowly picked up the bundle. It felt awkward to him. As he brought the baby closer, it squirmed and cried out.

"Relax when you hold him," the nurse instructed.

Cameron dropped his shoulders and brought his son to his face. The newborn seemed extremely tiny to him. It made Cameron smile. He laughed out loud. He could not believe he created life. His son's little arms stretched out in protest. He cried again. His son was not going to be the silent fighter like himself, he was going to make his mark by being heard.

Cameron smiled at Lisa. "He has a good set of lungs, doesn't he?" Cameron said. His fears slowly dissipated after seeing Lisa smile at him.

Cameron, Rhonda and Rochelle looked at the babies in the nursery. Cameron's attention was only on one. The little boy with the name "Johnson" over his head, slept peacefully. All of the other babies looked much larger than baby Johnson.

"I need to make a call. I'll be back," Cameron told Rhonda. He walked down the hall to the pay phones. He dropped the coins in the slot and dialed his mother.

"Hi mom. Lisa had the baby. It's a boy," Cameron said slowly.

"How is Lisa?"

"She's fine. She's a strong woman like you. She delivered the baby without the epidural."

"She is a strong woman. How is the baby?"

"Mom, he's so tiny."

"Is he premature?"

"They said he weighs seven pounds and eight ounces. I know I was much bigger than that."

Cameron could hear his mother chuckle lightly.

"He's a little larger than you. You weighed seven pounds even. He's an average size baby."

"The other babies in the nursery are bigger than him."

"Don't worry! He will get larger and eat you out of house and home like you and your brothers did."

Cameron always enjoyed hearing his mother make jokes. He believed he got his sense of humor from her. "When are you coming to Atlanta?"

"I'll come near the first of Fall. If you need me earlier, let me know."

"Thanks, mom. I love you."

His mother paused for a few seconds. "Lisa doesn't expect you to be perfect and neither do I. We do expect you to do your best. Running away never solves anything. I love you too, sweetheart.

Good-bye."

"Good-bye, mom," Cameron said and hung up the phone. His mother always knew when something was wrong. Already, he felt sorry for his son. He would never be able to keep a secret from Lisa.

Cameron called his father. His posture straightened when he heard his father's voice. "Hey dad, Lisa had the baby!"

"Great! What did she have?"

"A boy! Johnson men always produce boys."

Cameron could hear his father laugh. Charles Johnson had three brothers. He was used to being around males.

"How is my grandson?"

"Greedy! He wants to eat already."

"I see he has his father's appetite. How is Lisa?"

"She's resting. It was a tough delivery."

"How are you doing?"

Cameron gulped. "Why are you asking me that?"

"I know when something is wrong."

Cameron had difficulty swallowing. He thought he sounded up-beat and happy. How could his father know something was wrong? He concluded his son was really in for it. Everyone would know his business. "I feel like my son...helpless."

"When Lionel was born, I was the proudest father on earth and also the most frightened one too. I thought about the 'what ifs'."

"I want to do a good job. I want my son to be proud of me."

"Parenting is tough. It's trial and error. Each child is different. Your son will be proud of you. Don't expect him to tell you that. Sometimes it never happens."

Cameron hesitated a little. "Despite the things that have happened, I'm proud of you and so is Lionel."

"I know, son. Children should learn from their parents' mistakes. This child is a little different from Celeste."

Not only did the last statement occupy Cameron's attention, but Rochelle coming to the telephone did too. Cameron paused a little. He had forgotten about Celeste. "What do you mean? I love Celeste too."

"This one will get more of your attention. Do as much as you can to give yourself to Celeste."

"I will. When are you coming to visit?"

"Around the end of August. Jason wants me to meet some girl he likes. If I didn't know any better, I think he's in love. I guess he drank a love potion. I've never heard him talk about a woman like this before."

Rochelle's loud talking and laughing forced Cameron to end his conversation sooner than he wanted too. "I'll talk to you later, dad," he said and hung up.

"Wait a minute! Here he is," Rochelle said and handed the phone to Cameron. She picked up another phone and dialed someone else.

"Hello," Cameron said.

"Hey Cameron! I heard Lisa didn't have an epidural and that she was in labor all day yesterday."

"Who is this?"

"Alicia, fool!"

"I'm sorry, Alicia. I couldn't pick out your voice."

"So the baby is twenty-one inches and weighs seven pounds and eight ounces?"

Cameron couldn't determine if it were a statement or question. He decided to be agreeable as the woman rambled on about information he didn't know.

Paul, Marilyn and Gina were sitting in Lisa's room. She was resting with the help of an oxygen tube in her nose. Marilyn decided to call Barbara. It was time to pay their last respects to Debra.

Lisa opened her eyes. She saw Paul first. From his features, she could not pick out what she inherited from him. Her breathing became short when he approached her bed.

"The doctor says it will be awhile before you can travel. I would like for you and the baby to stay with us until you are strong enough to leave," he said.

"Where is Cameron?"

"He's at the nursery," Gina answered.

"I don't know what to say and I don't expect you to accept me with opened arms. I want you to know if I had known the truth, you would have never been without me."

Paul had rehearsed the last statement over and over. He wasn't one to lie. He felt betrayed by Debra and his brother. Since no real proof existed before the court papers, he felt safe to say he didn't know the truth.

"Did you know about me?" Lisa demanded.

"I knew about you. But like I said, I didn't know you were mine. I took the blood test and waited for the results. They never came and your mother was dead. When my brother claimed that he was your father, I thought it was the truth. He made sure you were taken care of. I'm sorry that neither one of us were in your life."

There was nothing more for Lisa to say. She closed her eyes and thought about her baby. She wanted to see him again, but she was too weak to get out of bed.

"Paul, do you mind leaving me alone with Lisa?" Gina asked.

Paul nodded and left the room. Gina walked to the bed. "Did you send me those papers?" she asked Lisa. There was no response.

"When Paul told me that he wasn't your father six years ago, I left it alone. When I received those papers, I wanted to confront him about it before calling you. I knew you already knew. My feelings were hurt after finding out that he was."

"Gina, I really don't want to discuss it."

"I hope you will stay at my mother's house until you are able to travel."

Cameron and Rochelle entered the room. Gina stepped away from the bed and Cameron took her place. "Mom and dad send their love," Cameron said. Lisa nodded. "I need to take Rhonda back to Atlanta and stay for the big production meeting. I want you to stay with Mr. and Mrs. Smith until I come back for you guys."

Gina excused herself from the room and Rochelle followed. After they left, Lisa looked at Cameron with a frown. "I don't want to stay with them."

"I know you don't. Please do it for the sake of me and the baby. I would feel much better knowing that someone is taking care of you. The doctor said you and the baby should be able to travel in a couple of weeks."

"How is he?"

"He's a big boy. All the other boys are crying like punks."

Lisa chuckled. "Remember, he's a baby. If he cries like a punk, he has the right too. He's my baby. I don't want him trying to be tough too early."

Cameron leaned forward and kissed her on the forehead. He rubbed the side of his rough beard against her face. She frowned a little but enjoyed the attention.

"You are a brave woman. Although I didn't see them give you the episiotomy it made me shaky just knowing that they did. I never imagined childbirth being so tough."

"It's wasn't as bad as I thought. I guess the squaw vine tea really works."

"What is Rhonda, some kind of voodoo woman?"

"Squaw vine is more natural than an epidural. And I want you to be nice to her. Regardless of what anyone says, she is the only real family I have. I want her to feel welcomed in our home. She will be our son's godmother."

"Have you decided on a name?"

"I thought about naming him after you."

Cameron shook his head. "I want him to be independent. I never liked juniors."

"Do you like Caleb William Johnson?"

Cameron smiled. "Sounds good. Where did you get Caleb

from?"

"From a list of names in my grandmother's bible. It was written underneath my name."

After Miss Mattie died, the only personal belonging Lisa wanted of Miss Mattie was her bible. After the funeral, Lisa looked inside it for the first time and saw several names. At first, she was confused seeing her name listed under Jennifer and Melanie. After talking to Miss Sweets, it became clear. All the names meant something to Miss Mattie. The names Corine and Coretta were listed too. Underneath Lisa's name was Caleb. She didn't know what it meant, but it sounded nice.

A knock sounded on Lisa's door. "Come in," Cameron said.

In walked Marilyn, Barbara, Susan and JoAnn. Both Lisa and Cameron looked confused.

"Lisa, I want you to meet some of your mother's closest friends," Marilyn said. She introduced Lisa to Susan and JoAnn. Lisa already knew Barbara.

"Cameron, do you mind if we talk to Lisa alone?" Barbara asked with authority.

"I'm going back to the nursery. Tina, Crystal, Tony, Brad and the others will be here later. They just made it back from St. Louis," Cameron said and left the room.

"I wanted you to meet your mother's closest friends. We all considered ourselves sisters," Marilyn said.

"I guess so. All of you are Kappas," Lisa said.

"It went closer than being sorors. All of us came from humble beginnings. We depended on each other for support," Susan stated.

"Didn't my mother get kicked out of the group from sharing some secrets?" Lisa said smartly.

"Not really. It was a misunderstanding that was mainly our fault. We each made amends with your mother before she died," JoAnn answered.

"Speaking of my mother's death Mrs. Stevens, the ceremonial cloth you gave me had a 1972 death date. I know that date is incorrect. This cloth is used to bury all Kappa sorors. Were you ladies at my mother's funeral?"

"Yes we were," Barbara answered.

"When did she die?"

"June 6, 1989," Barbara said.

Lisa closed her eyes. She began to breath hard. Her mother had lived seventeen years after she was claimed dead. Lisa began to cry. "Why did she leave me?" Lisa cried.

"She could never give you the things you wanted or for that matter deserved," Marilyn said.

"*Why did she leave me?*" Lisa barked

"I was with her the day she died. She asked if I would

apologize for her. She never meant to leave you. Sometimes when people make mistakes, it's difficult to face them," Barbara said.

"How did she die?" Lisa whimpered.

"She found out that you were getting married. She developed enough courage to attend the reception. She was planning to stay incognito. On her way there, she ran head on into Jennifer's car. The accident took her life. She was Mrs. Farrow. She has always been at important events in your life," Barbara said softly.

"Carleton Peterson said her body was shipped to Georgia," Lisa said to Barbara.

"I have the location to your mother's grave site. The one in St. Louis was for your purpose. It wouldn't raise any questions about her death," Barbara said.

"When we gave your mother the Kappa's Last Rites, we vowed to keep alive our motto, 'All for One and One for All'. All of our children look at us as their aunts. We hope that you can do the same thing too," Marilyn said.

Lisa never had a real family. All of a sudden, everyone was inviting themselves into her life. She didn't know what to say or do.

"If ever you need anything, just let us know," Susan said.

"I want to be alone," Lisa whispered.

"Sure, honey. We understand," Barbara said and looked at the document that Marilyn had given her.

The women left Lisa's room relaxed. They felt the conversation went better than expected. They rehearsed briefly the things Debra would have wanted her daughter to know. The discussion brought closure to years of separation, misunderstandings and secrets.

"Thanks for calling us, Marilyn. It broke my heart knowing that girl has gone so many years not knowing the truth," Susan said.

"I don't understand why Debra would do such a thing," JoAnn commented.

"Debra had her reasons. We all have our reasons. We never thanked her for giving us self-esteem. Had she not done the things that she did, we would probably not be where we are," Marilyn said, giving her last respects.

"She did have a good heart. She helped me get a 'B in math," Susan said, giving her last respects.

"She had more than a good heart. She was loyal to us, even after the disagreement," JoAnn said, giving her last respects.

Barbara said nothing. Only Barbara traveled to Georgia to put Debra Arvell to rest. She arranged for Debra and her sister to be buried side by side. Barbara never had a disagreement with Debra. She trusted Barbara with the final secrets, documents of information which many Barbara destroyed.

Debra was a survivor. She was shrewd to the point of being criminal. She had no problem falsifying documents to do whatever necessary to help herself and other people too. She never bolstered her ego.

Susan got her 'B because Debra typed the final exam for Mr. Greer. He, like so many other male instructors, trusted the very sweet, very pretty, flirtatious Debra Arvell. She overlooked them accidentally rubbing up against her for a few seconds of thrill. Men were to be used, as far as she was concerned. She only liked one, Bill Smith and trusted another, Carleton Peterson.

JoAnn was correct to say Debra stayed loyal after the disagreement. Had it not been for Debra working several jobs, one being a typist for the District Attorney's office, JoAnn's husband could not dodge child support payments. Barbara just could not determine if Debra did it for the sake of JoAnn or to make JoAnn's husband pay for being a man.

Barbara continued staring at the documents naming Paul as the father of Lisa Willet. There was something familiar about them. Then it came to her. The signature on the document, *Bernard Howard.* It had the indicator the three partners in crime used as their signature for revenge, the letters *BH* representing Benny Hayes. The documents were probably false, Barbara thought. She smiled.

"Is anyone coming to the President's reception tonight?" Barbara asked. The group agreed.

"Barbara, I hear that Lori will probably win. She has the support of some of the graduate chapters we were trying to pull," Marilyn said.

"Too much has changed over the years without our involvement," Susan added.

Barbara nodded. She heard the news from Floristine a couple of weeks ago. It all fell within her plans. It was best for Lori to win regional director.

Chapter Twenty-Nine

Linda instructed the young women to mingle in the crowd of older couples standing outside the banquet room. The young women were nervous at their first after-five affair. They were pleased with the dresses Melanie designed for them. All the dresses were black with a hint of youth and sex appeal. A few had short dresses with either sheer sleeves or sheer backs. The ones with longer skirts had splits that went pass their knees.

Tosha was first to offer assistance to the older women. She approached Barbara who was standing with Floristine, Gloria and Susan. Tosha smiled upon her entrance. Barbara stared hard at her. The gold tooth was gone. Barbara returned the smile.

"Hello, my name is Tosha. If I can help you with anything, please let me know," Tosha said with a huge smile.

"Thank you, Tosha. Are you still in college?" Gloria asked.

"Yes ma'am. I'm majoring in political science. I plan to attend law school next year. I want to be an attorney specializing in legal issues pertaining to women."

"How nice! Will you join the Kansas City Alumnae after graduation?" Floristine asked.

"Definitely! I thought about joining the younger chapter, but I think sorors coming out of college need to continue to learn from our older sorors."

Gloria sniffed and Floristine wanted to faint. They hated hearing young versus old. It appeared that Kansas City was considered old and Lee Summit was considered young.

"Tosha, can you direct us to table number three?" Barbara asked with a grin.

Tosha walked in front of the group of women. As she took strides, her long lean legs caused her short, swing dress to swish.

The sheer sleeves exposed thin firm arms. The group of older women took shorter strides falling a short distance behind her.

"My legs used to look like that when I was her age," Barbara whispered to the group, admiring Tosha's strides.

"My arms used to be thin and firm like hers," Susan added.

"I had a waistline like that... before the children, of course," Gloria said.

"I looked better than her when I was her age," Floristine said.

Linda directed the young women on the task of cleaning up. They were joyous as they performed their duties. Linda came to her mother's table after the reception. The women complimented her on the reception. She was ready to leave when the president came to her.

"Everything was wonderful, Malinda. Thanks for a wonderful job," she said.

Linda blushed. It had been a long time since she had done any catering. She contracted with another catering company. She cooked some of the food and did the majority of the presentation. It was a small crowd of two hundred people.

"Thank you Madame President. I could not have done it without the help of Zeta Chi chapter," Linda said.

"Isn't that chapter up for suspension?" the president asked.

"Yes ma'am. I'm working with them to correct some of their problems. It's been a long time since they had structure. They have an impressive list of projects they are performing in hopes of reconsideration," Linda said.

"Suppose the chapter is suspended?" the president continued.

"They know what went wrong. What they are doing is mainly out of remorse to the chapter founders," Linda said.

The president nodded. She chatted briefly with Barbara and Gloria. Floristine and Susan talked among themselves. Linda took the initiative to leave. The women looked happy to see her go. She was confused.

"It looks as if everything is cleared away. Keith and I are leaving to pick up the children," Linda said.

"Okay, sweetie. Tell Melanie I need to talk to her," Barbara said.

Linda bid everyone goodbye and left to find Keith. He was talking to a couple of friends from college. She saw him having a good time and decided to thank the young women. They were in a little group talking and laughing. Linda felt guilty about all of their hard work being done in vain. The way the president talked, the chapter would be suspended.

"Ladies, thanks so much. Everyone is raving over your appearances and performances," Linda said.

"This was fun! I can't wait to go to another after-five function," one said.

Linda kept her pasted smile as she looked at the excitement on the girls' faces. She had so much confidence that the chapter would be saved.

"I guess I will see everyone after the election on Tuesday. I want you all to come to my house for a celebration for the hard work. Don't think I don't know about the behind the scenes campaign," Linda said.

"Jessica Patterson, the girl who's running for regional representative, wants to talk to you," Tosha said.

Linda remembered the dark girl who reminded her of Jennifer. She thought about how nice it would be for the two of them to work together. "Tell her to call me tomorrow," Linda said and left.

Linda and Keith climbed the steps to Melanie's apartment. They could sense something was immediately wrong. Melanie's door was cracked opened. Keith rushed inside. Lauren was cuddling Indie and little Edward was sitting next to them on the floor. When Indie saw Linda, she broke free from Lauren and ran to Linda crying.

"Where is Melanie?" Linda asked nervously.

Lauren pointed to the bedroom. Little Edward began to cry. Keith rushed inside Melanie's bedroom. She was on the bed half nude. As he approached the bed, her eyes pierced him. He was shocked to see blood on her face. She looked as if she had been beaten badly. He sat on the bed.

"Get the hell off of my bed," Melanie said hoarsely.

Keith slowly got up. There was nothing about her that he recognized. It was difficult looking at her with ripped clothing and it was equally difficult for him to see her face puffy and blood staining the inside of her thighs. He turned around and faced Linda who was standing in the doorway with Indie in her arms.

"We need to call for help," Keith said.

Melanie raised slowly from the bed. "If you do, I will kill you," she said.

"Keith, take the children home," Linda said.

"I'm calling for help," Keith insisted.

"Get out of my goddamn house," Melanie said roughly.

Keith turned sharply and left the bedroom. Linda remained. She saw red marks on Melanie's chest. "Did John do this?"

"I want you to leave and take Lauren home with you," Melanie said.

"I'm not going anywhere," Linda said stubbornly. She put Indie down and told her to go to the living room. The little girl refused.

"I'm killing that son-of-a-bitch," Melanie said very low.

"If you do, you will need an alibi. I think the perfect thing to do is to go to the hospital to document this. At least you won't spend your entire life in jail. Keith and I will raise Lauren while you serve time in jail," Linda said sarcastically. She hoped the insanity of her statements would jog sense into Melanie.

"That's a good idea. I'm going to shoot his dick off," Melanie said a with wicked grin.

Linda became more nervous. Her comments seemed to humor Melanie. She looked and sounded different.

"This will be the last time he hit my baby and this will be the last time he fucks me," Melanie said. Her eyes widened. She looked at her closet. She needed to get to the shoe box. If only she had the chance to get to her closet, John would have left on a stretcher.

"Have you decided where you are moving?" Linda asked without looking at her.

"I don't know where I'm moving," Melanie said. She brushed her hair from her face roughly. Linda saw the side of her face. It was red.

"Put on some clothes so that we can take you to the hospital," Linda said with a little more force.

Melanie turned around sharply. "Do you have a hearing problem? I'm not going anywhere! Where is Lauren?"

"She's in the living room."

"I need some money."

"How much?"

"Not yours, his!"

"Angel, please don't do anything stupid!"

Melanie puffed out a laugh. "Angel? When I'm finished with that bastard, he will need Jesus to recognize him." Melanie struggled to get out of bed. She had difficulty standing straight. She bent forward. "That son-of-a-bitch will pay for this."

Linda put Indie down. She began to whine. Linda ignored her and rushed over to Melanie. She was able to catch her before she fell.

"We have to put our heads together on this. We can't let him get off easy," Linda said quickly.

"Who cares if a man rapes his wife!"

"You have to be careful. He can kill you," Linda said and eased Melanie onto the bed. Indie ran to her and reached for her. "Indie, go to your father," Linda said firmly. The little girl stood still and cried. Keith came into the bedroom.

"The police are here," he said and picked up Indie.

Melanie's eyes were blazing with fire. She pursed her lips. "Tell them to leave," she said low.

Keith understood Melanie's contempt. He often heard that

rape victims generally became angry with any man.

"Officers, in here," Keith said without losing eye contact with Melanie. He hoped that she spoke out of anger about killing him. From the looks of her eyes, she was ready to make good on the threat.

Melanie stared at the ceiling. She could feel Lauren ease her thin body next to her.

"How is my baby?" Melanie asked.

"Fine," Lauren answered.

"Are you ready to visit your dad again? He will be here in a few weeks to get you."

Lauren said nothing.

"Baby, what's the matter?"

Lauren began to cry. Her mother refused to get out of bed for two days. Barbara had to call the Youth Center to tell them that Melanie was assaulted by a stranger. One of the program directors gasped. They didn't know what to do, especially since the executive director was out.

Melanie turned her focus to Lauren and smiled. "You want to move far away?"

Lauren nodded. She began to sign. Melanie smiled as Lauren told her that she loved her. Then Melanie stiffened when Lauren told her that Lionel was coming to town soon.

"Did you call him?" Melanie continued.

Lauren shook her fist and looked sadly into Melanie's eyes. Melanie swallowed. Her throat was dry. She had not eaten or drank anything in a couple of days.

"Lauren, I told you about calling your father all the time. He's busy," Melanie signed.

Lauren shook her head and signed, "He will help us."

Melanie sighed heavily. Her head turned quickly when she heard the door open. Barbara entered the room. "The finance director is on the phone. You feel like talking?" Barbara asked.

Melanie moved slowly to the telephone. She picked it up and instantly, she was on automatic with the person who was responsible for disbursing funds. Melanie wanted to make sure Carlos got everything he needed for the basketball tournament. It was starting within the next couple of days.

Carlos worked well with the teenage boys. It was tough the first few practices. He had to put some of them out of the tournament. They tried starting trouble, but Carlos' magic touch was firm with them when he told them to either work as a team or stay out. He was able to get Dennis and a few more Lambdas to coordinate a small tournament. Melanie could tell that it was going to grow into something larger the following year.

Melanie hung up the telephone. She saw a glow in Barbara's

eyes. It was election day. According to Barbara's look, it appeared that Linda was the winner.

"Are you going to the conference?" Melanie asked. Barbara nodded.

"Will Linda be the new regional director?" Melanie continued.

"I don't think so. She spoke beautifully as she exposed the weaknesses in the sorority. She was quite eloquent and passionate when she talked about bridging the gap between the generations," Barbara said with pride.

Melanie's mouth was wide opened. She and Barbara talked about Linda winning and nothing less. Barbara played her trump cards on the election.

"I thought she had enough votes to pull if off," Melanie said in shock.

Barbara sat on the bed. She rubbed Lauren's face slowly. "Will you look after your mother while I'm gone?" Lauren shook her fist. Barbara took her pointer finger and lifted Lauren's chin gently. "I want you to talk to me."

"Yes, Auntie Barbara."

"That's better."

"Aunt Barbara, I thought it was a sure win," Melanie said.

"It is!"

"You've just said she wasn't going to win."

Barbara turned her focus to Melanie. She brushed Melanie's hair from her face with her fingers and smiled. "My daughter deserves something special. She has worked hard for something more than regional director." Barbara stood and looked at Melanie. "John will pay for what he's done to you," she said and left the room.

Melanie looked confused. She and Barbara worked together on calling in the favors. It wasn't making sense. Then it came to Melanie. The trump cards Barbara played were past presidents, not chapter delegates. Something big was about to happen.

Only voting delegates and national officers and officials past and present were allowed to be in the ballroom. The four candidates were seated on the dais along with the national officers in attendance. Everyone held their breaths as the sargent-of-arms delivered the envelope.

Earlier, Linda saw her mother sitting with some of the past national officers in the front of the room. Barbara was not there. Linda's heart pounded. Something had to be wrong.

The regional representative was announced first. Instead of calling names with the number of votes, the winner was announced, Jessica Patterson. Linda saw the tears of happiness in the young woman's eyes.

Linda tried preparing herself for what everyone was waiting

for. Her adrenaline began to flow as she thought about working with the young woman who called her the other day, asking for advice.

It was time to announce the new regional director. The room was still. Linda heard the names called in alphabetical order with the corresponding votes. Lori's name was first with fifty-eight votes. Linda heard squeals of joy. She felt the room slowly growing smaller. The next candidate received twelve votes. Linda knew she needed the remaining votes to beat Lori. The next candidate would surely receive more than ten votes. Linda's nervousness changed to disappointment.

The next candidate's name was called and eighteen votes were attached to her name. Then Linda heard yelling and screaming. She saw Lori jump up. Linda's name was called with forty-four votes. She wanted desperately to exit without looking like a poor sport. She hated the idea of congratulating Lori on winning, but it had to be done.

Linda pasted a smile on her face and approached Lori. Their looks became calculating.

"Congratulations, Lori. The better candidate won," Linda said and extended her hand. Lori accepted the offer graciously.

"It was a good race. You fought a good fight," Lori said.

Linda nodded and turned to walk away. She was standing face to face with her mother. Linda blew air and tried to smile. Barbara's look was stern. Linda could not determine if her mother was disappointed at her or the race. Barbara stood closer to her. For the first time, Linda wanted her mother to hold her.

"Sisters, please have a seat. We must finish our last bit of business. We must announce the nomination of a newly vacant slot for national official," the past regional director said.

The room quieted down. No one was aware that a vacancy for national official existed. Usually, the biography of a nominee would accompany the last sorority quarterly, but nothing was written on any candidate from the Central region. It gave voting delegates an opportunity to review the individual from their region who would represent the sorority worldwide before confirming the nomination at the conference. The individual would be confirmed at the conference in the region in which they lived. It meant high national presence because the national official could easily bring national officers to events. It was just a matter of a quorum at the conference.

When openings for national officials became available, they were usually nominated in the year of the conference by national officers past or present. Each candidate would be under review for a whole year before voted on by the executive committee in the following year of the convention. The individual could serve a maximum of four terms or eight years as long as the executive committee voted for them to continue. The position was usually held by older women who could financially afford to travel not only across the country but around the world.

Five past national presidents approached the podium. One president announced that Edith Saint resigned. She gave a biography of accomplishments on Edith Saint.

Linda looked at the person who was Edith Saint. She was one of the women at her mother's card party. She sat at Melanie's table. At the conference, she looked saintly but at the card party, she looked like a Vegas dealer.

Another past national president started on the list of projects Linda spearheaded, one receiving recognition from the mayor. Although Linda performed them under the auspices of Lori's leadership, she received credit.

The next past president talked about Linda visiting a past national official after hip surgery and how she cooked and cleaned for her. She talked about Linda visiting older sorors, outside the region, lending a helping hand.

The next past president talked about the letter Shontay sent to nationals telling about the problems of Zeta Chi. No one undertook the charge but Linda. She helped the undergraduates see the importance of belonging to the sisterhood. They were working hard on projects to bring honor back to the chapter. The president announced the projects and letters from directors of each project proclaiming the outstanding performances of the young women. The president announced that one letter was from a member of Alpha Theta Lambda Sorority. The audience gasped.

As the last past president stood at the podium, Linda remembered her. She attended her mother's brunch several years ago. The woman spoke clearly, articulating every word. "Sisters what an impressive resume we have just heard. We will bring to the floor, at the national convention next year, the nomination of Linda Stevens Reed as national official of Phi Kappa Psi. I present to you and introduce to others Linda Stevens Reed."

It took a while for Linda to understand that she was being nominated for national official. She was stunned. To hear others talk of her made her sound important. The things she had accomplished sounded impressive. She looked at her mother. Barbara returned the look.

"Do you or do you not accept the nomination?" Barbara asked sarcastically.

Linda walked out slowly. She heard loud clapping. Her focus was on the smiling face at the podium. When she arrived at the podium, she looked out over the audience of clapping people whom she hardly knew. She cleared her throat. "Madame President, had I not heard my name, I would still wonder who was this striking, charismatic, charming, intelligent, benevolent individual. But enough about me."

The audience laughed at Linda's quick wit and humorous remarks. When she said that she accepted the nomination, everyone stood. She stepped back and gave a soft wave to the audience. Each past president gave her a hug. She walked back to the sideline to her mother and wiped her eyes.

"Lori won the election," Linda said nervously to her mother.

"Thank God! Now she can continue her political career."

"Mother, I don't think I'm ready for this."

"You're ready."

"It's such a huge responsibility."

"You can do it. Besides, it's time for Edith to step down. We haven't traveled together since God knows how long."

Before Linda could say anything else, The Other-Side-of-the-Tracks members approached her and extended congratulations. They quickly turned their attention from Linda and talked to Barbara. Linda walked away. Lori was in her path. As she approached Lori, she could see a genuine smile on Lori's face.

"I think I under rated you. Zeta Chi called us first. Did Melanie help you?"

"Why did you kick her out of the group? You were the big sister she never had."

"I made a mistake! I heard she was in the hospital. How is she?"

It was clear to Linda that Lori knew what happened. It didn't make since to polish up the incident. "She's adjusting. She's going to need help."

"Tell her I will give her a call in a couple of days. It should give her time to regroup."

"She's at mother's."

"Oh? Now I have to face Barbara Stevens."

"My mother respects you a lot. You should not have kicked Melanie out of the group. She's my mother's goddaughter."

Lori nodded as she watched Barbara talk to her select few. Before she could turn her head, Barbara caught her eye and whispered to the group. The women approached Lori and Linda.

"I guess I have to pay the piper now instead of later," Lori said low and plastered a smile on her face. "Hello Mrs. Stevens," Lori said happily.

"Hello sweetie. How is your mother?"

"She's fine. She saw you at the reception Sunday."

"I know. Congratulations! I say the better candidate won."

Lori and Linda understood the double edge sword. Lori hesitated before speaking. "It was a class act finish, Mrs. Stevens."

"I guess you haven't lost your step, Barbara," one friend said.

"Even if you are an old bitch!" another said and the group

filled the hall with laughter.

Lori was filled with embarrassment. Barbara smiled at the younger woman. "Wait until you are an old bitch. It gets even better. I want you to give Melanie a call," Barbara said and looked at Linda. "Make sure the picture with all of us at the Lambdas' Cotillion, including Debra, replaces the one on the chapter room wall," Barbara said and walked off with her friends.

Linda took a deep sigh of relief. The chapter was saved.

"I really under estimated her. Do you mind asking your mother if I can talk to her?" Lori asked in a demanding tone.

Linda had to chuckle a little. She had been nominated to join the highest rank and Lori still kept her at local level. It didn't matter to Linda for Lori to keep the upper edge. Linda had a great amount of respect for her.

"Mother doesn't like talking business on the phone. When do you want to meet with her?"

"Whenever she's available! Estelle is having a victory celebration at her house this Saturday. I believe it is for the both of us. Will you and Melanie be there?"

Of course she will, Linda thought. No matter how big of a bitch Lori was, Estelle was just as bad. No way she could refuse an invitation from the two top angels of 1978. Even Barbara would chew at her if she did.

"Do I have a choice?" Linda asked with a grin.

Lori smiled back. "I think Estelle wanted you to win too. She's such a bitch!"

"Melanie and I will be there."

"You never answered my question. Did Melanie leak the information about Zeta Chi?"

"No."

"Who did?"

"I don't know."

Lori didn't know whether or not to believe Linda. Each pledge line had their secrets. Lori was the one who named the line S.S. Diamonds Are A Girl's Best Friend. The loyalty between the members on the ship deserved the title. No one broke under pressure when the big sisters pledged them harder after finding out the line silently retaliated against them.

Lori came to the conclusion that she had been beaten three times by the same group of girls. The performance at the step-show, between Annette and Melanie, deserved an academy award. Instead of kicking anyone out of the group, Lori decided to keep the women in close view. There had to be a smaller group of planners and controllers. The ones from her line. It was time to play another game.

Chapter Thirty

It was eleven o'clock Saturday morning. Avery was standing next to Paul receiving final instructions before the game began. According to his grandfather, all he had to do was hit the square box with the ball and it would fall into the net. With all of his might, Avery threw the ball up and it only hit the rim. He looked disappointed each time. Each of his other teammates was able to throw the ball inside the net except him.

"Don't worry about making a basket. Defense wins the game too," Paul coached. He was coaching ages eight and nine on Avery's team and ages fourteen and fifteen on another team. Paul was impressed with a couple of players on the other team. He worked the boys on making points as oppose to showing off and looking pretty in the process. A few boys weren't happy with his coaching style so they joined the opposite team and Paul received from the other team boys who would listen, ones he felt would win the game.

It was a small tournament. There were enough boys for two teams in each of the five age categories. They younger boys were starting first. The older boys, ages sixteen, seventeen and eighteen were playing in the evening.

Paul got the little boys in a huddle and gave final instructions. They put their little fists on top of his and shouted. Five boys walked out on the floor. Only seven were on a team. Each one would get a chance to play. Paul wanted them to enjoy the game, not necessarily win.

The whistle blew and the boys ran down the court. They were using the width of the gym. There were screams and shouts from the audience of mothers in the bleachers. Then Paul heard a familiar voice. She shouted at the referee for not seeing the foul against her son. He looked around and saw Gina standing with hands on hips. He saw Carlos tap her and she sat down.

The little boys continued running back and forth, throwing the ball into the air missing the net. Finally, Avery snuck behind a boy and hit the ball away. He dribbled the ball down the court by himself. Both Carlos and Gina shot up from their seats screaming. Avery made it to the goal but hesitated. All he heard was "shoot." He didn't think he could make the point, so he beckoned for a teammate and threw the ball to him. The boy threw the ball into the air and missed the net. The period was over and the kids ran to their coach.

"*Why didn't Avery shoot the ball!*" Gina shrieked to Carlos.

He didn't understand either. The smaller boys' teams were not as structured as the bigger boys. They even let the smaller boys get away with double-dribbling and traveling. Carlos tried offering an answer. "He's probably a guard. They are taught not to get point happy."

"Momma, did Avery mess up?" Sidnee asked.

"No, Sidnee. He's playing as a team," Carlos said and motioned for Gina to be quiet.

The boys came back out and started the routine of running back and forth, tossing the ball into the air. Avery tried stealing the ball again. A foul was called against him. This time, Carlos stood and shouted against his frat brother the referee. Even Paul had something to say. Avery had gotten into the game so much that he asked the referee, "Why?"

The little victim walked to the free throw line and gave his best two efforts. One shot tipped into the basket. The boy's mother jumped up and down with joy. The score was 1-0 in favor of the opposing team.

Avery was able to steal the ball again. He ran as fast as his little legs could carry him to the goal. He looked at the square box and decided not to try. He waited on a teammate and threw the ball to him. The little boy threw the ball into the air and it bounced off the rim. Paul called a timeout.

"What the hell is Avery doing!" Gina shouted.

"Gina, please," Carlos said while throwing his head toward Sidnee.

Gina stood to leave. She struggled to get pass Carlos. "I'm talking to Paul. He needs to tell Avery to..."

Carlos pulled her back. "Paul is an excellent coach. You will only embarrass Avery by going down there," Carlos said, wanting just as bad to talk to Paul.

The boys began their routine of running again. Avery skillfully stole the ball from the little boy who was dribbling. As he headed toward the goal, he saw Paul motioning him to shoot. He hesitated because he was afraid. When he saw Carlos stand, demanding that he shoot the ball, he looked at the box. With all of his might, he threw the ball into the air. The ball hit the backboard and fell into the net. Avery was shocked.

Gina and Sidnee jumped up and down. The crowd screamed loudly. Avery brushed it off as business as usual. He trotted down the other end like a pro. He could not wait to go home and tell Montez he made a basket.

As the game came to an end, a boy bumped up against Avery as he held a defensive posture under the goal. Avery stumbled. The boy threw the ball into the air and it went into the net. All Avery could hear was screams of protest. The basket was good and time ran out. The other team won.

Gina sat angrily with arms folded. Carlos was steaming too. He had to say something to the referee who seemed to be against his son's team. Carlos stormed down to the court.

"What's up frat? Didn't you see that foul?" Carlos demanded.

Avery watched as his father squared off with the referee. The other boys circled around to watch the adults stew over the game.

"He was in motion," the referee argued.

Before Carlos could say anything more, Paul rushed to the referee. "Let's not fight in front of these kids. It was a bad call like so many other bad calls in the NBA. The kids had fun so let's leave it at that," Paul said.

Carlos looked over at Avery and the other little boys who continued to watch him. He decided to congratulate his son on making his first basket. When Carlos began walking away, Paul pulled him back. "You must have pledged this young man because he definitely has something against your son," Paul said as an ice breaker and walked over to Avery. He left the men arguing playfully.

Avery was grinning as Paul approached him. "I made a basket, granddaddy. It was pretty. Did you see it?" Avery rejoiced.

"It looked like something Pippen would have done at your age," Paul said.

Gina and Sidnee made it to Avery and Paul. The expression on Gina's face had not changed. Even little Sidnee was pouting.

"Did you see that bad call? Avery held his spot and that little hoodlum hit him. Then the stupid referee let the basket count," Gina fussed.

Paul whispered in Gina's ear, "Let it go."

"Momma, did you see my basket?" Avery asked grinning.

"Do it again," Sidnee said with glee.

Avery saw how proud his sister was of him. "I can't. The game is over."

"Momma said that boy hit you," Sidnee said, slightly pouting.

"He did, but we can still beat them."

"Momma, can we see the baby?" Sidnee asked.

Since Lisa's arrival at her parents' house with little Caleb, Sidnee was on her best behavior, wanting to help with the baby. Paul went into the room often to see Lisa and his new grandson. Marilyn was quite attentive to Lisa's needs, showing her how to care for the baby as well as herself. To Gina's surprise, Lisa was receptive to the attention. She and the baby were leaving the following Saturday.

"Is everyone ready to go home?" Gina asked.

"Can I stay? I want to see Eric play. He's good," Avery begged.

"I'll bring him home," Paul said.

Gina left with Sidnee asking dozens of questions.

Lisa walked into the room while Marilyn was making her bed. "You don't have to do that. I can get it. I don't want to get too spoiled."

"I'm glad to see you're moving much better. How long did he nurse this time?"

"Off and on for twenty minutes."

"Seems like he's taking in more."

"I really appreciate you and your husband allowing me to stay here."

"I owe it to your mother. She was my closest pledge sister. She and I were going to pledge Alpha at first. It looks like our daughters did."

"What was her major?"

"I'm not sure. She helped me a great deal in my math class. She was able to look at something once and remember it."

"Why would a woman not spend time with her daughter or just plain leave her?"

The question struck a nerve in Marilyn. She was accused of not spending time with Gina because she worked so hard. Over the years, the communication had become better. Still, there were too many years Gina spent fighting for her attention.

"Your mother was a fighter. Everything was done on gut instincts. You can't expect a person to know something they were never taught. Your mother's friends vowed to help you. It's up to you to accept the offer."

Marilyn sounded so much like Gina during Lisa's pledge period. It brought back memories of times that were most enjoyable and yet painful, the college years. Gina often told Lisa that college was a period of growth and development. Friends made in college were usually friends through out life.

Gina entered the room with Sidnee. The little girl ran to Lisa. "Hi, Aunt Lisa. Can I see the baby?"

Lisa was taken by Sidnee's reference to her as "aunt." She sat on the bed with the baby so that Sidnee could get a closer look.

"Sidnee, let's wash our hands before touching the baby," Gina said.

Sidnee raced to the bathroom with Gina trailing. The water ran for several seconds. Soon they were back in the room with Lisa and Caleb.

"Carla, Cheryl and Rita will be by late this afternoon," Gina announced.

The last time Lisa had seen the women was at her wedding. She thought about how good it would be to see them again. Lisa let Sidnee touch Caleb one more time before laying him in the portable bassinet. It was one of many presents Paul had bought. She eased herself onto the bed.

"Let Lisa get some rest," Marilyn said to Sidnee.

"I want to see the baby," Sidnee whined.

"He's asleep," Marilyn said. Gina remained quiet as Marilyn did battle with Sidnee.

"I want to touch him," Sidnee mumbled.

"I was hoping you wanted to go to Toys 'R Us to pick up Barney for the baby," Marilyn said, baiting the little girl.

"Can I get Barney too?" Sidnee asked, biting the bait.

"Do you have any money?" Marilyn continued as she left Lisa's room. Sidnee was trailing behind, singing the Barney song.

Gina drove her mother's car to Toys 'R Us. Sidnee recognized the sign and immediately began clapping. They climbed out of the car and walked into the store which was a playground for children. Sidnee ran up and down the aisles.

"Momma, she might be a handful. You can't keep buying her things," Gina said.

"I wasn't planning on buying her anything. Stores like these take the place of a playground. I thought this would give us time to talk."

"What's wrong?"

"Nothing is wrong. I talked to Carlos the other day. His mother is going to need help. Carlos is her most reliable son."

Gina remained quiet. She watched as Sidnee took dolls off the shelf and cuddled them.

"Where are you in your career?" Marilyn asked.

"At a stand still."

"Where do you want to be?"

"With Carlos' research and the kids needing my time, I haven't given it much thought."

"Carlos is going to ask you to make a tough decision. It will require sacrifice on your end. What is the goal for the family?"

Sidnee ran up to Gina and pointed happily to the small cars.

They walked further up the aisle. Sidnee jumped into a Fisher Price plastic car and scooted up the aisle.

"Did Carlos ask you to talk to me?"

"He asked me my opinion and I gave it to him."

"And what was it?"

"I told him if I were sick and had no one to count on but one child, I would hope that one child would offer to see me through my last days. Dorothy is doing well for right now, but I don't know if she will be able to work again. I was able to find an organization to pay her hospital bills. Some undergraduates from Zeta Chi are doing housework and cooking for her."

"Why didn't Carlos talk to me about this before coming to you?"

"He's a very smart man. He wants to get as much information before approaching you. He knows you well enough to understand there should be a plan. I respect him enough to help as much as I can."

Sidnee scooted toward them in a little car. "Grandma, Barney's over here," she said.

Marilyn paused a little. It was the first time the little girl acknowledged her by 'grandma'. "Okay honey. We're right behind you."

Sidnee scooted away and met another child in another car. She forgot about Barney and began to play with a truck.

"If a job is what you're worried about, I have a few contacts in the home healthcare field that are looking for good managers. It's not a big operation like International Foods, but it's a start."

They walked up and down aisles behind Sidnee. When Marilyn figured the little girl was tired, she offered ice cream. Sidnee jumped up with delight. They left the store leaving Barney on the shelf.

Gina drove to Dairy Queen. They went inside and ordered ice cream. Gina had the clerk to put a small amount onto the cone for Sidnee. Before the girl handed the cone to Sidnee, Marilyn asked her to dip it in chocolate. When the girl came back with Sidnee's cone, her eyes were big. She never had a chocolate ice cream cone. She began to sing to herself.

They sat and ate ice cream. Marilyn and Gina talked about Lisa for awhile. Marilyn filled Gina in on the group's college commitment to each other: All for one and one for all. Marilyn also shared how the group did very little to uphold their end of the commitment to Debra. Marilyn shared a little on how Debra found JoAnn's ex-husband and he had to pay back support. Gina giggled.

"Paul doesn't want this new information to change anything," Marilyn said.

Gina looked confused. "What are you talking about?"

"He thinks you are a little jealous."

"*What?*"

"You have and will always be his little girl."

"He thinks I'm jealous of Lisa?" Gina panted.

"You know how men are. The things they should get excited about, they don't. The things they do get excited about are nothing."

Marilyn wiped her hands. She knew her daughter felt a twinge of jealousy. They had to put Lisa and the baby into one of the guest rooms. Gina didn't want to give up her old bedroom, claiming the children were more comfortable in there. Avery embarrassed her when he said he wanted a room by himself.

They left Dairy Queen and drove home. Gina saw Carla's car. She rushed to park the car and get out. When they walked inside the house, Lisa was sitting in the living room with Carla, Cheryl and Rita. They had brought gifts. They seemed to be having a good time. Marilyn left the women alone and went to her bedroom.

Carlos' team was doing warm-up drills. He was coaching the fourteen and fifteen year old team. A team of eight boys a piece. He and Paul were rivals. He looked around for his star player. He finally came in late. Carlos looked firmly at the young man.

"Sorry I'm late coach," the boy said.

"Give me ten laps," Carlos said and walked away. The boy took off running.

The whistle blew. Two boys went up in the air for the ball. It tipped to a boy on Paul's team, the gold team. The boy dribbled the ball down the court. They passed the ball back and forth. From the outside, a boy shot the ball and it went into the net.

Carlos' team, the black team, had the ball. They too passed the ball back and forth. It was thrown to the star player. He took a shot and missed. The black team missed the rebound and the ball changed hands to the gold team.

The boys played a fifteen minute half. They were at their bench taking half time.

"Phil, your game is off. What's the problem?" Carlos barked.

"Nobody's setting it up for me to get my shot off," the boy responded.

"Fuck you, punk! You missing them easy shots," one boy said as he wiped sweat from his forehead.

"Kiss my ass, nigga!" Phil said as he stood next to the boy.

Carlos stood in between them. "The next time I hear 'nigga', you can sit out for the rest of the game. I want you brothers to chill on the language. Phil, take a rest. Gary, you're in."

The boys returned to the game. The black team closed the

fifteen point gap to four. The crowd became more excited to see the comeback. Carlos called a timeout to get the team prepared for the last two minutes. He saw Gina walk in with Carla and Cheryl. Immediately he straightened his posture. He figured Gina came to pick up Avery. He and Eric were swimming.

"Man, old-school's team is pretty cold," one boy said, referring to Paul.

"Old-school has a record at Lincoln University that no one has been able to break," Carlos said to the boy who looked embarrassed.

"Phil, I want you to set up the pick-n-roll for Quontez. If he misses, you should be able to rebound and get the shot in. You down?" Carlos asked firmly.

The young man nodded. The team did their cheer and walked out on the court. Carlos pulled Phil over before he stepped onto the court. "What's up?"

"Neisha's pregnant," he said without looking at Carlos.

Carlos had to pause. How could a fifteen-year-old with raw NBA potential get somebody pregnant? When the buzzer sounded, Carlos told Phil they would talk later. Carlos took his position on the sideline. He saw Dennis enter with his team of sixteen, seventeen and eighteen-year-olds. Dennis' mere presence made Carlos want his team to win.

The boys played hard down to the last minute. The score was tied. Paul called a timeout. The boys came back huffing and puffing to Carlos.

"They know Phil hasn't been shooting, so they won't expect him to take the last shot. If the pick-n-roll don't work, Phil, get the rebound and pass it. I want the ball back in Phil's hand. Young brother, you either win it or put us into overtime," Carlos said and the boys walked back onto the court. Carlos feared an overtime. His team was losing steam.

Carlos quickly glanced at Dennis as he stood straight with his group of teenagers. The boys stood at attention next to him. He had no problem getting his team into shape. The boys respected him because he showed them that he still had the game in him.

The clock started. The black team passed the ball around to set up the pick-n-roll, but it failed. One boy mishandled the ball and the gold team scrambled to get it. The boy who mishandled the ball and a member of the gold team were holding the ball. The referee called "jump."

Carlos turned his back. The shortest person on his team had to jump against the tallest person on Paul's team. Carlos turned back around. He relaxed. He had to come to grips that it was only a game.

When the ball went up, the gold team player tipped it to Phil. The boy took two steps and jump shot the ball. The buzzer sounded and the ball sunk into the net. The boys barked. Carlos raised his arms in victory.

The two coaches shook hands. The black team fell on top of each other. When they got up, they lifted Carlos into the air. He grinned. "Okay young brothers. We did it. We need to give up the floor for the next crew."

When Carlos' team left the floor, Dennis approached him and asked about Phil. "I'll tell you about him later," Carlos said.

Carlos walked to Gina and her group and let the boys celebrate without him. Gina stood and stretched out her arms. She never displayed open affection in front of her sorors. Carlos took the invitation and hugged her tight. He decided to take Dennis' advice and get a hotel room. Dennis gave him money to do so.

"Good game, Carlos. I guess it's time for streetball," Carla said teasingly, referring to Dennis' team. She knew Dennis could play well. He played hard and rough. He was a schoolyard ball player.

"You don't know how good it makes a man feel to see his woman watching him at his best," Carlos said, still holding Gina.

"I don't think Dennis knows I'm here. I came to pick up Eric," Carla said.

"He knows you're here. Stay and watch him coach," Carlos said. He knew when Dennis brought his team into the gymnasium, he had to impress the most important person in his life and that was his wife.

The older groups' game was under way. Carlos sat with the women and explained the game. He explained why Dennis' team performed the way that they did and went into detail each call made from the bench. The women fussed at him, telling him to shut up.

Soon, a young program director came into the gymnasium with an upset Avery. He pointed to his parents. They rushed to the group of adults.

"Are you Mrs. Williams?" the man asked quickly of Carla.

"Yes I am," she said slightly nervous.

"I need you to come to my office. Your son was about to get into a fight," he said.

"Carlos, tell Dennis to come to the office," Carla said in a rush.

Instead of Carlos obeying, he accompanied Carla to the program director's office. The young man was new at his job. He made a big mistake. He left the two feuding boys in the office alone. When they came inside, Eric was on top of the boy pounding him with his fists. The program director tried snatching Eric off of the crying boy, but it was difficult. Carlos had to grip Eric hard and yank him up.

Carlos recognized the crying boy. He gave one of the Lambdas' coaches a hard time during practice. The boy picked at Eric constantly, calling him a punk. Carlos thought he might belong to the neighborhood gang.

"Eric, what's going on?" Carla fussed.

"He keeps fuckin' with me," Eric said angrily, eyeing the boy hard.

Carla's mouth dropped open. She had never heard her son curse before. "I don't want to hear you talk like that again! You here me?"

Eric ignored her and kept eyeing the crying boy. Carlos knew if the boy had a hard time whipping Eric, Carla wouldn't. She had a low tolerance for bad behavior and Dennis was even less tolerant.

"Punk, I'm kicking your ass," the boy cried as he came closer to Eric.

"Yeah faggot! Look whose ass just got kicked," Eric responded with his finger in the boy's face.

Carla shook Eric. She was ready to slap him until Carlos stopped her. "Let him calm down. He's in a neighborhood that only respects that type of language," Carlos whispered in her ear.

Carla understood, but she had never heard her son use inappropriate language. She talked slowly and told Eric to go home with her. He gave her no problem as he tagged along beside her.

Carlos went back inside the gym to talk to Gina and Cheryl. Avery looked shakened. Carlos picked him up and hugged him tight. "Are you alright?" Carlos asked him. Avery nodded.

"Eric is fine. He went home with his mother," Carlos told him.

At half-time, Carlos went to the floor to talk to Dennis. His team was leading by twenty points, but Dennis did not look relaxed. He began critiquing the boys. He saw Carlos and kept talking to the boys. When he began writing on the clipboard, Carlos approached him.

"Eric got into a fight with a gang banger."

Dennis showed no emotions when he asked, "Did he whoop his ass?"

"Yeah. I didn't know he had a bad temper."

"He got it from his mother," Dennis said and gave final instructions to his players. The teenagers, rotated a group out and new players went in.

"I wanted you to know his language was a little rough. Carla is upset."

"Shit!" Dennis hissed. Now he had to contend with his wife.

Chapter Thirty-One

Estelle opened the door. Linda and Melanie walked inside the noise filled house. It was a typical hen party. The surprise for both women was seeing many sorors from earlier lines and very few from latter lines. The familiar faces made Melanie stop in her tracks. The ice packs and makeup covered much of the pain and humiliation. Melanie knew everyone was probably aware of her situation.

"Melanie, do you have a minute?" Estelle asked.

Melanie looked around the room as women waved at her with a smile. The smiles looked genuine. It seemed as if everyone's attention was focused on her.

"I wasn't planning on staying long, Estelle," Melanie said.

"It won't take long. Sweetcakes, congratulations!" Estelle said to Linda and gave her a light hug. Estelle beckoned for Melanie to follow her to a back room.

Estelle entered with Melanie. Four other women were sitting. Wine glasses were on the table and the women spoke softly. Lori stood and extended her arms. Melanie took Lori's hands and kissed her on the cheek. Lori called Melanie after the election and asked if she could visit. Melanie refused the visit. It took Barbara to encourage her to attend the double celebration.

"You don't need to say anything. We are the only ones who know about what happened. I hear you are leaving...uh, moving to Minneapolis," Lori said.

Melanie looked curiously at the women who were responsible for setting the stage for her to become president of Zeta Chi. They were beautiful and cunning. She had always wanted to follow in their footsteps.

"I haven't made up my mind about where I'm going," Melanie said slowly.

"Sharon knows of an opening at a nonprofit organization in Minneapolis. Maybe you should give her your resume," Estelle said with a smile.

"Right now is not a good time to leave," Melanie said looking at a picture of a woman holding a baby.

Lori handed Melanie an envelope. "How is Lauren?" Lori asked, waiting for Melanie to look at her. Melanie finally looked at her.

"She's...doing well," Melanie answered.

"I think Minneapolis is a great place. It's cold as the North Pole, but it should do well for a small family. Doesn't her father live there?" Sharon inquired.

Melanie didn't answer. She just stared at Sharon who was the most serious one of the group.

"Doesn't he have a computer business or something?" another one asked.

"He's single isn't he?" the last one asked.

"He's divorced," Melanie finally answered.

"The last time I remembered, divorced meant single," the last one said with a chuckle.

"You haven't opened the envelope," Lori said.

Melanie opened the envelope and gawked at the check for three thousand dollars from Lori's personal checking account. Lori stood in front of her. "It's from S.S. Diamonds Are Forever and everyone from Lee Summit. We are wishing you well," Lori said and extended her arms. Melanie took the embrace slowly.

"My family is here," Melanie whispered.

"I know," Lori whispered back.

"All of my friends and sisters are here."

"You can meet new ones."

"It won't be the same."

"I know," Lori said and pulled back. "That man is crazy. He will stalk you. He already has. You nor your daughter deserve to live in fear."

The other four women approached Melanie and each kissed her on the cheek and hugged her. Melanie was settled on moving.

"In a way, I'm glad you're leaving. You ladies have pulled your last stunt," Lori said and put her arm around Melanie's shoulder. She looked puzzled at Lori.

"You don't know what I'm talking about?" Lori asked. She was grinning but yet confused. Melanie looked sincere when she shook her head. Lori looked at the group. Their eyebrows raised. They left the back room and joined the others.

Everyone was jovial. Linda talked happily to the group of

women who supported her, feared her (at one time) and disliked her. Everyone was on one accord. Zeta Chi won twice.

When Lori and the others entered the room, everyone became quiet. Estelle started the toast. She offered congratulations to Lori and Linda. Everyone took a drink from their glasses. Then Lori told everyone that Melanie was leaving. Many gasped. Even Melanie gasped internally. Lori had forced her into a position.

Everyone wished Melanie well. Melanie smiled when she saw five of fifteen line sisters: Linda, Denise, Courtney, Jill and Annette. She smiled more seeing four of the ones she pledged as a neophyte: Maria, Joni, Brooke and Danielle. She grinned internally as Lori left the room with her confidants.

"You forced her into a position," Estelle told Lori.

"It was necessary," Lori said.

"She's going to be a contender in three years," Sharon said.

"With her out of the way, I can breath a little easier. Did you see the expression on her face when I asked about that little stunt they pulled? She behaved as if she didn't have a clue as to what I was talking about," Lori complained.

"Suppose she didn't?" Sharon asked.

"It doesn't matter. They all stick together," Lori said.

"Come off of it Lori! You were upset to hear about her in the hospital. You were saddened when Barbara Stevens told you to convince her to leave Kansas City. Face it! You are trying to convince us that you won't miss your little protegee," Estelle preached.

"Estelle, did I ever tell you that *you* are a bitch?" Lori said jokingly before walking through the doorway.

"I'm going to miss her too," Estelle told her best friend. The women closed the door behind them.

The guests separated into their own groups. Melanie was the center of attention with her line sisters. They small talked for awhile.

"Where are you going?" Denise asked.

"I'm thinking about Atlanta."

"Why Atlanta?"

"I have family there."

"I received the letter from the young sorors at Zeta Chi. I want to thank you for thinking about me. I thought you hated my guts," Linda told Annette.

"Linda, it has and will always be about winning against Lori and the rest. Remember?" Melanie said low.

"Whether we are in disagreement personally, I thought we pledged to stick together when it came to those bitches," Annette whispered.

"They may ease you out of the group," Melanie whispered in Annette's ear. Melanie knew Annette always dreamed of the opportunity to be a part of Lori's circle. Melanie was convinced that Annette could be trusted.

"You should have heard Lori commenting on us at the step-show. She's not as smart as I thought she was," Annette whispered to Melanie. Both women laughed.

"Those heffas have always made me sick," Denise added.

"Despite losing the director's spot, we still won," Jill said as she looked around suspiciously.

"How did you get the nomination for national official?" Courtney asked Linda.

"I had help," Linda shared.

"Lori called Aunt Barbara an old bitch, so Mrs. Stevens had to prove a point. She has and will always play to win," Melanie said and laughed.

It took awhile for Linda to digest that her mother's help was only given to beat Lori. When she thought about the woman at the card table telling her that she won because she had heart, she ignored Melanie's comment. All national officials politic their way there.

When the women saw Maria approach the group, they changed the topic. "Hi sweetie. How are you?" Melanie said sweetly. She didn't want Maria to feel uncomfortable. Everyone knew she was living with a woman.

"I'm fine. I heard that Lisa is in town. Did she have the baby?" Maria asked.

"His name is Caleb William Johnson. She's at Gina Smith's house. You should stop by before she leaves next Saturday," Melanie said.

Paul had finished barbecuing. He put the last of the meat on a tray that was on the patio table. The patio was decorated with balloons and "We Will Miss You" signs. Cameron had come to take Lisa and the baby home. Cameron had arrived in Kansas City early that morning. Once he walked inside the house, he picked up his son. The baby rested in his arms the entire morning.

Gina and Carlos were going back to Chicago. They had made the decision to leave the children in Kansas City while they closed out business in Chicago. Gina could only support Carlos when he asked her to move back to Kansas City. She thought about how it was her idea to move to Chicago. Her only request was to make sure she was able to land a job with health benefits before moving.

Paul walked into the house to gather everyone for lunch. The house hummed with excitement. Marilyn was giving a full fledge party. She invited Barbara and her husband; Linda and her family; Melanie and Lauren. Carlos' mother was invited but Marilyn did not expect her to come. William was on his way from the airport.

The doorbell rang. Paul opened the door and paused. William faced him with a smile and his garment bag over his shoulder. "I came to see my grandson," William said with a laugh.

"Come in," Paul said.

Before William walked into the house, he stopped. "I told Lisa nothing has changed."

"The court papers said I'm her father," Paul said without looking at William.

"The birth certificate says that I'm her father," William said seriously.

"I didn't understand the medical jargon but the blood test matched."

"I took a blood test too. I wanted to make sure that she was mine."

"What were the results?"

"I don't know. I never got them back."

The men were silent for a moment.

"I talked to Cameron when I found out that Lisa was having fibroids removed. I asked about her blood level. He told me something about her being 'O negative. I'm not 'O negative and it appears it is a rare type. I talked to her doctor explaining I was her father and did Lisa need blood for surgery. The doctor told me, no. I asked about Lisa being 'O negative. She said Lisa is 'O positive but something about the antigens in her blood makes it difficult to match with the universal donor 'O positive. It behaves as if it's 'O negative."

Paul was silent after hearing William's explanation. The two men looked at the ceiling.

"Is she yours?" Paul finally asked.

"Does it matter? I've been her financial support for years."

"Is she yours?" Paul asked again.

"I really don't know. At this point, I refuse to put her through a blood test to prove otherwise. Are you going to make her go through a blood test?"

Paul shook his head. It was too embarrassing and insulting to behave despondent. The young woman probably didn't want anything to do with him anyway.

"You and I took advantage of Debra. You pushed and pushed until she gave in and slept with you in college. I used her as a sounding board during my marriage. She wanted to make sure we paid for our mistakes and we have."

Paul realized his brother was right. "Bobby called last week. He asked about you, as usual. He had surgery for prostate cancer," Paul said.

William took a deep breath. He had not seen his younger brother since he married Catherine. He felt awkward visiting now. "Did they get it all?"

"I didn't ask. I think we need to see him."

"I haven't seen him in years."

"So, you're going to wait for his funeral like momma?"

"I took care of Mildred until she died. I'm not going to feel guilty about momma."

"For God sakes, Bill, she was your mother!"

"I've seen enough suffering and dying!"

"What do you want me to tell Bobby?"

"When are you going to visit him?"

"Soon. Let's go and see your grandson."

Everyone made their way to the tables in the backyard. When William walked outside, he received a lot of attention. Paul went back inside the house. He sat in his favorite recliner. He thought about Debra. He thought about betraying her in college, just to see if he could do it. He thought about the hurtful look on his brother's face. It never dawned on him that he was selfish to leave Bill to care for their sister. Regardless of his mother's urging, he could have stayed in Tennessee. He never received his college degree. He closed his eyes until the doorbell rang again.

Paul walked slowly to the door. When he opened the door, Carlos was standing beside his mother. Paul smiled at Dorothy and graciously invited her inside. When she walked inside, she stopped and stared at the beautiful home. It was her first time inside the house. As Dorothy slowly made her way further, she was greeted by Marilyn who had come to get Paul.

"Hello Dorothy. How are you?" Marilyn asked with a smile.

"Fine thanks," Dorothy said with brevity. She wasn't rude, just brief.

"I'm glad you could make it," Marilyn said.

"If you don't mind, I would like to speak to you alone," Dorothy said.

Carlos felt uncomfortable. He didn't have to force his mother to come, but he did encouraged her to. "If you need me, I'll be outside," Carlos said and left with Paul.

Marilyn and Dorothy walked into the living room. They sat opposite of each other. Both took deep breaths. Dorothy looked around the carefully designed living room. Things were not very expensive. They were nice and well maintained. It surprised Dorothy. She thought everything would be extravagant.

"You have a nice home," Dorothy said.

"I'm thankful to Paul. Getting a house big enough for the children was number one. He designed and built the house. He's also a scavenger. He can find a bargain any where. In the beginning, we had to be careful not to spend too much because of the children."

"I look for bargains too. When my husband left, I had to really pull my purse strings. He left me with three boys and no money."

"When my husband left, he cleaned me out too. It wasn't difficult to deal with a man like Paul. Matter of fact, I might be stingier."

The two women laughed lightly. "I want to thank you for finding them folks to pay my hospital bills," Dorothy said as she clutched her purse.

"When I found out how hard you had worked to receive an organ, I became angry. There is so much racism in the health industry. I was determined that this black woman would not be overlooked this time. White people are vicious when it comes to taking care of their own."

Dorothy was surprised at Marilyn's anti-white attitude. She took her for a woman who sang and danced with white people. "How long you been working there?"

"Too long! I'm retiring in three years. I'm going to enjoy my latter years."

"Carlos says him and Gina moving back home."

"I guess we had better be ready for the grandchildren."

"That little Sidnee is somethin' else. That child is a talker, asking all kinds of questions. That gal talks more than grown folks. She talked me to sleep one day. All I heard was Grandma Dorothy."

"I heard she's a talker. She hasn't warmed up to me yet."

Dorothy was more surprised. She thought Marilyn would be the center of attention when it came to the grandchildren. The mothers always made sure the children were close to their mothers. "I also want to thank you for sending them young gals to the house to cook and clean. They do a good job cleanin' but they cookin' ain't worth much."

Marilyn tried holding back the laughter but she couldn't. Dorothy was very honest with her feelings. "Let's get some good food," Marilyn said with a laugh. She helped Dorothy up and walked her to the backyard. Before Marilyn opened the patio door, Dorothy stopped.

"I want to thank Gina for talking Carlos into coming home. He wouldn't uh done it on his own," Dorothy said without looking at Marilyn.

"Your son deserves more credit than you give him," Marilyn said. Dorothy nodded. She still believed her son would not have made the decision to move back unless someone whom he loved more than her suggested it.

"When are you having the baby christened?" Melanie asked

Lisa.

"I go to a Baptist church. They bless babies," Lisa answered.

"So when are you going to have him blessed?" Linda asked.

"At the end of August," Lisa responded.

"Who are the godparents?" Gina asked.

"My cousin Rhonda and Cameron's brother Jason," Lisa answered.

"I haven't met her, have I?" Linda asked.

Lisa shook her head. She looked over at Cameron who was still holding the baby. He was talking to Carlos and Keith.

"Not only is Lisa my sister, she's also my cousin. Our mothers were sisters. Lisa's mother had a twin sister who was Rhonda's mother. My grandmother gave them away because she was forced to," Melanie said calmly.

Linda and Gina remained quiet. Lisa stood. "I'm going to put the baby in bed. I think Cameron has held him long enough. Excuse me," Lisa said and left the small group.

Everyone watched in silence as Lisa left the small group. "Well, I declare! What other secrets have been left dangling?" Linda said with a southern flare.

"Besides dad not being her real father, I don't know," Melanie said.

"I feel terrible about not keeping in touch better. She only had herself for so many years," Gina said as she watched Lisa take the baby from Cameron. William approached Lisa and extended his arms for baby Caleb. She carefully placed the baby in his arms.

"Enough of this! Miss Melanie, when are you moving?" Linda broke in.

Gina gasped. "You didn't tell me that you were moving," she said to Melanie.

"I probably won't leave until the end of summer. It should give the Center enough time to find another director. I'm submitting Carlos' name as a recommendation."

"It will be the best thing that has happened to this family. He was overjoyed from working in the tournamentsince. We're moving back to Kansas City," Gina said.

"Wait a minute. You guys are moving back to Kansas City and Melanie is moving to Atlanta?" Linda asked exasperated.

"You're moving to Atlanta? Why?" Gina asked Melanie.

"Who said anything about me moving to Atlanta?"

"Look hussy, you said at Estelle's party that you were moving to Atlanta to be with your family," Linda corrected.

"I said that I was *thinking* about moving to Atlanta."

"Okay, where are you moving?" Gina asked firmly.

"Minneapolis."

Linda looked at Gina. The women's eyebrows raised. They

looked at Melanie for an answer. "Okay, I still want him," Melanie said.

The women's children ran to them and all talked at once. The women talked to their godchildren, giving them more attention than their own children. Only Avery did not share one of the women as his heavenly-earth connection. Melanie made sure he was attended to.

All of a sudden, Lauren squealed. She took off running toward the gate. Everyone turned around. "Speaking of the devil," Linda said low. Melanie hit her on the leg. Lionel picked up Lauren in one easy swoop and tossed her into the air. She giggled with delight. He carried her closer to the group.

Cameron got out of his chair and rushed to his brother. He had to tell Lionel how big the baby had grown and how much he could eat. Those were the only things he could report on a two week old baby.

"What's up, Ron?" Lionel asked and put Lauren down. He gave his brother a strong hug and a pat on the back.

"You should see the baby. He's getting big!"

"Where is he? I didn't come this distance for nothing," Lionel said loudly.

Gina leaned over to Linda. "He can sure lie, can he?" she whispered.

Melanie heard her and hit her arm.

"What's the matter? It's the truth," Gina said and burst into laughter. Linda looked at Melanie and laughed too.

"Mommie, what you laughing at?" little Edward asked.

"Go talk to your grandmother," Linda answered.

"She told us to come over here," Avery said.

"Go somewhere and play," Gina said.

"Why?" Sidnee asked.

"Because we are having an adult conversation," Linda said firmly to Sidnee.

"Can we see the baby?" Avery asked.

The three women looked at each other and connected.

"Why don't all of you go inside and visit Auntie Lisa," Melanie suggested.

The children took off running to the patio door leaving Indie struggling to keep up. Marilyn looked in shock as the children ran to the door. "Wait a minute!" she shouted. The children stopped immediately and looked at her. "Stop running," she snapped. The children walked for a moment and then rushed inside the house. Cameron followed them.

Lionel sat next to Melanie. He took her hand. "Are you alright?" he asked softly.

Melanie smiled. "I'm doing fine."

"Hello ladies. How is everyone?" Lionel asked with his widest grin.

"So, what brings you to Kansas City?" Gina asked with arms folded.

"I came to see my nephew."

"Nephew my foot! Fess up," Linda ordered.

Before Lionel could offer another answer, Keith and Carlos joined the group. Gina and Linda looked irritated. They wanted to cross examine Lionel some more.

"What's up Lionel?" Carlos asked joyfully. Lionel stood and gave him a bear hug. Then he shook Keith's hand.

"Thanks for saving me, brothers. Your ladies were getting ready to roll me over," Lionel said with a smile.

"We are gearing up for some dominoes. You want to play?" Carlos asked. Keith was grinning as he nodded in agreement.

"Do you know how to play dominoes, Keith?" Linda asked.

"They are going to teach me."

"Don't bet any money! Carlos is a starving college student. He will try anything to get our children's college fund," Linda said and faced Gina.

"Pretty soon, he will be Dr. Simmons, so watch your mouth," Gina said.

"How much do you weigh now?" Linda asked Gina.

The men knew it was time to leave. They quickly joined Paul and William for a game of dominoes. Before Carlos sat down, he walked over to the table where his mother was sitting with Barbara and Marilyn. Dorothy seemed relaxed.

"Let me know when you're tired," Carlos told his mother. She nodded. He walked away.

"He should run for a political office. He has a rough political savvy," Barbara said.

Dorothy didn't know what "savvy" meant. She believed it was something good. She decided to wait until Carlos finished his game of dominoes before leaving. It was difficult sitting long. It was equally difficult understanding some of the words the women were using. They didn't talk over her head. She had been standing too low for too long. She decided to take advantage of the adult education courses. If her son was going to be a doctor, she could not embarrass him as an uneducated mother. She stressed education too much when he was growing up. She had to live up to her sermons.

Chapter Thirty-Two

Melanie was packing away the dishes from the kitchen cabinet. She had almost everything in order. A bank account had been established in Minneapolis. The Center's search committee had ended their interviews for the new executive director. Carlos interviewed very well. The only problem was Carlos' lack of experience with a board. Knowing that he was receiving a Ph.D. from the University of Chicago had the search committee sold. He was considered the top candidate. Melanie convinced the committee that she would freelance her grant writing skills to help the new executive director. It was silently understood that the director had to be Carlos.

Everything was falling into place. She had several interviews in St. Paul and Minneapolis upon her arrival, which was the following week after Caleb's blessing. She and Lauren were leaving in three days for Atlanta. The most relieving moment was hearing that the divorce would be final in a matter of days. At first it was stalled but then it moved quickly. John called The Youth Center constantly. Melanie found out that he didn't get the bid that he worked very hard to land. He was depressed.

Melanie finished with all but a few things in the kitchen. She moved to her bedroom. She saw the bear from Camille's carousel lying on her bed. She picked it up and looked around the room for the wastebasket. It wasn't in sight. She decided to put it into her purse. Lauren asked about it earlier. It had to be available in case the little girl inquired about it again.

Melanie decided to start on her closet. It was faster packing alone. Lauren wanted to help, but she was sent outside to ride her bike around the parking lot. When Melanie reached to clear the closet shelf, her hand touched the gun she had removed from John's house. She quickly grabbed it off the shelf. She looked desperately for a place to put it. She put it on her night stand to remind herself to get rid of it.

Lauren rode her bike near the cars. She happily steered it in and out of empty parking spaces. She decided to venture further down the parking lot. She was not allowed to go pass the building before the steep incline leading into their section of buildings. She could only go around the the buildings across from hers.

She rode around the circle of buildings. When she became bored, she parked her bike at the curve pass her building. She sang a rap song that she had heard on the radio. As she became preoccupied with the rhyming words, a familiar car drove around the building. Her heart pounded with fear. She got up quickly and got on her bike. She was so nervous that it took her awhile to get her coordination together.

Finally, she was on her bike. She was about to turn back when she saw the car coming close. She had to go back to warn her mother. The last time John was around, all she heard were screams of pain coming from her mother's bedroom. Instead of steering the bike the other way, she went forward heading toward the "off limits" area.

She looked back to see if the car was coming close. It crept up behind her. As soon as she brought her focus forward, she was on her way down the steep incline. She panicked and the bike wobbled down the hill. Instantly, she was down the hill and lost control of her steering. She was thrown off the bike and landed on her arm. She screamed. The familiar car slowly left the apartment complex.

Lauren continued screaming from the excruciating pain on her right side. Miss Angel was in front of her. When she looked at her friend, the pain went away. "Don't be afraid. Your mother will be here soon," Miss Angel told her.

A car drove up beside Lauren and stopped. Miss Angel put her finger to her lips to motion Lauren to keep quiet as well as keep still. A lady that lived in the building across from her rushed out of the car.

"Honey, can you get up?" the woman asked.

Lauren began screaming again. Soon, other people came outside. Lauren could not talk. Her voice was injured. She continued screaming at the top of her lungs.

"Watch her. I'll get her mother," the woman said to another woman before taking off running.

All Lauren could think about was her father. She felt protected when she was with him. When he disciplined her, it wasn't abusive. He would tell her that he was disappointed in her behavior and his facial expression would show it. Knowing her actions affected someone was punishment enough.

Melanie ran at top speed down the hill. Jennifer's face came in her thoughts. Melanie imagined the worst, another death. She ran faster. Her heart settled when she heard her daughter screaming, but Jennifer's face was in view. She ran faster to the scene. She moved people out of the way.

"Mommie. Mommie," Lauren cried.

Melanie dropped her head. She moved Lauren. She screamed again.

"I think her arm might be broken," the woman said.

"Could someone please call for help?" Melanie whispered.

"I didn't mean to ride down here. John was behind me," Lauren explained.

Melanie stiffened. Her face became heated. Her ears felt on fire. When she touched her face, the heat on her face made it impossible. The only thing she could think about was too much abuse for too long. She was going to rid herself and her daughter of the monster that had robbed their happiness for two years.

Melanie began to feel strange. She smiled at Lauren and wiped away the tears from her face. "It's going to be okay."

Lauren's arm was broken in two places. It wasn't difficult for the doctor to set her arm. She was obedient. Although it was painful, she behaved like a big girl. She was quiet as Melanie drove home.

"Mother, will John come back?" Lauren asked fearfully.

The sound of Lauren's voice angered Melanie. It was her fault that her daughter was afraid to ride her bike in her own neighborhood.

"You want to visit Auntie Linda?" Melanie asked sweetly.

"Yes," Lauren muttered. She knew her mother was going to drop her off. She wanted to sleep next to her, to protect her. She wasn't able to do it the last time, but she knew how to call the police because Linda taught her.

Melanie helped Lauren out of the car. They walked to the front door. Linda opened the door. The solemn looks on their faces alarmed Linda. Then she saw Lauren's arm in a sling.

"I need to finish packing. Could you keep her for a few hours?" Melanie asked low and walked away. Lauren looked back at her mother in fear.

"Lauren, what happened?" Linda asked as she escorted Lauren inside the house. Lauren said nothing. She began to cry.

Melanie quickly placed items into the boxes. She jumped when the telephone rang.

"Hello," she answered roughly.

"Lauren told me what happened," Linda said.

"I need to finish packing. I don't have a lot of time," Melanie said and hung up. She took a deep breath. She needed air. She needed to be free. She had made so many mistakes. As soon as she began doing well, disaster struck. She should have left John after the first slap. She wanted to stay married to a well-established, financially secured man so that she could say that she married well. Now, her daughter was living in fear. She thought about what the woman at the card party said about her abusive "ex". It was a perfect idea. She had prepared for it.

No more, Melanie said to herself. She looked at the night stand. The small gun seemed to beam at her, inviting itself to tag along. She quickly grabbed it and put it into her purse. She looked at her black driving gloves in the box with her winter things. She removed them from the box. She grabbed the car keys and rushed out of the apartment. As she locked the door, she heard the telephone ring. She ignored it and kept walking.

As she drove to John's house, the anger inside exploded to flames, causing her face to feel heated again. She had no idea as to why she was traveling to John's side of town. She figured whatever happened once she arrived would free her.

She thought about ringing the doorbell and putting the barrel of the gun in his face. She wanted to see fear in his eyes as he had seen in hers many time. Then she wanted to pull the trigger and enjoy the aftermath.

She was two houses down from John's house, his pride and joy. Every time he was angry, he reminded her and Lauren that it was his house. When she thought about selling her house to be with him, she became more angry. She parked the car two houses away from John's. She put on the gloves; grabbed her purse and got out of the car.

She looked suspiciously around and ran lightly to the house. John had just finished cutting the grass. One of the garage doors was left up with the lawn mower in the center. She quickly entered the house. She saw a red canister of gasoline. Instinctively, she picked it up and kept moving. Before she opened the door leading to the basement, she reached for the gun. She pulled out the bear instead. She tossed it into the trash can and continued her search. She felt the handle of the gun and took it out.

She closed her eyes and took a deep breath. The scene of the first fight came to mind. He slapped her hard. She walked away and he came behind her. For the first time, she feared a man. The scene of Lauren's first whipping came to focus. He hit her with his belt and left marks on her legs.

The anger turned to flames. Melanie balanced the gun in her

hand and turned the knob. The door was open. She tiptoed into the foyer. She assumed John was upstairs so she tiptoed up the stairs. The plush carpet silenced any noise she made on her journey. Before she opened the door to the kitchen, she looked at the canister in her hand. All she needed were matches. She wanted to burn down the only thing John love. His house. He designed it and helped build it. Before she opened the door, she poured gasoline down the stairs.

Melanie adjusted the canister in her hand and slowly opened the door that led to the kitchen. She tried desperately to be quiet as she entered the kitchen. She saw a book of matches on the kitchen table. She quickly put them in her purse and silently hunted for John on the first floor. There were no sounds of him. She proceeded up the stairs to the bedroom. She poured more gasoline as she approached the master bedroom. She could hear the shower on. She poured gasoline in front of the door and place the canister outside the door. She put the gun in front of her and entered the room. She didn't know how to shoot or handle a gun. But the feel of the weapon felt familiar.

As John showered, she waited patiently. She practiced slowly lifting her arm and then pulling the trigger. Then she thought about simply burning down the house with him in it. But Linda's words came to her. If she committed a crime, she would pay for it. She wanted to leave. What she was doing was foolish. It was time to move on with her life. Everything was in motion.

She was about to exit when John came out of the bathroom nude. Then Melanie thought about the rape. She raised her hand slowly.

John looked at the gun and then at her. "What are you doing?"

Melanie said nothing. She pointed the gun at him. John's mouth opened, but nothing came out. "Put the gun down, Melanie."

"You will never hurt me again, you bastard."

"I'm sorry. I didn't mean to hurt you. I love you too much to hurt you," John pleaded.

"You will never hurt my daughter again either."

"I didn't make Lauren fall," John said nervously after hearing the gun cocked.

"You heartless son-of-a-bitch! You left her lying in pain."

"I didn't want you to see me," John said with his voice cracking.

"Why did you come to my apartment? Evidently, you wanted to see me."

Melanie's hand gripped the gun's handle tighter. John's eyes widen with fear. She saw it! She saw fear in John's eyes. She smiled. And then she laughed loudly.

John wrapped the towel around him tighter. When Melanie

continued to laugh, he frowned. He tried easing to the night stand. Melanie became cocky.

"I've been told that political payoffs are not business tax write-offs," Melanie said. She watched as John lost more ground in the battle.

"Put the gun down, Melanie," John said hoarsely. He could not think of how she found out about the information. She was total ignorant about tax forms. She signed them obediently without raising any discussions about his business.

"You paid a lot for this upcoming contract. How do you think the newspapers *and* the IRS will react if they knew this information," she continued.

John no longer treated the situation calmly. Too much was at stake. Melanie was too comfortable with him. He walked quickly to the nightstand and yanked open the drawer. His gun was gone.

"Are you looking for this?" she teased.

John paused for a moment. He frowned at her and began to walk toward her.

"Get back!" Melanie shouted.

John walked up to the gun. "Go on and shoot."

Melanie became nervous. Her hand shook. She gathered the courage to pull the trigger but nothing happened. John knocked the gun out of her hand. He became angrier. "Remember when you told me to take the gun out of the house? Remember when I told you I would remove the bullets instead?"

Fear slowly surfaced on Melanie's face. How could she have forgotten the discussion? The first time she saw the gun, she ranted and raved about keeping it out of Lauren's sight.

She didn't get a chance to continue thinking because John landed a hard slap across her face. She looked spitefully at him and then took off running down the steps. He was behind her. He pulled her by the hair and she screamed. He pulled her close to him. She could feel him breathing hard. She could feel him getting hard. She could not imagine being raped again.

John's grip became tighter. The odor of the gasoline caught his attention. He sniffed. His grip on her hair lessened. He looked around the house trying to find out where the odor was coming from. He became anxious so he gripped her hair tighter.

"Noooo," Melanie cried as he gripped her hair tighter. He began dragging her back to the flight of stairs. He kissed her roughly as he yanked her head back.

Loud banging on the door made him stop. "Who is it?" he yelled.

"Overland Park police."

John released Melanie quickly. "Just a minute!" he shouted and ran upstairs to put on some clothes.

Melanie rushed to the door. Before she opened it, she looked down at the gloves. It would appear strange wearing gloves in August. She removed the gloves and opened her purse. She saw the book of matches. She thought for a moment. She wanted to come back later and burn down John's pride and joy.

"Overland Police," the voice shouted.

Suddenly, the heat left her face. Her head dropped forward. The anger suddenly left. John was at the top of the steps frowning and sniffing, wondering where the gasoline was coming from.

Melanie saw him sniffing and looking around as he came down the steps. Then she began to relax. She knew it was going to be expensive for him to replace the expensive carpet. Her shoulders relaxed as she opened the door.

All were quiet as the preacher blessed Caleb William Johnson. The baby released a soft cry. As the preacher informed Rhonda and Jason of their responsibilities as godparents, they stared at one another. It was such a huge responsibility to step up to bat in case something happened to the parents.

As Caleb was being presented to God, Lauren snuggled closer to Melanie. She held Lauren's left hand and gently squeezed it. Lauren looked to her right at her father. He looked happy. She looked at her Granddad William and Granddad Charles standing next to Auntie Lisa and Uncle Cameron. The two men had a look of pride. Lauren looked at her only grandmother. She looked happy too.

All of her aunts were there, except Auntie Linda. She was in Aruba. Uncle Paul and Uncle Jason were there too. It was too expensive to bring her cousins.

Lauren felt a surge of energy enter her. Miss Angel was sitting between her and her father. Lauren smiled and was about to nudge her mother. Miss Angel smiled and shook her head. "Remember, it's our secret," she said with her finger at her lips. Lauren nodded as she swung her legs, waiting for her new cousin to be introduced to the angels.

Everyone dined at Cameron's and Lisa's house after church. Everyone formed little groups and chatted amongst themselves. Rhonda and Jason were in the kitchen talking.

"I want to take you to The City Grill tomorrow. I hear it's a very nice restaurant," Jason said with a smile.

Not only was The City Grill nice, it was expensive. She remembered what Lisa and Rochelle told her. If she didn't behave as if she deserved better, she would never get treated better. Rhonda looked shyly at Jason. "What's the occasion?" she asked casually.

"A new start. A new attitude. A new girlfriend."

"Me?"

"I was hoping."

"You live in Minneapolis. It would never work."

"So you're giving up on me already?"

"They say long distance relationships never work."

"I was hoping that it didn't have to be long distance."

"Are you moving to Atlanta?"

"I think you will like Minneapolis. It's an outdoors city."

"It's cold up there!"

Jason took a deep breath. His father had instructed him to be open and honest with Rhonda. It was his first attempt at something long term. It appeared she wasn't interested. "I was hoping that one day you would dance for me."

Rhonda felt she was playing it a little too hard. She did not expect Jason to suggest living together. "I just don't want to give up everything if it turns out bad between us."

"I wasn't thinking about you moving right away. You need time like I need time. If you don't feel comfortable with the idea, it's okay."

For the first time, Rhonda had a decent man asking her for a date and a committed relationship. She was treating him like all of the others. Sure she wanted to try it with him and all she could think about, since the day he left, was dancing for him. "Do you mind if I tell you that I'm scared?"

Jason smiled at Rhonda's honesty. Fear was written all over her face. He touched her face lightly and kissed her softly on the cheek. He saw her look down. He could hear her take a deep breath. He waited for her to look at him. When she did, he kissed her on the lips. "Will you dance for me one day?" he asked low. He kept staring into her large innocent eyes.

Rhonda nodded. She bounced a little. She smiled and kept her focus away from him. It was difficult looking at him because she did not want to see a lie in his eyes.

"Hey, look at me! I'm not that ugly," Jason teased. He grinned his biggest grin. Rhonda grinned too. "I heard that Phipps Plaza is a nice mall. Let's go and pick out a dress for tomorrow," he said.

Rhonda was flabbergasted. No man had ever offered to buy her anything. She wanted to thank him beyond words, but she was going to continue playing it safe. "You have pretty hair. I would like to see it down," she said.

Jason removed the ponytail holder and shook out his hair. He continued to stare at her but without a smile. "Is that better?" he asked.

Melanie was clearing the table when William walked beside her. "Hey dad!" she said cheerfully.

"How is my favorite girl?"

"Free!"

"The divorce became final?"

"Yes."

"I hear that John lost the big contract."

Melanie was silent. Barbara said he would pay for what he did. When Melanie visited Barbara on the day John told her about losing the contract, Barbara just smiled and said, Give me a big hug.

"Why didn't you tell me about the fighting?" William asked.

"I didn't want to bother you."

William was confused. He had to think back to the times he basically neglected his daughter. His career was more important. His little girl was a trophy that was set out as needed. He wondered if she endured the beatings because of his lack of parental support and guidance.

"Minneapolis is pretty far away. You won't have the instant support of Marilyn, Paul, Barbara and Ed," William said.

"I need to make a fresh start."

"I know I was never there when you needed me as a young woman. To be honest, I didn't know what to do. I remember the first time I combed your hair after Catherine died. I knew I wasn't cut out for a girl."

Melanie just smiled as she wiped the table with a dish towel. She remembered that time too. They lived in a two-family flat. She yelled ouch every time William touched her hair. She remembered him putting his head in his hands and waiting a few minutes before attempting the task again. After several failed attempts, he took her by the hand and knocked on the door of their next door neighbor. A woman with four girls. William offered to pay her if she would comb Melanie's hair. The woman said nothing as she included Melanie in the morning routine of combing hair.

"I want you to feel comfortable calling me when you need anything," William said.

"I heard you were good in track," Melanie said to change the topic.

"How did you know? I've never told you."

"Aunt Barbara told me. Lisa was good in track too. She was a middle distance runner. Weren't you a middle distance runner?" Melanie asked without looking at William.

William said nothing. He wondered what Melanie was saying. Then it came to him. He sighed. "I ran hurdles."

"I want you to stay consistent in her life, regardless of what has been found out."

"I told Lisa nothing has changed," William said. He was right. Nothing had changed.

"Lauren runs very well too, considering her hearing problem."

"Is that right?"

"I would like for you to sign her cast. She won't ask you

because she's afraid of you."

William was surprised. He was always cordial to Lauren. "Why is she afraid of me? I'm always nice to her."

"Her Granddad Charles plays with her and takes her places when he's around. Granddad William just speaks and keeps walking. You can give her what you never gave me."

Melanie did not wait for William to answer. She took the dishes into the kitchen. She saw Rhonda and Jason hugged up. "All right, break it up," Melanie said.

The couple grinned and looked away from each other. Jason cleared his throat. "Melanie's moving to Minneapolis. You won't be by yourself. You will know somebody," Jason said.

"You're moving to Minneapolis too?" Melanie asked as she loaded the dishwasher.

"I don't know yet," Rhonda said shyly.

Melanie put cleaning powder into the container inside the dishwasher. She straightened her posture and saw the hungry look in Rhonda's eyes. "Do you want to move there?"

Rhonda bit down on her bottom lip. She could hear Cameron laughing about the baby saying 'da-da' at close to two months. She heard Lisa commenting on Cameron spoiling the baby. They sounded in love. Rhonda concluded it was time to let go of her cousin.

"Yes," Rhonda finally answered.

"Then move! Life is too short to play it safe," Melanie said maternally and left the kitchen.

Lionel and Charles were in the living room. For the first time in years, Charles and Lionel were on decent speaking terms. The information about Jennifer's birth created a chasm between the two.

"I talked to Stacy the other day. She wants you to spend more time with Damon," Charles said.

"She's only saying that because Melanie is moving to Minneapolis."

"Do you want to spend more time with your son?"

"Of course! I'm damn tired of her childish games. She knows I travel from time to time. Every time I want to get him, there's always a problem."

"Have you told her that?"

"Yes I have!"

"Maybe you need to put it into terms she understands. Either she maintains a consistent pattern with visitation or she can raise him alone."

"I love my son."

"I know you do. Cameron and I had this same discussion about Celeste. Sometimes it's easy to forget about the ones that are out of sight."

"I will never forget about Damon. He's my son."

"How serious are things between you and Melanie?"

"I'm helping her get situated."

"Does she have to move to Minneapolis to get situated?"

"What's wrong with her coming to Minneapolis?"

"You have always had a special place for her. I don't want you to forget this conversation," Charles said and stood. He stretched. "How is business?"

"It's growing fast. I'm stretched. I need help."

"Talk to Jason. He's going to need something contractual while he's in school."

Barbara was in the sunroom with Marilyn and Paul. She felt drained. The summer had been busy. She was feeling sluggish. Her last visit to the doctor was the same diagnosis. She needed surgery. It wasn't something she was set on. She was determined to rest when she got back home. In another week, her siblings were due in town. It meant more entertainment.

Barbara removed the papers from her purse. It was time to give Lisa the final secrets. Then she looked at the death certificate of Caleb Arvell. Barbara decided to destroy the document. Debra was dead and Lisa did not need another interruption in her life.

Barbara left the sunroom and went to the baby's room. Lisa was in there with Gina. "Our flight is leaving in two hours. We're leaving for the airport. Here is the location of your mother's grave," Barbara said and handed Lisa the document.

Lisa took her time taking the paper. She paused before looking at it. The address was near Cartersville. No wonder she never felt life from her mother's grave in St. Louis. She wasn't there.

Lisa folded the paper. "Thanks for coming, Aunt Barbara," she said with comfort.

Lisa's greeting took Barbara by surprise. Finally, there was closure to the separation from Debra Arvell. Barbara gave Lisa a hug. "If you need answers or advice, feel free to call. A baby is a lot of work and husbands are more work," Barbara said as she hugged Lisa.

"Cameron will be here to help me," Lisa said with a smile.

"No sweetie. Don't count on him too much. Women are nurturers by nature. *We* are the smart ones. If I counted on my husband to help with my daughter, she would have kept diaper rash."

"Aunt Barbara, I'll see you in a week. Carlos and I are moving back to Kansas City," Gina said.

Carlos received the job at the Youth Center and Gina was able to land a job managing a healthcare facility. Carlos decided to take his time in completing his dissertation. The Center's board of directors was impressed that his paper was on the creation of urban ghettos. They were willing to compensate the completion of his research since it was almost over.

Carlos approached Dennis about buying their home. It wasn't difficult to start the financing because Carla was set on moving after the incident at the basketball tournament. Instead of Dennis jacking up the price as he wanted to, he decided to get enough on the house to use as a down payment for another house. There were repairs to be done and Carlos was excited about doing them. He saw potential for the neighborhood. He formulated ideas to keep out unwelcomed elements. Already, he wanted to join a political group to not only spring the Youth Center for funding, but to ensure the safety of all black neighborhoods. With Ray's contacts, it appeared inevitable.

"Your mother told me about the children. Why did you spoil them?" Barbara fussed.

Gina gasped. "I didn't spoil them!"

"You know how your mother is. Lisa, I'm leaving. Take care, sweetie," Barbara said and kissed Lisa on the cheeks. Before Barbara kissed Gina on the cheeks, the two looked at each other and smiled.

* * *

Linda waited impatiently on the surgeon. Her father and Indie were with her. Little Edward was in school. Edward senior was extremely nervous. The surgery was into the seventh hour. It was considered high risk. He could not imagine life without Barbara. She was a strong footprint in his career and personal achievements. She was strong in areas where he was weak. She brought balance to an ego that could have been distorted by accolades.

"Dad, are you okay?" Linda asked weakly.

"Sure, honey," he answered. Usually, he would put his arms around his daughter to comfort her, but he was the one that needed comforting.

Indie brought a coloring book to Linda. Brown and orange seemed to be her favorite colors on one page. Red and yellow were the colors on the other page.

"Look," Indie said.

"That's pretty," Linda said.

Indie could sense something was wrong with her mother. She patted Linda on the leg and pointed to her purse. Linda opened her purse to search for crackers. The bear from the carousel was in there. Indie pulled it out.

"What time is Birdie coming?" Edward asked.

"Her flight should have been here by now. She might be on her way from the airport," Linda answered. Her attention went to the very bright bear. "Dad, is mother going to die?"

"Honey, don't talk like that."

Finally, the surgeon came out to talk to Edward. Barbara was in recovery. The surgery went better than expected. Now, everything depended on Barbara.

"Malinda, how are you?" Birdie said as she entered the room.

Linda saw her mother when she saw Birdie. She rushed to Birdie and grabbed her hands. "Mother is in recovery," Linda said panting.

"It's going to be fine. Your mother is too mean to die," Birdie said with a smile.

Linda chuckled a little. Any other time, she would believe it, but her father was too nervous to believe it. He even wore his favorite, colorful, good-luck shirt.

"Kelly and her family will be here later," Birdie said.

"Sugah Doo, Rosie and Baby Brother will be here tonight," Linda said. She watched as Birdie took a deep breath. It had been years since the remaining family had been together. The reunion was going to be tough on everyone.

Barbara heard Catherine first. "Thanks for taking care of her. She will be fine now. I have one more favor. Don't you think she will make an excellent national president?"

Barbara loved a challenge, but she felt that Catherine was pushing it. "Why national president, Catherine?"

"The best! I want her to have the best!"

"I want the best for my daughter too!"

"Fine! It was a struggle getting her to this point. I thought for sure she was going to lose it with John, but she's protected. My baby will always be with her."

"Jennifer?"

"Um-hum."

"Do you know who fathered Debra's daughter?"

Barbara had a strong hunch, but she knew Catherine knew the truth. She and Debra were friends again. They had their own secrets now. Barbara relaxed knowing that Catherine and Debra were friends again before their death.

"Didn't Debra pull a good one?" Catherine said.

"She was always the smart one."

"She's at peace now...her and momma."

"What about you?"

"I was at peace the time I was going to meet Charles. Can you believe his sons are in love with women that he feared?"

"They are much smarter than him. They should be happy."

Barbara saw the light embracing Catherine. She was slowly leaving her view. Barbara didn't want her to go.

"Will I see you again?" Barbara asked sadly.

"Not for awhile. Cherub Cinderella is a real angel. I'm here to help you."

"To do what?"

"To hold on to life and enjoy to it. The memories, Barbara! You must keep them alive for our daughters and their daughters too."

"I guess we'll talk later."

"Sure we will. By the way, you haven't lost your step!"

"Thanks Catherine."

"But you're still an old bitch! Goodbye sweetie," Catherine said with a smile and disappeared.

Debra's voice became audible but Barbara could not see her. "Barbara Ann, you are the best. I would not have handled it that way, but it worked out fine."

"Debra, is that you?"

"I think Lisa knows that I really did love her."

"She loved you too. Who is her father?"

"The only thing that matters is she's going to be fine. One day we'll talk again."

Barbara waited for Debra to say something else but there was silence. "Debra, everyone says, 'hello'." Barbara heard nothing but Debra's familiar laugh.

Barbara heard singing. She heard her mother's voice. She opened her eyes and saw Birdie singing one of their mother's favorite songs. Barbara wanted to join her taking the low notes.

After Birdie finished, everyone clapped. Rosie noticed Barbara first. She put her hands to her mouth.

"What's the matter Rosie?" Birdie asked.

"She's gonna be fine," Rosie said smiling. Then she pointed at Barbara. Everyone's attention went to Barbara. They talked at once. Barbara couldn't respond. She saw Linda whisper something to Indie. The little girl kept staring at Barbara.

"Say it Indie," Linda said smiling as she rocked Indie. Linda prodded the little girl to speak to Barbara.

"Hi Gumma," Indie said shyly.

Everyone in the room laughed and said, "Ahh."

Barbara wanted to smile but like Catherine said, she was still an old bitch. Did Linda think it was cute for Indie to speak like a street urchin? Couldn't the child speak better than that? Then Barbara looked at Linda's hair. It looked as if chickens had pecked a style in it. If she were going to wear it short, then it needed shaping.

Unexpectantly, Edward bent forward and kissed Barbara. *Oh my God*, Barbara thought in horror. The first thing she noticed was Edward's ugly, favorite, good-luck shirt. It had too many darn colors. She wanted to fuss at him for wearing the shirt in public. It was okay for wearing around the house. One time, she tried giving it away to the Goodwill. He found it in the bag and retrieved it.

Barbara's stern expression didn't concern Edward because he understood the recovery process. His wife could not show enthusiasm right away. She had gone through a very trying task. He took Barbara's hand and rubbed it. He only hoped she would eventually smile.

Barbara closed her eyes to avoid the multitude of colors that were invading her space at her right side. She turned her head left and weakly motioned for Birdie with her hand.

Birdie walked to Barbara. Her siblings smiled with happiness. Barbara tried talking, but her throat felt like cotton. Birdie's eyebrows creased. She leaned closer. "Carl," was the only thing Barbara could muscled out.

Birdie leaned closer. Her eyebrows raised. She leaned in very close to Barbara's ear. "He's having surgery for prostate cancer today."

Barbara frowned. It was difficult for her to imagine Birdie leaving her husband alone at the hospital for something as serious as prostate surgery. She kept her eye contact on Birdie.

"When I get back, I want the nurses to tell me that he called for me," Birdie whispered. She took Barbara's left hand and gave it a gentle squeeze.

A smile formed at the corners of Barbara's mouth. She couldn't wait to get better. Her mother didn't die, she was still alive.